I0838362

AN UNCOMMON TRUTH OF DYING

BROKEN VEIL

BOOK 2

MARIE ANDREAS

OTHER BOOKS BY MARIE ANDREAS

The Lost Ancients
Book One: The Glass Gargoyle
Book Two: The Obsidian Chimera
Book Three: The Emerald Dragon
Book Four: The Sapphire Manticore
Book Five: The Golden Basilisk
Book Six: The Diamond Sphinx

The Lost Ancients: Dragon's Blood
Book One: The Seeker's Chest

The Asarlaí Wars Trilogy
Book One: Warrior Wench
Book Two: Victorious Dead
Book Three: Defiant Ruin

The Code of the Keeper
Book One: Traitor's Folly

The Adventures of Smith and Jones
A Curious Invasion
The Mayhem of Mermaids

Broken Veil
Book One: The Girl with the Iron Wing
Book Two: An Uncommon Truth of Dying
Book Three: Through a Veil Darkly

Books of the Cuari
Book One: Essence of Chaos
Book Two: Division of Chaos
Book Three: Destruction of Chaos

ACKNOWLEDGMENTS

I'm so lucky to have many wonderful writing companions on this journey—artists, editors, beta readers, and readers.

I'd like to thank everyone who has ever supported me, read chapters, edited, let me cry on their shoulder, read my books, given nice reviews, and/or bought me soothing beverages. I could never have done this without ALL of you. I can't list you all here, but you mean the world to me.

My awesome editor- Janet Tait—thank you for helping make sense of a lot of twisted ideas. My beta readers: Lisa Andreas, Patti Huber, and Lynne Mayfield. Proof reader extraordinaire- Ilana Schoonover. Any errors or mistakes are completely mine.

And to my very talented artist- Aleta Rafton, thank you for your lovely work. And to The Killion Group for their excellent and timely formatting of the print interior and print cover!

To all my readers—thank you for enjoying the crazy worlds in my head!

CHAPTER ONE

—◆—

AISLING CUT THE CALL AND threw her phone across the room. It bounced off the top of the sofa and landed softly on the cushion. Not at all satisfying, but probably cheaper than replacing another phone.

"Damn it."

"He still won't take your calls?" Maeve came in from her room in loose sweats with a towel wrapped around her hair. Maeve was taking this enforced temporary vacation much better than Aisling was. Or so she appeared.

Maeve was a semi-former MI-6 agent who had been also working as Aisling's partner in the L.A. police force for the past ten years. Currently, they were roommates in Aisling's brother's house as Aisling had her house explode in front of her, and Maeve's townhome was still under investigation. Maeve was extremely active, and sitting around for a week watching TV, eating junk food, and washing her hair every other day wasn't her style.

There had to be a reason for it. Aisling folded her arms and glared. "What have you been doing?"

Maeve had been walking to the kitchen, but she stopped and pointed to her towel. "Washing my hair. A week off and your detective skills go to the shitter, do they?" Her British accent always got heavier when she was being snarky.

"Funny." Aisling followed her into the kitchen. "You've been playing the lady of leisure this last week—what are you *really* doing?"

Maeve ignored her, went into the kitchen and pulled out a can of beans and a loaf of bread. "Just because Reece won't return your calls is no reason to get pissy with me." She waved a piece of bread in the air with an offering gesture as it was headed toward the toaster.

"No, thank you." Aisling liked beans on toast, but after a week, it was getting old. "I am currently annoyed at Garran, not Reece." Garran was their boss. Reece was her…she had no idea what they were, and that was part of the issue. He was pissing her off was what he was. A tall, well-built, handsome, super spook with deadly gray eyes. There had been something going on between them. Or so she thought. But he hadn't returned a single call all week. Like just about everyone else in her life.

"Garran told us to take time off. He was pretty clear about it." Maeve dropped four pieces of bread in the toaster and got out a plate.

"And it's been a week. If we were in some way a leak or compromised, he would have found out by now." Two weeks ago, a criminal fey named Nix tried to spread a deadly drug all over L.A. in his bid for control of the city. Most drugs didn't work on the fey, but this was iron. It was not only fatal to fey, but it was a horrific and painful way to go. Humans like Maeve would have survived. Elves like Aisling and the other fey would be gone, leaving the city wide open for the elven Nix and his cronies to take over. How he'd become immune to the drug himself was anybody's guess, and the focus of a lot of think tanks right now.

He had been stopped, but he escaped after they grabbed his massive stockpile of the drug. At the same time, halfway across town, a super-secret headquarters for the super-secret government agency Area 42 blew up. Or rather, it looked like it blew up, but in reality, the entire thing vanished. Luckily many of the people who worked there, including Reece and his spy partner Jones, were dealing with Nix and weren't in the building. But there were still a few hundred people missing.

Aisling, Maeve, Reece, Jones, and Aisling's brother, Caradoc, had been working on the clues—of which there were few—for a week. Then Garran, the captain of detectives, called and pulled Aisling and Maeve off the case. And Reece stopped returning her calls.

After a week of being ignored, Aisling was ready to start hurting people. To make matters worse, her brother Caradoc had been working on something with Area 42 and had not come home during the last week. Considering the house they were in was his safe house and had all of his gizmos and gadgets in it, that was annoying as well. He would answer her calls, but with never more than, "everything is fine".

"Oh, beans and toast, lovely." Harlie poked his head in from the living room. Harlie's full name was Harthinatle, and he was Aisling's thousand-year-old brother, the eldest of their siblings. He was alarmingly tall and thin, but he loved to eat.

"Harlie, don't you think it's odd that Garran has put us on indefinite leave, isn't returning our calls, and neither is Reece? Even Caradoc is blowing us off, and all of his things are still here." Not that Aisling thought he'd have noticed. Harlie was a mystic, a talented magic user who was often clueless about the reality around him.

Maeve handed Harlie a full plate and he went out to the dining room. Aisling grabbed a cup of tea and followed.

"I think Caradoc got his things." Harlie hooked a thumb over his shoulder to Caradoc's room with its closed door.

Aisling put down her tea, stomped over, and pushed open the door. The bed and dresser were still there, but the piles of tech were gone. "When did he do this? Did you see him? Talk to him? What in the hell is going on?" First her boss, then whatever Reece was doing, now her brother? Who was next? Maeve?

Maeve came out with her plate of beans on toast and another plate with three chocolate-filled croissants. She slid the croissant plate next to Aisling's teacup on the table. "Eat something, you're getting cranky."

"Caradoc snuck in last night to get his things. He thought no one saw him. But he sneaks loudly." Harlie had already polished off half his plate. "Very loudly."

"Seriously? That's it, I'm going to the station." Aisling came back to the table and ate two of the croissants. She did feel better, but she wasn't going to admit it. She'd gone to the police station the day they'd been cut off, but Garran had the station still under lockdown. The two cops on guard were apologetic, but they wouldn't let her in.

They would this time.

"Why do you want to know? Isn't a bit of rest a nice thing?" Harlie usually appeared to be doing little, but Aisling knew his mind had a million different tasks going on at once.

"I don't mind rest. I like vacations. This isn't a vacation but a lockdown. We have a case that hasn't been solved yet." She turned to Maeve. "And have you noticed that we're followed every time we leave?"

Maeve shrugged it off at first, then nodded. "You're right, but I think they are doing this for a reason. It might not be one we like, but something made Garran and Area 42 cut us off."

Aisling polished off the last croissant. "You could call your *other* people." She hadn't wanted to bring up MI-6. First of all, she hadn't known Maeve was still officially an agent until Reece's connection told her a few weeks ago. And secondly, Maeve clearly hadn't wanted to discuss her MI-6 involvement when Aisling first found out about it.

"I really don't want to until we have to." Maeve held up one hand. "And no, you getting cranky and frustrated is not a 'have to' moment. Besides, I know you. You're as pissed about Reece as you are us being sidelined. You just don't want to admit it."

Harlie glanced up but wisely continued to keep eating his beans and toast.

Aisling stalked over to the teapot and poured a refill. She *was* annoyed at Reece, more so because she wasn't sure what they were to each other. There had been a serious attraction, but near-death experiences and adrenaline can cause emotions to arise that might be exaggerated. Even the week before everyone dropped them like iron waste, he'd been pulling away. But at that point, she'd believed he was just working night and day trying to find the missing building and all those people. As he completely refused to call back, she began to get pissed. If there was nothing between them, fine. She'd live. But this was an important case, and him cutting her out needed to be addressed.

"Shit. It's because of our family's box being left at the building site, isn't it?" She aimed her glare at Harlie. All of the oldest elven families had boxes made out of the Hewlith tree, also known as part of the enchanted forest. The wood was from their original homeland beyond the veil, although there was a small grove of the trees in northern Wales. Their family's box was left in the wreckage of the missing Area 42 headquarters. Two others had been brought to Aisling by vallenians, a species of Old Ones left behind when the fey fled to this world. They weren't supposed to be able to come to this side of the veil. And if they did, anyone who saw them would soon die.

Aisling had seen them on three separate occasions and was still here.

Harlie had found a connection between their mother, the High Council, and attacks on Area 42 personnel. He hadn't been able to find out how far it went or what the connection was before the building vanished.

"We don't know that." But the slow response from Harlie gave her the true answer. That was his theory or his primary one, but he wasn't ready to announce it yet.

"You still haven't found the connection for the boxes?" Maeve jumped in, changing the subject from why they were being sidelined so quickly that Aisling almost got whiplash.

"No." Harlie scowled. "The other two families are connected to ours, well, to mother at any rate. They're First families too. But why their boxes were stolen and given to us, or rather to Aisling, I don't know." That admission cost him dearly. Harlie prided himself on his ability to figure out anything—that he wasn't able to on this was clearly annoying him.

"And they might not have been for me…" Aisling dropped her comment when both of them looked up with raised eyebrows. "Fine. Maeve brought me one and the vallenians dropped the other at my feet. But ours… was brought to me by Reece when *they* found it where the building had been. I don't know if that one counts." She leaned back and closed her eyes. "I would simply like to get back to being a detective. And doing detective things. Catching bad people. Solving this damn case."

"And what's stopping you?" Caradoc's voice came from behind her. He snuck into his own house most likely just to make her jump. And it worked. Teasing his baby sister would never get old for him.

"You took all of your things out, have been blowing off my calls, and now you come back?" Aisling narrowed her eyes at him. Why sneak his belongings out just to come back the next day?

Maeve laughed at the expression on his face. "They booted you too?"

Caradoc folded his arms and scowled, then dropped a large duffle and himself into the sofa. "It appears so. I moved my things to one of my other houses so they wouldn't think about them being here. Didn't work—they kicked me out anyway." Caradoc was taller than Aisling, but still a good seven inches shorter than Harlie's almost seven-foot stature. His blond hair, sharp blue eyes, and killer smile looked great on magazines—but he was also a savvy business owner and tech inventor. And extremely used to getting his way.

"Are you pouting?" Aisling stood and walked to the chair nearest the sofa and leaned forward. "Yup, pouting."

"I am not. I'm annoyed, frustrated, and put out. I do not pout."

Both Aisling and Harlie laughed at that one. Maeve looked ready to, but held back.

"And? What happened? Your sister is getting ready to storm the castle," Maeve said.

"Which castle? Eh, either one will kick you out right now. Garran isn't even letting Stella in. As for Area 42, they wanted my help at first. I thought it was because I was so gifted. Nope, it was just because I was part of this family and was less of a risk than Aisling because I wasn't attached to the police. When they figured that I couldn't help them with the family issues about our box, they politely escorted me out." He got off the sofa, got some tea, and came back. "And no, I can't tell you where they are. They had someone pick me up each day and kept me blindfolded. That should have been the first hint about their goals."

"Are we all suspects? The only connection really is our mother. And I was technically on loan to Area 42." A loan that ended when everyone else cut her off as well.

"I couldn't even be sure of that," Caradoc said. "I wasn't allowed to ask questions unless they were directly related to the project I was assigned to. They think the missing building might be trapped out of sync with our reality."

Harlie perked up at that one. "That was one of my theories. However, I still haven't been able to connect mother and her cronies to something on that level. None of the people she works with, that I know of, have the gifts for something like that."

"What if the vallenians were helping them?" Caradoc asked.

Aisling shook her head. "It sounds odd, but I think the vallenians were trying to warn us about something—I don't think they would be working with her or her gang." That was a weird thought that Aisling hadn't let surface much. By definition, vallenians were the bad guys—all of the Old Ones were. That was why they stayed stuck on the other side of the veil with the other dangerous and unstable beings thousands of years ago when the elves and the rest of the fey fled here. "The trio of them that found me when we blew up Old Town, for instance. It felt like they were trying to help."

Harlie nodded slowly. "Not much is known of the Old Ones, any of them. And look where the information that we do have came from."

"The High Council," Caradoc said. "The same people who formed a secret cabal intent on destroying who knows what."

Aisling hadn't been a fan of her mother for decades; this new possibly-trying-to-take over-the-world situation was making it worse. "So where does that leave us? I seem to be the only one willing to fight to get involved on this case. I know we can make a difference if they would just let us in."

Caradoc watched her and Maeve for a few pointed moments, then shrugged. "Which brings me back to my original question, why aren't you two great detectives out detecting? Yes, as free agents you won't have the access you had before. But you're both pretty damn good."

Maeve looked over to her, head tilted in question.

"We could do some groundwork, at least until we're back on the case officially." Having this case dangling in the wind was bugging the crap out of Aisling, both as a cop and on a personal level. She didn't like the bad guys winning. Being blocked from the case for the past week just made her more determined. Not to mention, whoever or whatever managed to remove a massive building in broad daylight scared the hell out of her. "But we're going to need some of your gizmos to block being followed. I'm not sure whether it's the police, Area 42, or someone else completely, but someone is watching us when we get on the roads."

"I thought we'd take my car." Caradoc smiled. "All the bells and whistles you could want."

"That's the real reason you want us to start digging, you're annoyed you got booted." Maeve laughed as she pushed herself away from the table. "No bother, your gizmos should stop anything after us. Let me get dressed, then we can head out. Any idea where first?"

Aisling smiled. "Stella's diner."

CHAPTER TWO

———◆———

"STELLA'S? WHY?" CARADOC WAS FOCUSED on something on his phone, so Aisling gave him a break for not thinking of it first.

"Because she's also been kicked out of the loop and she's got Reece's secret base hidden in her diner? If anyone can start us in the right direction, it would be her." Stella was a tiny, extremely old changeling who ran a classic diner down off Second Ave. Reece's secret hidey-hole was inside the diner and not connected to Area 42. Aisling wasn't sure if Stella could get into the hidden room if Reece specifically shut her out, but she would be a good source for info.

Besides, Aisling could do with some real food.

"Good point." Caradoc pocketed his phone and looked up. Then he held out his hand. "Hand me yours. I think it's best we upgrade the tech on all our phones before we go hunting."

Aisling handed hers over just as Maeve came out of her room. "Mine next. And I agree on Stella, she's a good source to start with."

Once Caradoc had finished dealing with the phones, they all got up to leave. Even Harlie.

"Where are you going?" He spent most of his time at home. Aisling theorized that a few hundred years in a cave in Nepal might have left him feeling uncomfortable in the wide outdoors. Especially in a city like Los Angeles.

He shrugged. "I like Stella, I like her food, and someone should watch to see if you are still being followed. Stella knows I'm your brother, but I can stay unnoticed by others." His grin was sly and looked more like it belonged to a teenager than a thousand-year-old elf. "I'll take my bike and go a different route. Don't look for me." With a quick nod, he grabbed his motorcycle helmet and left.

"I'm still trying to figure him out," Maeve muttered more to herself than anyone else.

"So are we," Aisling and Caradoc both responded.

"He's very different from the hermit we grew up hearing about. I only actually saw him twice as a kid. He stayed in Nepal the entire time I was growing up." Aisling led the way to Caradoc's black SUV.

"Maybe he just didn't like your mum any more than you two did." Maeve took the backseat.

Caradoc got in the driver's seat. "She could be right. I was just a kid when he went to Nepal, and you weren't even born yet. Let's face it, the rest of our siblings are pretty much jerks."

Aisling nodded. She and Caradoc were the two youngest. Harlie was the oldest. The ten more in-between were practically psychological clones of their mother and focused on power and prestige. Their father never appeared to follow in her world domination power trip, but he also didn't stand up to her. Even though it hurt, Aisling, Caradoc, and Harlie had cut off communication with him as well once they realized that their mother was far worse than they thought and was working in secret with the High Council to go after Area 42 agents.

Backing out of this driveway still felt weird to Aisling. Caradoc's house was old-school, in a high-end beach neighborhood and about a hundred years old. The area around it had all been upgraded to mansions years ago. But thanks to a magic hedge that surrounded the property, no one knew they were there.

It was the going in and out of the hedge that gave Aisling the chills. But it was far better to drive through than to walk through. That experience she never needed to repeat.

"So have you heard from Reece?" Caradoc waited until she was trapped in the car before bringing that up. Considering that he'd been around Reece far more recently than her, he was trying to be annoying.

"Of course not. You know that." She noticed he kept a sharp eye on the road and wasn't even slightly looking in her direction. Great for proper driving technique, not typical for her brother. "Spill. What do you know?"

"Are you holding back on your sister?" Maeve leaned forward. "She's been driving me bonkers this week with her sighing."

Aisling pushed her back. "I wasn't sighing. I don't like things left unfinished. If whatever it was is finished, I deserve to know."

Caradoc glanced over. "I thought I could draw it out longer, but I don't want to hear you sighing either. Reece fought to keep you in the loop—both of you. He insisted you weren't a leak risk and could provide valuable insight into the situation. He got shut down. Massively." His smile dropped. "Whatever is going on in the higher levels of Area 42, there is something bad connecting us to it. All of us. Even Jones stood up for you two. He and Reece are bewildered as to what's causing the shutout as it's above both their heads."

"I thought both of them were Area 42's black ops and high ranking?" Maeve returned to leaning forward a bit.

"They are." Caradoc's frown went into a full scowl. "And not only are they being shut down, both, along with the majority of agents, are now living in a concealed bunker outside of L.A. Where, I have no idea. They got bussed into the hidden working area as well."

"It's annoying as hell, and totally unfair in regard to us, but I can't blame them for being extremely paranoid. They are the most secretive agency in the world, and someone *stole* their extremely secret building. That has to mess them up." Aisling understood it logically. But she also felt that by shutting themselves off as they were, Area 42 was losing resources they might need.

"Then they aren't in contact with the police at all?" Maeve asked.

"Not that I can tell." Caradoc got on the freeway and hit a few switches on his dash. "They seem to be rebuffing all other law enforcement contacts."

Maeve nodded. "They don't know who to trust."

"I'd say they don't." Aisling tried to read the writing on the switches Caradoc hit, but she was at the wrong angle. "What did you just activate and why are we shooting past the exit for Stella's? Who do you think is following us?"

Caradoc didn't answer at first but hit another switch on the dash, then took a north-bound exit. "I'm not sure. These are external scramblers and should block anything that my normal protection doesn't."

"But we're still being followed." Maeve sat back in her seat and noticeably rechecked her seat belt.

Aisling double checked her own and braced herself against the dash. Whoever was following them was doing so too easily considering the amount of tech Caradoc was flinging at them.

"Yes, we are still being followed." Caradoc got off the exit ramp, tore through a yellow light, and then back down a side street toward the freeway they'd been on. Three large black SUVs, looking a lot like his own, came after them. Aisling saw two more continue on the freeway they just left, but they were heading toward the next off-ramp.

"Five? Who in the hell is sending five SUVs after us? Or at least five." Aisling hung on as Caradoc headed toward a massive freeway exchange. There were on-ramps and exits on both sides of this part of the freeway.

"There were two more that I picked up that stayed on our original freeway. All the same cars are kind of noticeable. They're sloppy and hoping to make up for that in numbers. Hang on." Caradoc swerved across six lanes of freeway at the last second—including a very rough exit island—and took an exit to the left.

One black SUV made it after them.

"Damn it." Caradoc got off the freeway and went down a winding side road. They were close to the southern end of the Glovin forest.

That forest was massive, covering a third of the state of California, and Aisling knew Caradoc had a fondness for it. She wasn't sure that it was the best option in this case though. "Why don't we just lead them back to the police station? That should get them to back off."

Caradoc gave a tight smile. "If that had been my plan, that would be perfect. It turns out that I have a different plan. And a new toy I want to test that could be dangerous to try on the freeway. Or any busy street."

"You're going to try to take them out?" Maeve looked back as they turned onto one of the narrower roads that went through the forest. Her gun was on her lap.

"Sort of. I want to disable both their vehicle and them, then find out who in the hells is sending this many cars after us."

"Don't think they radioed their buddies where they are?" Aisling also took out her gun. The other times they'd been tailed it had been subtle, watching but not getting caught. This wasn't subtle by anyone's definition.

"I hit a full block on anything being transmitted by them right before we turned to this exit. They won't even have a radio working." He raced down a few more increasingly narrow roads, finally spinning out where it turned to dirt. With a grin, he hit a red button as the SUV barreled right for them.

The black SUV slowed down; these roads weren't in

great shape. But it was still moving fast.

Caradoc swore and smacked the button a few more times. Finally, the SUV skidded to a stop five feet in front of the nose of Caradoc's car. Judging by the faces of the man and woman in the front seats, they hadn't been ready for that stop.

Caradoc jumped out of his car and aimed a round, metal gizmo at the SUV. Electric arcs engulfed the car and both people inside slumped against the dash.

"Damn. How did you…? Damn." Maeve beat Aisling out of the car but looked as shocked as Aisling felt. Caradoc was good, but what he just did was crazy.

"I see why that wouldn't have been a good idea on the freeway." Aisling was still a cop, even if she was benched right now. The idea of that type of tech falling into the wrong hands was horrifying.

"Yup." Caradoc had an electronic pad out and scanned the car as he slowly walked forward. "I'm not sure how long this will hold. I have some zip ties in the glove box." Aisling almost asked him why, then changed her mind, got them, and brought them over.

She and Maeve ended up hand-cuffing the two while Caradoc kept scanning and swearing softly. He also briefly aimed it at his vehicle and the swearing increased.

Once both were out of the SUV and secured on the ground, Maeve dusted her hands off and peered at Caradoc's pad. "Want to share what's making you so stressed?"

"I don't think this was as stealthy as I'd hoped. The good news is that it stopped the car following us and knocked those two out. The bad news is that they might have had a secondary GPS sending signal buried in their system—the rest of their people will be on their way. They might also actually be the FBI."

CHAPTER THREE

"WE JUST CARJACKED AND KNOCKED out two FBI people?" The FBI or Fey Bureau of Investigations was one of the agencies almost as powerful as Area 42. To say they would be upset about this was an understatement. Aisling peered down. The man was a fey; northern elf from his white hair and pale coloring. Although the northern elves were fond of keeping their hair long—this guy had a buzz cut. But no clan ear chain. Made sense, FBI agents wouldn't want anyone to use their clan affiliation against them. The dark-haired woman was a human or a human-fey breed. Human was always the dominant gene in those.

Maeve dropped down to the unconscious bodies and patted them both down. Two badges came out. "Yup, both are FBI, but why would FBI be that blatant about tailing us? Something isn't right."

Aisling kept an eye on the road behind them. "Look at their weapons." FBI was predictable on the type of fire-power their people were assigned.

Maeve swore. "There is no way they are FBI. They each have a naru pistol." Naru pistols were nasty little illegal weapons with a lot of kick and far more common with high-end thugs than any legit law enforcement.

"Someone wanted us to think they were FBI but didn't plan on us being around long enough to tell anyone about the naru pistols." Aisling took out the small knife she carried and stabbed all four tires of the other car. "Caradoc, we need to get out of here, now."

He jogged over, cut off the cuffs, and dragged both

unconscious bodies further into the road. "My gizmos should have left no electronic trace, and obviously the others knew who they were after, but let's make things a bit harder to prove."

They ran back to his car and took off down a side road.

"Wouldn't getting back on the freeway be faster?" Aisling kept looking behind them, but there were no dust trails of pursuit. Yet.

"It would if I thought we could get there. More people are coming the way we came in and I didn't want to go off-roading to get around that car."

"Which hopefully will slow them down." Maeve was also looking back. "I presume that was why you moved the bodies? Nice way to add to the blockade. Unless they really don't care about their people."

He swore as they hit a hole. The road was nothing but packed dirt at this point.

"Do you even know where you're going?" Aisling watched as the trees grew closer together and wilder looking.

"Yes. Maybe. Damn it. The trolls have to be here somewhere." Caradoc didn't fluster easily, but he'd been too cocky about being able to block their followers—epic failure wasn't helping his mood.

"You're trying to find the trolls? This wasn't your plan." Aisling gripped the dash as he hit another hole.

"It might have been? Grundog was quite taken with me after all." Caradoc managed to sound wounded at being accused of making this plan up as he went. Grundog was a half-troll, half-minotaur friend of Stella's who'd helped them when they were rescuing Maeve from Nix.

Maeve caught the look on Caradoc's face and laughed. "Right, sure she was. She hugged you a bit longer than the other males, eh?" She shook her head. "Troll females just like messing with the other species. But she did seem like a good person."

"And we don't have many options. I'm seeing enough dust for multiple cars rising behind us." If it came to a shootout, Aisling supposed being in the woods was better than on a street. Of course, whoever was after them might have backed off if they'd stayed on the freeway. Eventually.

Caradoc spun the car down a hill heading toward a ravine. They were almost there when a barricade dropped in front of them.

Aisling braced for impact and felt Maeve grab the back of her seat as they slammed to a stop. "You were planning on driving us off the cliff?" The barricade was about six feet high, made of huge logs, and most likely triggered once they crossed a set point. The ravine, from what she could still see of it, looked deep and wide. Last she'd checked, Caradoc hadn't made his car able to fly.

"No, Grundog said to come down this way if I ever needed her. Damn it. There must be some way to contact her."

Aisling saw movement in the woods. Someone was on foot in the trees. She rolled down her window. "We need Grundog! Stella sent us!" She hoped the person back there was a troll and knew Grundog and Stella. Leaving the people and the disabled car back there might have slowed their pursuers down, but it wouldn't for long.

The shape in the forest paused, then started moving toward them. Judging by the height, it wasn't Grundog, this was a full troll. Trolls kept to their own kind in their own towns, usually deep in the forest. They didn't get along in crowded places or with lots of people.

Yup, a full troll. One with primitive clothing, unshaven face, and a large club and who was stalking toward them.

"Do you know Grundog? We got lost." Aisling didn't want to shoot unless she had to. Not all trolls adapted to even the rustic living that most of their people did. Some were wild.

He kept coming forward. The tusks sticking up from his lower jaw were far longer than she'd ever seen. Then he grunted. It wasn't a muttered word; it was a grunt.

"Um, hello? We've lost our way?" Maeve decided to help and put a lot of emphasis on her British accent. Usually, it charmed people—this time it just made the troll's unibrow lower down to his eyes.

And give another grunt. He raised his club and charged toward them.

Aisling had her gun ready but kept it below the window.

The troll stopped and started laughing. "Sorry, mates, I couldn't keep it up. You were great sports though." He lowered his club and shook his shoulders out.

"We don't get visitors out here much. Where can I point you toward?" His accent was even a heavier British one than Maeve's and noticeably lacked the pidgin most local trolls used. His smile dropped and he tapped his ear. "Come in again? You broke up." He had a small earpiece. "More? Damn it, call out the troops. I'll deal with these."

"We're being chased by some fake FBI people in black SUVs like this one. Grundog helped us out a few weeks ago—Stella is our friend." Aisling didn't like the new frown on the troll's face or the way he'd taken a few steps back from them.

"Grundog is in town. I normally don't dress like this, was trying a bit of a wild walk. And those cars you mentioned are almost here." It looked difficult to fold his arms and still hold the massive club—but he managed.

Caradoc leaned down to be seen through the window. "Can you call Grundog? Fast? Those cars aren't good."

"Hold on." The troll turned away before he spoke to whoever was on the other end. "Need you to stop those cars, don't hurt anyone unless they fight. But stop them."

"The ones we saw had naru pistols," Maeve said.

The troll turned back to them. "Your FBI doesn't carry

those." He motioned to the back seat. "Move over a bit if you would, and follow exactly where I say."

Maeve slid behind Caradoc and the troll came in. One advantage of these massive SUVs, all species fit in them. Even if his head was brushing the roof. "I'm Reginald, most people just call me Reg. On a bit of a travel about from home, visiting some of the other outposts."

"I'm Maeve, from London."

"Nice to meet you, Maeve. I'm from just outside of Hebden Bridge, but I do love London." He laughed. "Aye, a troll loving one of the largest cities in the world. But the energy is intoxicating. Can't stay for more than a day or so—both for me and it makes others nervous."

"That's wonderful," Caradoc said. "But where do we go? Those cars have to be right behind us. I'm Caradoc by the way, and that's my sister Aisling."

"Nice to meet you both." Reg glanced behind them. "I wouldn't worry about those others though; they're dealing with a few larger problems. I wasn't the only one out walking today. Still, might be a good idea to move along." He held up his club, pressed the smaller end, and the tree barricade vanished.

"Where to? That ravine doesn't look crossable." Caradoc had calmed down a bit.

"Appearances can be deceiving. Just drive forward."

Aisling would have asked a few more questions, but Caradoc hit the gas. Having Reg in the car with them lowered the risk of it being a trap. She still hung onto the dash tightly.

As soon as the front of the car hit what looked to be the edge of the ravine the wheels sounded like they were grating on metal. Aisling looked down and saw the slight outline of a heavy metal grid.

"Nice! I'm still not picking it up on my sensors." From the tone of his voice, Caradoc was going to be bugging some trolls for secrets once they were safe.

"It's meant to fool everything." Reg tapped his earpiece as the scowl came back. "Hold them as long as you can, but don't risk our people."

"How many cars?" Aisling knew who he was talking about.

"Six. All looking like this one. Well, plus the one dead in the road. Whatever you did was good, it's still not moving, but they did carry their unconscious people away."

They reached the end of the ravine and the tire sound returned to dirt.

"Stay to the left. Damn it." Reg kept swearing. There was a barricade here too, but it was clear that it was real. He tapped his earpiece. "What happened on grid five? Trees and rocks are down." He listened for a bit, then spoke to Caradoc. "Back we go. Turn right here. We'll get a closer look at your friends than I wanted, but nothing can be done about that right now."

Caradoc muttered under his breath, but they went back through the woods. There was a bridge here too, but it was visible.

"We normally never let *guests* use this one." Trolls weren't fond of trespassers.

They had just cleared the bridge when gunshots rang out.

CHAPTER FOUR

—◆—

"I'M ENGAGING THE SHIELD ON the car, but where in the hell is it coming from?" Caradoc was watching the road and everything else.

Aisling looked around, but the woods were so dense that nothing could be seen beyond trees.

"I'd say it's whoever is engaging your friends. My people said two more cars, also plain black SUVs, have shown up but don't appear to be with the first batch. I have to ask; do you people use anything other than black SUVs? Very dramatic on their own, but a pack of them on multiple sides is a bit ridiculous."

Caradoc snorted. "I'll be changing my primary vehicle once we get out of this."

A loudspeaker crackled through the air. "Halt or we will use a rocket launcher and make you halt."

Aisling frowned at the voice more than the words. "Is that who I think it is?" The speaker distorted the voice, but it was annoyingly familiar.

"Stop your car and come out with your hands up." The loudspeaker confirmed her suspicions.

"Charge and hope they are bluffing or listen to the familiar voice?" Caradoc sounded like he was good either way.

"Stop the car. I don't care if you know him or not, no one threatens anyone with a rocket launcher while I'm in the forest." Reg waited until the car almost stopped then jumped out and raised his club.

Aisling did spare a thought that maybe he could bat the rocket out of the air—he stood like he thought he could.

"I'm Reginald Larksong of the Larksong trolls of the U.K..Who the hell are you and why are you threatening me?" He added a very impressive growl to the end of his words.

Aisling didn't want to ruin his thunder, but she knew who was on the other side of that speaker. She got out of the car, leaving her gun on the seat. "Do we have to put our hands up? What's the matter, Reece, we didn't stay home as you wanted, so you sent goons after us?"

Caradoc and Maeve got out on their side of the car. A quick glance showed neither had their hands up, but they left their weapons in the car.

"Damn it, Aisling. And Caradoc and Maeve. You ruined an op." Reece turned off the loudspeaker and came tromping through the trees. He was dressed in a black suit and a black dress shirt and had three people flanking him dressed the same. He looked good. Pissed, but good. Yup, one of the elven women with him had a rocket launcher sitting on her shoulder. That Reece didn't seem completely surprised at Aisling's appearance, and that he still had someone ready to blow up the car she was in, didn't make her happy to see him no matter how good he looked.

"I don't care who knows who." Reg strode forward and blocked Reece. "These woods are troll land."

"They are, and we apologize for this. I'm Agent Larkin with the FBI, and we were setting up a sting to catch a gang pretending to be FBI when your friends there got in the way."

Reg gave Reece a slow, appraising, and ultimately dismissive glance then turned to Aisling. "Is he for real? I know Stella and Grundog have had dealings with an Agent Reece Larkin, but this wasn't who I'd envisioned." More shapes were moving through the forest, but unless Area 42 had recently managed to recruit a tribe of trolls, they weren't with Reece and his people.

"He's that person." Aisling couldn't look at Reece. Yes, Caradoc said he fought to get her and Maeve to be part of the investigation, but that said nothing about their personal interaction. Or lack thereof.

Reg sighed and held up his right fist. The movement of the dark shapes around them stopped. He used his earpiece. "Did someone find Grundog? More of her friends have shown up." He paused as his call changed. "Hey Grunnie, some people are out here in extremely questionable circumstances and throwing your name around. Reece Larkin, a pair of elves called Caradoc and Aisling, and a Brit named Maeve." He listened for a bit then started laughing. "Thanks."

"She knows us?" Reece sounded almost nervous about that. Considering that if Stella had been cut off from the investigations, so had Grundog, he might have cause. Even civilized trolls weren't always as civilized as they could be when they were pissed.

"Yup, but she likes the other three better than you right now. My people will back down if you and yours take the rest of the black SUV gang and leave our forest." The entire forest didn't belong to the trolls, but this far back, they were clearly on troll land.

"I need to debrief those three, they interfered in a federal investigation." The words were there, but there wasn't much force behind them.

"Yeah, no." Aisling took a step closer to him. She noticed the people with him all dropped their hands to their sidearms. She didn't know them and at this point, she didn't care. "We were going about our business and your friends went after us. Not our problem." She folded her arms and glared. She found that she could stare at him much easier when pissed.

"You destroyed an operation we'd been working on for months. You looked like one of our contacts and the people we were after took the bait. You need to come with us." The female elf was pissed and looked like she wanted to shoot Aisling.

Aisling shrugged her off but watched the other two. Both reminded her of Jones with their silent stillness. A sting that had been in place for a few months? One that Reece hadn't been a part of at that time since he was focusing on Nix and the iron death killings.

Aisling smiled at the woman. "Just because you got replaced as head of this operation, and it blew up spectacularly, is not a reason we need to come with you. All three of us are civilians on troll land. We're not going anywhere." The snarl on the woman's face and a wince and glance away by Reece told her she was right. This type of job was below Reece's level. Most likely his defending her and Maeve hadn't gone well, and he'd been bumped down to replace the woman elf on an FBI case.

"As long as you stay beyond our borders and don't harass or hinder our guests in any way, you're welcome to do what you want. Providing you put down that rocket launcher." Reg nodded then turned to Caradoc. "I can guide you in. Grundog is looking forward to seeing you again. All of you." They all got back into Caradoc's car.

Reece kept looking down, but it looked to Aisling like he was hiding a smile. He quickly looked up as they started to drive away and gave her a tight nod.

Reg caught the movement. "He's not really FBI either, is he? What about the ones with him?"

"It's complicated." Even though Aisling was still pissed at Area 42 and Reece, she didn't want to compromise them. And the others could have been real FBI, it would depend on how much Reece annoyed his actual superiors. He often did work under the FBI badge, but given the severity of the current Area 42 situation, if he got bumped to an FBI case, he was on someone's shit list.

Reg grinned. "Not to worry, I know Stella has some interesting friends."

"Is she here, by chance?"

"No, she's back at her diner. She was here for a few days, so mad I thought she was going to break someone. Whoever this Garran person is, he'd better hope she's calmed down."

"Good, he deserves it." Maeve folded her arms and glared.

"Thanks for the save, but we were actually trying to get to Stella's diner." Caradoc was driving slower than normal, even in a forest. Most likely looking for a way to turn around.

"You know Reece will be waiting. He knows us too well. He might not know why we were out here, but he'll be waiting." Aisling wasn't sure how she felt about Reece right now. She'd been fully pissed for the last week but seeing him had changed something. That, and his standing up for them even if it meant he got bumped off the missing building case raised her opinion a bit. She was still annoyed, but both of them had times they couldn't tell anyone what they were doing.

"You might want to call Harlie, let him know it'll be a while," Maeve said.

"Good idea." Aisling dialed, waited until it rang through, hung up, dialed again, hung up again, then dialed and let it keep ringing.

"What was that about? The call not go through?" Caradoc picked up a bit of speed once it was clear they weren't getting out quickly.

"He's asked for a code when we're out and about. He didn't tell you?"

"I guess he figures my line is more secure."

Harlie picked up on the fourth ring. "Where are you all? I'm getting some odd feelings from you." He was a precog, but like most, they couldn't always control what they picked up.

"Caradoc took a detour. Then we got into some trouble."

"In the woods? Why are you all in the woods? Stella is looking forward to seeing you."

"Tell her we're visiting Grundog first, then we will be by."

"I'm going to keep eating without you." He hung up.

"He wasn't concerned enough to not eat, so that's good."

The troll town looked like a small rustic village somewhere in the alps. They didn't get a lot of snow here, but the sharply peaked roofs were more traditional than a necessity. Most trolls lived in colder areas.

Grundog was waiting as they drove up. She was almost willowy compared to most troll maidens, being as she was a troll/minotaur mix. But she refrained from picking any of them up in a hug. "Good to see you. Reece there as well?" Like most local trolls, Grundog usually spoke with a heavier pidgin accent. The fact she was toning it down while watching Reg out of the corner of her eye explained why she wasn't hugging.

"Good to see you too. Reece is still on the bad side, he wanted to take us in," Aisling said.

"He shouldn't be." She frowned.

"Since you're here, let's give you a tour." Reg and Grundog gave a quick tour of their town. Aisling had lived in the far north for a while in her youth and aside from the lack of ice, this reminded her of the troll towns up there. Minus the excessive brawling.

Caradoc vanished partway through the tour and they found him taking apart the bumper of his car. And swearing.

"What happened?" Aisling looked over the pieces he had next to him, but she couldn't see any bullet holes or other obvious damage.

"It wasn't just by chance those fake FBI people were following us." He held up a handful of tiny metal bugs.

Literally. They were shaped like flies, but the light glinting off them said they were metal.

"Those are all trackers?" Maeve came out to join them as well, but she dropped down next to him and poked through the things in his hand.

"Yes. And while I'd bet they came from the same creator, they aren't a design that I recognize. Mind you, they probably were added by different people. Or different groups at least. There are slight modifications between them."

Aisling took one. "Great craftsmanship—they even have tiny legs and wings." She flicked it and it started moving its legs. "They're still active?" She dropped it back to the pile he'd put on the ground. The one she dropped kicked its legs a few more times, then went still.

"I sprayed them with a neutralizer as I took them off the car, so that was just an automatic reaction. But who put them there?"

"And how did more than one group have the same supplier?" Maeve got back to her feet and dusted her hands off.

"That is disturbing too. Obviously Reece and his new crew put some on. But I'd guess that the fake FBI did as well."

"Which means they weren't following us because they thought we were someone else. They were following us for *us*." Aisling went back to thinking bad thoughts about Reece. "Reece probably knew that."

"Which meant he was trying to bring us in for something else?"

"Or making a good show for the real FBI agents he was working with. He might not be as removed from Area 42 as it appeared." She kept her voice down. Reg and Grundog had gone back to check on the status of the black SUVs lingering in their forest, but still better to not be flinging around that name.

A nearby door opened and Reg came out. "Your friends have left. Between the scouts I left behind and the electronic sensors, you're clear to the freeway." He shrugged. "Beyond that, you're on your own."

Grundog came out as well with a packet. "Give to Stella? It's something she was asking about." She was still fighting to keep her pidgin out, but it was slipping. Reg and his British accent were rubbing off on her. Or she was trying to lose it for him. She handed Aisling the large envelope. "Please make sure she gets it." The look on her face was serious.

Aisling almost asked what it was, then just took it instead. It felt like there were a few disks in there along with a lot of paper. "I'll make sure it gets to her." She held out her hand to Reg. "Thanks for helping us get out of our situation. Or both situations."

Reg shook her hand and grinned. "It was a pleasure. I'm sure we'll be seeing all of you around."

Caradoc had the bumper put back together and the bugs in a steel-lined case. He still didn't look happy as they got in the car. "I know we were going to see Stella, but I want to figure out where those damn bugs came from."

"I need to get this to Stella. Something in here had Grundog upset. Besides, if we can get into Reece's secret lab you can check out the bugs there."

"I know, but there's something about this entire thing that is odd. I have a sensor alert, none of these damn bugs should have been able to function on my car. When I removed them, all were live." The tone in his voice boded badly for whoever was behind the bugs.

"Someone out-geeked the tech king." Maeve was making light of it, but she sounded like she shared the same concern. Caradoc was one of the best, yet just in the past few hours his tech had been thwarted repeatedly.

"I wonder if Reece's bosses knew and that's why they

cut you loose." Aisling was more muttering to herself than them. But both had excellent hearing.

"That's a weird connection. You think Area 42 was testing Caradoc?" Maeve asked.

"Why not? Yeah, they weren't able to find any connection to our mother through him, but they might have also been testing his tech skills. When you take apart those trackers, can you tell how long they were on the car?" At this point, she didn't trust Area 42 about anything.

Caradoc was focused on the road and driving quicker than they'd come in. It took him a moment to shake himself free from wherever his thoughts had gone. "Yes, I should be able to. Damn it, if Area 42 was tracking me, then who else was?"

"That's what you get to find out." Aisling wasn't a huge fan of freeways, anyone who lived in L.A. got through them as quickly as possible. But she was extremely happy to see the onramp to the 5 freeway right now. She'd wanted to be doing something about the case, but being chased through the woods by unknown assailants wasn't it.

They were all silent as he drove to the exit for Stella's diner, but Aisling noticed that Maeve rode most of the way looking behind them.

"I do have a rearview mirror, you know." Caradoc cut off two cars to get off the freeway.

"And you don't always share what's going on." Maeve didn't change her position. "I'll keep my eye out if you don't mind."

Stella's diner wasn't in a great part of town, and unlike some areas, it looked like it had never started out great. Tiny houses with non-existent yards lined the street to the diner, along with a few larger new buildings that had little to no signage. But Stella kept her food prices low and made sure families in the area were taken care of. At 4'11" she looked like someone's kindly grandmother.

But people who crossed her only did so once.

Caradoc parked a way down from the diner and they walked to it. Harlie's motorcycle was still out front.

"You brought our friends I assume?" Aisling hadn't seen Caradoc grab the steel box, but he was extremely distracted.

He patted his jacket. "Yeah."

Maeve stepped up alongside. "He's still trying to figure out who's smarter than him. He'll get over it."

Aisling drifted to a small, seemingly empty parking spot near the diner. It could hold two cars, but more importantly, Reece had a cloaking system on it. If he were here, she'd be able to touch his car even though she couldn't see it. She picked up a small piece of gravel, hopefully not large enough to set off his alarm, and threw it where his car would be. Not a peep and the gravel didn't stop in its arc.

"Checking for him?" Maeve stopped while she did her test.

"Yup, better to be prepared if he's here." She wasn't sure if she was happy or upset that he wasn't there. They followed Caradoc into the diner and were waved down by Harlie to a large booth.

"I thought you were going to keep watch but stay separate from us?" Aisling slid in next to him.

"Seemed a bit redundant since you were already followed repeatedly. And if there is someone here watching you, I can spot them." Harlie had a few empty dishes near him and one of the busboys darted over to get them.

"The waitress will be right back." The busboy was a teenaged satyr and his voice managed to crack three different times in that short sentence. He bobbed his head, grabbed the used dishes, and trotted off.

"What'll ya have, sugars?" Stella came up so silently Aisling hadn't heard her approach. She did notice the frown and slight shake of her head as Stella handed out the menus.

"I'll start with a cup of hot tea if you would." Maeve flashed her best smile. She'd most likely seen the frown and head shake as well.

"Iced tea for me, please." Aisling looked over to Caradoc who was scowling at his phone. "For him as well."

"I'll get on those and be back for your food order. Our specials are on page *three*." She took off before anyone could respond.

Harlie frowned. "She wasn't like that before…oh." He pointedly looked to a group of young goths near the back. Who were pointedly not looking their way. "They must have just come in. Most likely following you three. You have acquired some extremely sloppy tails as of late."

Maeve flipped through her menu, grabbed Caradoc's and flipped through his, then turned to Aisling. "Well? Look at page three." She'd dropped her voice, and there were no occupied tables near them, but Aisling had a back-of-the-neck-feeling that the group in black was extremely aware of her.

Without a word, she flipped to page three. A slip of paper stuck out behind the daily specials. "Go to the back room. Wait for my signal. Tell others not to go."

Aisling read it twice, but if there was anything else to it, she was missing it. She folded it flat against the menu and slid it to Maeve. "I'm thinking I might get this one." She put her finger on the note.

Maeve nodded and read it. "What do you two think?" She elbowed Caradoc to get his attention, but Harlie nodded at once.

There was no way to tell what the signal would be, or when it would happen, but she didn't need Maeve, Caradoc, or Harlie jumping to their feet and running after her.

A minute or two later, yelling erupted from the group in the back corner. The three in black leaped to their feet and started shaking their hands as if shocked. That was as good a signal as any. Aisling jumped to her feet and ran for the back broom closet. She waited until she got the door to the diner shut before trying the second door, the one at the back of the closet. If Stella had gained access to Reece's hidey-hole, Aisling would have expected that she'd find a way to get all four of them in. The second door stuck briefly, then let her push it open.

"Hello Aisling, please take a seat."

CHAPTER FIVE

EVEN THOUGH SHE'D CHECKED FOR his car, seeing Reece there wasn't as surprising as she would have thought. He must have ditched the FBI folks as soon as they cleared the forest. However, seeing the holograms of Garran and Surratt standing there *was* surprising. Surratt was human, or appeared so. In reality, he was a changeling—but working so deep undercover that few knew. Even most likely calling in from his hospital room he looked sleek and well dressed. His dark hair and beard looked trimmed within an inch of their lives. Garran was a bit taller than Surratt, and pure fey. Just which fey species was unclear. His buzz-cut hair showed ears longer and more pointed than any other fey. Most likely a mixed fey breed of some sort. He never said what his lineage was, and no one asked.

Reece stood near the front of the table, closest to her. The other two stayed on the far end—most likely where the holographic receiver was. Holo-tech was a new science and she was surprised to see it. They were top-notch holograms, but it was clear what they were. In theory, scientists were working on making them indistinguishable from real people until someone tried to touch them. Aisling could see far too many ways for that to be a bad thing. Garran had been the one who spoke when she came in.

Aisling shared her glare with all three, folded her arms, and remained standing. "What the hell is this?" She wanted to add a lot more, but not in front of Garran and Surratt.

"I'll sit." Reece sat noticeably not in the chair closest to her. "I'll let them start, however."

Garran looked uncomfortable, something Aisling had rarely seen. He was acting chief of the department, having taken over when Surratt died. Or at least when they told the public Surratt died to bring out whoever had tried to kill him. He was still playing dead and Garran was still in charge.

"This isn't how I wanted things to go down. How any of us wanted them to go down." He shot a glare at Surratt. "But today's events are making us speed up the timeline and pull you into the loop. We can't bring in Maeve or Caradoc yet though."

Aisling raised her hand and turned toward the door. "Then I'm out. Maeve is my partner, and I'm sure somewhere deep inside you recall what that means. Caradoc is my brother and only one of two family members that I can stand. Not to mention whatever you're all up to, having them along is a good idea. Don't read me in if they're out." She wanted to be on this case, but she knew the others needed to be in as well.

She had her hand on the door handle when Reece got up and grabbed her arm.

He turned to the two holograms. "I told you this would happen. You can't have one without all. I'd say add in Harlie too—who knows what he'll pick up."

"This isn't open for negotiations." Surratt had been silent, and his voice was low.

Aisling let go of the door handle and glared at them. "And you're not my boss—since everyone thinks you're dead. Garran isn't right now either, since both Maeve and I are on indefinite leave. We all know, or none of us do. And if any of you added bugs to Caradoc's car, he will find you. He's working on reverse engineering them now. He *will* find out who created them."

A crash came from behind one of the electronic boards

on the left side of the room. Reece winced, the two holograms shook their heads.

"Whoever is back there needs to come out now. I am getting seriously sick of these games." Aisling stalked over but the board slid back before she got there.

"Hi, Aisling." Mott Flowers stood there, looking embarrassed. "Nice to see you again."

Aisling looked from the rumpled inventor to Reece and the other two. "He's involved but we're not? Let me guess who created the bugs." Mott was one of the few people who could out-tech Caradoc.

"Now see, I told them they made a mistake kicking Caradoc out. And not letting you in. Or Maeve. They wouldn't listen." Mott was an elf, a pure one. But his lack of height and permanently rumpled appearance made Aisling wonder if there wasn't a gnome or three buried deep in his family tree. He'd worked with Caradoc in one of his businesses and also in a brain trust.

"And they tried to keep you hidden from me?" She turned to the holograms. "This is where trust issues begin, boys. You want me to trust you, but you keep hiding things." This time she had the door open an inch when Reece pushed it shut.

"We need to talk." He was close enough that there were a few layers of meaning in that comment.

His face was close to hers and his gray eyes were almost pleading. Aisling let go of the handle then swore to herself—never look into Reece's eyes. Reece was damn good-looking, tall, slender but with a well-built swimmer's body, thick dark hair—and some sort of mojo-powered gray eyes. Even before she knew who he really worked for, she'd had a policy to stay away from those eyes.

She pushed past him and took a seat. "Talk fast, and don't say anything that you don't want me to repeat to Maeve and my brothers out there." She folded her arms and shared the glare around the room. Except Mott. As usual, he looked confused as he took a seat. He was brilliant with technology and weapons, not so much on social cues.

Reece sat as well but pointedly looked to the two holograms.

"And we're talking now?" Aisling was glad they had reached out to her, but she wasn't leaving the others out. Trust was earned, and she trusted the three out in the diner more than the four in here.

Garran broke the silence. "We cut you off, and them, because we needed to see if there were connections to the people behind the Area 42 attack."

"You thought that if we were involved we'd go running to Mommy the moment you cut us? Or what, that Maeve would run to MI-6?" She understood that there was a lot of stress going on, this was an unprecedented situation. But either they trusted her or they didn't.

"No." Surratt turned and partially vanished. When he came back into the picture he spoke louder. "We were watching to see if they would reach out to you. And we'd wanted to wait longer, especially after Area 42 cut Caradoc loose."

"Against my objections by the way. But I'm not on the higher-ups' good list right now." Reece shrugged.

That answered the question of if those three he'd been with were FBI or not. He'd been demoted to babysitting an FBI operation when he'd tried to stand up for Aisling and the others.

"Where'd you park? I checked your secret spot coming in."

Reece smiled. "I told Mott you would. I'm around the corner in a very staid unmarked FBI loaner. I can't use any car that someone might recognize." From the look on his face, that wasn't his call either. Reece was very attached to his cars.

"I'll cut to the meat," Garran finally said. "The main theory, that Area 42 won't admit to any of us, is that there is a cabal within the High Council. We don't know the motivation and since Area 42 won't tell us what, specifically, the group housed in the building disappeared was focusing on, we're not getting anywhere fast."

"You mean like my mother." Aisling shrugged. "Yup, I'd say she and her cronies are definitely involved. Harlie found some connection with them before Nix's drug operation blew up. The reason as to why they stole a building, however, is up for grabs. But my mother is a power mad bitch. If I were going up against her, the first people I would have included would have been people who know her well and can't stand her."

"Which are good points. But we're working around Area 42 on this and they have information that we don't. Judging by the way they excluded you after they recruited you, kicked out Caradoc, and semi-demoted Larkin, I'd say they might know more than we do."

"They said they didn't need me either, not that it seems to matter." If Mott was upset about being let go as a consulting-semi-prisoner from Area 42, he wasn't showing it. Mott wasn't fond of organizations in general.

"So here we are. Whatever this is." Aisling motioned around the table. "We call the others in, or do I walk?"

Garran and Surratt closed their mics to only themselves as they broke into a silent yet extremely animated conversation.

"It's all about them you know." Mott leaned over and nodded to the arguing holograms. "I'm not completely sure what they are, maybe a secret unit? But those two are leading it. When Area 42 set me free, Garran was driving the cab that picked me up."

"Which wasn't known to Area 42, by the way. I was still inside at that point, and they called for a regular cab. I didn't hear anything that the people who dropped

Mott off recognized Garran." Reece watched the other two, most likely to try and read their lips. Both were at enough of an angle to make that difficult. But it didn't stop him from trying.

"Did they pull you in before or after you got demoted? Thank you for trying to get Maeve and me back on the case, by the way." She still wasn't sure what was going on with them on a personal level, but she genuinely appreciated his attempt on the professional one.

"After. They just brought me in a day ago. Ironically, Area 42 removed me from the case before Caradoc."

"Was that op in the forest near the trolls anything at all connected to the Area 42 case?"

"Not a bit. I'm glad you refused to come with us though and good on Reg for the backup." He grinned. "I looked him up, he's not just any troll on walkabout. He's a high-ranking member of Ckiong, the agency that protects all troll interests. They aren't fond of the elven High Council, by the way."

"Good thing I'm not one of them." Aisling watched the holograms, but they were still arguing. "Why are you glad we didn't go with you?"

"Because you're not related to the FBI case, and it would have been a waste of time. The case they dropped on me is a mess. They got infiltrated a few months ago by a gang. Didn't even realize it for a month. Thought they had a trap set up to follow them back to their base, you guys show up, the fake FBI follows you instead and the operation failed."

"At least you have them. How many were in that group?" There had been seven SUVs. The first car only had two people, but there could have been far more in the rest.

"We have captured twenty of the lowest rungs in the fake organization. I left the questioning to Jazmyn since she's still pissed about me taking over."

"Didn't we go to school with a Jazmyn?" Mott asked as he doodled on an electronic pad. Possibly creating a new tech to change the world.

Aisling shook her head. She and Mott had gone to primary school together, but she hadn't thought of him until he became involved with the iron death drug case. "You're the one who remembers that better than me, I doubt this is the same one though."

The sudden sound as both Garran and Surratt turned on their mics again was startling.

Garran nodded. "Go get the other three. Actually, get Stella too. We fix this together or we all go down together." Neither he nor Surratt looked happy, so it wasn't clear which one had put up the bigger fight.

Aisling was out the door before they could change their minds. They were still in the booth, but Harlie was the only one with food. The goth gang from the corner was gone though, and Stella was hovering near the booth.

"They said you had something for me?"

Aisling had forgotten about Grundog's envelope. She pulled it out of her jacket. "Sorry, Grundog gave me this."

"I'll be right back." Stella darted away, vanishing into the kitchen.

"So? What was that about? And don't say nothing. You were in there too long for nothing," Maeve said.

"Let's wait for Stella, but yeah, all of you need to come to the back room—her too. I don't want to say anything until we get back there."

Caradoc looked ready to climb out of the booth that second.

"Seriously. We all need to go together. What happened to our odd little friends?" She looked toward the corner the goth gang had been in.

Harlie grinned. "Pretty sure they were Baobhan, the one that looked like a guy, wasn't. They took off not too long after you vanished. Stella might know more about them."

Baobhan were female vampires. They were a fey race but often tried to pass themselves off as human. Or, failing that, as evil ones from beyond the veil. Vampire legends notwithstanding, they were really only dangerous in large groups. They were frail and had no magic. If they could drug someone they might be able to take their blood, but most humans had a natural avoidance of them and most other fey would kill them if they tried anything. The majority of the race were decent members of society, but there were always a few in every group who had to push things.

Stella came back a moment later, noticeably without the envelope. "There now, all secured. So?" She directed the last at Aisling.

"So we all get to go into the back room."

Stella's eyebrows went up. Since the only way into the secret room was through the diner, she had to know who was in there right now. She might not know about the two holograms. From what Reg had said it was probably a hell of a lot safer for Garran that he was only a hologram when he was facing Stella. She obviously hadn't taken the exclusion any better than Aisling.

"Let me tell Nethi to cover the place." Stella nodded and went back to the kitchen.

"I'll keep an eye out here." Harlie watched the patrons around him all the while still appearing to be only keeping an eye on his food.

"Nope, you're being pulled in on this too." Aisling was about to flag down the busboy, but Stella caught him just as she came back out of the kitchen. He nodded at her instructions then went into the kitchen.

"I've set a low spell to cover us all going into the broom closet. Toby will keep serving this table to keep the images of you active." She counted to three then nodded toward the back. "We're covered, shall we?"

They all followed her, but looking back, Aisling could see that they still appeared to be chatting in the booth. She was reminded not to mess with a magic user of Stella's level.

Things were crowded with five of them in the broom closet, but they didn't want to risk anyone being seen.

Aisling was closest, so she pushed open the inner door.

"Reece, good to see you. Again." Maeve's tone was icy as she stalked in. None of the others looked happy either.

Aisling scowled. Mott was missing and so were the holograms. "I meant it, Reece, all of us get read in on everything or I walk."

The rest sat around the table as Reece rolled his eyes. "Certain people wanted to keep things secret. Just come out, Mott. If the other two want to play games, fine."

"Mott? What are you doing here?" Caradoc nodded as Mott came out from the restroom this time.

"Good to see you, boss." He nodded to the others. "Haven't met you before, Harlie, but I've heard of you since I was a sprout."

Harlie smiled then tilted his head. "Your family name is Flowers, but you're connected to the Olci family, aren't you?"

"Yes, my mother's side."

"And they're part of the High Council, aren't they?" Caradoc leaned forward.

Mott scrunched up his face and shrugged. Family connections, like most things non-tech related, weren't his strong point.

"Yes, they are." Reece pulled up the electronic wall screen. "Might as well start with them, since the theory seems to be that the High Council is connected in one way or another with recent events." The screen filled with elvish names. "These are the families and immediate ties of families who are members of the High Council. Most have been members since the crossing into this world. A few," he clicked on the screen in front of him, "are newer." The lines shifted a bit and some changed color. The original main lines were now dark green with others changing to light blue. Olci was dark green, as was Otheralia—Aisling, Caradoc, and Harlie's family last name. Aisling used Danaan, a common elvish last name, akin to Smith, as her last name to keep herself separate from the family. Caradoc went even further and used one far down the family tree. But few people connected Aisling Danaan or Caradoc Larfin with Lady Tirtha Lasheda Otheralia—their mother.

"And these three are the ones we have family boxes for." Reece's screen updated and Otheralia, Hthia, and Wolinshea—all lit up.

"And I assume you already looked into anything untoward about either family?" Caradoc was studying the screen far too carefully. If Reece didn't give them access to a copy, Caradoc would have them all memorized.

"Any other signs of the Old Ones?" Maeve had a close encounter with one and had been a bit freaked out about them since. Humans didn't fear the beings from beyond the veil the way the fey races did—it was instinct with the fey. Fleeing to another world to escape being slaughtered by Old Ones would do that.

Reece shook his head. "But to be honest, not sure that would be reported even if it happened. Either you and Aisling are lucky exceptions to the rule, and the vallenians do kill people who see them on this side of the veil, or it's just a myth to scare people."

Harlie glanced up on the screen then turned back to Reece. "Myth. Complete myth. Although I don't believe they want to be seen, so if someone does see them, it is because the vallenians wished it. But, I do believe they are staying on their side. For now."

Reece watched him, but Harlie just smiled.

"Then what are the connections with these three, beyond the fact they're part of the High Council?" Aisling was still missing something.

"They were all at the signing of the accord to save the humans during the Black Death," Caradoc said with a glance toward Harlie who gave a short nod.

"But so were other families." Reece shook his head. "They used the boxes of these three for a reason, something tied into whatever happened to Area 42.

"Something that is not yet completed." Harlie turned pale, stumbled to his feet, then collapsed. At the same time, the walls shook.

CHAPTER SIX

———◆———

AISLING GRABBED HARLIE AND STRAIGHT-
ENED him out on the floor. He was breathing
heavily, and his eyelids were fluttering, but he wouldn't
wake up. Mott made a pillow out of his sweater and put
it under his head.

"What happened? And what the hell was that shake?"
Aisling knew that this inner room was fortified with
massively thick steel and concrete. Nothing should make
it move like that.

"Let me get him a tonic." Stella was out the door in a
flash.

Reece rubbed his forehead a bit, then started pulling
up scanners on the far wall. He had cameras all over the
city, but right now he had the ones closest to the diner
showing.

"Garran? Surratt? You guys notice anything?" Aisling
didn't leave Harlie but yelled toward the far end of the
room.

Caradoc and Maeve both looked around.

"You see them in here?" Maeve raised her eyebrow.

Aisling waved her hand. "They were here as holograms.
Before. Reece? Did they leave?"

"They logged off." Reece scowled at the screen and
tightened the focus to a parking lot a block over from
them. Rather, something Aisling knew had been a parking lot when they drove in—but was now a massive pile
of concrete, girders, and steel.

Caradoc got up and walked closer to the screen.
"What's that?"

"A pile of what was a building. Or part of one. Dropped from a serious height." Reece flipped through a few more screens, working out from the parking lot.

"And where did it come from?" Caradoc moved closer to the screen then sat, never once taking his eyes off the image.

"That's what I'm looking for. There should be a damaged or missing building somewhere, something that exploded. That looks too small to be more than a shop maybe?"

Stella came in with a large mug. "Just a bit of the old brew to get him right. I don't think anything is seriously wrong, what we felt, he got slammed with." She held the mug up to Harlie's lips and Aisling raised his head.

Harlie's breathing slowed down and his eye movements stopped as he drank whatever was in the cup.

"You mean the explosion from *that* landing in a parking lot?" Maeve turned back to the screens. "A hopefully empty parking lot?"

Sirens echoed from outside and fire trucks, police, and paramedics all arrived on the scene.

Harlie started muttering, but Stella made him finish the entire mug.

"There is something wrong with the veil, didn't you feel it?" He opened his eyes and slowly sat up but kept rubbing his forehead.

Stella nodded as she set aside the mug. "I felt it. A nasty kick that one had."

"The shaking we felt?" Aisling hadn't felt anything else, but something did a job on Harlie and there was tension in Stella's face as well. Not to mention Reece rubbing his forehead when he thought no one would notice it.

"No," Stella said. "The two were probably connected in some way, coincidences don't happen like that. But there was a psychic kick that hit me right before Harlie collapsed."

"It's still open." Harlie got back into his chair and handed Mott back his sweater with a nod of thanks. "No idea how or where, but the veil is open."

"Didn't it have to open each time the vallenians came through?" Maeve asked. "No one got hit with a psychic slam when that happened, did they?"

"That was less tangible." Harlie still appeared to be in pain. "They came through as singles, or at the most, that group of three. Something far larger has forced it open."

"Like part of a building?" Mott had been focusing on his pad but looked up toward the front screen. "That came from somewhere."

Reece had run through all of his screens. "I'm not seeing anything within the range of my cameras that is missing a building or part of one. I don't have the entire city covered though." He got out his phone and dialed. "Garran? You two need to come back online in here. Yeah, we noticed. Harlie collapsed and said there's a problem with the veil." The rest of the conversation was one-sided, and Reece wasn't sharing. Finally, he hung up.

"They aren't coming back?" Aisling resumed her seat.

"Not right now. Whatever that was, it's fried some tech, including holograms. There have also been reports of more precogs collapsing as well." He rubbed his head again. Aisling knew he had shown some precog abilities before, but as a fey-human hybrid he shouldn't have them. So he kept them hidden. Right now, he looked like he needed a dozen aspirin.

Caradoc looked up at that. "They managed to get holo-technology to work? I'd love to see that. Do you know the limits?"

"Yeah, don't get fried by whatever opened the veil and dropped the mass of building on a parking lot." Maeve leaned over to Aisling. "Good to know you hadn't gone bonkers and were hallucinating people."

"Yeah, me too."

Reece's phone rang. "Yes. Yes. And yes. We'll be right there." He clicked it off. "They want Jones and me to go to the building crash site."

"He's here too?" Caradoc asked.

"No. He's on his way in. Even though I've been bumped down a few pegs, we're both still Area 42. That's who just called." He got to his feet and gave a quick look around. "You're welcome to stay in here, but it won't help you much without myself, Garran, and Surratt to read you in. Can you give Mott a ride home?"

Mott briefly looked up at his name, then went back to whatever he was building on his pad.

"I might like to use some tools if you don't mind." Caradoc pulled out the box he'd put the trackers in and dumped them on the desk.

"Ah, nice, aren't they?" Mott grinned and reached over for one. "I thought it added a bit that they look like real flies." His grin was more like a five-year-old with a new toy than a mad inventor.

"You made these? All of these? And what, sold them to the highest bidders? How many different people were tracking us?" Aisling asked.

Mott frowned. "I made them for Area 42. However, I believe someone there sold them to others." He started picking them up, peering at them closely, then sorting each into one of three piles. "Area 42, FBI, and unknown. The Area 42 ones are untampered with. The FBI ones have tiny antenna added here and here." He held up the tracker in question but without a microscope, there was no way to see the difference. "And these. They are totally modified beyond my scope." He glared at Reece. "Who did your people give these to?"

Reece got to his feet but held up his hands. "I have no idea and right now they aren't really *my* people. Maybe you and Caradoc can find out?"

"I'll bring in some food and cut the spell running on

your booth out front." Stella also rose as she turned to Reece. "But you had better keep us updated. And warn Garran I want a word with him." Her smile was not a nice one and seemed to be directed at both Reece and Garran.

"I promise on both counts. Now, if I don't meet with Jones, he'll come looking for me, and I'm not ready for that yet."

"He doesn't know we're going to be involved?" Aisling folded her arms.

"You, yes. The others, not yet." He opened the door for Stella. "I'll talk to him."

"You haven't really told any of us much, you know." Maeve sat next to Caradoc and Mott watching the tracker investigation.

"We will, I promise." He shut the door behind them.

Harlie sat back and watched the closed door. "It's not that he's lying, really. But there is definitely a level of mis-truth there." He winced and rubbed his forehead. "Or it could be the backlash from the veil being kicked open."

"Any idea what came through?" Aisling imagined marching armies of vallenians and other Old Ones. Nothing and no one left on the other side of the veil was harmless. In the thousands of years since the fey races crossed over to this world, they'd never looked back.

"Not a one. I might be able to figure out if they are still here, it could have been a test."

"You think the Old Ones are planning an invasion?" Aisling didn't like the look on his face.

"Their idea of an invasion and ours might be extremely different concepts. Those of us who crossed the veil have been changed by this world."

Stella broke up the cheery thoughts with plates of sandwiches, salads, and drinks.

She settled in next to Aisling. "So Garran was here, wasn't he? Even as a hologram, that's still rude. I helped them solve that case, and what does he do? Kicks me out of the police station!"

Aisling helped herself to the food. "I thought you didn't get involved in Reece's jobs. You just helped him stay hidden." Reece's former partner had been the one who created this room—her and Stella. But when Aisling first met her, Stella insisted she didn't like to get involved beyond watching over things.

From the look of chagrin on Stella's face, she recalled their conversation too. "This last case was different. I found I liked being in the action." Her eyes went round. "Speaking of action, let's see what Grundog sent." She patted Aisling's arm and scurried out the door.

"Any clue as to who the third group was that had the trackers? Or who put them on first?" Caradoc and Mott had dragged out at least fifteen small tools from Reece's storage and were so caught up in what they were doing that Aisling had to repeat herself. Twice.

"Hmmm?" Caradoc looked up finally. "Oh, not yet. But I think we may have a fourth group. But they only had two. If I had to guess I'd say Area 42 was first, the fake FBI second, and the other two sometime after that. But none of them had been on my car for longer than thirty-six hours." He looked to Mott. "I'd like to know how you were able to break my car's security and why. We *are* friends, you know."

"That was difficult. Extremely so. Your security measures are top-notch. But they told me it was a test, that you knew they were on there. As for the thirty-six hours, yes for them having been on your car that long, but I built them over a week ago."

"Serious bastards." Caradoc shook his head. "They didn't tell me about it even though they had you build them when I was still working with them. Damn. Part of me is glad their building got taken."

Mott shook his head. "They really aren't nice. Larkin

and Jones aren't bad, but the rest? Eh, we'll figure this out before they do."

Maeve turned back from watching the screens. "So that's what we're going to do? Just form our own group of rejects and solve things? Do we get a secret multi-colored van to travel around in?"

Aisling shrugged. "You wanted to get involved."

"No, *you* wanted to get involved. I was still enjoying being lazy."

Stella came back in; the envelope Aisling had given her was fatter now.

"Did you feed it?"

"In a way. Since we were excluded from the formal investigation, Grundog and I had been working on our own theories. We believe what happened to the Area 42 building had repercussions elsewhere in the world. It should be noted that Reg showed up days after the building vanished." She nodded as if that was important.

Aisling was sure it might be, she just didn't know what the connection was. "What did Grundog send you?"

Stella dumped the contents of the file out on the table. "Even though Reg won't help directly, as he claims to be just wandering around the globe, Grundog has other friends in the U.K.. These pictures came through one of her sources three days ago. They didn't want to trust them to electronic transfer and neither did we." She held up the top picture. An older elf, lean, scarred face, buzz-cut red hair, and no clan jewelry. Even just waiting to cross the street he looked violent.

"Is that Nix?" Aisling added a few choice swear words. Nix was a serious pain in the ass. A former elven gangster who decided he worked better as a ruler than a joiner and destroyed at least one entire gang when they disagreed. He was also the force behind the spread of the iron death drug and had come far too close to killing all of the fey in southern California before she and the others stopped him a few weeks ago.

Maeve was up and standing next to her immediately. She grabbed the photo, then another one below it. "That bastard. Why won't he just die?" Maeve had a long history with him, none of it good.

"I know. I'd hoped when he got sucked up into whatever that vortex was in the cave, he was gone. Judging by the date on these—he's alive and kicking in Cardiff."

Stella spread out more of the contents of the envelope on the table. "That does conclusively verify it is Nix. For some reason, your MI-6 mates won't confirm or deny. It's as if something big is coming and all the largest agencies are closing everyone else out. My theory is that Reg is trying to work with them, but they're shutting the Cki-ong out too, so he's doing his own thing."

"Where in Cardiff? I'll find him myself and take care of that still alive situation once and for all." Maeve patted her gun.

"He was heading to a coffee shop on Womanby Street. I doubt he's hanging around waiting for you." Stella rolled her eyes. "If we go after him, we need to plan it."

"We? Fancy a trip?" Aisling looked through some of the other documents, but most were in code. There were a few more pictures, but none looked remotely like Nix. She'd need to have Stella identify who else they were tracking.

"I haven't been out of California for far too long. Probably longer than you've been alive. A trip across the pond might be just the thing. I have a valid passport, might as well use it." Stella consistently lied about her age, and like most changelings, she could make herself look however old she wanted. But this confirmed what Aisling had started to suspect—Stella was closer to Harlie's age than her own.

"Damn it!" Caradoc grabbed a hammer and started smashing a number of the trackers. "Did you put a resurrection system in these? Now look! They're all turning back on!" He didn't wait for Mott's answer as he finished off the fake bugs. He then scooped the remains and dropped them into his steel box.

Mott looked as shocked as the rest of them. Except Harlie. He was focused on the screen with the camera on the parking lot.

"I didn't do that to them. In fact, I would have thought it would have been impossible with the secondary connections I'd added." Mott scowled and looked toward the closed box. "They messed with my invention." The tone of his words was that the most heinous crime possible had been executed on him personally.

"Area 42? They might have folks who could change things like that." Aisling didn't have a hard time imagining them messing with his inventions, but Mott clearly did.

"We need Reece to get his ass back here and start explaining." Mott glared at the screen as if looking for Reece on the camera would help.

"I think they are going to be busy for a while. They found a section of building that appears to be proving interesting." Harlie hadn't looked over but cut all the other screens so that the only one remaining was the parking lot and he enlarged it massively. "Yes, right there." He'd found a laser pointer and circled something in the far-left corner.

"I give up, what is it?" Aisling could see random letters on the concrete, but the damage was too severe to put together words. At least for her.

Harlie pulled up another screen and put the words in place—then filled in the missing parts. "This was part of the commissary for Area 42. I think we found part of the missing building. Or it's found us."

CHAPTER SEVEN

"ARE YOU SURE THAT'S WHAT it says?" Caradoc shoved aside his worry about the bugs for the moment and moved closer to the big screen. "There are very few intact letters."

Harlie glanced away long enough to give his little brother an eye roll. "This program was extrapolated from one of yours. Plus, they are making the same connection. Look at them."

He was right, the gaggle of people in suits, as opposed to the cops or firemen, were now swarming that one corner, effectively blocking it from Reece's camera.

"And now they are chasing off everyone else." Stella shook her head and made a tsking sound as the cops and firemen returned to their vehicles, with a few suits making sure that happened. "They can't keep trying to do this on their own."

"But that won't stop them." Aisling spotted some familiar people. "There's Jones and Reece as well."

"We need a sample of that building debris." Caradoc narrowed the camera as tight as it would go, but the Area 42 people were doing a great job of blocking it.

Harlie peered at the image. "Agreed. If there is any psychic resonance on it, from wherever it came from, I might be able to pick it up."

"I was thinking more along the line of Mott and me doing a study on the elements on it." Caradoc looked like he was already deciding what instruments to use.

"Now, boys," Stella said. "Both avenues of study are valid. But first we need to get a piece of that building."

"I doubt Reece would do it," Aisling said, "even though he's pulling us into this secret group with Garran and Surratt, he is still trying to stay in Area 42."

"We need to hide a piece from them, then pick it up once they leave." Maeve broke away from staring at the two Nix photos. "We know they're going to haul it off soon."

Middle of the day, middle of L.A., and Aisling knew Area 42 would still find a way to remove all the rubble. She had no idea how they were going to get a piece free before that happened.

"That might be possible." Stella was rubbing her chin and a small grin formed. "I know I couldn't get close enough to steal a piece, but with the right disguise, I might be able to wander close enough to that far edge there to magically hide a piece."

As a changeling, and a powerful one at that, Stella was good at disguises. It was illegal for changelings to use their abilities for nefarious reasons, but she was just going to wander by a place of interest.

"What spells are you thinking?" Harlie and Caradoc were both powerful magic users, but unlike Caradoc, Harlie actually followed the practice. Caradoc kept trying to find ways to do the same things magic could with technology instead.

Stella tapped her chin as she thought. "I believe a shali hiding spell combined with a usibik repulse spell. There are several small, broken pieces in that far corner and it's a good distance from the piece with the letters." She was already planning her attack.

"How much building do you need?" Aisling aimed the question squarely between Caradoc and Harlie. She agreed with Stella that both areas of study could help.

"I won't need much," Caradoc said. "A spectral hythinator should give us some answers as to where that came from and what it is. It works on small amounts. Maybe a handful of material?"

"That should work for me as well. It should also tell me if that is actually the building that left here or not. Depending upon who or what took it, they could have sent material to confuse the search."

"I'll spell what I can. There will be a marker left by the hiding spell, once the Area 42 people leave you should be able to grab it." Stella got to her feet. "Keep an eye on me on the screen."

Before Aisling could ask what she'd be going as, a short familiar black man appeared in Stella's place.

"Nice, but Reece and Jones will recognize you. Not to mention, you know Garran probably has eyes in the area as well." Stella had used that disguise before when the police station had been attacked.

Stella looked down with a scowl. "That's what I get for not changing very often. Spell fall-back contamination." She closed her eyes and a taller woman appeared. She looked human and possibly homeless. Or at least rough around the edges. "Bother. I was aiming for a man." Stella looked down at herself. She changed again and appeared as a small male gnome. One who also had seen better days. "Perfect." She started for the door.

"We'll watch you and call if anyone looks too interested," Aisling said.

"I'll have my phone on vibrate. Ring if I need to bug out." With a nod, Stella left.

"What are the odds that's not truly the missing building?" Aisling hadn't thought of that until Harlie mentioned it. If someone could steal a building, faking part of it coming back to mess with Area 42 was possible. It depended on who took it and why. Neither of which they had answers for.

"It's hard to say. But everything must be examined." Harlie winced as he scanned through a few of the closest cameras.

"Your head still hurts?"

"Yes. I have a bad feeling that building is directly responsible for the veil being open." He scowled at the screen.

"I wish I could—" Aisling cut off as she saw a dark shape on the camera. It was in all black with a tall old-fashioned hat. "A vallenian?" It was hard to tell as it kept drifting between the pieces of rubble. But considering that no one on the ground appeared to notice it, it could be. Or Aisling could have finally snapped.

"Where?" Mott had drifted back working on his pad, but his head snapped up immediately at her words.

"Right there. He's by the edge where the partial words were." He wasn't easy to see, but there was no doubt that he was there. Aisling looked around but saw the same level of confusion on Mott's face as that of everyone else. "Seriously? Harlie? Tell me you see him."

Harlie squinted at the screen. "I'm sorry. There is a disturbance of some kind in that area, something beyond our ken, but I don't see an Old One."

"Damn it, why do I keep seeing them?"

"Hey, I saw one before I knew what it was, but I don't see it now." Maeve gave an encouraging smile. "It doesn't mean anything bad though. They might just like you."

"Or she's somehow tuned to them." Caradoc squinted at the screen and looked annoyed. "I was in the area where she saw one, but I never saw it. Reece was there in Old Town, right? When you saw the three?"

Aisling kept looking away, hoping the creature would vanish, but it was still there each time she looked back. "He was. He did see them right as they left that time. But not the first time they appeared. We had one follow us and he looked right where it was and saw nothing."

Harlie nodded slowly and kept his eyes on her. "I think we need to find out what is unique to you that you see them when your blood relatives don't. But not right now."

Aisling rubbed her arms as a chill hit her. Logically, she agreed. They had a few more pressing things on their plates. Emotionally, she wanted them to fix it immediately.

"Is that Stella? She moved fast." Maeve called their attention to a smaller screen that was a block away from the parking lot. A semi-drunken appearing gnome was meandering down the street. He appeared to be wandering, but he was making good time.

"And the vallenian is right in the corner she's going to visit." The vallenian had stopped passing through the rubble but was watching everything from the corner in question.

"And no one is even looking over there," Maeve said.

"I have to distract it." Aisling got to her feet. She wasn't sure what she was going to do, but if the vallenians kept appearing to her and not others, it might mean there was a connection. That thought didn't make her happy, but it might come in handy in this case. Having Stella run into one could be a bad thing. This wasn't the time to test their theory that vallenians didn't kill people.

"What if it is helping us out?" Harlie watched Aisling carefully. "You want Stella to be successful and now no one in a group of thirty are remotely near the spot she's heading toward."

"You now think that because I can see them, I'm influencing them?" Aisling looked around the room. No one was disagreeing. "Seriously? How can I control them? And if I could, wouldn't I have used them to save me? On any number of adventures, such as facing off against Nix?" He'd buried her in a landslide of rock in the tunnel he was using to store his iron death drug. She still had nightmares about it.

"Like when they appeared when you and Reece were trapped in that gang war? And they appeared to save you both from certain death?" Caradoc's face now echoed Harlie's.

"I didn't call them! They were there when I came running out." Aisling didn't like the way this was going. Creatures used to scare fey children, shouldn't be connected to her. At all.

"And they just happened to freeze time so fifty or so gang members, heavily armed, mind you, didn't even see you." Now Maeve was getting in on things.

"Everything happened extremely fast."

"Point is, we can't prove or disprove any impact Aisling might have on them right now. And Stella's getting awfully close to that corner." Maeve pointed toward the screen.

"The vallenian is still there." Aisling shook her head. "I don't think we can count on him being on our side to keep the Area 42 people from noticing Stella. Or to leave her alone. They have their own agenda." It was specifically hanging out in that one spot for a reason. Just because their recent encounters with the vallenians hadn't left anyone dead, dying, or dragged back through the veil didn't mean that was their new status quo.

"Agreed. Let's make you look less like you." Caradoc rubbed his hands together.

"Can't I just wear a baseball cap and sunglasses? It works for vid stars."

"Actually, it rarely works for them but that's what they want." Mott's eyes lit up. "Which might work too."

"A vid star walking by that group of hardened Area 42 agents isn't going to distract them." Maeve shook her head. "But one being chased by something large and scary might?"

Caradoc and Harlie looked at each other and grinned.

Aisling didn't like that grin. "Just what are you two thinking about?"

"Not a thing that will harm a hair on that lovely

blonde head, sister mine." If Caradoc's grin got any larger it could be used to flag down wayward ships from rocky shores. "I have a baseball hat and some fancy shades in my car." He threw his keys at her.

"I need to know what's going to happen."

Maeve shared a look with the brothers then turned back. "Might be more realistic if you didn't."

"You too? Fine, keep an eye out and move fast." She opened the door. "Because I will be." She vanished. Or appeared to. When elves wanted to, they could move faster than most beings could see. Except other elves.

Aisling ran to Caradoc's car, found the hat and shades, locked the car back up, and started walking quickly—but not elf-running-for-her-life quickly. Whatever they had to surprise her would be moving quickly too. There were enough elves in the Area 42 group that they'd see her high-speed run, but it would be better if all of them first saw her.

She slowed down as she came out of an alley a block away from the parking lot. She was surprised that Area 42 didn't have the zone blocked off. Then again, they were shorthanded, and blockades caused questions. Whenever they'd been involved in needing a blockade before, it had always been something set up by the L.A. police. Since they were avoiding them, she could get why Area 42 didn't have one. She kept an ear out for whatever it was her brothers were planning on surprising her with. She got a few stares from passersby across the street as they tried to figure out which tall, leggy, possibly famous blonde might be drifting through the bad part of town, but no sign of anything scary.

The only tip-off she got was a slight scraping sound as a huge, clawed foot lifted off the ground behind her. She spun and screamed. A real scream, they'd worked that surprise out well. A snog monster was right behind her.

Snog monsters didn't exist outside of a fairy tale her

mother used to tell her. About three feet high, they were all claws and teeth and ate bad elf children. Yes, as an adult she knew they weren't real. But the five-year-old child inside of her screamed again and took off running.

The timing was perfect. She tore past the parking lot at almost elvish speed and the Area 42 people instinctively went after the monster.

Everything would have gone great if the vallenian hadn't appeared right in front of her.

CHAPTER EIGHT

S HE SKIDDED TO A STOP, the snog monster behind her scrambling as well. The Area 42 people were almost upon her when the vallenian tipped his hat and motioned to the people behind her. Which shredded the snog monster image and pushed back the Area 42 people hard enough that most of them fell.

Then he vanished.

Aisling couldn't be caught by the Area 42 people, so she kicked back into full speed and ran. She was still running a good five minutes later when her phone buzzed. She slowed down. "What?"

"You're clear." Caradoc sounded like he'd been laughing before he called. "Not sure what you did to our monster or the agents, but none of them are following you, and Stella has our sample. You did such a good job pulling them away, she didn't hide it, she grabbed it. You up to running back or should I come get you?"

"I'll get back there on my own. Just you and Harlie remember this moment—revenge can take time. But it *will* happen." Sending a fictitious childhood monster after her was not cool. She clicked off the phone and took some deep breaths. After the vallenian had appeared, then vanished, she'd really sprinted. She wasn't in bad shape, but she also rarely ran that hard. She jogged away, making a wide circle of the area to make sure she was clear of any straggling Area 42 agents. Then she kicked up speed and ran back to the diner.

Reece still wasn't back, and the others were all clustered around the far end of the table. They jumped collectively when she came in.

Aisling gave all of them a long look. "I know all of his toys are tempting, and that in theory we're going to be one happy super-secret family, but are you ready for Reece to see whatever you're doing? Not to mention, not sure how long until they can come back, but Garran and Surratt's holograms appear about a foot from where you are. The receiver is in the ground right in front of the screen."

Caradoc sighed and uncovered the equipment he'd thrown a jacket over when she came in. "We could have kept it hidden."

"Can you do the same study with your own equipment?" Aisling knew patience wasn't one of Caradoc's strengths.

"Yes." He packed everything up, storing what looked like crumbled concrete and shards of steel and wood into yet another steel-lined box. Then he put back the large tech toys he'd borrowed into the storage area along one side of the room. He did give them a small pat and wistful sigh.

"One advantage of magic." Harlie smiled. He had a small portion of the same rubble Caradoc had, but his pieces were sitting in the middle of a brightly colored piece of silk.

"And Garran and Surratt could still appear, and you'd have to scramble to hide it. Not to mention that I'm not even sure Reece hasn't got the place bugged."

"Oh, he does." Stella was back to looking like herself. "But I can turn it off. You are correct though unless you want to share what we just did with them, you might want to wait until you all get home."

Harlie didn't look as annoyed as Caradoc, but he carefully tied the corners of the silk square together and tucked it in his pocket.

"So the vallenian was still there?" Maeve grinned as she

finished a salad.

"Yes. The nice snog beast these two sent got me in full speed as I passed the parking lot. The vallenian appeared directly in front of me. It defused the snog beast and sent the Area 42 people tumbling." She hadn't seen Reece or Jones in the ones following her, but it all happened too quickly.

"That's what happened—well, part of what I saw." Stella got up and hit the replay on the screen. "They showed me this when I got back, thought maybe I'd sent a spell. But I was busy grabbing the rubble." She showed the clip of Aisling and the snog beast running past. Aisling watched as the vallenian popped into place. She looked around the room. "None of you see him, do you?"

"Not at all. It's only you and that creature. I am sorry you are going through this." Harlie's concern was genuine. "But this reinforces our hypothesis that the vallenians are tied to, and protecting, you for some reason."

"No box this time?" Maeve looked more curious than concerned.

"No, nothing."

"What's that?" Maeve frowned, got to her feet, and came closer. "That necklace that's barely showing under your shirt? I've never seen it before."

"I'm not wearing a—" Aisling dropped her words as her hand went to her throat. She did own a few necklaces, just didn't wear jewelry much. And she knew she didn't put anything on this morning. How she hadn't felt this before, she had no idea. But yup. There was a silver Celtic knot pendant within a triangle on a chain, simple, but unusually delicate. And not one she'd seen before. She tried to find the clasp, but the chain was a solid link.

"Lift it over your head, it's long enough." Maeve looked ready to start pulling.

"I didn't have this thing before I went out there." Aisling tried, but it wouldn't budge past her ears. "That vallenian gave me a necklace that won't come off? Someone help me get this damn thing off." She tugged on it, but while it didn't hurt her as it should have, it also wasn't coming off. She could lift it enough to look at the pendant, that was all.

Everyone clustered around and took turns trying to remove the necklace. Even Harlie's magic didn't work. Caradoc was breathing down her neck as he looked at the chain. "This looks like pure silver. No links, just a strand of unbreakable, unnatural silver."

They heard the first door open and everyone scattered along the large table pretending they were focusing on the screens. Of course, Area 42 had taken all of the rubble and left so there wasn't much to look at.

Reece and Jones came in together, neither looking happy. Jones held back as he saw everyone who was there. He was a tall, thin human, deliberately nondescript in appearance with short black hair and an angular face. He always looked like he was thinking of the best way to disable or kill someone. Aisling used to be a bit on edge around him, the trained killer persona was painfully evident. Now it was comforting to have someone that deadly on their side.

"You weren't kidding." After his initial pause, he came into the room, nodded his hellos, and took a seat. He was unflappable.

"Shouldn't you still be with them? They just hauled it all away." Aisling wanted to figure out the necklace and that damn vallenian, but she wasn't bringing either up to Reece or Jones yet.

"They asked us questions, had us help chase the LAPD out, then sent us on our way." Reece threw himself into a chair.

Jones looked around the room. "So we're all working together now? I'm fine with that if we are, not happy with certain agencies. As long as we don't do anything that should be reported to them within the guidelines that both Reece and I have in our contracts—I'm good."

Even Reece lifted an eyebrow at that. Aisling was sure that was the longest thing she'd ever heard Jones say. "Yup, that's the plan. Now, what were you all doing?"

Stella nodded to the remains of food. "We were eating and watching you all do your important work. Caradoc and Mott were trying to take apart those trackers. You two want something to eat?" She was all ready at the door when she finished her question. Which, from the look on her face, wasn't a question. They were getting something, it just depended on if it was going to be something they wanted.

"The usual for me. Thanks, Stella." If Reece had an idea that there was something else going on, he wasn't showing it.

Jones smiled. "A bowl of stew would be lovely. Thank you."

She nodded twice and left.

"Now, what were you really up to?" Reece looked around the room. "Something caused a mess at the crime scene. I didn't see them, but the reports were that a blonde woman and some weird creature ran down Towsling Street. Then both vanished, and something blew most of our agents over. There was no evidence of any type of explosive device, yet a few agents went back as far as ten feet."

"And why would we have been involved with that? Just because your people got tossed about by some wind doesn't mean we did anything." Maeve folded her arms and glared.

"Jones and I were being talked down to by Captain Driyflin at the time and missed most of it." He smiled at Aisling.

"What? It's not my fault she went after you. Or was it?" He might have been grinning because the person with the monster was a blonde woman. She'd lead him away from that.

"She wasn't happy about the lack of people brought in on that FBI case, but I convinced her that you all had nothing to do with the fake FBI crew, or whoever was behind them. I was thinking that since a blonde had been involved in the parking lot…what's that necklace?"

Aisling was willing to take the distraction. He might not have actually seen her, but her description with shades and a hat could be any number of a few thousand women in a ten-mile radius.

"This? I've had it for ages. You've never seen a triskele before?" She held the pendant up.

"You weren't wearing that when I left." He narrowed his eyes.

Caradoc gave Reece a raised eyebrow. "Yeah, she was. She's been wearing it since everything went into the shitter a week ago. It's a family good luck charm."

Reece got up and sat in the chair next to Aisling. "I would have noticed that."

She tucked it under her shirt. "Even if it was covered by my shirt? You only saw me for a short while."

Stella came in with food for Reece and Jones and refills for any who wanted them. She sat the food down then looked at the Aisling/Reece tableau. "What's wrong?"

"Reece thinks he's never seen Aisling's necklace before."

It was still hidden by her shirt, but Stella nodded. "The triskele? She's been wearing it each time I've seen her. Are you just not paying attention? And I thought you were a super spy."

Reece looked around the room, even Jones shrugged. "Don't look at me, I haven't seen her since we lost Nix." He slid over the photos that had been left out on the table. There were only two and both pictures had familiar red hair. The rest of Grundog's file must have been scooped up by Stella when she left. "Speaking of which.

We have a lead on the bastard?"

"One that I found, thank you very much." Stella looked ready to take the pictures back but folded her arms instead. "Grundog has some connections and got those two photos to me. She knew Aisling and Maeve would be interested."

Aisling hid her smile. Stella was good. She'd sacrificed two pictures to keep the rest of the items hidden. And distracted Reece from the necklace. She didn't want him or Jones knowing about it until she had a better idea where it came from and what in the hell it did. Those two might be currently estranged from Area 42, but they were still agents of it.

She resolved to wear turtlenecks until summer came or they could figure out what the damn necklace was and how to get it off her.

"Where were these taken? When? Does MI-6 know?" Reece asked without looking up as he and Jones examined the photos.

Aisling shared a smile with Stella as Caradoc moved over to the other two.

"A coffee shop in Cardiff, a few days ago, and no idea. They don't share things with us." Stella got just the right amount of snark in the last line.

"This has to be reported." Reece looked up earnestly.

Maeve shook her head. "I'm the closest thing you have to an MI-6 agent. And they have not thrown me under the shitter as some people have. Yet I say let them find their own copies."

Aisling knew the comment was for show. If Maeve seriously thought MI-6 didn't know where Nix was, or at least where he had been, she would be scanning those photos to them in a heartbeat. Maeve was in a non-active but still on-call status with them and had been the entire time she'd been working with Aisling. With Aisling only finding that out a few weeks ago.

"Do you want to show them to Area 42?" Stella didn't sound concerned which meant she had far more interesting things in her envelope that she wasn't sharing yet.

"We can talk about it," Reece said as he stacked the photos in the center of the table.

"Okay, so then do you want to tell us about that pile of building?" Aisling held up her hand before Reece could respond. "Yes, I know that you two weren't included in the investigation, which doesn't mean you weren't noticing things." She still wasn't sure what was up between her and Reece, but that was a separate, and definitely private, issue. Depending on what Reece said here, and even Jones would help determine if they could all trust each other professionally.

"Not a lot. That section of building hit with enough force to crack the parking lot like a glass plate. It didn't come from high above, but appeared five, maybe ten feet above the ground."

Harlie nodded. "It was falling for a while before it broke through. That makes sense."

Jones narrowed his eyes. "Broke through?"

Aisling nodded. "Harlie believes the building, or whatever that chunk was, is what popped open the veil."

"And what's keeping it open," Harlie said. "It's quite wedged open at the moment.

"Seriously? That's not possible." Jones looked like he was about to reach for his phone, then dropped his hand.

Aisling looked from one to the other. Yes, they'd been censured by Area 42, but for them to not pass on important information? That wasn't like them. "What's really going on? I don't believe you two wouldn't report things like Nix or a possible break in the veil to your captain."

Reece ran his hands through his hair. "Something in Area 42 is compromised. The system was showing cracks before the disaster, and it's only been worse since then. We're working with Captain Driyflin but there's something wrong with one or more of her bosses above her. She doesn't know exactly what's wrong and we sure as hell can't tell. She cut all of us, and kept you all out, to try and keep people safe."

"That's why you and Garran and Surratt formed your little support group." It made sense in a way. Before the building had been taken, Area 42 had a problem with agents being taken out in their private homes. Their hidden, secretive, private homes. Aisling had speculated they had a mole. Reece had insisted it was something else. One of the times she'd hoped to be wrong.

"Yes. Speaking of which, neither were happy about us expanding our group, nothing personal, everyone is just a little paranoid now. We should see if we can pull their holograms back." Reece tried calling both, but from the sound of the voice mails, neither picked up.

"So these bad higher-ups are who gave my inventions to the fake FBI and possibly a few other random evil groups?" Mott had been watching everyone. At least once he'd finished building whatever spec he'd been working on his pad. He didn't look any happier than anyone else.

"They might have been. We don't have a lot of information." Jones joined the unhappy club.

"What *do* you know? We gave you Nix, what do you have?" Aisling looked between both of them.

Reece nodded. "That building was part of the Area 42 complex. I believe Harlie might be right that it crashed through the veil. Which means the rest of it is probably still on the other side."

CHAPTER NINE

"I DON'T SEE HOW. BUT IT'S not my area of expertise." Jones shook his head and turned to Harlie. "I'll be the first to admit that I don't know as much about the veil as the average fey, let alone you. But wouldn't we have noticed if the veil opened long enough to suck an entire complex up? The building was large, but the underground portion was massive. I crawled around down in the pit for two days. It's all gone."

"You're right," Harlie said. "There was a psychic impact, one that was felt by precogs when the building portion crashed through the veil just a short while ago. It also caused a physical disturbance. There would have been an even worse one when the entire building vanished if it went through the veil."

Jones narrowed his eyes. "You're saying it didn't go through the veil, but this piece of it came back through the veil? That's a direct contradiction."

Aisling settled back in her chair. She hadn't known Harlie most of her life. But in the past month, she'd learned a lot. Such as his dropping into lecturing mode on topics that most normal people had no clue about. Jones made the wrong observation. She noticed that Caradoc and Maeve settled back as well. The others, including Mott, were leaning forward.

"Now, that is what it seems to be, isn't it?" Harlie's current grin probably terrified the Nepalese in the village below the cave he lived in for a few hundred years. "But time is different between the land past the veil and here. Oh, it moves the same, but at a different rate of influence. A fascinating phenomenon but it would take a few months to explain it to anyone clearly. Not to mention that there was an impact." He turned to Aisling. "You mentioned that this Nix person got pulled up and a massive wind filled those tunnels? Right about the time Area 42 was being taken?"

"Wait, you're saying that Nix was taken beyond the veil and managed to come back?" Reece wasn't narrowing his eyes like Jones, but there was a good amount of doubt on his face.

"Yes." Harlie's smile had gone beyond scary and into the complete and utter terrifying range. "Makes sense, doesn't it? Things from our world aren't meant to be on the other side. The building had never been over there, so it had no resonance with the old world. Even if Nix had been one of the ones who crossed originally, thousands of years would have changed him too much to fit there either. None of us can go back."

"The veil spit them out. I agree with spitting Nix out." Maeve snarled whenever she said his name.

"In a manner of speaking, yes."

Aisling was following things, barely. "Wait, so if the things that got pulled through the veil are coming back, where in the hell is the rest of this massive building? Not to mention the people who were in it." She turned to Reece and Jones. "There were no people or bodies in what you found, right?" They hadn't seen any on the screen, but they couldn't see below the top layer of rubble.

Reece gave a quick head-shake but didn't say anything. At least that was good news. Hopefully.

Harlie barreled on. "That's where the time displacement issue arrives, I'm afraid. The rest could come through anywhere or any when. The people could be alive or dead. Others might have been pulled through as well. You might want to have a global search for mass missing persons about the time the building vanished. However, the thing we need to focus on is the displaced reaction."

Everyone was giving him the same look Jones had.

"You lost us." Caradoc shook his head.

"Only the more powerful precogs felt the true impact of the veil opening this time and that chunk of building falling into this world. But all of us felt the physical side—the building shaking." He waited until everyone nodded. "That was only a small portion of the actual power that opening caused. The rest will hit us at another time. Earthquakes, tsunamis, who knows. The point is that was part of it, not all of it. The impact wasn't the reaction of the building or Nix being pulled through the veil—it was *how* it went through. The physical and psychic impact will be massive. And could hit at any time. It could come in waves."

Reece still looked lost. "We're waiting for a reaction of some sort, one that will most likely be catastrophic wherever it happens. We might also have more extremely large sections of building crashing anywhere. Also, I assume, random and unpredictable." He looked to Harlie for confirmation but frowned more when it was given, "And there's nothing we can do about any of it?"

"You were right until the end bit." Harlie wiggled his fingers at him. "I believe that Caradoc, Mott, and myself can create a program to predict the returns. It will still take time and require all of your equipment here plus more that you'll need to get."

Maeve stood, leaned on the table, and glared at everyone. "What can we do now? *Right now.* I'm glad you three can hopefully figure out how to stop things from destroying us unexpectedly, but I need to do something now. And Nix is alive out there somewhere. I'd like to take care of that situation."

Reece's phone buzzed. "Garran, I assume that you

and Surratt saw? They kicked us out not long before the clean-up." There were almost five minutes of talking from Garran's end with only minor sounds of agreement from Reece. "I agree on all of that. However, we have a roomful over here and there's been some updates you two need to know about."

There was a flicker near the front screen, then a second one. Then both Garran and Surratt shimmered into being.

Reece hung up the phone. "Let me start by saying, everything is worse than we thought."

"We've news as well, but judging by the looks on your faces, I'm going to suggest you go first." Garran nodded.

Reece and Harlie filled them in about the veil, the building, and the possible world-destroying return of the energy used to move the building and its parts coming back into this world.

"That's hard to believe, and if it came from anyone other than Harlie, I'd say you're all drugged. Not enough people know about the mechanics of the veil to even come up with good questions. I think our ancestors thought that once we were over here, we didn't have to worry." Surratt leaned back on something outside of the range of the hologram. He was still pale and gaunter than usual, and he was leaning back because he needed to, judging by the wince on his face. Even though he hadn't been killed, he'd still been injured when he was ambushed.

Harlie nodded. "I know you're not old enough to remember coming over, even I wasn't born yet. But that was very much the way they felt when they arrived. Things were bad over there, far worse than they let be known to casual research. None of them will talk about it even now."

"Even your mother?" Surratt folded his arms.

"Especially her," Caradoc jumped in. "She doesn't talk

about that time—and neither will our father. But she did a bit when we were kids."

"She is hiding something. But to find out would mean exposing us to her powers, even I don't want that." Harlie frowned.

Aisling shuddered. "I *really* don't want that. Okay, so you know what we know about the veil. What do you have?"

"We have a lead on Nix." Garran tossed it out too lightly; he had something larger he was holding back.

Jones picked up the two photos from the middle of the table and held them facing the holograms. "So do we."

"Ah, nice shots. Where?"

"Cardiff, Wales, a few days ago. Maeve desperately wants to hunt him down."

"Well, she might need some help. We received information that he was in Cardiff. He was also spotted in London, Birmingham, and Stirling. And a possible, but not confirmed, sighting in Galway. All within a half-hour of each other." Garran shared an image of all five sightings. Same face, different clothing, and various locations.

"No one could be in five places at once." Caradoc stepped up closer to the images.

"He's either changed what he is, or there are now more of him. Neither is a good option," Surratt said.

"Were there any sightings of him before a few days ago?" Aisling looked at the faces carefully; they all had the same haircut, same cruel mouth, narrow eyes watching everything. Just different clothing.

"Nothing from *my* source." Stella hadn't pulled out her envelope of notes from Grundog, but she was willing to admit she brought the photos.

If Garran was surprised at her admission, he wasn't showing it. "Nothing that we've found either. It's as if he just popped out of nowhere—all over. We have every agency we can keeping an eye out. His stomping ground was the U.K., but there could be more of him elsewhere."

Maeve looked ready to be sick. "There are five of him? Maybe more? Is this a trick?" She had gotten to her feet but now slid back into her chair.

Stella left and came back with a pot of tea and a single cup which she sat in front of Maeve. Maeve drank without noticing.

"This has to be a trick. Maybe he didn't get pulled past the veil and has been hiding, just waiting to pull this off." Aisling wasn't sure if she believed it herself.

"Really?" Caradoc shook his head. "How is appearing as multiple people going to help him? Not to mention that he had to risk being seen to pull this off."

"He's in cred recovery." Stella studied the images. "Criminals live and die on their cred and his failed attempt to destroy L.A. and take over the Celtic gangs cost him a lot."

"This is just to freak people out? We're back to thinking it's some sort of trick." Caradoc seemed happy with that, but Harlie didn't look like he was.

"I don't know." He reached over and patted Maeve's hand. "This may upset you, and I am sorry. But there is a chance that something happened to him when he was beyond the veil. They are all the same being; I can feel that on a level beyond normal ken. But it might not be Nix."

"We can't do anything at this point but gather information." Garran rubbed the back of his neck. "And that's all I have right now. We can send more detailed information about the sightings once it comes in. Will you be working here?"

Harlie glanced around the well-stocked room, then shook his head. "No. We'll need to move to Caradoc's house. I'll gather a list of what we'll need."

Garran and Surratt nodded and the holograms blinked out.

"You don't want them looking over your shoulder, do you?" Caradoc was already pawing through Reece's collection of portable-sized tech.

"Neither do you," Reece said. "Not that I blame you. Is there anything else you need? There might be a pen or two you missed." He added as the collection on the table grew larger.

"Just so I know whether to have a full breakdown, do we have multiple Nixes, or not?" Maeve went to pour another cup of tea, but the pot was empty. Stella darted out of the room and came back with a fresh pot.

Aisling had had Stella's tea before. She loved strong tea and often made pu erh—an aged and very strong Chinese black tea—Maeve would be awake for a day or two at the rate she was drinking.

Caradoc stopped his pillaging and came next to her. "That's what we're going to find out. I promise we'll get answers about him."

"And the veil. We need to…make sure Nix isn't replicating further." Harlie caught Caradoc's look midway through his comment. He flashed Maeve a grin, but she was staring into her teacup.

"Wait, this could be ongoing?" Maeve's voice went into the dog whistle range.

Caradoc winced. "That's what we're going to make sure doesn't happen. Right Harlie? Reece? Aisling?"

Caradoc looked at a loss to help Maeve, but he was trying. Aisling smiled. Maeve had a crush on Caradoc since Aisling first introduced them, but life made it impossible to pursue. From the flustered look on Caradoc's face, he might share the feeling.

"Right now, let's just get you all relocated to Caradoc's place." Reece waved to the diminished wall of tech. "Take what you need and give Jones a list of what else you want him to get. He's on better terms with our bosses than I am right now."

CHAPTER TEN

THE MOVE BACK TO CARADOC'S house took longer than expected; in part because Stella had to keep casting a spell on the diners every time a load went out.

"You guys need to consider a back door to the place." Caradoc moved the final load into his car. They'd made it all fit, but Reece was going to have to give Maeve and Aisling a ride home. Along with dropping Mott off at his place.

"That would endanger the protection the place offers." Reece looked at the diner front. "But I have thought about it. If things would settle down long enough for luxuries like remodels."

Caradoc grunted, then got in his car and took off. Even though they'd packed everything extremely well, he drove away like a five-hundred-year-old gnome out on his first drive in eighty years. Harlie gave a nod to everyone and took off on his motorcycle.

"Can I stay and help?" Mott had been silent during the conversations and the move. He'd helped carry out what was handed to him, but he was clearly thinking of things far from where they were. "I might have worked out a way to track things that crossed through the veil. And possibly people." He gave a wincing smile to Maeve.

"It's okay. I'll just have a few more blokes to kill." The smile Maeve gave him back was vicious and seriously caffeinated.

Jones walked with them to the end of the street then nodded. "I'll go talk to the captain in person. This will take some work." He held up his note screen with the items Harlie and Caradoc had requested. The list was long and wasn't going to be easy to get. Even with almost clearing out Reece's tech equipment, there were things on there that even Mott had never heard of.

Reece led them to his car. He was right, it was a very boring car, and was even painted an odd beige color that Aisling had never seen before.

Aisling slid into the passenger seat with Maeve and Mott climbing into the back. It was weird after being so pissed at him to be back sitting in a car with Reece. She waited until they were on the road. "I have something to tell you. We weren't sure about telling you yet, but I asked Harlie before he left and he said you should know. There was a vallenian at your building crash." She watched him closely, but he kept his eyes on the road. Too focused on the road. "You knew? How could you know? None of your people reacted to him at all." That was something she hadn't thought of. Reece had been around three of the four prior sightings, even if he only saw them the last time. Maybe somehow he could pick them up.

"I didn't see it." Reece gave her a quick glance then went back to navigating the freeway onramp. "I felt something. I honestly couldn't have told you what I felt, but there was an odd chill."

"Displaced air?" Mott leaned forward from the back seat. "There is a theory that items from beyond the veil displace molecules when they cross to this plane. That's what ties to my proposed tracking system. The theory isn't well known, and quite old. It took me a while to hunt it down again, but it could be valid. Reece might have sensed that. We need to look at the camera footage again and see if he and it were near each other."

Aisling looked back at Mott but didn't know what to say. He had been searching in his own memories for an obscure theory that he might have read decades ago. The scary part was Aisling knew once they found it, it would be exactly as Mott said.

"It might be?" Reece shook his head. "I would have brushed it off as part of a messed-up day if you hadn't told me you'd seen it. Did the vallenian attack the agents? None were seriously hurt, but it took a lot of force to push them back like that."

Aisling still wasn't up to admitting she'd been there too; besides, she knew he suspected it at this point. "Yes, or so it appeared. It waved toward them and everyone tumbled. It vanished right after that."

"I'll have Jones tell the captain to look for elven family boxes in the rubble. We can go over the footage again when we get to Caradoc's place. If we give you a tracking pointer, you should be able to show us where the vallenian travelled."

Aisling nodded and sat back. She doubted there was a box. This time the vallenian had been far more personal. She hoped that Harlie and Caradoc could figure out what the necklace was, and what it might do, before it did something nasty. Like strangle her in her sleep.

Reece slowed down as he went down the off-ramp, but still barely missed the sinkhole that appeared right in front of them. Aisling grabbed onto the dash as he swerved and hit his brakes. Maeve started swearing and Mott looked ready to be ill.

"Hold on." Reece backed his car up and off to the side of the exit. The hole was massive, taking out the entire off-ramp and would have easily swallowed Reece's car. He grabbed an old school police car radio from his dash. Maybe this car was a reconditioned cruiser. An extremely old one. He'd massively pissed off the powers that be to have them make him drive this thing. "We have a major sinkhole on the 17B off-ramp. Request emergency back up." He nodded at the confirmation, then got out of his car.

Aisling and the others were right behind him. There

wasn't a lot of traffic, but Reece grabbed some orange traffic cones from the trunk of his car and set out warnings at the top of the off-ramp.

Aisling met him on his way back down. "Your own car had a secret Interpol connection; this one has an old cop radio and traffic cones. Bit of a change."

He gave a crooked grin. "Yeah, that'll teach me to open my big mouth."

"We do appreciate it, and knowing that it might have been to protect us all helps as well. How have you been?" She'd known Reece for over a year, but he acted like an ass to keep her and the majority of her cops at bay while he looked for moles within the station. She'd only known the real Reece a short while. Trying to sort out her feelings for him was a mess, but there was no doubting that there was something there. Damn it, she gave herself a headache.

"I've been good." He laughed. "Well, as long as I survive working with certain FBI agents anyway. And missing a particular stubborn elf." He smiled.

"You guys might want to see this." Maeve interrupted from where she and Mott stood at the edge of the sinkhole.

Sinkholes weren't unheard of in Southern California, but they were usually associated with heavy rains. It had been bone dry for four months now.

Aisling slowly stepped as close to the edge as she dared. "Crap. Is that what I think it is?"

Reece followed and started a steady stream of swearing. "We'll have to check, but yeah. That looks like part of our building."

The mass of concrete, framing, and steel was wedged about ten feet down. Actually, the upper part was about ten feet—there was no way from this angle to see how far down it went.

This time Reece used his phone to call it in. "We

found another *anomaly*. 17B off-ramp. Emergency crews already on their way." He listened for a moment, then disconnected the call.

"We need to have the emergency crews officially shut down the off-ramp but keep them from the sinkhole." He didn't look happy.

"If chunks of buildings keep falling around town, people *are* going to notice eventually." Aisling peered into the hole. It was horrifying and perversely fascinating. They hadn't seen anything fall. One minute the road was clear, the next it had a massive hole in it. She mentally shoved aside what would have happened if Reece had been driving just a little faster.

"I know. But we have to try." Reece walked back up the off-ramp toward the approaching fire engine and cop car.

"Is there any way we can get a building sample before the Area 42 people get here?" Aisling watched the street across from the sinkhole carefully. Most likely they'd come from there as the access would be easier.

Mott started hitting his chest, then finally reached into a vest pocket and pulled out a mechanical hummingbird. "Can't get much, even less than what Stella grabbed. But something is better than nothing." He appeared to pat the hummingbird, then released it. The bird flew down into the hole and came flying back with a bit of building. It got in three more rounds before Aisling spotted a trio of black SUVs heading down the cross street. Reg was right, there was a serious obsession with heavy-duty all black vehicles in the local law enforcement communities.

Mott pocketed the hummingbird and shoved the building rubble into his pants' pockets.

"What are you doing here?" The dark-haired elf who approached on the other side of the sinkhole wasn't rude, but he also wasn't happy.

"Reece was giving us a ride home when that thing

opened up on us." Aisling folded her arms and did her best bored cop stare.

Maeve came up and echoed it, but hers had more of a snarl added. "It wasn't something we *did*, mate. Back off."

The elf studied them for a moment, went to the edge of the sinkhole, pondered that for a bit, and then went back to his car. The rest of the unsmiling Area 42 crew got out of their cars as well and multiple low-level discussions went on. Aisling didn't recognize any of the agents.

The firemen used their engine to block the off-ramp, and it looked like the police car had gone back up on the freeway to head off traffic further down.

Reece came back down the ramp. "They'll move so we can get back on the freeway, but first I want to see if we can help." There was nothing in his voice that indicated the Area 42 people would let him get involved, let alone allow her, Maeve, or Mott, but Aisling knew he had to try.

Before he could talk to them, the fire engine moved over enough to let a small green car in, then it resumed temporary barricade duty. Whatever Reece had said to them was keeping the firemen up top, but Aisling knew that wouldn't last.

Reece scowled when the car first appeared, then schooled his face back to neutral as it parked off to the side behind his own. A short male gnome got out and marched over.

"Good thing you didn't dump your car in the pit." His tone was less sarcastic than his words and he nodded to everyone on this side as he stomped up to the sinkhole. "Yup. Big old mess." He shook his head and muttered to himself as he walked back and forth along the lip of the hole.

Aisling looked over to Reece, but he just gave a tight shake of his head.

"What are you doing over there? We're supposed to be

on this side. Actually, are you even supposed to be out here?" The tall elf with dark hair looked annoyed at the gnome, as did the other agents.

The gnome grinned. For a moment Aisling wondered if he was related to Garran. That was one of his grins, and it wasn't a nice one.

"And it's good to see you too, Rockquet. And your little friends. I was sent down here by New York HQ—they needed someone to keep an eye on all of you." He rocked back on his heels, folded his arms, and smirked.

Rockquet didn't say a thing but turned his back to make a call.

The gnome turned toward them with a real smile. "I know who that one is," he nodded toward Reece. "Let me guess, Aisling Danaan, Mott Flowers, and Maeve Halithi. Nice to meet you folks. Read all about you." He shook all of their hands. "I'm Agent Barthlinio Churchill. You can call me Bart."

"I've heard of you." Mott's eyes narrowed and he tilted his head as he obviously searched that massive data bank of a brain to find the data on Bart. "Ha! You wrote a paper on veil transmutations and the aggregation of stray particles."

Bart pulled back and his eyes widened. "Yes, I did. Fifty-three years ago, in an obscure science journal. I'm impressed."

"We're supposed to stay here too." Rockquet called out after he finished his phone call. "They're sending choppers with heavy grav lifts."

Bart rolled his eyes then turned to the agents on the other side. "That's wonderful. Did I say you couldn't stay? I believe I said I was keeping an *eye* on you." He shook his head and turned back to Aisling, Maeve, and Mott. "I am sorry that I didn't get to meet either of your brothers, Detective Danaan. Like Mr. Flowers, they are renown in certain circles."

Aisling wasn't sure what to think of that. Yes, Caradoc was. He was an odd combination of eccentric billionaire inventor and social butterfly appearing on magazine covers. Unlike Caradoc, Harlie didn't crank out scientific papers every month and his studies were less tech and more out-of-this-world.

"I'm sure they would have liked to meet you." She had no idea what else to say. Reece was standing a bit behind and to the side of Bart with his arms folded but a neutral look to his face.

"Might I ask why you're here?" Reece stepped forward.

"Like I told the dolt over there, New York headquarters wanted me to keep an eye on them."

"Ignoring the fact that you've been watching us far more than them." Maeve smiled.

"Eh, I know what they're doing." He dropped his voice. "They're all young agents, even younger than pretty boy here." He motioned to Reece. "New York is worried about the repositioning of so many untried agents. I've spent a lot of time out here in past years, but I am part of the New York office. You might say that I'm internal affairs for Area 42. Or as close as we get to it. But I'm watching them, not you all."

Any questions they might have had were lost as three massive helicopters flew into range. They were the military grade, grav lift copters, but even with them Aisling wasn't sure they would get the building section out.

"Ahh, the cavalry has arrived." Bart watched as the helicopters hovered in place and another car drove down the cross street to the gathering of agents. This one wasn't black but was less bright than Bart's.

Aisling recognized Captain Driyflin as she got out of the passenger side. The driver stayed in the car. Captain Driyflin was Reece's direct boss. She was a gridgen, a small species of fey. A bit shorter than Bart, but far less stocky than a gnome. She called a few of the agents over and from the look on her face she was chewing them out.

"How'd they piss her off that fast? She just got here," Aisling said.

"There is a lot going on with this branch." Bart scowled across the sinkhole. "And it started before that attack on their building." He peered over the edge of the hole. "I do wonder how many more pieces will be landing around here. Seems a bit stupid to go through that much work to pull something like that off, only to drop parts randomly around town."

Captain Driyflin finished whatever she was chastising Rockquet about as a military truck pulled up on their side. People clad in camouflage got out and came to the edge of the sinkhole and started motioning to the choppers. Lines dropped and an electric arc formed over the hole. The magic charge it emitted crackled through the air.

"Shouldn't you be on their side of the hole?" Maeve had stepped forward to make sure she looked down at Bart. Aisling recognized the stance; she was still deciding if he should be on her shit-list or not.

"Nope. I can watch them better from here. Missed the first drop in that parking lot, was just landing at LAX when they found it."

"You were on your way here before the building pieces started showing up?" Aisling saw the answer on Reece's face as she asked. Bart's visit really was about the agents. The issue of random and potentially deadly chunks of buildings crashing to the ground was a chance for him to see how the agents performed, nothing more.

Except Mott mentioned that Bart knew about veil issues. Which brought him back into the knows-more-than-he's-letting-on club.

Chapter Eleven

———◆———

Bart SWITCHED BACK AND FORTH between watching the agents on the other side and keeping an eye on the maneuver with the building. The concept behind the grav lift utilized magic and tech combined to encase and lift heavy, awkward, and dangerous objects. The agents had used smaller versions to gather the rubble from the parking lot, but just to get it into trucks. They still couldn't see how big the chunk here was, but there were no trucks around for hauling.

"Are they planning on carrying that through L.A. airspace? Because that will be noticeable." Aisling jumped as her phone buzzed in her pocket. "Hey Caradoc, what's up?"

"Where are you guys? If you just didn't want to help carry things into the house you could have said something."

"And then you'd still make us do it." Aisling laughed. "Nope, not avoiding. A big chunk of a certain building made a nice sinkhole at the exit near your house. Right in front of us."

"Damn!" Caradoc covered his phone, most likely yelling at Harlie. "We'll be right there."

"I wouldn't suggest it, the place is swarming with agents, cops, and what look like military." She looked over to where Bart was still inspecting the slow upward movement of rubble coming out of the sinkhole. "Hold on a sec." She walked next to Bart. "My brothers are close by. If you want to meet them, this would be a good time."

"Excellent! We can go over…that's not what you meant." He gave a smirk that was similar to Garran's when he was about to pull something over on someone. "They could both be extremely helpful in their observations. And being as I outrank everyone here, it's my call. Send them over quickly. This move will take a while but I want them to observe as much as they can."

Aisling nodded and flashed him a smile. "Okay, you and Harlie get here ASAP." She looked around, the other side wouldn't be the best idea, even if Bart outranked them all, they weren't going to be happy about more people being involved. "Go north and come off the 17B ramp. The cops and firemen will be asked ahead of time to move."

"On our way." He disconnected.

"Larkin? Could you do me a favor?" Bart was still watching the move and the agents across the sinkhole. "Make sure that Caradoc and Harlie have no trouble getting down here past the officers up top. I'd like their feedback on this."

Reece nodded to the crowd of agents on the other side. "They are going to be pissed."

"I know. It's good to have power, isn't it?" Bart gave a sigh of contentment.

Reece jogged up the ramp and stayed there.

Aisling knew Caradoc would probably break every speed law to get there. "You like egging them on, don't you?"

"Everyone needs a hobby." Bart frowned. "Not all of them are bad, but there is something evil coming to L.A., or it might already be here. The entire reason for Area 42's existence is to keep the bad things in life from destroying the good. I don't think this crew can do what they might need to."

"What happens if they can't?"

"We have to pull from other Area 42 locations and we

rebuild." The grim look on his face didn't bode well for the agents who were found to be wanting. Aisling had no idea what was done with people who no longer fit a super-secret agency. But it couldn't be good.

The front helicopter's engines started a high-pitched whining and it dipped a bit, then steadied. But it still didn't sound right.

Maeve had been near the lip of the sinkhole but stepped back. "There's something wrong." She wasn't looking at the helicopters but down in the ground.

"Are those cracks?" Aisling pulled on Bart's arm and moved them both away from the hole. Lines radiated out from the edges, deep ones that hadn't been there a moment before. "Get back! Something is happening to the sinkhole!" She yelled across to the agents on the other side, but they were still in argue-and-debate mode. Captain Driyflin finally looked over. "The cracks are spreading!" Aisling yelled even louder as the helicopters increased volume, but eventually the captain nodded and had the cars moved back.

The military people kept steadying the lines of the grav lift and the building.

The fire engine moved aside and Caradoc's SUV came down the ramp and parked off to the side. Both he and Harlie ran out.

Harlie looked like a crazed prophet with his waist-length hair flying behind him in a long ponytail and a look of terror on his face.

"Everyone has to get back! Now!" He grabbed Maeve and Reece since they were the closest to him and pulled them toward the cars.

Caradoc didn't grab anyone except Mott, but motioned for Aisling and Bart to follow him. "Harlie started freaking out the moment we got on the freeway." He looked at the helicopters and the people on the other side. "They need to drop the grav lines and go higher." He pulled out his phone. "Captain Driyflin, you need to get everyone out of there. Get the helicopters out too. No, I can't explain it. Just move!"

Aisling saw the captain yelling at the agents. All three helicopters jerked up suddenly. Then an explosion rocked the area as at least one of them slammed into the sinkhole. Aisling barely stayed on her feet, while Mott tumbled over like a toy. The rest were tossed about, but upright. A wave of heat slammed into her as smoke and flames shot out of the sinkhole. Yelling came from both sides, but there was no way to hear anyone with the ringing in her ears.

The fire crew brought their truck down and were putting out the flames in seconds.

Looking up, it was clear that only the lowest helicopter exploded and the other two had cut their grav lift lines and were hovering much higher. Aisling wasn't an expert in helicopters but neither one sounded good.

One of the cars across the way got hit by debris, but it looked like the captain and the rest had made it clear.

Aisling kept low as she went over to Harlie. "How did you know that was going to happen?"

He still looked rattled, but not as bad as when he first arrived. "The air is permeated with…something is leaking." He looked disturbed, but not freaked out. Yet anyway.

Reece looked back to them. "Leaking, as in another explosion?"

"No. Leaking as in something is coming through the veil down there. You probably want to destroy that chunk of building. Maybe a corrosive agent." He nodded to himself as he looked at the sinkhole but didn't move closer.

"Something is using the building to cross over to this side?" The vallenians weren't the only Old Ones, nor were they the worst. Aisling didn't want to think about what else might come through.

"Not sure," Harlie said. "But it's not good. Caradoc? Do you have gas masks?"

Caradoc started to shake his head, then stopped. "Actually, I have some prototypes." He opened the back hatch of his car and brought out a small box. He took what looked like a piece of cellophane out, put it over his face, and handed the box to Maeve. "Just touch it to your face, it'll do the rest. Pass them along."

The results were a shimmery glow that Aisling saw on the others and also slightly colored her view once she got hers on. The box held way more than they needed, so Reece ran some up to the cops. The fire crew already had their own masks on.

"There's definitely something coming out from the sinkhole." Harlie's voice was slightly muffled by the clear mask.

Bart had his phone out. "Captain Driyflin, get all of your people and anyone else over there to back up. There is something leaking through that hole. And tell the helicopters to land somewhere safe, away from everything." He paused as he listened to her. "We're testing a new gas mask from one of my consultants, don't worry about us. Get out. That's an order."

Driyflin put away her phone and started barking orders.

"Something is coming out of the hole." A nasty green ooze crept out along the edge of the hole on the other side. Maybe it was a gas leak, or her imagination, but it looked to Aisling like there were small, misshapen bodies in the ooze.

"Damn it." Bart didn't move any closer to the hole but raised his voice toward the agents on the other side. "Get out now, you idiots!"

There were still two agents not far from the hole as the ooze crept forward. One was the dark-haired elf, Rockquet. Both agents appeared more interested in what was going on across the hole than in it. They finally started backing away, but it was too late. The green ooze made a lunge and engulfed both agents.

"That stuff is sucking out their life force. We have to stop it!" Harlie ratcheted back to hysterical as he frantically looked around. "Car keys." He held out his hand to Caradoc.

Caradoc looked confused but handed them over. Harlie ran to the car, started it up, and raced toward the hole.

Everyone, even Mott, ran after him as they realized what he was doing. The car stopped, then the engine revved higher. Harlie rolled out as the car shot off and flew into the sinkhole. Which sent a fireball fifty feet into the air and the fire crew ran forward again. Two more fire trucks came down the ramp and soon three crews were fighting whatever was still burning in the sinkhole.

The green ooze attacking the agents vanished and their desiccated bodies collapsed to the dirt.

Sirens echoed down the freeway and ramp as more fire crews, more cops, and another unidentified car came into the area. The two remaining helicopters vanished during the car explosion and Aisling hoped they got away and managed to land without trouble.

"I should have known that you all would find a way to be involved in this." Garran got out of his car and stalked over to them. "Did you make the hole or the explosion?" He folded his arms but was saving his glare for Caradoc, Harlie, and Mott. Fair enough, if there was anything weird going on it would be those three.

"Neither." Caradoc paused as Reece raised an eyebrow. "Technically the explosion was caused by my vehicle entering the sinkhole at an excessive rate of speed." He held up his hand. "But it was fully justified and probably saved everyone on that side of the hole. Well, most everyone."

Garran squinted at the other side and took a long, deep

breath, then turned back. "They don't look so good right now. A few of those bodies look like skeletons."

"That's what they were saving everyone from." Reece stepped forward. "There was a weird green substance coming out of the sinkhole. The car crash cut whatever it was off." He gave a quick glance to Harlie, and Aisling saw him give a nod. "There was something coming through the veil."

Bart stepped into Garran's space with a scowl. "If you'd use your eyes, you skunkwaffle, you'd see what happened." He growled the last bit.

Considering how much Bart clearly didn't like the L.A. Area 42 agents, and yet was mostly civil to them, Aisling was surprised at the nastiness he was sending toward Garran.

"Peace, ya fat guts!" Garran peered down and snarled back.

Bart got an inch away from Garran with his hand reaching for his gun. Then burst out laughing. "Ha! Henry the fourth, part one. Try and fool me!" He punched Garran in the gut, but not hard.

"At least I'm not making up shit. Skunkwaffle? Will had naught to do with a waffle." Garran laughed.

"Ah, but he would have liked that one, I know it. I was a bit rattled what with sinkholes, deadly gases, exploding helicopters and cars. It's been a day. How the hell have you been and what are you doing here?"

"Things have been changing out here. Surratt is out of the picture, and they made me chief. Crazy idea. You here to see what's going wrong with Larkin's crew?"

Bart's levity vanished. "With what's left of this branch of Area 42. As far as I can tell Larkin and Jones are both legit; I've no reason not to trust them. The rest of this branch is under investigation at the moment."

Garran shot a glare to where ambulances were arriving on the other side to take in the injured Area 42 people.

And two coroner's wagons. None of which said County of Los Angeles. "They've shut everyone else out. Our people were the first on scene at the parking lot where the first piece landed. That crew showed up, wouldn't say anything nor share with anyone as they cleared us out."

Bart shook his head. "*I'm* working with you now. There's no one left standing in this branch that outranks me and even if there were," he pulled out a badge holder and flipped it open. "I'm internal affairs now, so they can't say boo."

"Wait, there's no higher-ranking people left?" Reece had been standing back but came forward with a frown.

"Your captain over there is the highest one left. Apparently, the rest were all still in the building when it was taken. Now tell me that isn't suspicious."

CHAPTER TWELVE

"BUT YOU SAID CAPTAIN DRIYFLIN was cutting us out to protect us because she didn't trust her superiors." Aisling had only met the captain twice, but she seemed like a good person. Then again, her former longtime friend Heike had tried to get her killed, so maybe she was just becoming a shitty judge of character.

"She said people above her, she could have meant New York." Reece narrowed his eyes. "It's interesting that information didn't come up at all in the past week. They kept everything moving, so unless we knew someone who was missing personally, we didn't know."

"Explains why they kept us out of things and eventually booted us." Jones was suddenly there. Silent as ever and no car. Just there.

"Where'd you come from?" Aisling was facing up the ramp, the barricade of cop cars was still in place. She would have noticed him.

"There's an access road a bit that way. I parked there and walked in. I gave the captain our list but then she and almost everyone in the building took off. They kicked me out before they locked up though." He held out his hand to Bart. "Nice to meet you in person, Agent Churchill."

Even more than the fact he was obviously good friends with Garran, the tone of respect in Jones' voice made Aisling believe Bart was trustworthy.

"Eh, just call me Bart. Everyone else does. And I've read up on all of you, so I feel like we're old friends."

Caradoc handed Jones and Garran gas masks. "If what

Harlie was trying to do worked, then the danger is probably past. But since we've no idea what was sent up in the air, might as well be cautious."

The other side had cleared out, with Captain Driyflin the last to get in her car. There was still enough wafting smoke to partially obscure her, but Aisling thought she was looking at them for a while before she got in the car.

A call crackled from one of the fire engines and one of the fire crews started packing up. The fire was out and now they were just doing mop up.

One of the firemen came over. "Not sure why there was a helicopter and an SUV down there. It looks like there's only one fatality, the chopper pilot. I take it here was no one in the car?"

"No there wasn't." Garran stepped forward. "Thank you. We'll take care of it from here." He flashed his badge and Bart flashed an FBI badge. The fireman clearly wanted to ask more questions, but he nodded and left.

The cleanup was done in twenty minutes and then it was only them and the sinkhole.

"Area 42 is simply going to leave it here?" Maeve went closer to the edge then stepped back. "These masks don't block the smell at all, by the way."

"I'd like to know that too." Bart scowled. "They took some losses, but that's still a big mess to leave behind." He stomped away from them and started yelling into his phone.

"I'll give him a call or two to get them back out here, then I'm calling in our department." Garran also moved closer to the hole but he stayed there. "I'll also notify the Highway department; this ramp will be down for a long time while we get everything out and make sure that breach is closed." He stepped away to make his own calls.

Harlie stood there with his eyes closed, but opened them suddenly. "It's closed. But the veil was down and not in any way I've heard of before. There are people

I need to talk to." He glanced around as if looking for Caradoc's car.

"You destroyed it, remember? It looks like it was the right thing to do, but still. Good thing all the equipment was already unloaded." Caradoc clearly wasn't happy about losing his car, but not as upset as Aisling would have expected.

"You were already planning on dumping it, weren't you?" Maeve laughed as she picked up on the same thing Aisling had.

"There are far too many black SUVs running around." He shrugged. "That wasn't the way I wanted it to go, but it served a purpose."

Jones nodded. "Once we know if Bart needs us or not, I can take you and Harlie home."

"Thanks."

Harlie looked agitated. "I know where we are, I can get there myself. I do need to talk to some people. Privately. Hermits like privacy." He took off running before anyone could respond.

"There's a hermit connection where they all compare notes? Why hadn't I heard of this?" Caradoc watched as his brother picked up speed and vanished.

"Because you're like the anti-hermit?" Mott had been silently watching everything. "I've heard of it. But I'm closer to being one than you."

"A secret club for hermits, what next?" Maeve's phone chirped and she scowled at the number. "I have to take this." She also moved away.

"I feel like I should call someone," Aisling said and turned to Reece and Jones. "What are you going to do now? It looks like Bart can get you both back in with Area 42."

Jones watched Bart who was still up the ramp yelling into his phone. "I have a feeling we'll all be working outside of the L.A. Area 42 group. His jurisdiction is higher than Captain Driyflin's, but I think he's trying to gather people he trusts so he can sort out the bad ones. There is something wrong with this branch."

Reece nodded. "I just wish we had a better clue how everything is linked. The fact that all of the higher-ranking agents were lost and it was hidden even from us? That's not good."

Bart stomped back down the ramp. "I just got off with New York and you are all now working with me. Well, except Garran over there, but I told them I'm sharing all intel with him." He looked around. "You lost one."

"Harlie needed to go talk to some other scary people about whatever scary thing just happened. He did say the breach in the veil here is closed," Aisling said. "For now."

"Good. We'll need that ability of his and others like him to sort this. Or you will." Bart nodded to Garran as he came back from his own calls. "I'm assuming you'll be reinstating these two?" He pointed to Aisling and Maeve. "Less suspicious if they're back on the active roster."

"I thought you were annexing them?"

"Easier to grab active detectives than benched detectives. They'll still be working for me while this investigation is going on."

"Do we get a say?" Maeve came back from her phone call and looked to both of them.

"Nope." They echoed each other extremely well.

"And I do know that you are still involved with MI-6." Bart smiled. "I'm sure, if we need to, we can pull them in as well. My job here officially is to look at what in the hell is going on with the L.A. branch. Unofficially, I'm looking at a lot of weird shit that's threatening everything and everyone. I want all of you focusing on that."

Maeve didn't say anything, but the sour look on her face said MI-6, or someone connected to them, had been on that call. Aisling would wait until they were back at the house to find out exactly who and what.

A pair of black cars appeared at the top of the ramp and came down once the cops moved their cars aside. There were trucks up top with cement berms to put in place to block the ramp.

The first car had Captain Driyflin and three other agents that Aisling didn't think had been there before. The second had five agents—also not familiar. To be fair, aside from the two who'd been killed, she didn't get a good look at any of them before.

"Agent Churchill, thank you for taking care of things until I could return. Seattle will be sending down the special crew you requested to analyze and take apart the wreckage in the sinkhole." She gave a stiff nod to Jones and Reece. "I understand you'll be reporting to Agent Churchill. I'll officially notify the FBI that you're off their cases."

Bart walked around the new batch of agents. "Keep an eye on things until the Seattle crew gets here. I'll be going back to your temporary office and reviewing the findings on the first building drop. I'll also be sharing it with the L.A. police." He'd timed his walk around to finish directly in front of the captain. He watched her carefully as he spoke.

She gave a start at the sharing of information, but recovered. "My understanding was that information concerning these events was to stay internal only."

"Who told you that?" Bart folded his arms.

"The NYC office." She kept her gaze focused over his head.

"Who? Please do not mistake my jovial manner for something other than what it is. I am still internal affairs, and this *is* an active investigation."

"Toril Kjai. He said it was crucial to keep anything associated with the missing building under wraps." Her eyes darted around the group. "Since we still have no idea who was behind it."

"We have no idea who is behind it because you have cut off resources that we could be using. Closing in on ourselves is not what is needed. However, I'm not surprised at Kjai's actions. He's always been a bit of an ass." He turned toward Aisling and the others. "I'll be in contact with you all, but there's no reason to stay and babysit with us." His smile was tight.

Aisling knew she was missing some dynamics going on between Driyflin and Bart but they weren't her concern right now. Besides, the odd smell from the hole—death mixed with burning rubber and rotting vegetation, was giving her a headache. "I'm all for that." She started toward Reece's car, along with Mott and Maeve. Then she noticed Reece was still standing with the other two. Even Jones and Caradoc were moving toward the embankment that would lead to the access road where Jones had left his car.

"Ya coming? You are our ride home." Maeve folded her arms and glared. From the scowl on her face, she had a headache as well.

"Just a moment." Reece held up his hand and he, Bart, and Driyflin had a short but intense conversation. He nodded and turned to his car. Bart looked smug. Driyflin looked pissed.

Aisling waited until they were in his car and he'd turned around to go back up the ramp. One cop car was gone, and a pair of cement berms were locked in place where it had been. The car that remained moved to let them out. "Are you going to tell us what that was about, or just let us guess?"

Reece swore, but it was at trying to get onto the freeway from an exit ramp. Once he was properly on the freeway he shrugged. "Nothing too secret. I just told them that if Jones and I are working under Churchill, we want separate offices from the rest of Area 42."

"You don't trust Captain Driyflin." Mott said.

"I'm not sure. Neither is Jones. I'd been focusing on some high-level moles in the L.A. police department for the past year and possibly missed some in our own organization." He held up his hand before Aisling could speak. "Yes, I know you said there were some a while ago. I was wrong."

Aisling's look of shock was wasted on him as he kept looking forward.

"There might be a problem," Maeve said as she looked at the side window. "I'm being reactivated for MI-6. I want to talk to Bart and Garran alone about it. But I'm not sure how much I can refuse this reactivation. Not only have there been three more Nix sightings, there was a sinkhole in a town outside of London. A section of the town of Noth was destroyed before they locked it down."

CHAPTER THIRTEEN

"WHAT?" THAT GOT REECE'S ATTENTION. "We need to tell Churchill."

Aisling watched Maeve, but she was still just looking out the window. "And Garran. But this came to Maeve through MI-6. If they wanted the others to be involved they'd say something."

Maeve finally looked over. "They didn't specifically comment on my sharing the information one way or another—so I feel okay to tell Garran and Bart. But I have to report back in London within two days. They only gave me the briefest intel on the sinkhole."

"Caradoc can find it." Mott looked over. "I probably can as well."

"They can force you back? What if you don't want to go?" Aisling still wasn't sure how she felt about Maeve lying to her for the past ten years about being completely done with MI-6. But there was an apparent chance that she hadn't had a lot of say about remaining connected to them.

"Not sure. But I do want a chance to get Nix, however many of him there are. I want them all dead."

They all were silent as Reece drove to Caradoc's house, through the hedge, and parked beside Jones' car.

Maeve sighed. "The gang's all here, might as well sort this out."

Aisling had wanted to get into the action, but now they might have a bit more action than they could deal with. Still, it felt better to be actually doing something. Or about to be doing something.

Jones' and Caradoc's conversation in the living room dropped as the rest came in. Harlie was nowhere to be seen. He'd claimed one of the rooms in the upper level of the house so was most likely up there dealing with his hermit group.

"Anything happen after we left?" Caradoc watched Maeve stomp into the living room.

"Yeah. There are now eight sightings of Nix, all close in time, all over the U.K. and Ireland. And MI-6 is reactivating me and calling me back in. I have to be in London in two days." Maeve flung herself down onto the sofa. "Oh, and a sinkhole opened up outside of London and destroyed half of a town."

Jones sat down near her. "I thought you wanted to kill Nix. Isn't being in the U.K. the best way to do that?"

"Yes, but not as much as you would think. I'm more limited as MI-6, ironically. Partly because I wanted to leave. They didn't want to let me go completely, but they also don't fully trust me. It's been ten years since I was an active agent." She rubbed her forehead. "Is it too early to drink? I could use a pint."

"Not at all." Caradoc went to the kitchen and came back with a bottle of beer. "Need a glass?"

"Nope." She took the bottle with a grateful smile.

Harlie came running down the stairs. "We have to go to England. Specifically, Noth. North of London. They had an accident."

"A sinkhole that swallowed most of the town? Yeah, we know." Maeve took a long pull of her beer.

"What? How?" He waved his hands. "Never mind how you knew. Did you know it happened at the precise time that the one here did? Or that I believe it was also caused by a piece of the Area 42 building?"

Reece and Jones had taken seats at the dining table but both stood back up and stepped closer to Harlie. Jones looked the most interested. "Are you sure? That would mean we'd need to go as well." There was a violent gleam in his eyes. There were a lot of people who wanted a chance at killing Nix. Good thing there might be enough of them to go around.

"Even if we get there, you're going to have to fight Maeve for killing Nix." Aisling watched Maeve carefully.

Harlie started pacing. "My connections are sure. Noth was a small town, but a contact of mine has lived on the edge of it for fifteen years. She verified the sinkhole time and the appearance of what looked like a building. The sinkhole kept growing until it swallowed a row of cars. The resulting explosion stopped it."

Reece rubbed his forehead. "Did your friend have the ability to sense a veil intrusion?"

Harlie pulled out a chair from the dining table set and flopped into it. "Yes. There definitely was a veil breach. They are still looking for missing people. They did evacuate the town though. Wasn't clear exactly who, but it appeared to be MI-6." He watched Maeve.

"Seriously, just because I'm MI-6 doesn't mean I'm going to do something every time it comes up." Maeve glared at them all, then finished her beer.

"True. Besides, the Area 42 group out of London should have stepped in quickly," Jones said.

"That's a good point. Why haven't they?" Aisling looked around the room. She knew Area 42 was focused in the US, but they had branches in most major cities of the world. London being the largest U.K. one.

"One we might want to speak to our new boss about." Caradoc pulled out his phone. Then frowned and hung up. "Bumped to voice mail. But what of it, you two? Why is MI-6 kicking in but not Area 42?"

Both Jones and Reece shrugged.

"I'd say they are there. Even though London is larger than the other U.K. branches, it's still a smaller office than anything we have here. They probably work with MI-6."

Reece started to call someone, then put his phone away. "I was automatically going to call the captain."

Harlie studied everyone for a few seconds then leapt out of his seat. "When do we leave?"

"I think we have to sort things out first." Aisling shared a look of concern with Caradoc.

"Yes, yes, travel. Papers. I know. But we need to go quickly." Harlie was bouncing in excitement.

Caradoc walked over to Harlie. "Are you okay? Is there something that you're picking up that we aren't?" He turned to Reece. "Have you sensed anything?"

Reece responded first. "I'm not a precog. I keep telling you that." He saw Aisling raise her eyebrow. "Okay, I have picked up on some weird things in the past, but nothing right now. Including back at the site."

Harlie kept nodding his head. "Different people connect to different things. Since the blood of yours that started beyond the veil is diluted you wouldn't feel everything. But for me, I just know that things will happen. Lots of things. And we," he motioned around the entire living room, "all need to be in England. Soon. My friend outside of Noth can put us up." He frowned. "The city of London is too much for me. I can visit, but not stay there for long."

"Well, not sure about the rest of you, but I need to report in." Maeve got to her feet. "I'll be packing, it won't take long." She left for her room. Most of her things were still in storage from when Nix had cleaned out her townhome. She'd been saying she would deal with it, and go back to her townhome, but hadn't moved forward on either yet. Aisling thought she didn't want to live alone right now and couldn't blame her.

"I'll try Bart again," Jones said. He'd just dialed when both Reece and Harlie collapsed. He hung up the call.

Aisling reached Reece first, while Caradoc and Mott grabbed Harlie.

Aisling checked Reece's pulse. "He's alive, his breath is short and choppy and his eyes are fluttering under his eyelids. What the hell happened to them?"

"Harlie's the same." Caradoc looked from one to the other. "Unless someone else here has talents we don't know about, I'd say something just smacked the precogs hard." His phone beeped and he grabbed it. "Yes, Harlie is out cold." He caught himself before he mentioned Reece. "Understood." He hung up. "That was Bart. Whatever hit these two also hit a precog at the sinkhole site and there are calls coming in from all over the county. Precogs are collapsing where they stand. Or sit. There are traffic accidents being reported all over L.A. as drivers pass out."

Aisling gave both Jones and Mott a worried look. She didn't know if they knew about Reece, nor if he'd want them to. Not only could Reece's secret mean problems for him, it could mean prison or worse for others who knew and didn't turn him in.

Caradoc nodded as he saw who she was looking at. "It's okay, Reece told me who knows a while ago. They're safe."

Aisling nodded.

"Just in L.A.?" Not that Aisling wasn't grateful, the amount of damage that could happen was already huge, but if it was global, it could be horrific.

"As far as they know. Not even in Ventura. They're trying to map the reactions."

"And they probably all radiate out from the sinkhole." Mott pulled out his pad and was wiping through a lot of screens if his arm movement was any indication.

Groans came from both Harlie and Reece and it seemed to Aisling that their breathing was returning to normal.

Caradoc went to the kitchen and came back with two glasses of water. "This will help." He handed one to

Aisling.

"Is it supposed to be so…thick?" She swirled the glass a bit. It looked normal from a distance, but almost gelatinous up close. It didn't look like something she'd want to drink.

"Yup. Harlie showed me where he had the packets to put in water in case this ever happened to him. Supposed to help against the overload that knocked them out, but this is the first time I've used it. Make him drink it all." Caradoc dropped next to Harlie, lifted his head, and started slowly tipping the liquid into his mouth.

Aisling pulled Reece's head into her lap and did the same. Although neither seemed conscious, they did appear to be drinking. If the growing frown on Reece's face was any indication, the drink didn't taste good.

The glass was half empty when his eyes opened and he pushed away the glass. "Ack. What is that? And what the hell happened?" He looked around, realized he was on the floor, and tried to get up.

"It's what's helping you. You can sit up if you finish drinking it, or I can continue to force you where you are." Aisling was a bit surprised that whatever knocked out Harlie also hit Reece this time, but if Harlie left instructions for this situation, she was following it through.

Reece looked ready to argue, then nodded. "I'll drink it. Let me up. Then I'll need a dozen aspirin."

Harlie was still drinking with his eyes closed, but he pushed the glass away when he'd finished. "That wasn't good. Not the drink, what happened to me." He glanced over to where Reece was still struggling through his glass. "Nor is the fact that Reece was hit also. Something punched through the veil at an extreme velocity."

"Again? Damn it, what is this? No action from the veil or anyone on the other side for centuries, now everything is coming through at once?" Caradoc was freaked out by things he couldn't track through technology—

like the veil.

Harlie stared out into the distance—at something only he could see. "This breach happened a few decades ago, but the psychic impact was delayed. Somehow. It's only in this area because it was tied to an event here—decades, or possibly centuries ago. I don't know that the sinkhole is connected, or maybe the weakening of the veil in the location of the sinkhole helped push this through. I can't tell." He shook his head.

Aisling took the two now empty glasses, went to the kitchen, and came back with a bottle of aspirin and clear water in the glasses. "How can a psychic impact be delayed? Who could delay it? Why?"

"Delay what, now?" Maeve came out of her room rolling two suitcases behind her. "What did I miss and why are they on the floor?"

Aisling caught her up as both men took seats at the dining table.

"In answer to your questions, yes, a strong enough magic user could delay something like this. But the larger question is why." Harlie first shook off the offer of aspirin, then shrugged and took two. "And why it came back now. If there was a reason for something to be delayed, then it would only come back at a set time. I'd think. Or if the magic user who delayed it grew weaker, lost control of the spell, or was killed." Harlie frowned. He, even more than Caradoc, didn't like not figuring something out.

Aisling turned to Reece. "Now maybe you'll stop trying to deny the whole you-being-a-precog thing?" She understood his denial, he was a breed, one parent was fey, the other human. Breeds always stayed human in likeness and abilities. Reece had shown talents as a precog and also channeled his naiad side by swimming in an extremely non-human manner to save her and Jones a short time ago. If the High Council knew there was a breed with fey talents, they'd want to investigate. Reece would probably never see daylight again. But for his own safety and sanity, he needed to accept what he was.

Reece sighed. "I'd rather still keep denying it, for now anyway."

Aisling let it drop for the moment. He didn't look as freaked out as he usually did about the precog gifts, so maybe he was finally admitting that's what they were and not just extremely good intuition. He also looked like his head was trying to crack open, and pushing someone when they were injured wasn't nice.

"Solving this issue will take a while, and I can do it anywhere. How soon can we get to England?" Harlie might have been slammed to the floor by a decades old psychic event, but he stayed focused on his task.

"We need to get Bart on board first." Reece rubbed his head and took a sixth aspirin.

Mott kept looking at his pad, but shook his head. "I won't be going. If you don't mind, I'll stay here. Can I take one of those extra rooms upstairs for a bit? My own place appears to have been compromised." He flipped his pad around. Split camera screens showed three people, clad in black so effectively that it wasn't clear what gender or species they were. They were systematically going through everything in his apartment. Carefully. Everything was replaced after they scanned and documented it.

CHAPTER FOURTEEN

"YOU'RE EXTREMELY CALM FOR SEEING strangers pilfering through your things." Maeve dropped her luggage by the front door then came closer to Mott for a better look at the screen. "At least they're not destroying the place. What are they looking for though? And who are they?"

Mott turned the screen back to himself and did a few more swipes. "Regarding the who, my bet is the L.A. Area 42 goons, or some other formal organization. Thugs aren't that neat." He continued swiping. He might have a small apartment but he had cameras everywhere judging by the number of different angles he switched to. "They broke in about five minutes ago."

Caradoc leaned over his shoulder to look at the images. "They're looking for something small. See what they're picking up? Books, vases, plates. Maybe looking for a chip of some kind."

Mott nodded. "Ah, I believe you are right. They probably want the override code I liberated before the Area 42 building vanished."

The silence was loud in response to that.

"You did what now?" Caradoc got his question out first. And he was nicer about it.

Jones and Reece might be under a different boss, but they were both still Area 42 agents. The look on their faces indicated they would have been a lot harsher.

"It was for security; mine, not theirs, although I might have the only version left now so they should be glad I took a copy." Mott set down his pad but continued to glance at the images from time to time. He didn't seem concerned, so the odds were good the chip wasn't anywhere near his place.

"It was the morning of the big Nix show-down. They left me alone when some argument popped up among the ones watching me and a higher up." He shrugged. "I downloaded the security codes for everything in their system and pocketed it. Figured it might be good to have in case something came up."

Neither Jones nor Reece looked happy—Caradoc looked pale.

"How did you…I don't…" Caradoc was at a loss for words, something Aisling had rarely seen.

"Wasn't that hard. But never fear, I have the chip in a secure location." Mott looked over to Reece and Jones. "And no, that's not anywhere on me or my belongings. Equally, no, I'm not going to tell you."

"Are you actually talking about a way to access all of Area 42's records?" Aisling glanced over at the methodical search still going on in his apartment. She was surprised they were trying to be so careful in placing things back exactly as they had been. They must guess that the chip might not be there and didn't want to provoke Mott into bolting. He had a history of going on the lam if he felt threatened.

"Wouldn't a group like Area 42 have the equipment to block cameras?" Maeve asked as she also watched the slow search.

"We do." Jones ran his hand over his short hair. The look he favored Mott with was split between horror and admiration. Jones wasn't a tech-head, but he clearly knew how hard it would be to have done what Mott did.

"And *I* have ways of breaking their camera blockers. Ha!" Mott had his hand up for a high-five but no one gave one back. He dropped his hand with a shrug.

Caradoc was still looking torn between proud and terrified. He finally held up his hand. "I think for all of our safety, we should stop talking about this. No idea if that chip could pull data back from beyond the veil."

"Which brings us back to getting us to England," Harlie said. He'd been the only one not looking at Mott's screen. "I believe all of us besides Mott should plan on going."

"But you said this recent attack, if that's what it was, originated here, shouldn't we stay?" Caradoc asked.

"Yes, it did. But I can continue looking into it over there. The event that caused it was so long ago, unraveling things will take time. What happened there needs to be looked at in person." He frowned. "She couldn't give a reason why, she's not sure herself, but my contact is extremely worried about the attack on Noth. I believe it's more important than it appears. It's urgent we go there quickly."

"Jones and I can't just take off because you feel that we should." Reece's phone rang. He narrowed his eyes at Harlie, but answered the phone. "Hello Bart. Yup, Harlie is up and fine. He isn't sure what caused the collapse, but feels we need to go to England to resolve the current crisis. That newest sinkhole over there might be a key to something bigger."

Aisling found it interesting that Reece's forehead scrunched up when he lied. Good to know.

Reece nodded as he listened to Bart. "Mott isn't joining us. But the rest can be ready to head out tomorrow." He paused at something Bart said. "Agreed. I'll keep in touch."

Aisling scowled at that. She wasn't certain they should leave so quickly.

"Seriously? How did you do that?" Reece stared at Harlie once he hung up his phone. "Bart and Garran think we should go there. You four even get official Area 42 badges."

Harlie shrugged. "Bart seemed like an intelligent individual. And as that sinkhole was more destructive than the one here, in terms of size and connections to psychic energies. It makes sense to have the experts go."

"We're not experts," Aisling said. "Even you aren't an expert. Has this ever happened before?"

"No." Caradoc folded his arms.

"No, as he says. Which means that we are as close to experts as they have." Harlie's grin was teetering on manic. "I suggest we get ready. I'm sure Caradoc can get us plane tickets, etc. Let's not fly into Heathrow, though. Too much London there." He darted up the stairs.

"Great!" Maeve smiled. "Will be nice to have some mates there. I need to head down now, my flight got bumped up. Maybe I could get a ride to the airport?"

Caradoc started to open his mouth, then shut it. "I don't have my other car here." This had been Caradoc's rarely used safe house until everyone started moving in. He had a townhouse in one of the fancy neighborhoods, most likely with extra cars.

Jones stood up. "I can take you. I have a few things to take care of before our trip." The look he gave Reece spoke volumes, but nothing that was clear to anyone other than Reece.

Maeve hugged Aisling. "I'll see you soon. Try not to get into trouble before then?" She grabbed her luggage and left.

"Could you drop me off at the townhouse? I'd feel better with a car." Caradoc already started out the door.

Jones rolled his eyes. "I live to serve." With a nod to the others, he followed Caradoc out.

Mott looked around. "I believe I'm going to go claim my room upstairs. Once the spies are gone, I'll need a ride over to get some things from my apartment." He nodded and went upstairs.

Leaving Aisling and Reece alone.

"This is awkward. I have been channeling a lot of annoyance your way the past week." Aisling finally broke the silence.

He shrugged. "I can't blame you. I wanted to call… but…." He shrugged again.

"They wouldn't let you? They were tapping your phone? They thought I was working in cahoots with the spawn from the abyss known as my mother? Any of those?" Aisling folded her arms and took a step back. Maybe she wasn't ready to deal with this, she was still pissed.

Reece gave a crooked smile. "Honestly? All and none. There was a concern from the higher-ups about your mother working through you; one which I tried very hard to convince them they were wrong about. You've made it clear how you feel about her. The investigation into her and the Council has been thrown off by the attack on the building. But there is something else there. It's beyond my paygrade, so I've no idea what it is."

"And? Why didn't you call even once?" She wanted to say more, but there was something in his eyes that she didn't like. She'd started having strong feelings for him once she got to know the real him, as annoying as that had been. She'd thought that went both ways.

"How do you feel about me?" That was blunt and unexpected. He watched her carefully.

"I…I like you? I think we had something starting."

"But you didn't feel that way before. You've known me for over a year, but only felt that way recently." He looked like he was going to be ill.

Aisling was confused. She wasn't sure what had been going on between them, but this wasn't what she'd expected. "Because you spent most of that year deliberately being a jack-ass to me and everyone in my department."

"True, but there might be more than that." He rubbed

his temples. "I've always had a feeling about things, precog if you want to call it that. I also could swim better than others my entire life. But none of my abilities came out as strong as they are now until a few weeks ago. Something is changing in me and I don't know why or how."

"I'm not going to tell anyone. You know none of us will." Had that been his issue? He'd been afraid she'd rat him out to the High Council?

"That's not the only thing. I did some research into my naiad family line a week ago as part of a study for the department. Turns out there was more than just naiad. Three generations back there was a siren." He winced. "I deleted that information from all the records that I could find."

Aisling pulled back. Sirens were dangerous fey. They could make others do what they wanted, with or without singing. They crossed the veil thousands of years ago, as did the rest of the fey races. But they were under the watchful eye of the Council. Sirens could lure humans and fey to their doom. Or make them fall in love. Aisling backed up into the living room chair and sat down hard. He'd used magic against her?

He held out his hands, but didn't come closer. "I had no idea. And it might not be what happened, I didn't try to do anything to you. But like my precog sensitivity, I might not have control." His attempt at a smile faded. "I could be reading too much into this. My feelings for you are sincere." There was a lingering doubt though, and it showed on his face as he sat at the dining room table.

She wasn't sure what to think. Sirens were extremely powerful, and the fact that his family had tried to hide one in their line wasn't good. "Is there any way to test what is happening to you? Not just the siren issue, but all of it? That wave of whatever just happened dropped you as badly as it did Harlie."

"I have no idea. Kind of hard to look into things like

breed powers suddenly appearing when to do so means a visit by the Council. I've done what searches I can, but I'm limited."

They sat in silence for a few minutes. Aisling had no idea what to think. Her feelings toward him had changed in the past month, but she thought it was simply because she was now getting to know the real him, not one of his personas. What if it had been the magic of a siren?

"We need to talk to Harlie about it. He's the only one who might have a clue as to what's happening." She couldn't look at him. It might be nothing. And he didn't have to tell her, she wouldn't have known. But this was shocking.

"Agreed. But I think I should leave now. Caradoc can take Mott to his place once he gets back." He got to his feet. "I'll see you when we fly out. I am so sorry; you know I wouldn't have tried to…I am sorry." He left the house.

Aisling wasn't sure what to think. Her love life had been in the crapper since her former fiancé ran off days before their wedding a few years ago. Then she starts falling for Reece, of all people. And now it might be just a bad bit of magic mojo. Great.

"I'm ready." Harlie bounced like a five-year-old as he came down the stairs with a single piece of luggage. "What's wrong?"

Aisling didn't want to discuss it with anyone, least of all one of her brothers, but like she told Reece, Harlie was the best chance they had to figure it out. Logically she understood that. Reece was freaked out about this as well, but emotionally that didn't help. She quickly explained the situation.

He frowned. "Sirens are supposed to be registered; all the fey of their magic class are."

"And obviously this one not only didn't register, they hid themselves from the family as a naiad. They look enough alike for it to work." Aisling now understood why Reece had looked ill—she was feeling that way herself right now.

"It would explain more about his precog sensitivity. I mean, as a breed he shouldn't have any abilities, but it appears he does, and precog is more in keeping with the siren genome than a naiad one." Harlie smiled as if that resolved everything.

"Could his growing fey powers, and it does appear they are growing, have caused an unintentional love spell or not?" She knew Harlie had a different world view than most people and she usually was fine with that. But this wasn't the time. Her heart needed an answer.

Harlie's dark eyes softened. "I don't know. We've got two issues—that he's a breed with fey abilities and the siren component. They aren't very well studied because they aren't common." He didn't add that when the fey first started mingling with humans, thousands of years ago, many of the more dangerous fey had been killed. By other fey trying to stay hidden, as well as by primitive humans. Sirens were killed the moment they were found out. "Even if he were sending out some siren magic, it would mean that while you weren't truly falling for him, his feelings for you would be true."

"Unless the magic, that he shouldn't have at all, is wonky. Not to mention, what if what I feel isn't real? We can't continue based on weird magic." She got to her feet. "Just find out what you can, please?" She glanced at his luggage. "You realize that we're not leaving for a day or so, right?"

The grin was back and he patted his suitcase. "Always be prepared. Never fear, I will track the answers down for you."

Aisling hugged him. "Thank you. I'm going to lie down for a bit. Mott's upstairs and the others are driving around. Caradoc should be back soon though." She was shutting her bedroom door when Harlie turned to her.

"Did Maeve take the scroll with her?"

Aisling opened her door. The scroll in question was one Maeve received under mysterious circumstances years ago and had kept hidden all of that time. Aisling found it when Maeve and all of her belongings had vanished. Harlie couldn't translate it as it was locked to Maeve. He'd been teaching her an ancient elven dialect so that she could translate it herself. Progress had been slow to say the least.

"I doubt it. Unless you took it out of my case." The scroll was an unknown power and something Nix had been desperate to find. To keep it safe, Aisling kept it in her opal charged case, the one she kept her family clan earring in. Only she or Harlie could open it.

"I did not. However, I believe she needs to have it with her there. That was where it was given to her, so that is where we find its secrets." He'd been muttering more to himself than her. He suddenly looked up. "Bring your clan jewelry. Caradoc and I should as well. We might need to enforce our actions over there."

Aisling wanted to find out what he meant but really needed to lie down before dinner. She nodded and shut her door. She walked over to the opal charged case and lifted the lid. The scroll was tucked in behind her ruby earring. The earring would start at the tip of her ear, with a single magic charged ruby, then a delicate chain led to a string of smaller rubies and connected to her ear-lobe. All higher-level elves had these earrings and other forms of clan jewelry. Aisling only wore hers when she had to. She wasn't proud to be part of her mother's clan.

CHAPTER FIFTEEN

—◆—

"WAKEY, WAKEY. TIME FOR DINNER."

Aisling tossed and fought to open her eyes. She'd only meant to rest but ended up falling asleep and having weird dreams that were no more than disturbing emotional remnants as she fought to ignore Maeve's voice.

Her eyes opened. "Maeve? Aren't you supposed to be on a plane?" She might be sleep confused, but that was definitely Maeve hovering over her.

"Should have been. But apparently the airlines are worried about the recent building drops in the L.A. area and are waiting twenty-four hours before resuming flights. I had a cab drop me a block away from here so no one would see me walk through the hedge." She shrugged. "You have to admit it would be dangerous if some random piece of Area 42 appeared mid-air where a plane happened to be."

Aisling rolled herself out of bed. "You don't seem upset."

"I'm not. I love to go back; England is my home. But I don't like being ordered about by an entity that couldn't even cover my arse when I was trying to help them."

Maeve had supposedly gone home to help her family a while ago. But it turned out she was trying to help a former MI-6 boss—who was already dead when she got there. MI-6 wasn't as helpful as they could have been and Maeve ended up being secretly flown back to the U.S. as a prisoner for trade. The more she'd found out about what MI-6 knew and what they didn't do, the more pissed she became.

"Okay." Aisling rubbed her eyes and stretched. The dream had vanished, but she still felt the edges of it.

Maeve took her arm. "Are you okay? You look out of sorts."

"A weird and terrifying dream that I can't recall." She reached around Maeve and shut the door. "And I had some things to think about." She told Maeve about Reece.

"That sucks." Maeve gave her a hug. "I'm not even sure how to process that."

"You and me both. Harlie knows because I need him to figure out if something magic did go through that could have modified my perceptions. But I don't want anyone else to know."

"Good idea. It's going to be weird between you two, though. This is a sharp group; they'll pick up that something is off."

She hadn't gone that far in her thoughts yet. "You're right. They know I was pissed at him for blowing me off, we'll just keep letting the others think that's the issue. I'm sure once we get to England he and Jones will have their own agenda. They might be making us honorary Area 42 agents, but it's for their benefit, not ours. Reece and Jones will be doing something beyond us, I'm sure." She pushed aside what would happen if it turned out Reece *was* magically influencing her. Not only would that bring their budding relationship to a quick end, but what if he was unconsciously manipulating others? They wouldn't turn him into the Council, but he'd be too dangerous to keep out in the world.

"Not a great look, love." Maeve peered at her.

"Sorry. Just thinking what our options would be if he is actually exhibiting siren powers. Uncontrolled siren powers. That's a problem."

"That's an understatement. Come on, he's not in the

house and neither is Jones, just the family. And Mott."

"I thought he was going back home to get his stuff?" She'd do better if she just didn't think about Reece at all for a bit. After a solid week of being pissed at him, it shouldn't be too hard.

"Caradoc's taking him over after dinner. Come on."

Dinner was an odd conglomeration of a lot of food that would go bad while they were gone. Mott was staying behind but he couldn't eat everything, so Caradoc had pulled what he could together. They were just sitting down when a knock came at the door.

"Are you expecting anyone?" Maeve was the closest so she went for the door but held back from opening it. She didn't have a weapon, but looked ready to jump whoever came through the door.

"No." Caradoc joined her. He had his hand raised for a spell. No one should even know this place existed, let alone be able to get through the hedge.

"It could just be Jones or Larkin, you know." Mott was focused on piling tuna casserole left overs on his plate.

"You're the one who says suspect everything." Caradoc shook his head and nodded to Maeve to open the door.

"Sorry to barge in like this, but I've brought dessert." Stella stood there just as if she'd come from next door and the house wasn't hidden within a magically secured hedge.

"How did you find us?" Caradoc asked as he and Maeve stepped aside to let her in. She had a large cake box with her.

"I have my ways, my boy. Not everything has to be known to you."

Mott looked up. "You tracked the equipment from Larkin's room."

"He is such a bright lad." Stella went to the table, sat down her box, and handed Mott a cookie from inside it. "There ya go." She turned to the others with a frown.

"I had a feeling you were up to something. I picked up on the report on the sinkholes, both here and the one outside of London. Something bad is coming, mark my words."

"You're right. We're all flying out to London tomorrow to look into that sinkhole." Caradoc motioned toward an empty seat. "I welcome you to our table."

Stella smiled. "I would love to join you all. Rare it is that I get to eat something I didn't make. So when are we flying out?"

"I don't know that they're going to let us loop you in." Aisling picked through the hodgepodge of food. "Besides, can you leave the diner for any length of time?" The diner itself wasn't so much the issue, but Reece's spy room needed to be secured. Alarms only went so far.

"Oh, the Area 42 folks don't need to know why I'm over there, it's none of their business. I have friends over there whom I haven't seen in a long time and are due for a visit. As for the diner, Grundog and Reg are coming down to keep watch. Shorter hours than I normally have it open, they really don't like a lot of people, so keeping their exposure down is a good idea. But they know about the room. I want to give them access, but only Reece can set that up." She looked around. "I thought he'd be here."

"No. He had things to address before we leave." Aisling wasn't sure how she'd explain things to Stella, but she'd have to do something. Caradoc and Jones might not notice her behavior, but Stella would.

"I see. Anything new about your necklace?"

Aisling hadn't realized her hand was even on it until Stella looked right at it. "No. I forgot about it with the sinkhole, being annexed to Area 42, and now flying to England—for another sinkhole." She looked at the pendant again in case it had changed. Nope. She dropped it back under her shirt. That was something to consider, she might need to watch what shirts she packed so it wasn't noticeable that she was wearing it all the time.

Harlie had been matching Mott bite for bite, but he paused and tipped his head. "I'd almost forgotten about that as well. I'll look into it before we leave."

"I think we have to figure it's connected to the building coming back in pieces, which means the Old Ones are connected to the building," Caradoc said.

Stella came to Aisling's side. "I didn't get a good look before; might I?"

Aisling pulled it out from her shirt and held it out by the chain.

"Ooo, there's a bit of a tingle, isn't there? It's okay little one, I'm a friend." Stella patted the pendant and kept cooing to it.

"I don't feel anything when I touch it. I didn't even notice when that vallenian put it on me."

Stella nodded. "Makes sense, whatever it is, it is tuned to you. I can't tell what it is, nor what it's supposed to do, but it is lovely."

Harlie left his feeding frenzy and came over. "I've never seen anything like that. The triskele is well known and it's used by many human and fey cultures. But the work itself is uncommonly delicate." He peered closer. "There might be words on it."

That caused Caradoc, Mott, and even Maeve to gather around, until Aisling finally pulled the pendant back.

"There's no way to get it off, and I'm not having you all hovering over me for however long it will take to sort it out. After we finish eating, Caradoc can scan what he can of it with his machines and you can work off that." The chain wasn't that long, but hopefully he had some way of scanning items that didn't involve a huge machine but would still keep the resonance of the actual pendant. She'd like to know what the pendant was and if there were words there, they definitely needed to know. Words often meant spells. But there was only so much room between her neck and the pendant.

Caradoc begrudgingly returned to his seat, but he drifted into his own thoughts, and the discussion of their upcoming trip swirled around him. Maeve had to call his name three times before he looked over. "What? Oh, the flight. We're all in business class. British Flyways direct from LAX to Gatwick. I also reserved a car, but we may need to get two."

"I'm flying into Heathrow. But will meet you wherever." Stella nodded.

"I'm booked to Heathrow as well. Might be a few days before I can catch up with you. MI-6 was vague as usual," Maeve said

"They are spies, after all," Mott said.

"True, but it would be nice if they would let the person they are dragging back know what was going on." Maeve turned to Stella. "How'd you get Grundog and Reg to agree to babysit? Trolls aren't fond of big cities."

Stella had tried a bit of everything and was working her way through it all. "They aren't. But Grundog is more used to L.A. than most and Reg has had to spend a fair amount of time in London. Plus, I promised I'd share pertinent information with them. We don't need to mention that to Reece or Jones—might cause them to have a conflict of interest." The look on her face clearly said the issue would be more of them trying to slow her down than she getting in trouble by them.

Once they'd finished eating, Caradoc dragged them all to his room. He'd just brought his things back, so it took him a while to find what he was looking for.

"A vacuum?" Aisling took the seat he pointed to but sat away from the thing he was waving about.

"This is a top-of-the-line scanner; well, the tube for it." Caradoc handed the vacuum-looking tube to Maeve, then moved more things around. "If they had just let me keep things like I had them." He muttered to himself, then pulled out a small box, took the tube back, connected them and smiled at Aisling. "Now we're ready. Hold out the pendant as far from yourself as you can."

Aisling did as he asked but it still looked like a vacuum. She kept her second hand on the chain just in case. The chain shook as the tube passed over the pendant, but it didn't pull it in. A screen on the small box came to life, and lines of data filled it.

"There *are* definitely words there." Harlie watched the small screen while Caradoc kept his eye on the pendant itself. "And in a language that I don't recognize. Or it could be that the words are too small."

Aisling squirmed a bit. "The chain is getting warm."

"Just a bit longer, there is a lot of data coming in." Caradoc glanced to the intake box.

The back of Aisling's neck was burning, just like a low sunburn, but not something she wanted to continue. "This is starting to hurt." She jerked the pendant out of Caradoc's hand. The chain cooled down immediately.

"Sorry about that, but it was getting worse. I don't think it liked whatever you were doing to it."

Stella peered at the pendant but didn't touch it. "Wasn't it all silver before? It's got a bit of gold running through now." She held up the pendant to verify.

"That wasn't there before." Aisling twisted the pendant to look at it. A faint line of gold shimmered throughout the knot work. "There's more than just words…a design within the design of some sort?" She let the pendant drop and pulled her shirt over it. "Can we focus more on getting it off of me? Then you can all run as many tests as you'd like."

"We need to figure out what it is before we try to take it off." Harlie frowned at Caradoc. "Or try technology on it. Cursed jewelry is not unheard of. There are too many things that could be behind it." With a nod, Harlie left and they heard him going upstairs.

"Well, that was interesting." Stella nodded. "I'll just show myself out. I'll find you when we're all over there. I believe the village of Noth is the destination?" She smiled and left.

"She must have gotten that intel from Reg." Caradoc downloaded the data from the pendant scan. "I'm taking the data with me on the trip, but leaving a copy here for Mott. See if you can find anything out about it."

Mott looked up from whatever he was currently working on. He looked distracted but he nodded. "Will do, boss. Can we get my stuff now? Those agents have been gone for three hours; I think we're good."

"But aren't you concerned they planted bugs?" Maeve asked.

Mott looked like a child on naming day. "Oh, they did! I saw all of them. They're deactivated now, but they won't know it. I'll reactivate them and give them to some avian friends to scatter for me."

"You have bird friends?"

"Yup, a flock of wild parrots. Well, semi-wild. They like me so they help me out from time to time. Trust me, those bugs will be all over L.A. County by morning." He whistled to himself as he left the room. Everyone else followed.

Aisling turned to go to her room and pack, but Maeve caught her arm. "I changed my mind. I know you too well and there's no way you're going to be able to keep your reactions to Reece normal. Not until you figure this out. Maybe you should take a later flight, wait a few days until Harlie figures out if he's gone siren on you."

Aisling ran her fingers through her hair. She'd been trying to ignore those same thoughts. "I don't know that I can. I wanted to get involved in this case and now we are, but that means I have little say over where I'm going. My best bet is to keep acting like I'm pissed at his cutting me out—and avoiding him when possible. On another topic, did MI-6 give you any more details on Nix? Or whatever is out there pretending to be Nix?"

Maeve shook her head. "Like everything else, they're being tight about it. You think it's not him? Or are you just trying to keep me from freaking out that there are way more copies of that asshole roaming around than should be?"

"Both." Aisling grinned. "I don't want those to be clones, or copies, or in any way related to that bastard beyond looking like him." She held up her hand. "I have no idea what that would be, but until proven otherwise, that's what I'm hoping for."

"Something harmless that just happens to look like one of the vilest bastards in the world? That's not even close to normal."

"We have a building that was pulled out of the ground and is now being randomly dropped in pieces. I'd say we left normal a while ago."

CHAPTER SIXTEEN

SINCE THERE WAS NO WAY to take care of anything right now, and Harlie wasn't coming down to tell them he'd resolved anything either, Aisling packed and went to bed.

She'd just shut off her alarm after three attempts, when a feeling of soul-freezing cold flowed around her. It was early morning, dawn was coming through the curtains, yet she couldn't see anyone in her room. The chill grew painful as her fingers and toes began to freeze. Never mind that they were tucked under her blankets.

But the worst was the feeling of her soul being frozen. She couldn't move, couldn't fight, and couldn't tap into her magic. A deep blue glowing dagger appeared directly over her and she couldn't even open her mouth to scream. The dagger came down to her throat and a flood of warmth shot out from the pendant. The light dagger exploded like a shattered glass and the invisible bonds controlling her vanished.

The scream she'd been trying to get out came out as well.

Maeve slammed the door open, followed closely by Harlie.

"What happened?" Maeve had a knife at the ready.

"There's steam coming off your necklace." Harlie didn't have a weapon, but he did have his right hand up and slightly curled for a spell. He didn't use magic much beyond his own odd inquiries, but Harlie was at least as powerful of a magic user as their mother. Most likely even more so.

Aisling reached and touched the pendant. Her fingers and toes weren't frozen any more, but its radiant heat felt good. She looked around the floor as she swung out of bed, if there had been any shards of the dagger left, they were gone now. She kept her hand on the pendant and slowly walked around her room. Nothing.

"I'm not sure, but I might have to rethink how I feel about this necklace—I think it just saved my life."

"From what? There's nothing here." Maeve duplicated her stalking, but it wasn't a large room.

"There was though." Harlie got his mystic-in-the-cave look on his face as he also walked around the room. "I can't tell what it was. But it definitely meant harm." He held up both hands and closed his eyes. The spell he muttered was faint and vanished as he said it. A second later he was flung off his feet and slammed through the doorway into the living room. Good thing the door was still open, that amount of force would have flung him through it the hard way.

Aisling and Maeve ran after him. The sofa helped his landing, but he'd still hit it with enough force to move it a foot backward.

Aisling grabbed his wrist and sighed when she felt a pulse. "I don't see any injuries. He's alive, just knocked out." She carefully moved him so that he was actually stretched out on the sofa instead of piled on it.

Caradoc came running down the stairs. "What the hell just happened? I was checking out some of Harlie's research and thought I'd screwed something up."

"No idea, but I'm pretty sure it wasn't you." Maeve scowled. "Your sister was attacked by something invisible. Your brother tried to cast a spell to find out what it was and got slammed halfway across the house."

"And I think the pendant saved me. But I don't think it's what attacked Harlie." Aisling put her hand on Harlie's forehead. Her strongest magic was healing magic, but she wasn't considered a powerful magic user. First, she needed to feel what was wrong, so she shut her eyes and pushed through to his core being.

And found herself flung up against the wall.

Caradoc reached her first and pulled her to her feet. "Is that what happened to Harlie?"

"Similar, but I'm not unconscious." She rubbed her forehead. It hurt far more than the back of her head where she'd hit the wall. Whatever that had been, it didn't like her or her magic. She felt like someone had smacked her with a board in the middle of her forehead. "Whatever attacked me got chased off by the pendant—both times." She came back to Harlie, sitting down on the floor next to him instead of standing, and took hold of the pendant in her right hand before putting her left hand on his forehead. She tapped into her healing magic slower this time. She couldn't see inside Harlie's mind, but she felt chaos and confusion all around. The pendant didn't seem to be doing anything, it didn't even feel warmer, but she didn't get slammed across the room either. She focused on getting the wild storms flying around Harlie's mind to slow down.

She had no idea of the time, but she didn't stop until his hand pushed hers away.

Harlie's deep brown eyes looked weary but aware. "Thank you. That was…unique." He lifted his head a bit, then dropped it back down.

"What happened?" Aisling stayed next to him and kept one hand on the pendant.

"I would ask you the same thing. There was a presence in your room. It didn't like my trying to communicate with it."

Maeve stayed back. "An evil presence I'm assuming? Aisling was terrified and it smacked you hard."

"My house is sealed against magic." Caradoc walked around the living room windows with one hand up.

"The seals are still in place."

"I don't think it came through the windows or doors or anything on this plane. It was like it punched a hole into my room." Aisling dropped the pendant and rubbed her arms as the memory of the cold hit her. "From somewhere far from here."

"A vallenian?" Maeve asked.

"No, I've never felt anything strong from them when I've seen them—not good or bad. This was horrifying." She quickly explained what happened, but didn't want to linger on the topic. Even thinking about it brought too much back.

"You're right, that doesn't sound like something that would have come from this world. And there are more than just vallenians on the other side of the veil." Harlie still wasn't moving from the sofa, but he looked more alert.

Mott came clomping down the stairs. He normally looked like an elf/gnome breed, right now he was all gnome. His hair stuck up in tufts around his head like a deranged halo. His pajamas had tiny pink, blue, and purple unicorns on them, and there was a bit of cookie in his hand. "What happened?" He also looked like he actually hadn't slept much regardless of his attire.

"There was an attack on both Aisling and Harlie." Maeve turned to look at him, then scowled at his cookie. Part of it appeared to be in his hair. Or maybe it was part of a second one.

"I was working on a project…but I think I dozed off."

Caradoc and Maeve filled him in and Aisling helped Harlie sit up. "How are you feeling?"

"As…as if I can't describe what went through me. Oh, and something definitely went through me. Very upset at me it was. Then it felt something it didn't like and tossed me." He winced as he got to his feet. "It's gone now, but I need to go write it all down." He was up the stairs before anyone could say anything.

Caradoc's phone ringing made everyone jump. He grabbed it quickly. "Sorry, had the volume up high." He glanced down at the number. "I'll take this in my room. Probably want to get ready to leave for the airport." He had his door shut before anyone could respond.

"I'm going to take a shower and hope that settles my nerves." Aisling left Maeve and Mott debating breakfast.

She normally liked the fact that all the bedrooms had their own bathrooms, but right now it was taking a lot just to walk into her room. She didn't think she was crazy to keep one hand on her pendant the entire time.

As she showered, she tried to recall what, if anything, she'd sensed before the attack. That was the problem of it coming on the edge of waking up, if there was something that preceded it, she couldn't pull back enough of it to help. She'd never felt such a horrifying cold. And a feeling of being cut off. That had been there too. Along with her soul being pulled away, she felt no longer part of this world. All in all, it was a lousy way to wake up.

She got dressed and finished the last bit of packing—the only thing left was her opal spell case with her clan jewelry and Maeve's scroll. A shock went through her hand as she picked it up and she almost dropped it. She got it into her suitcase and shut it, but her fingers still tingled. The case should defend itself against anyone not of its family—but not her. Maybe it could sense how unnerved she was.

She picked up the pendant. "Is this you too? Look, I appreciate whatever you did to help me out, but you can't mess with anything else, okay?" She felt a little odd talking to the necklace, but Stella thought it could hear her, and she didn't have anything to lose.

Everyone was waiting out in the front room—including Reece. He must have come in while she was showering. He gave her a nod, but then finished talking with Caradoc in low voices. Finally, he looked up. "Maeve is on her own, MI-6 takes precedence; the rest of you report to me until we get over there, then you'll be assigned to a team. Because they are heavier spell users, Caradoc and Harlie will probably be with the magic squad. Aisling will be assigned to another team, I would believe." He didn't even glance her way. Yes, Aisling was a magic user, but not on the level of her brothers. Healing was a recovery magic, not an aggressive one.

"I'm ready to drive everyone down." Mott was grinning in a manner that would make anyone nervous.

"Does he even have a license?" Maeve looked him over.

"I have a license," he said. "It might be a bit old…"

Reece smiled for the first time that morning. "It expired fifteen years ago, Mott. Bart is coming by to drive you all down. I just had a few last-minute things to discuss with Caradoc."

Harlie's eyebrows dropped lower, usually a sign he'd had an idea. "Actually, Reece, could you come help me with this equipment up in my room?" He didn't wait for an answer, just started up the stairs.

Reece shrugged and followed.

"That's odd, what was that about? I helped him bring his things down already." Caradoc looked ready to follow them.

Aisling had a feeling that Harlie wanted to get Reece alone for a reason more related to her issue than anything else. "Actually, I think we might want to get the rest of this stuff out front and waiting for Bart. He does know about the hedge, right?"

Caradoc shrugged. "Hopefully. I just found out he was taking us down when you did." He glanced up the stairs, then shrugged and picked up some bags. "Let's get out in the driveway."

Reece came outside, holding up his bandaged right hand and looking back at Harlie with a frown, then back to them. "I guess you are all ready."

"I am sorry about that Reece; I didn't realize the spell was still running. Are you sure you're all right?" Harlie might have sounded concerned, but the grin that kept popping up said otherwise. Aisling would bet he'd done something tricky to get what he needed to find out of Reece was showing siren powers or not.

Reece held up his bandaged hand. "I'll be fine. Sorry I got blood all over your equipment."

Harlie gave a wink to Aisling. "Never worry, everything is fine."

Aisling studiously looked anywhere but at Reece or Harlie. Not a terribly graceful way to get blood for sneaky blood tests, but it apparently worked.

The sound of a car revving its engines came from the other side of the hedge. Caradoc held up his hands and threw out a spell as a massive silver SUV charged through. The spell caught the vehicle as soon as it crossed the hedge and before it could hit Reece's car or any of them.

Bart was rattled as he got out. "This thing has a lot more kick than my other rental. Not to mention that hedge is a bit disturbing. Sorry if I startled you."

Caradoc shrugged. "It happens."

Once they got everything in Bart's car, even Maeve was riding down with them, Caradoc pulled Mott aside.

Aisling couldn't hear the conversation, but there was a lot of stern regard on Caradoc's end and random nods on Mott's. She was honestly surprised that Caradoc was letting Mott stay in his house while they were gone. Then again, Caradoc most likely massively increased the spells around the place, and as long as Mott had his own mysteries to track down he'd be distracted enough to stay out of trouble. Hopefully.

Caradoc finally got into the car. "I also gave Reg and Grundog access to my house, just in case." He shot a final look of concern toward Mott as they backed up.

Bart backed out of the hedge with more surety than Aisling had the first time, and Reece's car came out after. Reece turned down another access road as Bart got on the 5 freeway and headed to the airport.

Aisling wanted to ask about what Harlie did to Reece, but she had a feeling it was related to finding out what mojo Reece was packing and she still wanted to keep that information as limited as possible. "Any news on the building parts? The two that fell here?"

Bart grimaced as he turned off the airport exit, but traffic was relatively light, so the reaction wasn't from that. "Three. There was a third drop reported as I came to get you. Small, hit out in the ocean, so no injuries. Tracked by a fishing vessel off the Santa Monica Bay. ASAB is sending a ship out to get it, and a few of our agents will be on board. It depends how deep it went whether we can get any of it back." He paused. "They found two bodies deep in the building of that sinkhole of yours when they were able to remove the helicopter and the SUV. They were identified as two Area 42 medical agents who had been reported missing when the building vanished."

"Damn. Then the agents who were lost are assumed dead?"

"Not that we know. Those are the only two. Even the section in England didn't leave any dead in its building wreckage. We still have no idea what is causing any of this. The metaphysical team in New York hasn't slept since the building was taken but is still coming up empty." He pulled up to the unloading zone. "Be careful out there."

They got their luggage out and Aisling and her brothers headed for the flight desk. Maeve followed a bit, then turned off by a waiting area. Aisling waved her brothers to go on.

Maeve waited until both were almost out of sight. "Do we think Harlie got enough of Reece's blood? It's a good thing it was him and not Caradoc who did it. He was sloppy and Reece doesn't suspect Harlie like he does Caradoc."

"Harlie looked pretty happy with himself, so I'm thinking he did. Good thing he has medical immunity or someone would question him carrying blood on a plane and into a foreign country." Aisling had medical immunity as well. Not as exciting as it sounded though. It just meant both of them had healing magic. Harlie just had a hell of a lot more skills on top of it. They wouldn't be questioned for things related to medical studies when they travelled.

"You'll call me once he knows for sure, right?" Maeve sat down her bags and stretched out. Her flight wouldn't even be preboarding for a few hours, so she'd snagged one of the reclining chairs to wait. "I've no idea when I'll be able to catch up with you all."

"I promise to call you. Take care. And no going after Nix on your own—even if MI-6 sends you after him." She leaned over to hug Maeve.

"I promise. Besides, after the report of how easily he took me out got to them, I'm surprised they even want me there." She waved her hands and pulled out a book to read. "Now be off."

Aisling smiled and followed her brothers to the bag check, then to their gate area. The waiting area was a large one, so they had room to spread out. But aside from a seat saved for her, the two were staying close to each other. They stopped talking when she came up.

"What ya doing?" She took the saved seat and kept her carry-on suitcase on her lap.

Harlie grinned, shut his mouth, and pretended to turn a key. She gave him a sideways stare. There was no way he would have told Caradoc about Reece. Not to mention, Caradoc looked too mischievous for something that serious. Most likely brotherly shenanigans.

"Just talking about my little sister's crush. Harlie wanted the details." Caradoc grinned but Harlie gave a quick shake of his head out of his range of sight.

"There's no crush. Reece cut me off for over a week. I know it's his job, I also know he could have at least said something. As far as I am concerned, the further I stay away from him right now, the better." She folded her arms and sat without looking at either. Nice set up on Harlie's side though, he gave her a chance to reiterate to Caradoc her annoyance. She didn't like keeping this from him, and she'd tell him once they knew for certain. But Caradoc, for all of his sneakiness, could be too easy to read if someone knew him.

"Now, give the guy a break. I was there, he cares about you. Captain Driyflin gave him a bad time." Caradoc was trying to be encouraging.

"But she liked me. She even said they were planning on recruiting me."

He shook his head. "Something changed after the attack in those caves, or right before. I got the idea that she was there in person because of something to do with you. But I couldn't get information out of anyone, and Reece didn't know."

She was just about to bug him for more answers he probably didn't have, when an alarm echoed through the massive gate area. It wasn't their gate but the one that was two over judging by the lights and the six-foot-high red cones that shot up from the floor. Magic powered; the force field raised by those cones probably hit before the alarm did.

Aisling leapt to her feet. The day after Nix's attack in the cave, Garran had her LAPD badge tattoo replaced. She also had her badge back. Both were done right before he put both her and Maeve on leave. She'd help if she could, depending on what caused the alarm response, but many times airport law enforcement didn't like others stepping in on their turf. Not that she could blame them.

Aside from the alarm and the cones, and a general nosy mob standing around looking, there appeared to be nothing wrong.

"Do either of you sense anything?"

Both brothers shook their heads.

Caradoc stood and looked over to the gate, then sat back down. "Probably just someone opened one of the flight loading doors by mistake. That happens all the time, but the airport still has to investigate."

The words were just out of his mouth when the screaming started.

Chapter Seventeen

—◆—

THE PEOPLE WHO HAD BEEN milling near the alarmed forcefield cones were now running back toward Aisling and her brothers. It wasn't clear if whatever caused the screaming had been seen by everyone, or simply terror breeding terror.

Aisling pulled back the sleeve where her badge tattoo was and ran against the crowd with her arm up. Yelling LAPD wouldn't help much but it did seem some folks were getting out of her way as they saw the badge tat. Caradoc was right behind her. A glance back showed Harlie still in his seat, but his eyes were closed. There was more than one way to find out what happened.

The cone force field was trapping people who had been in that gate waiting area and whatever else was on that side was making them frantic to get out. She couldn't see any airport security, but they probably had further to run than she and Caradoc had.

Finally, three airport guards ran up from behind her. "Stand back! Everyone return to your seats."

Aisling flashed her tattoo. "Detective Danaan, LAPD."

Caradoc held up a badge holder. "FBI." He ignored Aisling's glare.

"Look, there's nothing either of you need to—" The security guard's words were swallowed by a muffled explosion and more screaming.

"You need to let them out!" Aisling yelled over the noise. The people on the other side of the cones were hysterical and trying to climb out. "Drop the cones!"

The guards started to shake them off, when Reece and

Jones came running up. "Drop them now."

Aisling couldn't see what badges they both flashed, but it worked on the guards. The cones sunk into the floor and everyone stood aside as the screaming crowd ran out.

"You get to explain why we let potential criminals go." The front guard growled at Reece. He was a minotaur, and about a foot taller and twice as broad as Reece, the result was almost comical when Reece snarled back.

"Or why you weren't letting potential victims go. Did you notice that a lot of them had electrical burns? If I were you, I'd go get them some medical help." Reece ran into the area without waiting for a response. Jones was a silent shadow alongside him.

Aisling started to follow, then stopped since the guards still stood there. "Seriously, those people need help and they might have seen what happened."

Finally, two of them took off after the screaming masses. The third nodded to her. "I'll call back up, but we'll keep the cones down unless things get worse."

Aisling followed Caradoc and the other two. At first it was hard to see what had caused the screams. There was a large group of unmoving people huddled behind one of the flight boards, but she could only see their legs below the board. They must have huddled there for protection, but she wasn't sure why they remained there. Reece and Jones had gone around to the other side and both came out waving their arms.

"I'd stay back, it's not good." Reece said, but Jones was taking photos.

The smell of burnt flesh hit her as she skidded to a stop. "I do have healing abilities; I might be able to help."

"They're dead." Reece stepped out of the way. He obviously just wanted to warn them, not stop them.

Caradoc gasped, covered his mouth, and stepped back.

Aisling was expecting horror, but this was almost too much. The people whose legs she'd seen were now one giant mass of burnt and slimy flesh. Judging by the number of legs, there could have been twenty or so people there. The legs were untouched but heads and torsos had all merged together. The faces she could see were locked into horrified screams. A green ooze, not unlike the one that had murdered the two Area 42 agents, was dripping down from the bodies and the fried flight board. Arcs of electricity popped from the board but seemed to be weakening.

"I don't want to step closer, but are those extra bodies in the goo?" The bodies in question were twisted and almost skeletal but they didn't look to be part of the airport people. There looked to be something in the green mass that sat atop the tortured remains.

"You might be right, study what you can quickly, I'm calling in Bart." Reece stepped away from them and Jones kept taking pictures.

"Damn it, most of my equipment is in my luggage. But still might be able to get something." He reached out toward the mass and scanned it with a small device. He got far closer than she would have, but she had no idea what he was scanning for. Caradoc had a gadget for everything, so hopefully this one could give them something useful.

Bart came down the corridor barking orders a few minutes later. He must not have gotten far after dropping them off and most likely left his car at the front of the airport. Rank did have privileges. He had two Area 42 agents trailing him. The remaining airport guard had been joined by three others and it looked like they were debating their options. Bart strode right through them with his badge held high. "Airport security is now under the FBI in this case. Please go down the corridor and make sure all passengers stay clear and the injured are taken care of. Keep any who saw what happened directly in a separate room, my people will want to interview them."

The airport guards shrugged and left as the two agents with Bart took over their positions.

"What do we know?" Bart came forward alone, but by the checking-in calls coming from his radio, there were a lot of agents coming into the airport.

Everyone stepped back for Bart to see what happened. To be fair, he didn't gasp, but his face was a shade paler when he stepped back. "Damn it. Are we thinking it's the same substance as what killed those two agents at the first sinkhole?"

"That would be my guess, except why aren't they dissolved? At least the new ones don't seem to be." Aisling pointed toward the skeletons in the goo. The closer she looked the more they looked disconnected and not related to the mass of bodies. Like maybe they came with the goo. She stepped back a few feet, looking closer wasn't good for the contents of her stomach. The goo was piled above the bodies, but didn't appear to have come through the ceiling. Or if it had, it didn't leave a mark.

Reece shook his head. "Good question and no answer. It looks like the same stuff, but not sure why it didn't react the same. Those people look like they died immediately though. And there's no building part here—the goo came through on its own."

"Damn it, we need to get you all out to the U.K., but I think I need Harlie here." Bart stepped back and answered some more calls and watched down the corridor.

Aisling saw Captain Driyflin down the way and at least two dozen agents, police, and airport security. None of them looked like they were coming closer, most likely because Bart wasn't letting them. "Are we even going to be able to fly out? They shut the airport down because of the sinkhole. They might not know these are connected cases, but this one is far more personal for them." There were at least two reservations desk people who had died in the mass judging by what she could see.

A loud female voice with a distinctive British accent was heard just beyond the agents blocking the corridor to this gate. "I'm with MI-6, let me through."

Bart leaned around from the flight board and yelled to the agents blocking the way.

Maeve and her carry-on luggage came stomping through. "What in the hell happened?" She paused once she saw the mass. The massive filter for the airport was removing most of the smell, but she still looked ill. "How did that…what is that…" Her words trailed off as she took it all in.

Caradoc reached out to steady her. "We don't know. Right now, Harlie might be staying here to figure it out, but our *boss* wants us in the U.K.."

Bart nodded. "I'd rather that all of you stayed here, to be honest. But what's happening over there needs you at the moment. I received new details, I wanted you to get them when you were there, but this isn't far off from what happened to that village, Noth. Like here, electricity stopped the movement of the attacking substance, but not before ten people were killed and a portion of the village swallowed." He shook his head. "It's not my area of expertise, but Noth is a magic nexus. That status is making everyone above me more worried about it than the other drops."

"But they had a piece of building crash though, I'm missing that here." Maeve was looking less ill and more pissed and ready to fight. Something.

"That worries me. And there have not been any reports of sections falling since the last one in the ocean. Here or elsewhere in the last two hours." Bart glared around a bit more, then stalked a few feet away to chase down people on both his phone and radio.

Harlie came through the crowd with all of their carry-ons. It was interesting that no one tried to stop him even though Aisling didn't see him hold up any type of badge.

"This was an attack." He studied the body collection with a studious eye. It didn't shock him; he'd probably known what it was from his seat in their gate area. "The sinkhole was a test, to see if it could come through. This was something more aggressive."

Reece watched him carefully. "Then we're sure this came through the veil? Is this some sort of creature your people left behind?"

Considering that he was part fey as well, the comment about their people was undeserved. Aisling wasn't the only one who caught that.

"*Our people*, yours included, left many things behind." Harlie lifted an eyebrow. "Those who left were fleeing for their lives. It stands to reason there were many things on the other side of the veil to flee from."

"You don't know what this is though." Jones was standing by, looking stoic as usual.

"No. I don't. I agree I need to stay here after you go to England, but only to gather data. I can look into this from over there as well. I can join you in a few days."

Aisling was going to ask how Harlie knew Bart now wanted him to stay behind. But there were a lot of things Harlie knew without being told—starting to question them all at this point was useless.

"I can get all of you, even Maeve, out on a military transport." Bart's scowl was deep and he raised a hand. "Don't talk to anyone beyond stating who you are, that you all work for the FBI, and this is a top-secret mission with an extremely intense time issue." Whoever he had to work on to get them this flight, it hadn't made him happy.

"What about our luggage?" Caradoc had hidden his scanner, but Aisling was pretty sure Bart had seen it and not said anything. Clothes could be replaced when they got to London, most of his gadgets couldn't. He'd have a few in his carry-on, but she knew he'd taken almost everything he had that could fit in a suitcase.

"I'll have it taken off the cart and forwarded to the military. You'll need to spend a day in London, then go to Noth. Agent Greely will get a hold of you, but that's where you'll stay at first."

Aisling hadn't known that Area 42 worked with the military, but neither Reece nor Jones appeared surprised.

The rest happened quickly as Bart now seemed determined to get them out of there as soon as possible. One of the agents who first walked in with him led them all to a van and drove them to the Los Angeles Air Force Base. Rather, to the far side of the base that had a fifteen-foot high electrified and spelled wall surrounding a secret airfield. Few people even knew it existed. Jones told them about it on the way over.

"You Area 42 people work with the military a lot, do you?" Maeve asked as they drove through a tunnel out of the official Air Force Base and into whatever the secret area was.

"Sometimes." Reece looked uncomfortable. "We used to help them out on some odd cases. But now, due to the lack of people left in our L.A. office, we're relying on them to help pick up the slack." He glanced over to Aisling and gave her a small smile.

Aisling wasn't sure if Reece had some sort of siren mojo or not—he shouldn't. But he also shouldn't have his other breed abilities. But the fact he didn't know himself must be hard as hell. And he might have known some of those agents who'd been killed. Cutting him some slack might be viable. For now.

They'd come through a tunnel, but there was no light when the van stopped. The entire area was cloaked both physically and magically. It was strong enough that

Aisling felt the spell brush up against her as she got out of the van. No one was going to notice this place unless the people involved okayed it.

The airport was small and filled with so many armed personnel that it felt like they were under siege. Considering what just happened and Harlie's comments, maybe they were. The rest of the world just didn't know it yet.

The scanner directly past the entrance was massive and clearly far more intense than the one at LAX. Aisling was the first in line, so she put her belongings on the conveyor belt. The belt stopped on her carry-on bag.

"We need you to open your bag. There is a spell being detected."

"I have an opal charged spell case." She tilted her head when the elf in charge didn't react. "For my clan jewelry?" That should be known to any fey, especially another elf. That was the only reason for the boxes. Granted, hers also blocked that scroll of Maeve's.

They didn't react or back down so she, her entire bag, and two guards went to a metal table along the far wall. She pulled everything out—including the opal charging box. They were polite but went through all of her items twice before looking up.

"Please open the case."

Aisling stepped back. That was as bad of a violation of her privacy as if they demanded she strip down in public. Wearing the clan jewelry was one thing, opening the private case was another. Clan jewelry was vulnerable for the first hour or so when it came out of charging. Attacks could nullify or destroy the power of the stones. Not to mention, she didn't want anyone seeing that scroll.

Reece stepped forward. "Really? A violation of the clan laws?" He whipped out a pad and noted the badges of the two guards. "I'm Agent Larkin, senior FBI. There will be some serious conversations for you later. Right now, get me your commander."

Aisling had noticed before that Reece stepped into personas even when he wasn't in disguise. Right now, his voice had deepened, he appeared taller, and he remained leaning into the airspace of both guards even after he wrote down their badge numbers and names.

The first guard didn't flinch, the second one called someone on a radio. That they hadn't stood down about such a violation even when they knew who Reece was, wasn't good.

A fey of mixed heritage strode forward. He was easily eight feet tall, but it was impossible to tell what his heritage was. "Agents Larkin, Jones. What is the problem?" He barely glanced to Aisling, Maeve, or Caradoc but still managed to dismiss them.

"Captain Trillio, you did receive the call from Agent Churchill at oh-nine-hundred, correct?" Reece took a step back so he didn't have to crane his neck.

"We did. However, he didn't indicate that there would be violations of our travel procedures. Anything emitting active magic can't fly on our planes. You know that."

"It's a *clan spell box*." Reece narrowed his eyes and folded his arms. A move that put his right hand close to his gun. "Those have always been excluded for reasons you can take up with your superiors."

The captain pulled back and looked at his two guards then at the items on the table. "A clan spell box? It sure as hell looks like one to me. You want to tell me why you're trying to launch a war against the first families?"

The guards had been sure of themselves, but both looked at each other now.

"We were told to question everything for all non-military personnel." The first one finally responded.

"These people are to be treated as our own or they wouldn't be here. What part of that is debatable?" The captain was pissed but he also looked perplexed.

"The Secretary of the military sent a memo…" That

had been the second guard, but he let his words stop when he saw the look on the captain's face.

"I hate to interrupt, but we do have a plane to catch. Class one clearance." Reece had been watching the back and forth, but finally interfered.

"Understood." The captain nodded to Aisling's carry on. "Please accept our apologies. The cases are never to be opened."

"Thank you." Aisling gave the two guards her best family glare, gathered her things, and stepped back.

The rest finished their scans and Reece led them down a low corridor as he nodded to Jones. "You want to tell Bart?" He wasn't running but he was moving fast and his right hand stayed near his gun.

Jones made a call and started talking fast and low. "Yes sir." He cut the call. "We need to move fast and get on that plane. Something is going on and Bart's not sure how far it goes, but he's sending people over to take those two guards into custody."

Reece picked up speed.

"They think someone has taken over *here*?" Aisling kept her voice down. She had no idea how whatever happened at LAX would be connected to a potential breakdown of security on a secret military base, but the look on both Reece and Jones' faces said that's what they thought.

Reece picked up speed. "Hard to say, but we have to question everything right now. That they broke protocol for a memo? No way that would have happened. Had they questioned our weapons, I'd be less concerned. Those they were fine with."

Caradoc had been pensively quiet. "Both guards seemed honestly confused at the reprimand. I wish we had Harlie with us, he's better at reading those things."

"They did." Maeve dodged a slow-moving soldier. "They were shocked when the captain not only didn't back them up but took them down."

Reece grabbed his phone when it rang, but didn't slow down. He picked up speed as soon as he disconnected the call. "Regardless, we need to move faster. Bart thinks there could be something seriously wrong with this base. His people are now flying the plane, but we'll be the last flight out for a bit."

The corridor was mostly clear, except for a single black-clothed military person. A very heavily armed one. "Larkin?"

Reece raised his badge and the man let them through.

The plane was a military cargo transport, big and lumbering. The passenger accommodations weren't great but it had seats and belts and that was enough for Aisling. The past few minutes a nasty chill had been climbing up her back. She'd fly on the wing at this point if it meant they could get out of here.

The plane was rumbling and a runway appeared before them.

"How did it do that?" Maeve looked like she wanted to get up for a better look, but a stern glare from Reece kept her seated.

"Optical runway? Wow. You don't think they'd let me check it out later, would they?" Caradoc was almost drooling.

"No, they won't. Now sit back, once this thing gets cleared, it's a fast shot out of here." Reece pushed himself deep into his seat. A quick look showed that Jones had as well.

Aisling had only briefly heard about the optical runways, or paths, as they could be used for other things besides planes. Most of the details went right over her head. These runways could exist out of phase, then be called up when needed, only to vanish again after they had been used. A scary combination of magic and technology creating something that should never work.

Reece had been right about the shot, it felt like they'd been loaded into a gun at the speed the plane raced across the optical runway and lifted into the air.

The lift off was amazing, if a bit disturbing, but as the initial burst required for take-off leveled out the flight was almost normal.

No one said much as the plane reached cruising altitude and quickly went on its way. Aisling was closing her eyes for a nap when the alarms came.

CHAPTER EIGHTEEN

—◆—

AT FIRST AISLING COULDN'T FIGURE out where the alarms came from. Then she realized the plane's nose was pointed down and there didn't seem to be anyone in the pilot's seat. There was a crashing sound followed by a massive rush of wind.

Jones and Reece both unbuckled their belts and got up.

"Stay here, all of you."

"I can fly," Caradoc said as he undid his belt.

Jones put his hand on Caradoc's shoulder. "One of these?"

Caradoc sat back down and re-buckled his seatbelt.

Reece sat in the pilot's chair, fighting to pull the nose back up. "The pilot and co-pilot are here on the floor, both are dead." He had to yell to be heard over the wind.

"There was a third person hiding onboard?" Maeve twisted around but since the plane had no cargo beyond them it was fairly open. If anyone had been hiding, they should have seen them when they came in. There was no one around now.

Jones had taken the co-pilot's seat. Wind still whipping through the plane.

"Can't we close the door? I can get up and get it." Caradoc again started to unbuckle his belt.

"The door is gone." Jones was flipping switches and swearing. Considering he was usually unflappable, that was a bad sign. He picked up the radio. "This is cargo liner zero-zero-five-nine, we are possibly going down." He repeated his message twice more, the response was only static. Then he started taking apart the control panel.

From what Aisling saw, the "possibly" was wishful thinking. They'd hit cruising speed before the attack, but they were still aiming more down than up.

Jones turned back toward them. "The mage-line is fried. When we used the path, there was no more magic to support it. Either of you two elves packing any spells that might keep us airborne long enough for me to fix it?"

Aisling turned to Caradoc. He wasn't as strong as Harlie in the magic department and he didn't like using it. But he had more than she did. Unless there was a healing spell for a crashing plane that she didn't know about.

This time he was reluctant to undo his belt, but it was more that he looked like he was trying to figure out what to use than anything else. The wrong spell could bring the plane down faster.

He went to the front, the little bit of magic that the plane possessed was being used to keep all of them from being sucked out the open flight door. A lot of wind still went through, but nowhere near what would happen if that shield fell completely.

Caradoc and Jones were working trying to get the magic parts of the plane back up again. Reece was keeping them from crashing, but not much more than that.

A crackle of electricity shot out of the panel and slammed Caradoc and Jones all the way to the back of the plane. Aisling and Maeve ran to them. Both were breathing, but they were also out cold.

"Secure them to this netting." Aisling yelled as the wind grew worse. Maeve nodded and Aisling fought her way to the front. The good news was that the nose was definitely pointing up. Bad news, the shield sealing the open door was weakening, and air from the outside was already leaking in

"Are they okay?" Reece didn't look over as he yelled, the controls on the plane were fighting back.

"Alive, but knocked out. Where is the mage-line?" Aisling didn't know what she could do, but she was going to have to do something.

Reece pointed with his elbow toward a singed box.

Damn it. Aisling's magic wasn't like her brothers'. But maybe there was something. She looked around the line, it looked cut, but that could be figured later. Harlie always said thinking about things made them workable. She took a deep breath and tried channeling him.

"Think of your mother!" Reece yelled. Even this close the wind force from the missing door making speaking a yelling match.

Aisling smiled. She still had no idea what she was going to do, but at least now she'd have more power. They'd discovered that counterintuitively to what healing magic should be, hers really liked anger. And no one pissed her off more than her mother. Especially since to one degree or another she was behind everything that had been going on lately.

She was certain there was far more involved in fixing it properly, but the shield around the plane was failing and while they weren't going down right now, neither were they going up. Aisling went old school, grabbed both ends of the cut mage-line and thought of all the crappy things her mother had done during her life. The wind pressure eased and the plane felt like it was going up, but she couldn't stop to check. She was literally healing the mage-line as if it had been a living thing and it was taking all of her focus. She felt a presence behind her and vaguely heard Maeve ask if she could help.

She couldn't acknowledge her. Focusing on twisting a healing magic designed for biological beings into a mechanical system was pulling everything she had. Colors, energies, light, all flowed through her. But it seemed to be doing something—at least they hadn't crashed yet.

Aisling had no idea how long she'd been running her

magic through the system when she was pried free of the mage-line by a very concerned Reece.

"The plane!" She frantically looked around.

"We've landed in New York. Bart has a team from his office coming to get us." He stood back. "Can you stand?"

Aisling felt like she'd run the entire way from Los Angeles to New York. Standing would take a while. "What time is it?"

"A bit after one pm, L.A. time. We got here in less than forty-five minutes." His gray eyes were grave. "Do you need me to help you stand?"

Aisling held out her hand. The flight should have taken them three hours. "How did we get here so fast?" She leaned harder into him than she intended. That bugger better not be sending out siren mojo, she had the energy of a wet noodle and wouldn't be able to avoid doing something stupid.

"That's a good question." Reece held up one of her hands. It was covered in electrical burns—ones she didn't feel yet, but she knew she would soon. "I'm thinking your anger at your mother could be used as a major power source."

Aisling let him lead her off the plane. Jones and Cara-doc were both conscious, sitting on cots, and arguing with the medics. Maeve ran up to her as she and Reece came down the ramp.

"You gave me a serious scare."

"I think I gave *me* a serious scare. I want someone to tell me what I just did, but at the same time, I'm think-ing it might be better not to know." A medic team with a gurney came up and Reece handed her over to them.

"Take care of her. She's got serious burns on her hands and who knows what else." His phone buzzed before he could add more, but he definitely had a mother hen look in his eyes before he walked off.

"How are you feeling?" Maeve dodged the medics

who were settling Aisling on the gurney.

"Like someone just ran the power of this entire city through me." She looked around the medics to her brother and Jones. "They're okay, I take it?"

Maeve rolled her eyes. "Yes. Caradoc took the heavier hit, but your brother has a head made of stone according to the medics. They want the two of them to stay for observation for a few days, that's what the current argument is about."

"Reece doesn't look happy either." He'd walked off for his phone call, but was now arguing with a short human in a dark suit.

"That's the Area 42 second in command for this base. He and Bart aren't seeing eye-to-eye on us staying here or not." Maeve looked down at her. "I might have to leave you all if they can't work this out. My people were fine with my coming in with all of you given the circumstances of what happened at LAX, but they want me in London ASAP."

"Any clue as to what is going on? Or how someone snuck on board a secret military flight, unseen by any of us, killed the pilot and co-pilot, fried a bunch of tech, then jumped out of the plane? How were they killed by the way?"

Maeve stepped back as the medic team continued their work up. "No clue on most of that. But they were shot at close range. Reece thinks that they used naru guns with silencers judging by the small entry and the massive damage they did, but won't be certain until they check ballistics."

"We have to take her in for testing." The first medic said as they started to move the gurney away.

"Stay with Reece as long as you can, Caradoc too if they don't lock him up in a hospital room." Aisling wasn't in the mood to go for medical exams, but she could also barely close her hands, and her legs were still shaking.

"Will do." Then Maeve was out of sight, but they were going past Caradoc and Jones. Jones was sitting on the edge of a gurney, arms folded, and a sullen look on his face. Caradoc was arguing with anyone who would listen that he was fine.

Now that she had nothing to distract her, Aisling studied the airstrip they'd landed on. And it was a strip. Only a strip, not part of an actual airport. Didn't look military, but also not general population either.

The building she was wheeled into looked suspiciously nondescript aside from a small, closet-sized doorway to the right side that the female medic in the back darted into. The unlocking panel for the entrance to the next hall must have been in there as the doors opened wide as soon as she returned. Aisling wished Reece had followed them in so she could ask questions. The New York branch of Area 42 was supposed to be the largest of them all. At least in theory. That they might have their own secret airstrip wouldn't be shocking. But she still had a lot of questions about all of it.

The long hall they entered turned down into a shorter one. Everything was white and well lit. "How long will it take to fix my hands?" She was pretty sure that the weakness and shaking was due to an extreme over-use of her magic. But her hands didn't look good.

"The doctor will know," the first medic said and the second one nodded. The second one was following behind Aisling and since they had her facing backwards, she watched her as something odd caught her eye. A weapon on the woman medic. This was most likely part of the New York branch of Area 42. They had a lot of secrets and their agents were always armed.

But who armed a medic? Even in the paranoia of the world's most secret agency, would medics be armed? She thought about the nurses and doctors who had been in Mott's room in the L.A. branch a few months ago. Granted, they'd only been by in passing, but like most cops, Aisling's instincts caught when weapons were involved. And no weapons came to her memory.

This woman not only had one, a small gun outline on her right hip, but what looked like the butt-end of a larger weapon protruding from her back. Her scrubs and a sweater covered them mostly, but Aisling knew what she saw. And even though she'd been out of it when they put her on the gurney, she was pretty sure that those weapons hadn't been there before.

The small hallway the medic darted into prior to this corridor had more than the place to release access for this part of the facility. She'd had weapons stored there.

Aisling's brain was screaming to get out, but she didn't think her legs were ready yet. Her hands sure as hell weren't. Even if she could get to her gun under her jacket without setting the medic off, there was no way she could hold it.

They went through a third set of doors, then down what looked like a service corridor. If she hadn't been suspicious before, she was now. The white and bright of the other two corridors had been replaced by service gray and minimal lighting.

"The main route was flooded when a line broke this morning, we're going the back way." The first medic kept looking ahead as he spoke, so he didn't notice when the second one grabbed the gun on her right hip.

"Gun!" Aisling yelled and threw herself off the gurney.

The second medic wasn't aiming at Aisling but shot the first one in the back of his head. He dropped.

Aisling scrambled under the gurney, but there wasn't anywhere to hide.

The second medic grabbed her arm and jerked her up. "They don't want you dead, but they didn't say I couldn't injure you. Get back on that gurney and stay still or I will shoot you." She also reached around and took Aisling's gun. "Just in case those hands aren't as bad as they look."

With a wince, Aisling raised her hands and awkwardly climbed on the gurney. No idea who this woman was working for, but either it wasn't Area 42 or she'd been turned. The gurney continued down the service hall and into what could only be a morgue.

CHAPTER NINETEEN

—◆—

THE ROOM DIDN'T HAVE A sign, but was dark and cold and had a wall of small steel doors. They weren't supposed to kill her but they were going to lock her in a tomb? This wasn't getting better.

"Don't worry, this is just a stopping point. But, as we can't have you running around, in you go. This will help keep you calm." The medic shot her in the arm with a small needle, then nudged the gurney close to the lower door. It slid open and the platform slid out.

Aisling waited until the medic moved forward to get her onto the platform. Whatever she'd been shot with was slow acting and while she felt a vague sluggishness starting to hit her, it wasn't moving fast enough to stop her. Yet. Aisling had never been fond of enclosed places, but after Nix buried her in a pile of rocks, she *really* wasn't. Fear and anger helped her to overcome the pain and fatigue as well as what she'd been shot with. She touched the medic's arm and focused on pain. It was the other side of her healing powers and she'd only used it a few times in her life. The darkness that flooded her as she sent pain through the healing conduit almost made her throw up.

But she was not going into that box.

The medic screamed and dropped to her knees. Aisling hung on to her, following her to the ground. She kept sending the disruptive pain until the woman finally blacked out. Then Aisling crawled to the side of the room and threw up. The feeling that accompanied doing what she just did was horrific.

Once she'd calmed her stomach, she crawled back to the unconscious woman. Whatever she'd shot Aisling with might not have knocked her out, but it did help null the pain in her hands. They still hurt like hell, but she could move things now. It was hard, she was still shaking from the magic drain and what she'd just done, but Aisling managed to take the white jacket, including her badge, off the woman, and tumble her into the body box she'd planned on holding Aisling in. The medic would have a few more bruises than she'd started out with, but she was lucky Aisling hadn't done more. The damage she'd done with her magic wouldn't be permanent. While some healers could inflict death through the reversal of the healing conduit, Aisling wasn't that powerful.

She took back her gun and added the two that had been on the medic. Her hands screamed in pain with each move, but there wasn't a choice. She was glad she could use them at all.

If there were more turned agents on the other side of that door, she needed to be able to use her hands. Healing oneself was a tricky endeavor for most healers and Aisling had never been able to do it. There wasn't an option at this point, she only hoped that if she failed, the attempt didn't knock her out. She stood behind the door. If someone came in, she didn't want to be the first thing they saw.

She took a deep breath, ignored the residual shaking in it, and forced healing on the burns on her right hand. The marks slowly vanished. She slid to the floor before she finished, but she could move that hand completely now.

Fast moving footsteps coming down the corridor on the other side of the door made her forget about trying to heal the left hand. She got to her feet and had her gun out and up as the door opened.

"Damn it, here's the gurney, but I don't see her." Reece

ran into the morgue with his gun up. Jones was right behind him.

"I'm here." Aisling wasn't sure how much she could move at this point, any slight recovery from the initial over-use of magic had been totally wiped out by the recent events.

She must have looked as bad as she felt. Reece ran to her and held her up. "What happened?" He looked at her white coat and badge. "You're a doctor now?"

"The woman medic is inside on that shelf. She's still alive. She killed the other one as they came down this corridor. I took her jacket in case this was widespread. But I don't feel good." Everything was catching up to her and things were getting woozy. She leaned into him to stay upright.

"Let me get you back on the gurney." He started to walk her over but Aisling had enough strength to pull back.

"Yeah, not unless I'm unconscious, if you don't mind."

Jones opened the box and scanned the medic. "Work's been done on her face. The woman on that badge is a real Area 42 medic, but she was replaced at some point. We need to scan the body we found in the corridor too."

"If she killed him wouldn't that mean he was on our side?" Aisling shook her head at her own comment. "But he did lead us down this side corridor."

"Which only leads to the morgue and the dumpster. He was probably working with her until she decided he wasn't." Jones slid the woman back in. "She'll be okay in here. It's been modified to keep her alive but unconscious. Or rather, to keep you that way."

Aisling started sagging more. Whatever had been in that shot didn't knock her out but was making it hard to focus. "She shot me with something before I took her out. I might need some help, but seriously, no more gurney rides."

Reece put his arm around her waist and got her moving. With Jones in the lead, they left the morgue.

"How did you know to come find me?"

"Your brother. Not Caradoc, he's still fighting with the medics. Harlie called and said something was wrong and you were missing. The medical center didn't have you, but vid footage showed those medics taking you this way."

They stopped at the body of the first medic. Jones scanned the man's face, frowned and scanned again. "It looks like this one had work too, but not on the level of the woman. He only vaguely looks like the man he replaced."

"Why did Harlie say I was missing? This is part of the base, isn't it?"

"It is but something down here was blocking Harlie. The feed has been doctored as well. We saw them wheel you through those doors at the front of this corridor, yet the vids just show an empty hall right after that." Reece got them outside and sat her down on a chair. "I need to find someone I trust to get the body. Bart said to do as little as possible until he could get here."

"Great, so this branch is compromised too?" The fresh air helped Aisling's focus but things were still fuzzy. She wasn't up to fighting off more enemies.

"Hopefully, it was something limited to those two. But Bart's bringing Harlie with him. He can search on a level our tech can't."

"I'm going to set up a scanning for all personnel, just to cover the tech side." Jones nodded and vanished back into the building.

Reece took the chair next to Aisling. "Are you sure you're okay? You really don't look good."

"Flatterer." Aisling winced as she moved her left hand without thinking. "I'll be fine once this gets healed by a real medic and we are out of here."

"You too, huh?"

"What?"

"The need to get out of here. It hit me right before Harlie called me." Reece rubbed the back of his neck. "We can't leave here soon enough."

"Precog feelings? Or a hunch?" Aisling kept her voice low.

"Who knows? I sure as hell don't." He bent down closer to her. "There is a seer outside of London, not Area 42, but I know of him because of the agency. He thinks he can help determine if what I'm experiencing is actually fey." His eyes met hers. "All of it."

There were too many different emotions in those gray eyes for Aisling to deal with. But for once they didn't seem to be pulling at her. She almost told him about Harlie running similar studies but couldn't do it. They'd come clean later, once it was clear he wasn't linking into some secret siren ability. His precog had helped in the past, and his ability to swim far beyond human abilities had saved both her and Jones from a watery death. But siren abilities were too dangerous. Might explain about his eyes though.

"That would be a good idea. Just to be safe. If fey abilities are somehow coming through into the breeds…" Aisling left the rest there. If it was happening to Reece, it had to be happening to other breeds. The High Council would never tolerate that. The years of fey ruling over humans were gone, but they would see the breeds as siding with the humans since they all looked like them.

"Yeah. That's what I thought too." He gave a tight smile and stood up. "Let me get the medic who was with Jones to look at your hands."

Aisling held up her right one.

"They healed you in there?" He took her hand and turned it around gently.

"I did it." She shrugged. "I had no way to use my gun,

so I self-healed."

Reece rocked back. "Didn't know you could do that."

"Neither did I. But I know I couldn't do it again right now."

His smile was genuine this time. "I'll get someone to fix the other one. Without going inside and no gurney." He jogged over to the medics standing out front.

Caradoc, Maeve, and a medic were discussing Caradoc's freedom, and/or his extremely hard head, off to the side. Reece had figured out something had been wrong, but hadn't shared it with them. Better that he came to save her first. Aisling thought about going over there to tell them, but her energy was shot.

The woman medic dealing with Caradoc finally shook his head, raised both hands in the air, and walked off. Caradoc and Maeve must have noticed Aisling watching them and they both came directly to her.

"What happened?" Maeve took the seat Reece had just left. "Jones and Reece went barreling inside after they took you in and told everyone to stay out."

"The medics who were taking me in to be treated weren't who they were pretending to be." Aisling quickly told them what happened. "They're still trying to determine if this base is long term compromised or if it was short term and I was just a spur of the moment grab. But they were prepared to grab someone I think. There's no way anyone could predict what would happen with the plane or that we'd land here."

"Or that you'd be injured." Caradoc frowned.

"That's not a good look. What?" Aisling asked.

He sighed and ran his fingers through his hair. "One of the things Mott had been working on, before everything blew up for him months ago, was a predictive algorithm program. He didn't get as far as he'd wanted but it could predict weird events."

Maeve watched him as if waiting for a twisted joke,

then shook her head. "Like this? That our airport would be slimed, the military airport would be under attack, someone would kill the pilots, and Aisling and Reece would have to land the plane here because we'd probably crash into the Atlantic if we kept going?"

"Yes." Caradoc looked unhappy. "Let me check in with Mott. Don't go anywhere—we stay in sight of each other until we get out of this." He stalked off but true to his word, stayed within visual range.

"He's getting his stalking skills from Reece and Bart. Wonder if he realizes he's mimicking them?" Aisling watched him go closer to the plane and pull out his phone.

"How are the hands?" Maeve had been watching Caradoc but pulled back when Aisling held them up.

"Yeah, I healed one, no, I'm not sure how, and yes, the left one still hurts like hell. Reece went to go get someone to fix it."

Maeve looked at her injured hand but didn't touch it. "It sounds like Bart is going to get another plane to get everyone over to England. I get to fly with you guys as long as they get us off the ground in ten hours or less. After that MI-6 has another flight for me."

"Why so fussy on the time?" Aisling swore. "Something else has happened, hasn't it?"

Maeve looked around, but no one was nearby. "Yes. There's been an attack on a science lab in County Meath, Ireland. They are still tabulating what was taken. But all personnel were killed, twenty-two highly skilled brainiacs murdered where they stood. The lab was extremely hidden, and unknown to most agents. The only reason they told me after the attack was because of who they caught doing it." She pulled up a grainy image on her phone. It was a lab, there were bodies on the ground, and three people were ransacking the place. All three looked like Nix.

CHAPTER TWENTY

"**S**HIT." AISLING TOOK THE PHONE with her good hand, but the image was still extremely grainy. There was no doubt who those three were. "Then there are three more of them. Or could these be some of the ones we've already seen? And he, they, knew of this top-secret lab, and took it out before anyone could stop them?" She handed Maeve her phone back. "What in the hell is happening?"

"That's a good question." Reece walked up behind Maeve with a medic, the one who'd been with Caradoc originally, coming behind. "Not whatever has caused you both to look sick, I'd like to find out that later, but what's happening here. All the agents we found are who they are supposed to be. Any who come in later will also be scanned. The two medics who took you transferred in two days ago. Only thing anyone could recall of them is they were arguing about something this morning and both came in a few hours early for their shifts."

The medic who'd come with him gave a scowl. "They didn't interact much with any of us, but made sure to be polite when they did. They didn't give anything away." She motioned to Aisling. "Can I see your hand?"

Aisling held it out and smiled as a healing gel was gently applied. The medic also looked over her other hand. She didn't say anything but she nodded in approval.

"The two that attacked you were new? That can't be a coincidence." Maeve watched the medic closely until she finished.

"You should be fine now." Her eyes said she'd rather

have Aisling in a medical room for a full examination, but Reece must have explained her view on going back in right now. She smiled and left.

Aisling was sure that Reece wouldn't have brought over someone unless she was cleared, but she still waited until the medic was out of range. "Caradoc thinks Mott might know something about predictive algorithms. He thinks someone could have predicted that we'd land here." Aisling watched Reece's face, she expected him to look incredulous or surprised. That he looked neither was disturbing.

"I wasn't in the loop for Mott's project in that area. Only found out about it when he disappeared a few months ago and I found out how many think tanks he'd been involved in."

Caradoc came back. He still looked annoyed but not as much as before. "Mott says the people he was working with were still years away from an algorithm generator that could have predicted this many jumps with any accuracy."

"Then this was all just a weird coincidence? I take it we're stuck here until Bart and Harlie arrive?" Aisling didn't want to think about things for a bit. She was tired.

"Indeed." Jones came up. "We have a VIP guest suite to put you all in. Multi-layer guards and alarms. It looks like this base is secure, but I personally don't believe in coincidences."

They went around to a different door than the one used by the fake medical personnel. It took both Jones' and Reece's ident cards to unlock, and opened to a short hall with three doors.

"You guys get the big one." Jones led the way down. "Well, *we* get the big one. Bart wants us to wait here too."

Reece shook his head. "There's something wrong with this base, even if that woman is the only one alive who was in on it—there is something wrong. We could be looking while we wait for Bart." If he'd had a precog event, he wasn't disclosing it.

"And we could be targets." Jones shrugged. "I already went a few rounds with Bart. It's going to be unique working under him as opposed to Captain Driyflin. Trust me, giving in on this is a good idea."

The suite they entered was massive. A front room had a multiscreen set up in front with a dozen chairs, and past that was a kitchen, two bathrooms, and four small bedrooms.

"You know if you just added a few things this could be like your lair." Maeve walked around the space nodding to herself.

Reece shook his head. "I don't want to encourage too many people to hang out there. Besides, it's not my lair. Makes me sound like a mastermind of evil."

Caradoc was already pulling out things to make coffee. "Good guys can have lairs too. It's all how they use them. Yours is definitely a lair."

Jones shook his head. "Nerds." Then he settled down in one of the chairs in front of the bank of screens and started searching. He didn't say what he was looking for, but what looked like personnel files filled the screens.

Reece led Aisling to the first bedroom. "You look ready to fall over. I told the medic who healed your hand about you being drugged and gave her the syringe that I found. She said it should work its way out of your system in a few hours. Go sleep."

Aisling thought about debating it for a split second, then went for the bed. Rejecting his sound and intelligent idea would serve no one. She had her shoes off and the covers pulled back before he got to the door. "Thank you."

"Thank you for keeping me from crashing that plane." Reece looked like he wanted to say something more, but just smiled and left.

Aisling thought she heard the door shut, but once her head hit the pillow, she was out.

With everything that had happened, odd dreams weren't too surprising. Beyond the fact that she'd would have guessed that she was too exhausted to dream. Unfortunately, they were vague and terrifying. The same feeling that had hit her back in Caradoc's house struck again. Only this one was just coming into focus, something was chasing her, chasing all fey, destroying them as they were caught, but she couldn't get a good vision of what it was.

"Aisling! Wake up!" Reece's face was right in front of her and he was holding her upright.

"What happened? Are we under attack?" It took her a bit to orient to where she was, and when. The haunted feeling from her nightmare was slow to fade.

"You were yelling in your sleep." Reece brushed back her hair. "Whatever you were dreaming about, it did not look good."

"Nor sound good. Dang, girl, you are loud when being attacked by something in your sleep." Maeve was right behind Reece. "The screams alone should have chased whatever it was away."

Caradoc hung in the door way. "She used to have nightmares when she was little. A lot of them. Our mother called in healers, but nothing seemed to work unless they knocked you out. They stopped sometime around when you were five."

"I don't remember that. How come no one told me?" Aisling patted her hair but it felt like it was still sticking up. The bedsheets were tossed off the bed as well. "Whatever that nightmare was, thank you for waking me. I feel more tired than I was to start with."

"Only one thing for it. Tea." Maeve turned and shoved Caradoc out of the doorway to go to the kitchen.

"I don't think caffeine is going to help me sleep." Right now, Aisling felt that horrific combination of so tired she could barely keep her eyes open and too wired to sleep. The wired part was coming from the vestiges of her nightmare. Her heart still felt like it was beating too fast.

"Not all tea has caffeine." Maeve came back in with a steaming mug. "Although technically, this is an herbal tisane, no tea leaves involved. Chamomile is good for soothing the soul and body. Now drink it all."

Aisling took it but narrowed her eyes. "Only chamomile? Although right now I'd probably take anything. Especially if it could help chase away the dreams."

"There might be a few other components, but nothing you are allergic to nor anything that will react against what she shot you with. I can't guarantee it will stop the dreams, but it should knock you out enough for you not to notice them." Maeve used a lot of alternative medicine in her life, and from time to time shared it with Aisling.

"If I can just sleep." Aisling took a sip. She couldn't identify everything in it, but there was a fair amount of honey in there. Honey was the base for nectar, an alcoholic drink favored by the fey but on its own it was soothing and healing.

"Let's try this again." Reece got to his feet. "Finish your drink and go to sleep. We'll wake you if anything attacks here."

"Or when Bart and Harlie get here." She added around a yawn. The chamomile, honey, and whatever herbs Maeve had added were helping. They all left her room and shut the door. Aisling finished her drink, sat her cup down, and slid back into the bed.

There were only voices in her dreams this time, nothing scary. And they coasted through Aisling's sleeping mind gently. "I don't know that I can help her." It was Harlie, but at the same time, it wasn't. He sounded younger, scared, and pissed.

"You need to fix her. It's too dangerous for her to have those powers, she can't contain them. Not to mention I haven't slept in a week because the nanny keeps waking me up every time she has a nightmare. I don't care what you have to do—fix her. You owe me."

Aisling shivered. She knew that voice. Her mother. But when had that conversation taken place? Before he came to Los Angeles recently, Aisling had only seen Harlie twice—and neither time had there been much interaction. Then what was she hearing?

"Child, sleep." Again, the Harlie-not-Harlie voice, but now she felt someone brushing back her hair. "Let go of this." She felt something push at her mind. Taking something away…or blocking it. But the feeling was soothing, like the hand on her forehead. "Sleep now."

Aisling woke up sweating. It was great that Maeve's chamomile had gotten her to sleep, and there hadn't been a repeat of the terrifying nightmare, but she felt like she'd just finished a sixty-mile run. On the plus side, she felt recovered enough to have been on that kind of run.

Like the rest of the suite, this bedroom didn't have windows, so it was completely dark. But Aisling could see the outlines of the sparse furniture enough to move about without switching on the light. Had the voices she'd heard come from the front room? The idea of her mother being here was more terrifying than the nightmares. But whatever happened had felt so real. She could even smell her mother's perfume.

She marched to the door, intending to find out who in the hell brought her mother into a secret mission, but instead waited and listened.

The voices were low, but with concentration she sorted them out. Maeve saying if they didn't get a new plane quickly, she was going to have to leave. Jones and Reece debating something with Bart. Caradoc and Harlie were the loudest because they were in the kitchen which was next to her room.

"I don't know how that could have happened. Aisling

shouldn't have been able to do what she did to the plane. That's beyond her abilities." That was Harlie, sounding more agitated than Aisling had ever heard.

Outside of the weird dream she just had.

"She healed herself too. After doing what she did on the plane, then being kidnapped and drugged." Caradoc didn't sound freaked out, but he wasn't happy. And he kept his voice low.

"I...I don't know what's happening." That level of uncertainty and confusion coming from Harlie, along with the echoing voices of the conversation she'd dreamed of, was enough to make Aisling open the door and march up to Harlie.

"I think you need to talk and talk fast." The guilt and surprise on Harlie's face solidified things. Something was very wrong with her. Something that her brother and mother had done to her almost two hundred years ago.

CHAPTER TWENTY-ONE

———◆———

"AISLING." HARLIE SAID WITH AN uncertain smile.

"No, don't *Aisling* me. Something happened involving our mother," She stabbed him in the chest with her finger. "And you. Talk. Now."

The others all stopped talking. No one came closer, but the room wasn't large enough for them not to hear. Aisling didn't care at this point. She felt the wrongness in her. Whatever had been taken or blocked from her as a child was there. Hovering on the edge of her consciousness. And she was pissed.

"This isn't something that should be public." Harlie went pale and slid into one of the kitchen chairs.

"This isn't public, this is me and the people I trust. Which right now doesn't include you. What did you and our mother do to me?" Bart was a new addition to her inner circle, but she trusted him and this couldn't wait. Something had been changed and she needed to know what.

Harlie stared at her for a few moments, his eyes growing sadder as he did. Finally, he shook his head. "You had a bad nightmare. One that left you screaming and scorched the walls." Neither was a question.

"The walls are fine." She folded her arms and nodded for him to continue.

"Not these, although the nightmare here could have left damage we don't see yet. When you were a girl. No more than four or five. You almost destroyed the family home because of a nightmare." He leaned forward. "How did you know?"

"I had a nightmare. Here." She folded her arms tightly. She'd fight him if she had to, she knew that nightmare had been real.

Harlie grew even sadder, but just nodded.

Caradoc looked between them. "I wasn't as young as her, but I still lived in the house. Her nightmares were annoying for us and bad for her, but she never did any damage. I would have noticed if she almost burned the house down."

"That's what mother and father wanted you to believe. The housekeepers, security, everyone in the house needed to believe. They even blocked our siblings from the knowledge, although none of them lived there any-more." Harlie's voice was still filled with sorrow. But there was an anger there as well.

The room was silent and Aisling felt every eye on her. "That doesn't make sense. I'm not a strong magic user, ask mother. I grew up being the disappointing last child."

"That's what they wanted you to believe. Instead of training you to use your abilities, *she* made me hide them." His eyes were sad. "Your potential was unprece-dented. You had far more than just healing abilities."

"Then why in the hell did you people block her? Things are going in the shitter right now; in case you haven't noticed. Having some kick-ass powers might come in handy." Maeve was pissed.

"Had she been trained two hundred years ago, and taught to use them correctly, yes. She would be a force to be reckoned with. One that…" His words drifted off and he shook his head as he muttered to himself.

"What?" Caradoc was pissed too and got in his older brother's face. "What else did you and she do to Aisling? To me? I don't care about the rest of our siblings they can rot in the abyss—but what did you do to us?" Caradoc had been the only one to keep in contact with Harlie over the years, and the feeling of betrayal was clear on his face.

"I blocked her magic; I created a well for it to funnel away from her and not cause problems. But I just realized that had Aisling's magic been trained, and she been raised using it, she might have been stronger than our mother. I'm not convinced that I am stronger than her and I am the strongest of all of the children. But mother could have seen Aisling as a threat."

"Your mother had you block her, not to help Aisling, but to save her own arse?" Maeve turned to Aisling. "I am so sorry if at any time I doubted the level of evil in that woman."

Bart, Reece, and Jones had been standing by, watching the family drama, but Bart finally spoke. "Like your friends here, I am one of the few who know your family connection to that woman. I think it's best to keep it hidden. I don't have much magic, never have and never will. But what she had Harlie do was vile." He turned to Harlie. "I need you on this case, but this seriously causes me problems."

Harlie ran his fingers through his hair and wouldn't look up. "I don't blame you. I moved to Nepal to get away from her before Aisling was born. However, I stayed there after what she made me do. I can never be forgiven."

Caradoc watched his brother closely. Finally, his face relaxed. "I don't believe you had a choice. The question is, why did she have you do it, instead of doing it herself? I know her magic is different than yours, but could she have done what you did?"

"Yes." Harlie pulled on the ends of his hair, but he did that when thinking sometimes. "She could have definitely done what I did. Instead, she flew across the world to meet me in Nepal. Why?" His eyes were haunted but he wouldn't look at anyone for more than a few moments.

Aisling stayed silent. Mostly so she could work through the emotions before she started yelling them again. "She was threatened by my potential abilities, things that were somehow connected to my nightmares, so she had you block them. I didn't know you then, but I don't think you're the type to do something like that lightly. Especially for her." There were layers here that she couldn't deal with right now. As long as it didn't interfere with her job or life at this point, everything could just stay shoved in a corner. Except the why. Bart was right, they did need Harlie in on whatever in the hell was going on. But not if he couldn't be trusted.

"I think we know why. She didn't want to be connected to the issue or the blocking on a magical level." Caradoc shook his head as he looked to Aisling. "But she's still connected to you. She gave birth to you after all, and has spent the past ten years trying to get you back into the family fold."

"That was only a public face thing. Plus, she might have decided that my abilities could be used now that they're two hundred years delayed." Aisling poured herself some black tea from the pot on the counter. "What were my powers? The ones she had you block?" It was hard to ask, but necessary.

Harlie's eyes had tears in them. "That's the problem, it wasn't clear. You were so young and they were just developing."

"I'm not a magic user, but this doesn't sound like something we can resolve quickly." Reece shot Aisling a glance at the first part of his sentence. "Can you release her? Maybe if the block stopped the nightmares, removing it could resolve them now? Her stronger powers are already leaking through based on what happened today."

"I should be able to." Harlie looked up. "I'll find a flight back tomorrow, once we're sure the block has been removed."

"Not so fast." Bart stepped forward. "Aisling? How do you feel about your brother, what he did, and your mother?" He folded his arms but his face was neutral. She knew that Bart would back whatever she said.

Aisling watched Harlie. She hadn't known him growing up, but had learned to love and trust him in the last month. No matter what their bitch of a mother made him do, she found that she still did feel both. He was a victim here as well. She finally nodded. "I trust Harlie. I'm not sure what I feel about what he did beyond that it was our mother who made it happen. I hate her for what she did to *both* of us." She'd said it all quickly, so the emotion behind all of it could be felt by Harlie.

"Thank you." He sighed and leaned back. "If you need me, I will stay. One question though, how did you know? I was afraid to be around you in case you could tell I'd done something, but why now?"

"I have no idea. After Maeve's chamomile cocktail I didn't dream. But I heard words. You and her, talking about me. She forced you to do it." She repeated exactly what she'd heard and felt.

Harlie was back to looking pale. "That hand was mine. Everything you said was what happened. How did this come back? Mother had you asleep with a spell when she brought you to me. That's probably why you didn't see anything. But to have felt and heard that while you were under her spell." He gave a tight grin. "You might not end up being as strong as she feared you would be, but I think you'll still give her a fight once we train you."

"Good. Let's get started." She didn't care why her mother didn't want her to have her powers. She just hoped that getting them back would provide some much-needed payback. Her mother feared her potential powers, she'd make sure that fear was realized.

Reece, Bart, and Jones headed for the door. Bart turned toward Aisling. "We have more mundane things to deal with, such as securing a plane for you all. Do whatever you need to do to get a handle on this. But be ready to fly out in two hours." He gave a nod to Maeve, that must have been within the MI-6 timeline. The sound of the door locking behind them said even in the secret suite, things might not be as safe as hoped.

Caradoc and Maeve took up kitchen chairs on either side of Harlie, leaving the one facing him open.

Aisling took the open seat. "Do we have an idea what exactly is going to happen? Just so I can brace myself?"

Caradoc leaned forward, but he was watching her, not Harlie.

"I'm not going to grow horns, and he hasn't started yet." She folded her arms and stared back at Caradoc.

He grinned and leaned back in his chair. "Just remembering you as you were, before the change. You have to admit though, horns might be cool." He was laughing, but there was real concern in his eyes. Typical Caradoc, trying to help with humor.

It worked. The tension Aisling had felt since she woke up vanished.

Maeve reached over and took Aisling's hand. "Even with horns, we'd still love you."

Harlie gave a cough. "If you're all done? I'm not sure exactly how to remove the block completely, mother would have been feeding it with her own magic to keep it secure. Especially the first twenty years. It's a good thing you moved north about then. She couldn't have kept adding to the spell and you were far from her range of influence."

"I just needed to get away." Her move to the northern realms had come as a shock to everyone, especially her mother. Aisling hadn't been sure why she wanted to leave beyond getting out from under the family influence. Good to know her subconscious might have had a better reason.

Harlie took her hand. "It's going to feel weird. Even though you've had cracks of power lately, this is going to let a lot of power flow through you."

"I thought you said she wouldn't have much, since she was blocked for that long?" Maeve released her other hand and Harlie took that one as well.

"She will never be as strong as she would have been without the block, this is true. But she is still going to be accessing a lot more magic than she had."

"Be prepared to duck, then?" The more he was talking, the more he was freaking Aisling out. More magic would be a good thing. More magic she couldn't control, would not be.

Harlie looked to her with a grin. "Might not be a bad idea."

Before Aisling could retort, the feeling she'd had during her non-dream with Harlie and her mother slammed into her. Darkness filled her vision even though she knew this time that her eyes were open. "I can't see."

Harlie squeezed both hands. "We have to go back in your head. Remove the blockage and free the magic. You're back two hundred years ago."

Aisling clenched his hands as she heard the same conversation she'd heard in her sleep. She wanted to reach out and smack her mother, but knew that wasn't an option.

"It's okay, relax." The voice was coming from outside her and inside her. Harlie sounded like he did now and yet also different. It wasn't aging really; two hundred years wasn't that much to an elf. He'd been changed from who he was two hundred years ago. Aisling had a feeling he'd changed because of what he'd been forced to do to her.

The moment the block was installed flowed away from her mind. It was as if they had gone back all those decades and at the last minute, and stopped it from happening. It didn't have to be removed, because it simply didn't happen. But at the same time, it did happen, and she felt the emptiness and loss crawl into her five-year-old self.

Light, sound, vibration, and heat all crashed into her. She pushed Harlie and the table away and found herself on the floor at the far end of the room. Caradoc and Maeve, along with the table and chairs, had been flung up against the opposite wall.

Aisling scrambled to her feet, but vertigo slammed into her and she collapsed. She leaned over and threw up in a trash bin.

Maeve helped pull the table away from the other two. Judging by their faces as they got up, they were freaked out, but not injured.

"That wasn't fun." Aisling pushed up the trash can, but stayed on the floor.

"I'm sorry. I had no idea it would react that way. Well, I had no idea what would happen at all, so that had to have been one of the options." Harlie nodded but didn't come closer to her. He turned and fixed the chairs and table instead.

Caradoc and Maeve came and helped her to her feet.

"You're not going to get sick again, are you?" Maeve held her hand but stood as far away as possible.

"I don't think so." Aisling sat back in the chair Caradoc aimed her at and dropped her head in her hands. "Everything hit at once. Sounds, colors, light, heat. It was weird. And things won't stop spinning."

Maeve started to bring over the trash can, but Aisling held one hand up. "I think I'm fine. Or will be. Might need to go lie down again. Was that all of it though? You don't have to do anything else?" She lifted her head out of her hands to look to Harlie. He still looked freaked.

"I'm not sure. I'd just started reversing the spell when you took over. I heard myself, two of me actually, our mother, and you. Not as now, but as the child you were."

"I didn't hear that. Are you certain? What did I say, and

how did I say anything since you said mother had me spelled?" She hadn't heard her own voice, now or as a child.

"You repeated the spell as I said it. As the me of now spoke the words to remove the block. You did it word for word." Harlie's surprise was gone. Now he looked lost-in-thought-neutral. Not an improvement.

"Does she have all of her potential powers back?" Caradoc stayed near her but he watched Harlie.

"You can't sense it? I can. But since I was uniquely tied to them that makes for a good reason. I feel a change in her. I can't pinpoint what it is, but something is different." Harlie peered at her like she was an unusual rodent. "Not everything she could have been, but there is a change."

Aisling took a deep breath. New magic was good, but she'd spent her life with the knowledge that she wasn't a strong magic user. This would take some getting used to. A flare of fury at what her mother took from her hit her, but she shoved it aside. She'd deal with that later—right now she needed to focus on what she had and how she could use it. Hopefully, against her mother and whoever she was working with. "Should I try to do something with it? I feel the same magic-wise, but still spinning head-wise."

"Probably not a good thing to test right now, given the circumstances. Give your mind and body time to adjust." Harlie walked around her slowly. "My block is gone though. That I can tell. How much or what your magic will do with that, remains to be seen."

Maeve watched Aisling carefully, then turned with a frown to Harlie. "Your mother can't tell what you did, right? The way Aisling broke the tie when she went up to troll town as a rebellious youth, this is the same, right? Too far from her to sense?"

"That's our mother, even people who have never met her hate and fear her," Caradoc said.

"She has a good point," Aisling frowned. "I know Caradoc managed to block our tech from her, but she can't track us magically because of this, can she?" That would be a side-effect she didn't want to think of and she'd have Harlie put the block up immediately if it were the case.

"No. At least I don't think so." Harlie shook his head. "Everything about this is unknown, but I do think the further away we are from her the better."

"My sources say she is back in the pacific northwest. On a retreat of some kind." Caradoc managed to make the word retreat sound like a four-letter word. Their mother didn't retreat from anything, she gathered with allies for the destruction of others.

A knock at the door preceded Reece and Jones.

Reece took over one of the chairs in the front area. "Everything better now? We have a flight, a private plane that Bart is piloting himself and leaves in one hour. And no, he won't say who the plane belongs to or how he borrowed it."

"I have done what I can. Did he say if I was to stay here and look into the airport issue?" Even though no one was sending Harlie packing, the attack on the airport might be something he could find answers about.

"Actually, no. He wants you back in the group going to England. Even though he's flying us out, he's not going to be staying at this point. No leads on the airport mess, beyond identifying the victims, but he has other people he can tap for it."

"Has the fake medic said anything?" Aisling asked.

"She hasn't woken up. She should have, but her brain activity is off somehow." Jones added with a thoughtful look at Aisling. "They're looking to see if it was something in the body storage. It had been rigged to keep you, or her, alive, but there are some chemicals there that are attacking her memories and higher brain functions."

Chapter Twenty-Two

———

THE GROUP WENT SILENT. IT might have been something related to the woman herself, or it could have been what they'd planned for Aisling. Or because it might have been set up at the last minute, it might have been a horrific mistake.

Reece's phone rang and he said a few words then hung up. "Bart's ready for us to load. Let's go see what he found for us."

The airfield was far emptier than it was when they arrived. The damaged plane they'd come in on was rolled off to a large hanger. The only plane on the strip was a very expensive looking private jet. The nose was long and pointed and judging by the elaborate designs on it, pulled in a lot of magic to augment its speed.

Caradoc snorted as they walked closer. "Seriously? At what point do we realize magic and tech don't always play together?"

"I was going to ask at what point do we find out what the owner does for a living and switch jobs to that?" Maeve walked along the plane in awe. "I could get used to one of these."

The boarding stairs lowered and Maeve was the first onboard. Aisling followed. She understood Caradoc's view, but didn't completely agree with it. Technology and magic had been working together fine for a few centuries, there was no reason to think that was going to change.

Bart welcomed them onboard with a smile that looked like he was showing his first born.

Aisling had to admit the plane was amazing. Only ten seats in the main cabin, all looking more like fancy massage chairs than anything found on an airplane. Each one could fully swivel, recline, and had an attached arm with a micro screen and an adjoining table. "You even gave us snacks?" Aisling picked a chair and riffled through the basket on the table. Food, water, sodas all packaged and waiting for them.

"I didn't want anyone getting hungry. Nice, eh? And it's been fully scanned—three times. I've been onboard with the doors secured since then."

Even though Caradoc had been annoyed at the use of magic for the plane, he was pulled into the technology end of it and was already checking out the cockpit. "This is amazing. I almost bought one of these but didn't because of the magic. Might have to rethink that."

Maeve laughed. "Right. Because we could all buy one of these." She rolled her eyes.

"He probably could. He doesn't always act it, but Caradoc is sort of rich." Aisling continued her inventory of the snacks. She was peckish, so this would be helpful.

Harlie was last on the plane and he walked in like a small child seeing the circus for the first time—excited, but also terrified. "The shielding is powerful." He made his way to the centermost chair and slowly sat, still wide-eyed.

Maeve narrowed her eyes and looked to Caradoc as she took a chair near Aisling. "If you can afford things like this. Why don't you?"

Caradoc was still examining the cockpit but shrugged.

"Because he doesn't want anything that would be like our mother. She's rich, so he's in denial." Aisling opened a packaged fruit bowl and an iced tea.

"No." Caradoc came out and took a seat. "Well, mostly no. I like having a nice reserve. I donate to charities."

"And you don't want to be in any way like her." Maeve

grinned.

He sighed. "I don't. Our other siblings have all gotten rich by supporting her schemes and from her directly. You're looking at the only three self-supporting family members of the clan."

Reece and Jones took their seats. Reece stayed near the cockpit and Jones took the chair near the emergency exit.

Bart retracted the steps and locked the door. "Now then, shall we finally get you all to England?"

Reece looked over to Aisling and looked ready to speak, then shook his head and buckled in.

"What? You're looking for horns now too?"

"Horns?"

"Long story, but I won't be growing any."

Harlie had been looking around but leaned over. "Yet. That we know of. There *are* elven fey with horns you know. They look fine." His grin indicated he was joking, but Aisling still rubbed her head to make sure.

Bart taxied the plane and they lifted off.

"You could really buy one of these?" Maeve asked Caradoc.

"If I ever do, you'll be the first one I take up." His smile looked like it escaped from one of his magazine covers.

Aisling covered her laugh and turned to the folders on her table. Along with the snacks, a small portfolio sat at each table. Most of what was inside they'd already heard. Information about the attack in Noth, and comparisons to verify all three building sections were from the missing Area 42 building. She didn't know that an analysis of that sort could be done on building material, but apparently Area 42 had unique markers in all of their structures. If anyone would be that paranoid, it would be them.

The building pieces were the same at their core, but there was a serious breakdown in the cohesiveness of what landed. The first to hit, the parking lot one, was fairly intact. Or had been until it smashed into the parking lot. It hadn't gone deep either.

The second piece, the one in the sinkhole, had been less sound when it came out of wherever it had been. The Area 42 people were obviously avoiding the term 'veil' in all of their documents. Part of the reason it created the sinkhole when it crashed through was that a section of it merged with the ground as it made impact. Literally.

Noth was the third event, and the building piece was extremely fluid as it landed. It was also the most aggressive with the green goo; although had Harlie not crashed Caradoc's car into the sinkhole in L.A., that might have been a different story.

The event in the ocean was looking to be useless. They were pulling up what they could but it was already breaking down in the salt water.

The slime in the airport was now being treated as the fifth building drop, even though there were no visible building remains nearby. Analysis showed mutated markers that matched those belonging to the building present in the green goo. No actual building section, but it still managed to be there. The theory was that because it had hit the electrical flight panel, it was stopped. Sadly, not before twenty-two passengers and three airport personnel were killed.

She looked up and found Caradoc, Maeve, and Harlie reading the same report. Reece and Jones were watching out the windows, but they'd most likely already been read in on the situation.

"The green goo is part of the building? How did it break down like that? It doesn't say anything about the veil in here, but is that still the assumption? Something pulled the building through the veil and it's now coming back in pieces? There are no other options I can think of." She would ignore the images of skeletons she'd seen in the goo for now, but she had a bad feeling the people from Area 42 who'd been in the building when it vanished were dead.

Harlie nodded. "Beyond the veil is definitely involved, whether Area 42 wishes to admit it or not. I just wish I knew how or why."

"And if your friends from the other side are involved." Caradoc nodded to Aisling.

She didn't respond, but she hoped the vallenians weren't involved.

"Area 42 is officially in denial about the veil being compromised. But I agree with you all about that." Reece nodded to Aisling. "And you never did explain about that necklace. Yeah, I do know you weren't wearing it when I first saw you in my bunker." He was looking at her neck and Aisling realized she hadn't pulled it under her shirt.

She ran her fingers through her hair and sighed. At this point secrets weren't going to help anyone. "I was the blonde woman you saw near the parking lot at the first building drop. We figured you'd be limited in what you could tell us, so I went in to distract the agents while Stella gathered samples. The thing chasing me was a spell meant to also distract everyone. When I stopped, it was because a vallenian at the site popped up right in front of me." It was still hard to say their name. Should be easier now, she and the vallenians were obviously good friends at this point. She coughed to stifle the laugh that followed the thought. "He blew back the agents chasing me, vanished, and I ran on. I didn't notice the necklace until I got back to your hidden room. Sorry, bunker sounds as wrong as lair."

"Impressive. We tried to get intel off the vids we had of you, but couldn't break them," Jones said.

Reece looked torn between being pissed and something else Aisling couldn't identify. "Did Stella find anything? And what has this to do with your necklace?"

"No idea about Stella, but we moved everything to Caradoc's so I doubt it, unless she did some magic mojo, or she might have sent the sample or part of it to Grundog. This necklace appeared on me when I got back. Or rather, we noticed it when I got back. I think we can assume the vallenians are changing from family boxes to jewelry."

"Can I look at it closer?" Reece asked before he got out of his chair. He was possibly as weirded out about the siren issue as she was and didn't want to push closeness that might or might not be real. The entire situation was made worse by the fact that as much as they trusted him, they couldn't let Bart know. The most dangerous secret they had was that Reece appeared to be a breed with fey powers. Even Area 42 couldn't protect him if the High Council found out.

"Sure." Aisling stood up, the plane had leveled out at cruising speed already and it would be easier for him to see it if she was on her feet.

His hands were cold as he lifted the pendant up, but he kept the chain as extended as he could without pulling at her. "That gold line running through it is impressive. I've never seen such fine detail. The entire design is extraordinary." He released it and stepped back a foot. "Any idea what it does or why they gave it to you? I'm assuming since you're still wearing it you can't take it off?" He resumed his seat.

Aisling looked at the pendant, then tucked it back under her shirt and sat down. "Not at all. It did seem to stop something that tried to get me in my sleep, but aside from sometimes flinging people around and fighting off a bad case of the chills, even Harlie doesn't know what it does. And you're right about the not-able-to-remove part. It won't come off." To demonstrate she tried to lift it over her head. There was enough chain to easily clear her head, yet it wouldn't go past her ears.

Harlie had been looking all around the plane in slow motion as he studied everything, but he turned toward them at the sound of his name. "I think it's a ghau pendant. A source of great power on the other side of the veil." He smiled as though that wasn't the first time he'd told anyone that.

"A what? Why didn't you mention that before? Are those even real?" Caradoc was on his feet, next to Aisling's chair, and had the pendant in his hands immediately.

Harlie's grin faded as he saw the same looks of confusion on everyone else. "I didn't tell you? I'd meant to. I realized it when we were waiting for our first plane. Then things happened and I must have forgotten. Sorry. I believe it's a ghau pendant from the early dynasty of the elven rule on the other side of the veil."

"That was ten thousand years ago…this couldn't be a fraction that old." The chain around her neck suddenly felt heavy.

"Oh, the odds are extreme, but I believe I am correct. The addition of the gold line tipped me off. To bring it through the veil, they must have brought it to the base metal. As it adapts to this side of the veil, more aspects of it will appear." He looked way too happy.

Aisling hadn't been happy about the necklace before. Yes, it might have saved her back at Caradoc's house, then again it could have been whatever called that knife to her. But now she was becoming freaked out. Elven history from beyond the veil wasn't taught in most schools. At least nothing beyond that things were good, then they weren't, so all the fey left before they were killed. But she'd heard of the powerful, and unpredictable, ghau pendants.

"Are we sure we can't get this off me?" She tugged on it. "It's feeling warm."

"Because you're pulling on it?" Maeve stayed in her seat.

Aisling dropped it. "Still warm."

Harlie came closer to her. "This is interesting. I think it's changing again. Might not be optimal here on a plane flying over the Atlantic Ocean."

"Do you want to tell it to stop? It's not listening to me at all." Aisling tried to stay calm, but if the pendant lashed out or did pretty much anything, it could crash the plane.

"Take calming breaths. I can't stop it, but perhaps we can contain it. I'll need you and Caradoc to help me. The rest of you might stand near the exits. Life vests would be a good idea too."

CHAPTER TWENTY-THREE

CARADOC GOT ON THE SPEAKER and warned Bart. The swearing from the other end was clear throughout the cabin.

Aisling stayed still as her brothers stood near her to create a triangle. Harlie held out his arms and placed them on each of their shoulders. Then he turned to Maeve, Reece, and Jones. "Whatever goes on here, don't touch us until I break the containment. Which I won't do until we've landed. If the plane starts going down, save yourselves. I'll protect us if I can." He nodded, then faced Aisling and Caradoc. "Link arms."

Caradoc and Aisling both held out their arms as Harlie had and sealed the triangle.

A flow of energy crossed through Aisling's wrists and up to her shoulders. Her magic responded, but not in a way she was used to. It was as if it wasn't hers, and not something she could control. She had an odd feeling that this was her formerly repressed magic testing its range, not the pendant.

"Don't fight it or try to help." Harlie shot a glare to Caradoc. "Just focus on our arms."

A green shield surrounded them. Aisling could still see through it to the others, but they were faint. The pendant was definitely getting warmer, but seemed to have slowed down increasing the heat. She closed her eyes. If she was going to have to stand in the middle of a plane the entire way to the U.K., it was better if she wasn't watching her friends waiting for them to explode. Or implode. Or something else equally unsavory.

"Aisling? Can you hear me?" It was Harlie's voice, but coming through the connection he'd made. Not outside her, but also not in her head.

"Yes. This is weird."

"It is." Caradoc's voice came in also. "Not that you asked, but I hear you also. Both of you."

"This is an old spell, one used when our people first came here and there was a concern that human magic might be a probability. It's a way to keep things out, or in this case, keep them in. Try to think about nothing if you can."

Aisling gave a mental snort that was echoed by Caradoc. "Not going to be easy to forget we might crash this plane."

"We won't crash this plane. The shield protects us and isolates the pendant. The pendant is our friend." Harlie's voice was almost hypnotic and Aisling was pretty sure he was talking to the pendant itself. Great.

Aisling couldn't control her thoughts to nothing, but she did enter a dream state. There were trees all around her, massively old ones. Hewlith trees from beyond the veil. There was a small grove of them in Wales, where the fey had first crossed to this world. They needed a lot of magic to survive on this side of the veil. And they couldn't grow anywhere in this world outside of the Snowdonia Mountain region in northern Wales.

But the trees she was looking at weren't from the Welsh forest. They were hundreds of feet high and at least ten feet around. And they spread out as far as she could see. There was no one nearby, just a chill that felt like it came from the trees themselves. She circled the closest one, the chill stayed and so did the silence. Nothing threatened her directly, but she felt ill at ease. As if she'd come into a place of comfort that wasn't for her.

She passed a few more trees, but stopped when a low howling echoed in the air. Like the forest itself, it sounded like it came from everywhere yet nowhere. Figuring this wasn't what Harlie had said to do, she tried to pull herself out of the dream. Slightly disturbing trees were one thing—something that howled wasn't conducive to any sort of relaxing.

She couldn't wake up. Dreams were tricky, even for fey, but this wasn't a sleeping dream, just an extremely vivid daydream. One she couldn't get out of.

Dark shapes started appearing in the woods around her, and a dense fog rose from the ground. Some of the shapes were the size of massive wolves, others bipedal but with unusually long arms. There was nowhere she could run as they surrounded her. Then the howling became words.

"Why did you leave us?"

"You left us here to die."

"Save us."

The voices were all slightly different and there were dozens of them. The coldness increased and a pressure filled her mind.

"Let go! Aisling! Let go of the pendant!" Harlie's voice twisted around Caradoc's but both said the same thing.

A coldness hit her heart and a bright glow came from her hand. In the dream she had grabbed the pendant and not noticed it. She still couldn't pull free, but she opened her hand in the dream.

The voices stopped, the howling vanished, and the trees began to fade. She felt two strong hands shaking her shoulders. "Wake up!"

She almost let go of her brothers' shoulders, but remembered what they were doing in time and didn't let go. Grabbing the pendant must have only happened in the dream as her hands were still on their shoulders.

"Is it closed?" Caradoc's voice was still in the weird connection they had but he was talking to Harlie.

"Yes, and I want to know how that happened." Harlie sounded confused, and worse, frightened.

"All three of our magics combined plus this shield sent her through. Somewhere." Caradoc's words were strong, but there was uncertainty behind them.

"But where? I felt her *elsewhere*. I knew she was holding the pendant, and her heart was racing like a rabbit. Yet, where was she?"

"I can hear you both, you know." Aisling took a few deep breaths and opened her eyes. Okay, her heart had been racing a bit. Her brothers were trying to look supportive, she felt that in her head. The other three outside the shield looked freaked and all had life vests on under full parachute packs. Great. Whatever she'd just gone through in her head, something of it came out here.

"What did you do?" Harlie's voice was calm and measured, but Aisling felt Caradoc wanting to know the same thing.

"I tried to meditate. Or relax. Or something so I wasn't thinking that I was standing in the middle of a super fancy plane over the ocean, trying not to cause it to crash. Apparently, that wasn't the best idea. What did you two see?"

"Nothing directly, but your necklace was giving out sparks." Caradoc lifted his chin toward her.

Harlie was annoying her with how closely he watched her face. "I did see a shadow you, holding a shadow necklace. But neither of us could see where you were. The others can't hear us, but all three were disturbed by something and I think Bart called back to tell them to put on parachutes."

"We're not crashing, are we?"

"No. But we did dip a bit. That's when we tried to pull you out, but you didn't hear us."

"I did finally. I was in an odd forest. Massive, full of Hewlith trees. No, not the one in Wales. There were shapes…they were saying words." She tried to recall what was said. The words had been in her mind, but it was as if coming back here made them vanish. Like only recalling part of a deep dream. "Damn it. I can't find them again." She closed her eyes and focused, but all she recalled was the howling. "Nope. But they were very upset."

"You couldn't tell who they were? Where?"

"I couldn't even tell *what* they were." Aisling described everything she'd seen, but still couldn't recall the words. "They were angry at me. Or at the pendant." She wanted to look at it, but didn't think releasing the other two right now was a good idea.

"It's changed." Caradoc leaned as close as he could without releasing either of them. "There is now a line of trileium? That can't be right."

Harlie had been about to say something but leaned forward instead. "There's nothing else that's green like that—no metal. It's not from this world."

"You said the pendant was pulling metals through to this world? So the pendant might have sent me on a little out of body experience to get its trileium back?" Aisling was proud her mental voice didn't squeak. Trileium was only heard of in stories. An incredibly powerful metal that the first-comers were unable to get through the veil when they fled. It supposedly could transmute other metals, conduct spells, some even claimed it was sentient. And there was a tiny bit of it stuck on her pendant. That she couldn't remove. Part of her wished she was back home in L.A. still being shut out of everything. Be careful what you wish for indeed.

"I think so. Don't pick it up, but it is touching your chest. Does anything feel different?" Harlie was doing his slow, soothing voice again. If they got out of this, she was going to point out that all it did was freak her out more.

Aisling closed her eyes and focused on the place where the pendant touched her skin. The weight came first, it was cool now, no longer warm, but feeling more like a pendant should feel. "It feels more balanced. Not sure if that's the right word, but it feels content." Not a good thing that a metal that might be sentient, but it was what she felt. "Do you still think this is a ghau pendant?"

"Yes. This makes it a more reasonable deduction in fact." Harlie gave a tight smile but didn't elaborate.

"Interesting." Caradoc scowled at the pendant but the hand he had on Harlie's shoulder was twitching.

"Don't let go of each other." Harlie squeezed their shoulders. "It could have been that the pendant was trying to do what it needed to and so acted up to make it happen. Or it could be playing games. Either way, we stay in this shield until we've landed."

"Fine, but I want to see it closely afterwards." Caradoc kept staring at it. "Do you know what this could mean? If we can find a way to get trileium into this world? Under our control of course; it would have to be regulated carefully. The damage that could be caused by a large enough collection of it is insane. But think of the applications to technology."

"Seriously, Caradoc, you're drooling." Aisling didn't like the look in his eyes. Especially since it pertained to something that currently only existed attached to her.

"The pendant is a separate entity." Harlie narrowed his eyes. "I don't think you'd be any more successful getting the metal to cross the veil than the first comers."

Aisling watched Caradoc consider Harlie's words. "Not to mention, you'd have to cross the veil from this side first. Even if it's possibly getting thinner, that isn't going to happen. And look what's happened to the people who were pulled through trapped in Area 42. Those bodies in the goo don't look like they had a good time." She shuddered and reminded herself she couldn't break the circle to go find an airsickness bag.

"Bah. No sense of possibilities with you two." Caradoc shut his eyes. "I'm going to think right now, please keep your negativity to yourselves."

Harlie shook his head at Caradoc, then turned to her. "I could help you relax if you'd like. This plane is incredibly fast though, we should land in Gatwick in an hour or so."

"No, I'd rather not risk going back wherever that was. Might have only been in my head, but it wasn't a comforting place. I'll just stand here and wait."

Harlie nodded, then shut his eyes.

Aisling kept her eyes open but her mind as blank as possible. She noticed that the other three had moved to the chairs nearest the cockpit and were sitting. However, they all still had their life vests on and parachutes with them, and none of them looked relaxed. She had a feeling whatever happened out here when she'd been in the forest, had been more than just a dip.

<hr>

She'd managed to not think of anything for the rest of the time. Nothing like the fear of slipping through some psychic dream world to keep one focused on the present.

Harlie waited until the plane had not only touched down, but came to a complete stop and the engines shut down before dropping the spell.

Aisling was proud that standing still for a few hours hadn't wiped her out. Until the spell vanished and she stumbled forward. "Damn, that thing was holding us up. Everything hurts now."

Reece was next to her in a moment and took her arm. "Maybe sit for a bit? It's going to take a few minutes for Bart to clear us through. Apparently, the entire plane vanished from the air traffic control—all of them—for about ten minutes. He's got some fancy talking to do since everyone is on edge." The tight smile he gave her said what he wasn't asking was if she and her brothers caused the plane to vanish. He was wondering it though.

She returned the tight smile and let him lead her back

to her chair. Telling him what had happened would make more sense when they had a clue as to what actually happened.

Reece glanced over and noticed her necklace. "Did you know it now has something green running through it? Nice, but is it supposed to do that?"

Aisling lifted the necklace to get a good look at it herself. The line of green counterpointed the line of gold. It was striking. She'd be more impressed if she didn't know what that green line probably was, and if she could remove the necklace. "I think it's changing, just some trick of our friends who put it on me. The green is new though."

"Ah, you just rest then. I'll come to get all of you when we're clear to leave." The look on his face, and yet an even tighter smile, said he didn't completely believe her but wasn't going to push.

Maeve came over and sat near her when Reece moved away. "The weird scary pendant has changed again. I'm not familiar with any metals that green color. Or did it add stone this time?"

Reece, Bart, and Jones were at the open door where the stairs extended. They were talking to at least one other person in low, but intense voices.

"It's just messing around again." Aisling dropped the pendant back under her shirt. "What happened when we were in that shield? Harlie said there was a little dip." Aisling knew he'd lied to keep her calm, but something obviously had happened. How did they vanish from radar and all trackers for almost ten minutes? Was it related to her odd adventure?

Maeve laughed. "If he calls us dropping like a stone for three minutes a dip, sure. Bart got us back up and we ended up being fine, but it was terrifying. You three didn't feel it at all?"

Aisling watched her brothers locked in their own animated conversation. "They probably did. I sort of blacked out for a bit. When I came back, the green line appeared in the necklace."

"You might want to hide the pendant as much as you can. There are some wicked smart magic users in MI-6 and they might see things we might not want them too." Maeve glanced down at her phone. "They haven't called me yet, but I'm thinking they'll pull me off here soon. Regardless of what the others are doing."

Harlie came over to them. "Actually, let me put a spell on the pendant, just make it look less like itself." Aisling held it up to him. When he released it the gold and green lines were gone. He clearly didn't like the idea of the green showing, and she couldn't blame him.

Aisling looked at the changes, it now looked like it did originally, but she found that her eyes slid off of it. Nice spell. Folks would avoid looking at it but if they did, it just looked like a silver pendant. She dropped the pendant into her shirt and pulled the collar up. The longer chain meant she could hide it with most shirts she owned. But she might buy a few higher neck ones just to be certain. Harlie might not be the only magic user or historian to recognize it, even with a spell on it.

CHAPTER TWENTY-FOUR

"WE CAN DEPLANE NOW." REECE and Jones came back but Bart and whoever they'd been talking to were gone.

Maeve's phone chirped. "Yes." She listened for a few minutes while she gathered her things. "Understood. I'll be at pick up." She ended the call and slipped her phone in her back pocket. "That's it for me for a bit. Don't worry about finding me, I'll find you." She gave Aisling a nod, then left.

"We have a nice van that will take us to our first lodging." Reece grabbed his things. "No one is happy with our vanishing off the radar and once they realize that we actually lost power for part of that they'll be even less happy. They are requesting that we wait a day in London while they check it out."

"I know we knew they might do that, but shouldn't we go to Noth immediately? Timeliness of whatever happened and all?" Caradoc asked.

"That would make sense," Jones answered. "But there's not a lot of that going on right now."

Once the bags were collected, they followed Reece and Jones off the plane. Bart stood at the emergency exit door glaring at the two guards standing there.

"Come on, we need to shut this door and get out of sight." Bart snapped as he stomped past the two guards. The guards waited until everyone was inside, then they secured the door. One stayed outside and one stayed inside.

Bart led them down corridors that were clearly

designed for airline staff and held his badge up the entire time. At first Aisling was surprised that neither of the security guards followed them, but there was more than enough down this direction to make up for it.

A van waited at the curb, again, with another guard. This one had no visible weapons, but there was no doubting that he had them and that he was some sort of military. Bart got in on the right, Reece took the front passenger seat, and the rest funneled into the back two rows. The stealth guard loaded all of their luggage.

With a few swear words as he adjusted to a different side of the car and road, Bart got them moving out.

"I thought you were planning on returning to L.A. as soon as you got refueled?"

"I had been. Before whatever dropped us out of the sky and off the world's radars happened. They want to investigate the plane and find out what in the hell happened before I take it back up." He sighed. "I'd like the answers to that question as well, but I want a nice stiff drink before I hear them."

"Where are we staying?" Not that it mattered to her right now. That spell of Harlie's on the plane had kept her from feeling fatigue, but it was wearing off. Neither of her brothers seemed that tired, but they didn't have the weird adventure in dreamland that she did.

"I would have liked a nice low-level hotel. But we have an Area 42 safe house, fancy division, waiting for us." Only Bart would grumble about a nice place to crash.

Caradoc was silent but there was a grin on his face as they drove through London. "When this, whatever this is, is over, I might relocate my base to here. Or at least buy a flat. I forgot how much I love London."

"Not me." Harlie looked miserable as he hunched in on himself. "Everything is too closed in."

Aisling watched the history of the place flow around them as they drove. Right now, her thoughts were on what was going on with the necklace. Along with the issues with the veil and what had almost dropped them out of the sky.

"It will be okay, I promise." Harlie was in the seat next to her and he turned away from the window to take her hand as if he'd seen the turmoil in her head. His dark brown eyes grew sad. "Can you ever forgive what I did to you?"

That had not been in her thoughts. It said a lot that enough other things had shoved something that major out of her head. "It wasn't your fault. Even as old as you are, she is far older, trickier, and stronger than you. If you hadn't done it, she would have found someone else, or done it herself. Either would have been much worse." She squeezed his hand.

"Thank you. If that wasn't what was upsetting you just now, might I ask what was?"

"What happened for those ten minutes we were out of contact with the air traffic controllers?" She turned to the others. "And I'm not just asking Harlie—anyone can step in. And no, given what was going on at the same time, I don't think they are going to find anything wrong with the plane."

The silence said way more than she would have liked. Lots of smart folks in this van and none of them felt up to making a good guess. Very not good.

Finally, Bart coughed. "I got some more intel; we didn't completely vanish from the screens for ten minutes. It was more like we faded out, then technically vanished completely for three minutes then faded back in. The first thought when we vanished was that a piece of building hit us."

"Not sure if that's better or worse," Aisling said. "What did you three notice while we were in our little spell capsule?"

Reece turned back toward them. "The shielding

around the three of you turned dark green. We could still see you but only barely. When the plane lost power, you three didn't move at all. Maeve, Jones, and myself were tossed about a bit. Your spelled area stayed perfectly still."

Harlie nodded. "That would stand to reason. Technically we were a bit out of your reality while I had the shields up. Just enough to not be affected by the plane's movements."

"What? You didn't tell us that." Aisling looked in the backseat to Caradoc but he looked as concerned as she felt. She knew Harlie had some odd magics, but pulling them out of reality should have been forewarned. Granted, there hadn't been much time, but still.

"How did I not feel that? Where the hell were we?" Caradoc might not use his magic as much as Harlie, but he was still a strong magic user. And right now, a pissed one.

"I didn't think it was pertinent. The pendant was acting up, so I did what I could to pull us free so we wouldn't crash the plane. Had Aisling not been thoroughly shielded when she went on that mental trip, we would have crashed."

Aisling shook her head. "You still could have told us what you were actually doing. And wasn't the spell bubble and the power from you two part of what sent me wherever I went?"

Harlie flushed. "Possibly we contributed to whatever in your psyche sent you to that dream state." He waved his finger. "But it would have been worse otherwise, mark my words."

He was too defensive to make Aisling feel better either way. He got defensive when he was seriously unsure, and it wasn't a common experience.

"Wait, Aisling went somewhere? I saw her right there with you two," Reece said.

"I had a weird dream happen when we were inside the

spell. Don't recall much beyond it was scary." She had a feeling more of it would be coming back to her. She wasn't sure that was a good thing.

Caradoc leaned forward with a scowl. "And I bet once we get the data on exactly when the plane vanished, it will correlate with your adventure."

"How can you tell exactly when I went into that dream? It was my head after all."

"I can tell." Harlie tapped the side of his head. "Once we get the data, as Caradoc said, we can see what matches."

Bart didn't look away from the road, but raised his voice. "I get the not-so-subtle hints. You'll get the data once we're inside." He drove up a long road to an extremely old fey neighborhood. The houses all looked like classic Victorians with an otherworldly twist. Thin turrets made of spun glass weren't found on anything under a few hundred years old, and were uncommon as hell to start with. Spelling that much glass so it didn't break required a serious number of heavy magic spells used just to look cool.

The mansions in the area were huge, but the one Bart drove to was a bit smaller than most of them. Still a good three times the size of the place Reece had tried to hide her at in Gossamer Hill in L.A. The drive dipped down to an underground garage and the door shut behind them once the van was inside.

Mage lights lit the wide garage and three dark suited agents stood waiting for them.

Bart got out first. "Good to see you, Greely." He shook hands with a tall, dark-skinned elf.

"Agent Bart." He put emphasis on the causal name and his grin was genuine. "I do hope this will be sufficient for you? Might I introduce agents Locke and Wastegirdle. We're here to make sure no one followed you and your stay here is secure."

Aisling and the rest stood behind Bart as he introduced

them. Then he folded his arms and scowled. "Three top-level London field agents for a few people waiting for things to clear? What's really going on?"

Agent Greely dropped his smile. "Might be better to discuss inside. There's food and it's far more comfortable."

Bart narrowed his eyes but motioned for everyone to follow and went for the door.

Aisling had been raised in luxury, but this place would make her mother green with envy. Understated, and pricey as hell, elegance graced every corner including the door from the garage into the mansion.

Agent Greely led them to an expansive front room filled with enough expensive, yet comfortable looking, seats for everyone and a dozen more.

Bart flopped down, then waited until the rest of them sat before turning back to Greely. "One, where's this food? Two, start talking my lad, there is something more serious than what we were already dealing with going on, and that isn't making me happy."

"Ten years and you haven't changed a bit." Greely shook his head. "They'll bring in the food, just easier to eat in here. What did they tell you at the airport?"

"They recommended a nice little hotel near the airport while they sorted out how our plane vanished off all of their sensors over the middle of the ocean. *Our* people called me and sent us here."

Aisling forced herself to stay awake as they talked. The sofa was a bit too comfortable and leaning back was an invitation to give into the fatigue. She'd wanted to get back into the action, next time she'd be more careful what she wished for.

"At the exact moment that your plane vanished off the sensors, another piece of a building dropped out of the sky. In the middle of the Atlantic." Greely held up a pad with a diagram. It showed an image of their plane, and superimposed directly over it was a much larger picture of a piece of building.

Bart, Reece, and Jones all leaned forward at that. None of them said anything as the horror of what would have happened hit them.

Aisling held back from speaking, then looked to her brothers. That Harlie, and more importantly, Caradoc, said nothing as well said she'd made the right choice. Letting other people, even high-ranking Area 42 people, know that a mysterious necklace, one that might be a ghau pendant of ancient times, could have pulled the entire plane out of this reality and thusly avoided a fatal impact, would need working up to. Still, her heart was pounding at their near miss. At least she wasn't sleepy anymore.

"We should have slammed into it. I couldn't have moved the plane away in time." Bart's voice was sober with an edge of fear as he stared at the image. "I didn't even see it on my radar."

Neither Reece nor Jones said anything, but both watched Harlie. They might not know what happened, but they both had an idea where the saving came from. They were partially right.

"Watch." Greely attached the screen to a big screen TV and pressed a few buttons. The image transferred and a vid clip played. "Here's where we picked up the building." A dark mass appeared on the screen. Their plane was there as well. "It wasn't on top of you, but you're right, you would have been going too fast to avoid it." He played the short vid a few more times, then shut it off. "Our bosses want to know what in the hell happened?"

Harlie frowned, but stayed silent. Since he was the only one of them who possibly understood what had happened, Aisling wasn't going to say anything. He'd already told Reece, Jones, and Bart about pushing the spelled trio into another reality for a bit. From the way he kept looking at the screen, even when the image was frozen, it looked like he was wondering if he pushed more than just the three of them out. It was scary enough that he might have pushed them out of reality for a bit within the spell bubble. That he might have caused that to extend around the entire plane and not been aware of it was terrifying.

Caradoc sat on the same sofa as Harlie and twisted around to stare at his brother. The word "Well?" was projected so hard, Aisling could almost hear it.

"Something did happen up there, even though you were unaware of the building debris." Greely sat back and nodded after watching all of them.

Harlie got to his feet and started pacing nervously. "There are things I can't say, not yet. Speculation, if wrong, would be worse than staying silent right now. But I can say we did have an external reality situation during the flight. One that might have reached past my spell shield. But it might explain the plane vanishing off the radar as well as us missing the building."

Reece, Jones, and Bart said nothing about Aisling's necklace. That was a relief. Aisling trusted them, but the more they were involved with Area 42, the harder it would be to keep it secret.

"If we could find out what happened it might save others as more of these events occur." Greely leaned forward.

"Has anyone checked to get an estimate of how much mass of the building is left?" Caradoc asked. "I know that the ones that went in the water would be estimates, but how much are we still waiting for? And have there been any incidents outside of L.A. or London? Beyond the two known water landings."

Greely watched Harlie continue to pace for a few moments, then turned to Caradoc. "If we presume that the entire mass of that building went through the veil and is now coming back, then there has been less than fifteen percent seen so far."

CHAPTER TWENTY-FIVE

AISLING LEANED FORWARD. "YOU SAID veil. The rest of Area 42 doesn't seem to officially like that word."

"We don't either. Officially." Greely gave a grimace. "The idea that the veil has become flexible enough to pull something that massive in and is now spitting out pieces, apparently randomly, is horrifying. I'm almost as old as Harlie. I grew up being told stories about the other side of the veil. If the things they left behind are truly able to come through, and they are as dangerous as the myths say, we will lose. I don't think there's another veil we can escape through this time."

"And so, to avoid mass hysteria, even among their own agents, they just won't use the word? I didn't think Area 42 agents were that delicate." Caradoc glanced around the room.

"I think the higher ups have more information on all of these events than they are letting on, and they're freaking out is coming from that." Reece had been sitting back, but he'd been watching everyone. "If the horror that the fey fled from is coming through the veil, everyone needs to be prepared. Avoiding the word doesn't change the threat."

Bart's phone cut in before anyone else could add anything. He saw the number and got up. "I'll take this upstairs." With a nod he left the room.

"What say we bring out some food? Nothing can be resolved right now, and we still have a lot to talk about." Greely was cheerful as he went to the kitchen, but his eyes seemed to darken when he glanced at Harlie.

Jones went to help Greely and Reece moved over to the sofa Aisling was on. "How are you feeling?" He kept his voice low.

"I'm fine, just tired. Do you know Greely or the other two agents?" It was great that Bart knew Greely, but even in her fatigued state something felt off. Of course, it could be from the whole fake Area 42 medics trying to kidnap or kill her. Bound to make a person suspicious.

"Only by name. Greely is old school, like he said, he's almost as old as Harlie, and has been in Area 42 since it was formed three hundred years ago. He being the one to meet us kinda makes me think things are far worse than we thought. Even after that cheerful conversation we just had. He is admitting that the veil breaking down is a possibility and not trying to deny it."

Aisling watched him as he watched the others in the kitchen. "But? There is a but hanging there."

He turned back to her. "But, I think we've all been too complacent that Area 42 was unassailable. That smacked us all hard. Outside of the people on that plane we just came in on, I don't know who can be trusted."

"Agreed." Caradoc dropped down on the other side of her. "And something is setting off Harlie. He used to go into these trance states when he was living in his cave in Nepal when something serious got him thinking. He could stay in them for weeks." He looked up to where Harlie had stopped pacing but seemed to be in a quiet argument with himself. "We can't afford for him to fall into one of those right now. No one else has his understanding of the veil."

Aisling leaned backwards. "Harlie? Can you come over here?"

At first he didn't acknowledge her, then with a forced shake of his head blinked. "Yes?"

"Can you come here?" As she spoke, Reece left the

spot next to her and went back to his chair. "I'd just feel better if you were with us."

Harlie came over and sat next to her. "Is there anything wrong?"

"Lots of things are wrong. But we need you to stay with us."

"I was just looking for answers. Sometimes the only way to find them is to go inside."

Aisling took his hands. "You can't do that right now. We need you to figure everything out here."

The blank look in his dark eyes indicated he was drifting back in wherever he went in his trances.

"Harlie? I need you to help me. No one else understands the pendant." Aisling shook his hands.

He shook his head and his eyes focused. "Oh yes, that is essential. Must not lose that." He smiled. "Is there food?"

"It's coming." She smiled and released his hands. She figured he was speaking more of not losing the thought of the necklace and what it could mean, not actually losing the necklace. Aisling still wasn't sure if it was helping them or hurting them, but until they figured it out or got it off, she wanted Harlie close by.

Bart came stomping back into the room. If the saying of smoke coming out of his ears was real, he would have two massive plumes coming out. "This is becoming an exercise in stupidity."

Before he could expand, Jones and Greely came out with trays filled with tea and sandwiches. Bart didn't expand on his statement but kept his glare aimed at Greely.

That wasn't a good sign. He knew Greely and supposedly liked him. But something in that call had gotten him rethinking that. Not enough to attack him, so he probably wasn't someone other than who he said he was. However, something had changed for the worse.

"How long do we have to stay here? I think I need to

get to Noth quickly." Harlie ate like a starving man. Most likely when he'd lived in his cave, he mindlessly ate when he finally ran out of steam.

"That's a good question." Bart folded his arms and narrowed his eyes at Greely. "I've been told that you'll be leading the team to Noth, but you want to wait?" Even though he'd requested the food, he noticeably left it untouched.

Greely didn't look comfortable. "I'm not certain that rushing in is the best idea. The initial crisis is over, we need to proceed with caution."

Bart started laughing, but it wasn't a friendly laugh. "What did they do to you? You were one of the go-getters, stayed in the field because of the action, long after you could have moved up and stayed in an office. What changed?"

Greely looked down. "I'm feeling old, Bart. Just old. Someone wants this case kept quiet, not sure who, but they are high enough in the organization to apply pressure. I do what they say, they let me get out."

Bart had just picked up his sandwich but dropped it back to the plate. "Out? As in completely out? I ask again, what in the hell happened to you?"

"There are too many changes coming about. At least in the London branch. More things we're supposed to ignore. I am tired. Seriously. Settling in to a nice cottage in the Cotswolds and spending my days puttering around my garden sounds wonderful."

Aisling didn't know Greely, and she'd only just met Bart, but he was easy to read. He was concerned and pissed in equal measure. However, he wasn't going to force his friend to divulge his issues—not yet anyway. He also wasn't going to let things sit there.

"You're wrong. We need to get there even sooner if higher ups are saying we need to ignore it. And you know it as well as I do. I'll stay here if I have to, but this team is leaving in the morning for Noth, with or without you and those other two. I assume they are assigned to Noth as well?"

"Yes, yes, yes." Harlie cut into the strained atmosphere. "Talk as you must. But we need to get there tonight."

Reece and Jones had been silent. They were used to having autonomy but in an official capacity, both Bart and Greely outranked them. Reece nodded to Harlie. "I'm with him, although, unlike him, I don't feel it like he does. But I believe we need to get to Noth soon."

Aisling noticed that Reece had tension lines across his forehead and had rubbed his temples twice. And so did Harlie. Reece couldn't admit to being a precog, but he was reacting to whatever Harlie was on some level. That alone was enough to make Aisling want to run for the van immediately.

Bart nodded toward Harlie. "We have an expert in the obscure and odd things about the veil. He says we go now. I never ignore my experts."

Greely pinched the bridge of his nose. "I can't pass this up, Bart. I need out."

"At the possible risk to more people? The more we know about how and why these things are happening, the quicker we can stop it. You'd risk lives for retirement?" Jones was almost snarling in his response. He usually kept his emotions out of things, but obviously Greely's actions pushed him over the edge.

"I—" Greely's response was cut off as a low-level rumble went through the mansion. Not enough to knock them off their seats, but enough to knock a few photos off the wall.

"If we were in L.A., I'd say that was a 4.3, maybe 4.4 quake, nearby. As far as I know, London isn't prone to earthquakes," Caradoc said.

One of the two agents from the garage stuck his head in. "Everyone okay?"

Greely looked around, then nodded. "Yes. Check the neighborhood, that couldn't have been far away." He was far less upset than he should be. Since London really didn't have earthquakes, the only answers were an explosion or possibly another gift from beyond the veil. Or something he hadn't told them.

Bart got to his feet and the rest of them did as well. "You know what that was?"

Greely ran his fingers through his short hair and swore to himself. "Possibly. Another thing we're supposed to ignore, delay, deny. There have been things coming up out of the ground for the past two weeks. Horrific creatures who die once they come out of the ground."

"In London? And no one has noticed?" Aisling knew the British could stay calm under pressure, but that was pushing it.

"They haven't been in London—yet. They started just outside of Bath, then kept creeping closer. We've gotten to the locations before any locals saw the monsters, and no one had been injured. Judging by what I've read and what we felt, this incursion was nearby."

Bart started stomping and swearing so fast that individual words couldn't be determined. "You kept this from us? Who in New York knows? I'm going to remind you that I am now internal affairs and that means *everywhere*." He wasn't threatening Greely, but he was getting in his airspace.

"Toril Kjai knows. He's been working with the big guns. We were told to listen to him."

If Bart's face got any redder, he was going to pop. Gnomes had a reputation for being cranky and difficult—he was feeding the stereotype right now. "I'll take care of Toril Kjai myself when I get back. Let me make two calls, then we're finding whatever just came out of the ground. If it's nearby, you're going to send me reports on everything, and this group is leaving for Noth." He started to add more but instead shook his head and stomped back upstairs.

"I will say my head feels better now." Harlie rubbed his temples. "A bit uncomfortable for a bit there with that pressure. I would like to know what's coming up out of the ground, but I feel it is even more urgent we get to Noth."

Greely was busy doing something on his pad, so Aisling looked over to Reece. The tension lines on his face were gone and he gave a small nod. Whatever was going on, it wasn't the building pieces that were causing Harlie and Reece to have reactions—or at least not *only* the sections of building. As far as she knew there were no fey, here or on the other side of the veil, who lived underground.

"I'm just going to go look around outside." Harlie got up but even moving quickly couldn't get to the door before Greely called him out.

"Please don't. I need all of you to stay out of sight as long as possible. There are too many things going on." He might have had more to say, but his phone cut him off. "What?" Greely had dark skin, but right now it was drifting down to the pale range. "How? Damn it, call for back up. I'll bring these people too." He looked around just as Bart came back from his own calls. "The hole is a few blocks over. A giant mansion was swallowed and some weird things are crawling out. And they aren't dying."

Chapter Twenty-Six

——◆——

"**D**AMN IT, AND YOU DON'T have enough people close by to handle it." Bart marched through, grabbed the keys for the van, and kept going to the door to the garage. "Ya coming, or what?"

Harlie was already near the door, but the rest quickly followed. Greely brought up the rear.

Reece gave up his front seat to Greely so he could direct them and squished in with Jones and Caradoc. There was probably a little more room with Aisling and Harlie but she appreciated his keeping physical distance at the moment.

The house was three blocks down the street, and impossible to miss. It collapsed in on itself as the ground underneath it vanished. Pieces stuck up wildly but there wasn't a crowd around as she would have expected. Just the two agents working with Greely and two security guards.

Aisling shook her head as they got closer. "How come there are no lookie loos? I know L.A. is very different than London, but this *is* noticeable."

"A massively detailed spell shield." Bart moved the van forward slowly. "You see everything because you're involved through me and Greely. But anyone else wouldn't see the hole or the collapsed house, would be convinced that the rumble was only a passing truck, and would have an overwhelming urge to stay in their homes. Wastegirdle is a clauthin mage. He can't keep this level of spell up for long, so I'm assuming more of Area 42 is coming in." He parked the van and they all got out. Greely might not have been happy about their involvement, or his own for that matter, but he took charge once he stepped out of the van. He marched to the other two agents and moved the housing area guards out a bit further.

The odor hit Aisling as they opened the van doors. Death, decay, and an overused sewer crashed into her before she used a small spell to deaden her sense of smell. "Where are the creatures?" Then she noticed the second spell shield inside the first. This one was tight along the hole and had green oozing marks. She was stepping forward when a greenish, impossibly long, clawed hand slammed up against the shield. A scream came from below and the hand vanished back into the hole.

"There." Greely looked over the edge into the pit. The secondary shield spell flashed as he got too close. It would limit what they could see, but better that than one of the creatures getting out. Whatever they were.

Caradoc leaned into the shield so far that he was going to have burn marks on his forehead. Not that it would have stopped him. "What are they? Are these the same things that you said died before?"

"We don't know, yes, and could you step back? I don't think Bart would appreciate you getting eaten. This shield spell should hold, but we also shouldn't have monsters collapsing homes in the middle of London." Greely was taking charge, but he wasn't happy about it. Aisling just met him, but she could tell there was something more going on than him being burnt out.

Harlie held back and stared at something in the empty space where the mansion had been. "They are fey." His voice was quiet, more because he was speaking to himself rather than holding a secret. "Long lost fey. We forgot them." His wide dark eyes looked incredibly sad.

"There have never been underground fey. We would have known." Caradoc narrowed his eyes. "Are they from the other side of the veil?"

Harlie started swaying a bit. "We're all from the other side, aren't we? Except the humans. This was all theirs. We came. Those stayed but came another way." His speech was slurring and his swaying got bad enough that Reece and Jones each grabbed an arm to keep him upright.

Aisling ran to her brother. "What's wrong?" She tried to get Harlie to focus on her, but his eyes were rolling back in his head.

Caradoc grabbed his shoulders and shook them, but Harlie started sagging. "Damn it, Harlie, you can't slip into a trance. Not here or now. We need you."

Bart ran to the van and opened the side door. "Get him in here. Did anything hit him?"

Caradoc helped Jones and Reece move him. Harlie might not weigh a lot, but he was taller than everyone and had gone completely limp.

"He used to go into trances when he lived in Nepal." Caradoc adjusted Harlie inside the van. There was no way someone his height could stretch out, but he made him look less uncomfortable. "He hasn't gone into one since he moved to L.A., though."

Bart's scowl dug itself in deeper. "How long will he be out?"

"No idea. Hours, days, weeks?" Caradoc got out of the van.

"What was he talking about, fey we left behind? Things from the other side are coming through the ground now? And they're fey?" Aisling glanced back into the van. Caradoc might think it was simply a standard trance, but it hadn't seemed trancelike at all. He'd acted like he was drunk. Or drugged. But no one had been that close to him and the food he ate earlier was shared by all of them.

"No idea." Caradoc said as he followed Reece, Jones, and Bart back to the hole. "He'll be fine there."

Aisling stayed at the van and stuck her head in one more time, but Harlie was snoring softly. She wasn't certain, but she doubted snoring was part of a trance. She'd trust Caradoc on this for now, but hopefully Harlie would come out of it soon—whatever it was. She was concerned about him. But she also needed him to help her with her weird pendant, whatever happened on the plane, and getting back the magic he'd blocked.

More agents arrived. Most were fey, but there were at least three humans or fey-human breeds. Instead of the standard dark suits, all were fully clothed in white hazmat suits.

That was reassuring.

Aisling hung back; she had no idea what she could do that wouldn't get in the way.

"What happened? Another building?" Stella appeared at her side so silently, and Aisling had been so focused, that she almost yelled when the tiny woman spoke.

She looked down to where Stella stood next to her watching the goings on. "You weren't kidding when you said you'd find us. The Area 42 people won't be happy that you did so this easily, by the way. This doesn't seem to be another building drop—things are coming up from under the ground now." She'd expected Stella to share her confusion, but the changeling's face drained of color and she looked ill.

"When did it happen? How many?" Stella stared at the activity around the hole, but didn't move forward a single step.

"This one just happened a short while ago, but they said there have been more." Aisling watched Stella's freak out level increase. "You know what they are?"

Stella took a few steps back. "I've heard of them. My aunt was a witch, one who'd crossed the veil with the first-comers. She told me…where's Harlie? He should know about them."

"He collapsed a few minutes ago. Caradoc said it was a trance, and he's prone to them, but he seemed drunk.

Or drugged."

"That's not good. None of this is good. My aunt told me tales of the ones left behind." She dropped into silence and stared at the hole.

"What of them? Harlie mentioned lost fey before he collapsed. But he meant Old Ones, right? The fey all crossed over."

"No, they didn't. The High Council wanted everyone to believe all of the fey crossed and they only left behind evil and vile things. They set massively heavy spells to make certain those would be the stories people remembered. But my aunt was strong and kept the old tales." Stella watched the investigation, her face a combination of fear and annoyance. "There were fey left on the other side."

"Can we speak to her?"

Stella gave a snort. "I know you're a healer, but she was murdered ten years ago in a forest in Slovenia. I don't even think you could bring her back."

"I'm sorry."

"Eh, she was a handful. At the time I was sad, but not surprised. I believed she had annoyed someone more powerful than herself once too often."

"And now?" The news was almost not as bad as Stella's behavior. Dragging words out of her usually wasn't a problem.

"Now I wonder if someone knew she was right and silenced her for it."

"Ten years ago? Agent Greely said the ground attacks only started two weeks ago."

"Exactly. Things move at the time they need to move, and crossing over the veil, above or below, wouldn't be easy. But given time, they could have done it. They could have been in that part of the world for decades. Appearing as little more than myths and old tales. I should have listened to her more."

Aisling rubbed her arms. Her mother would know and she was the one person they couldn't ask.

"Where is Harlie?" Stella shook off whatever darkness she'd gone into.

"This way, we put him in the van." Aisling brought her over and opened the door. Harlie was still snoring, but also muttering. Unfortunately, it seemed to be in a tongue she'd never heard before. "Okay, do people in trances snore? Or sleep talk? He seemed like he had been drinking nectar before he collapsed."

Stella climbed into the van and put her hand on Harlie's head. She stayed there for a few moments, then pulled back. "He's in a trance, but not one he did to himself. He's not in danger right now, but I have no idea how long it will take to bring him out of it."

"Is it something that I could use healing magic on?"

"Not a clue." Stella grinned. "Can't hurt to try, eh?" She climbed out and Aisling took her place.

Unlike a physical injury, damage to the mind or psyche was tricker to deal with. Aisling needed to try though. She put her hand on his forehead, first establishing a connection. Physically, he was fine. But there was a fog around his mind. She sent a healing tendril near it but it evaporated. Knowing she supposedly had access to more magic now, she sent a stronger tendril. No connection with Harlie, but an instant later a force surrounding Harlie shoved her and flung her out of the van, bowling over Stella in the process.

Aisling shook off the residual tingling from whatever pushed her out. It had felt almost like an electrical charge. Luckily, it dissipated quickly. "There is something inside him that didn't like what I was trying to do." She got to her feet slowly, it didn't hurt her so much as startle her. She helped Stella up as Caradoc ran over.

"What happened? Good to see you Stella, but why is the van open?"

"Your brother isn't in a self-induced trance. Something or someone did this to him. It's good to see you too."

Aisling shut the van doors. "I tried to reach him, but whatever took him out has a massive fog on his brain. A vicious one. It flung me out of the van."

Caradoc opened the door. "He looks calm. Are you certain?"

Aisling folded her arms. "I didn't toss myself into Stella and push both of us five feet away. There's something in there."

"Is he going to be okay? How do we get him out of it?" Caradoc knew nothing of healing or medical issues, and his concern was clear on his face.

"Out of what?" Reece came over and smiled at Stella. "I knew you'd catch up to us. What happened here?"

Aisling repeated everything she'd just told Caradoc.

Reece scowled. "We need a mind healer for him. Area 42 London should have someone. If not, Bart can get him back to New York. He's not in immediate danger?"

"No," Stella said. "I'm not a healer or a mind doc, but I am familiar with this. He'll recover. It just might take a while."

"Good. Not that it will take a while, Bart was counting on his unique abilities for the case. But good that he's safe. I wanted to come get you, the creatures seem to be dying."

They all went to the hole, avoiding the hazmat suited agents as best they could. Stella walked to the edge, looked down, then stepped a few feet back and watched with folded arms and a worried look. There still wasn't much to see, so Aisling stepped back to her.

"Are these what your aunt knew of?"

"I think so. They are definitely dying, whatever they are. They don't look right though."

Aisling watched her for a moment, then finally prodded. "I couldn't really see them, but why don't they look right?"

"You have to look at more than just the physical aspects, which, granted, aren't very visible. I do hope that they will let me see the photos. But regardless, there is an off-ness. They don't belong here."

"Because they are from the other side of the veil maybe?"

Stella watched as one of the hazmat covered agents crossed the spell barrier. Thin, gray-green and impossibly long arms reached for him but they were too weak to do anything. "The vallenians have been here numerous times. One was nearby when I was stealing rubble from Area 42, right?" At Aisling's nod she continued. "I never felt anything wrong. Harlie's never noticed anything wrong. And they don't seem to be dying when you've seen them, have they?"

"No. They've seemed fine. But if both groups are from beyond the veil, why are these dying? Not to mention how in the hell are they crossing through?" A few weeks ago, it had been pointed out that the veil was thinning. Something her mother and her cronies would have been extremely aware of. Yet nothing had been said to anyone even though that could cause serious disturbances all over the world.

"I believe there is something wrong with the creatures coming through. My aunt's belief was that a race was left behind, one more powerful than the elves, but in far fewer numbers. But something made them stay when the rest of the fey escaped. I think the High Council spelled them." Stella pulled her arms tightly around herself, scowled, then came to some sort of conclusion as she nodded. "Stay here, there might be blow back." She stepped to the shield, closed her eyes and walked through it. She was walking on air, literally, as she stepped toward the few creatures still trying to get to the agent in the hazmat suit.

Aisling felt a wave of magic flow from Stella as she raised her arms. Comfort. Pure comfort came from the tiny changeling. Reece started after her, but Aisling grabbed his arm. "Let her do what she needs to."

Stella took a deep breath and spoke softly. The words slowly grew louder so others could hear the spell. "Rest. Go back. This can't be your world. Go back. Rest. Be at peace." She repeated them a few times, all while the feeling of immense comfort flowed over the area. None of the agents moved to stop her, or even moved at all. Aisling found she didn't want to move—most likely a component of the comfort spell.

There was movement in the hole, the beings that had still been moving vanished. Stella stood still for a few moments, then came back across her invisible bridge, crossed through the shield, and collapsed at Aisling's feet.

CHAPTER TWENTY-SEVEN

AISLING GRABBED STELLA AS ALL the activity that
had been frozen by her spell sprang back into action.

"What did she just do?" Reece looked around frantically as Aisling dropped next to Stella.

"Cast a serious spell." Aisling checked her pulse, she
seemed fine, just unconscious. A moment of panic hit
her as she feared that Stella had been struck by whatever
took Harlie down. But her healing magic reached out
to Stella gently. With Harlie, she'd had to force it. Stella
murmured softly as Aisling's magic revived her.

"Oy, won't do that on an empty stomach again." Stella
spoke before she opened her eyes, but her eyelids fluttered
and then opened. "Are they gone? And does anyone have
a snack bar?" She sat up with no assistance and glanced
around owlishly.

Reece glanced to the hole. "It looks like the only ones
left are dead, but the agents said they'd vanished in the
past—these haven't."

"That's good, it will help the agents find out exactly
who they were." Stella gave him a narrow-eyed glare.
"But I'll thank you to remind them these are our sisters
and brothers, no matter what they came across as. I expect
them to be properly cremated and their ashes released to
nature after the examinations." She put enough force in
the words that Aisling knew she'd come back to check.

Aisling was also aware that Reece would have little to
say on that, but she knew he'd try.

Bart came over. "Hello, I believe you are Stella. I've
heard much about you, but we haven't met." Bart stuck

out his hand. "I'm Agent Barthlinio Churchill, please just call me Bart."

If he was upset about Stella being there, or at what she'd just done, he didn't show it.

"Very nice to meet you, Bart. You'll have to come to my diner when we're all back in L.A."

"I shall. Which does bring up why are you here and what did you just do? Greely, the agent in charge over here, is having palpitations." Bart didn't look upset at that at all.

"I am here to visit some friends; thought I'd drop by here and see how things were. As for what I did…it's complicated." She gave him a broad grin. "However, I believe this is the first time they have bodies remaining, so that might be helpful."

"They had live ones."

"Who were slowly dying. They can't survive here, although they keep trying. I am surprised that they are so far south however." She looked around as if the London skyline was suddenly going to morph into something else.

"South?" Aisling had been having fun watching Stella and Bart fence without actually fencing. She had a feeling that Stella might have as much background on Bart as he did on her.

Stella nodded with her eyes now fully on Bart. "They should have been aiming for northern Wales. Near the Snowden mountains, where our people first came through. The movements and changes of the two worlds in the last thousand plus years, here and beyond the veil, have thrown them off." She tilted her head as something flashed across Bart's face. "Unless there *have* been some events up there?"

Bart's smile vanished. "I just found out. Greely insists they aren't related to these events and no one was ever officially sent to look into them. A few months ago, there were a series of small earthquakes in the Welsh mountains. Mostly distant wilderness, and a few hikers were reported missing, but nothing else." He looked around and glared at the London Area 42 people going about their business. "They didn't even investigate. There is too much complacency going on here. I might need to stay in an official capacity."

Greely might have felt the glare as he came over and Bart introduced Stella as another consultant.

"Very nice to meet you. If possible, we'd like to debrief you on what you just did? No one seems to know exactly what it was." He smiled at Stella then turned back to Bart. "You have a large number of consultants for an internal affairs agent."

Bart shrugged. "This is a complicated case. And getting more so by the hour."

"I will tell you what I can, but is this the best location? And I really could use some food, that spell took a lot out of me." Stella gave a charming little old lady smile.

Greely nodded. "I don't need to be here now, they have it under control. Head back to the safe house and I'll meet you there." He looked around. "I don't see Harlie."

Bart patted him on the shoulder. "It's complicated, we'll see you back there."

Jones and Reece stayed at the site as well and would come back with Greely, but the rest climbed into the van.

"How is Harlie?" Bart asked as he pulled away. Stella was in the passenger seat, with Caradoc and Aisling in the very back, looking over Harlie.

"Same as before. He looks like he's sleeping off a serious nectar binge." Aisling filled Bart in on her attempt to reach him.

Stella turned around to watch Harlie. "Whatever grabbed him, I don't believe it was connected to the poor souls in that hole. Before I touched them, I'd thought it might be. But now, I don't believe so. It was taking everything they had just to stay alive."

"Then who, or what, did this to him?" Aisling still felt no pull from her healing magic toward him and wasn't going to push at this point. "And why now?"

Bart glanced back in the rearview mirror. "It could have been a delayed spell. One that hit now just by chance? If we can't get him to recover quickly, we will have to leave him here." The tone of his voice said he knew how well that was going to fly.

"Harlie is essential to our investigation of Noth, we need him. Plus, no offense, but I don't trust these people with my brother." Caradoc shook his head. "Fake Area 42 agents kidnap my sister, and now something has taken Harlie down right when we need him most? Not leaving anyone I care about with Area 42. No offense." He added the last bit, but Bart hadn't looked like he disagreed.

Stella was still facing them from the front seat. "Would you mind if I found him a place to stay with friends of mine? I wasn't lying when I said I had people to visit here. I arrived in London a few hours before you did. My friends can protect Harlie from everyone." Her eyes had darkened a bit, and there was no doubt to her words. Whoever her friends were, they had power and she trusted them.

That was good enough for Aisling. She gave her a smile of thanks. "I'd feel better if he was with people you know and trust. Also, no offense, Bart, but your agency isn't trustworthy. Greely might look the other way if someone wanted to hurt or take Harlie."

"I hate to say it, but I agree. He's not the same elf I knew years ago." Bart had been driving toward the safe house, but slowed down as they approached a crowd of vehicles and people.

A pair of fire trucks were outside the safe house, mostly doing clean up. Whatever had happened, it was out now. As they drove closer, it was clear that half of the house was gone. Very neatly done, the garage and the front portion of the house were nothing but burnt timbers.

Aisling had seen fires and explosions before—but never one that could take out half of a building and leave the rest, and adjoining houses, untouched.

"Stay here." Bart pulled the van over a distance away from the burnt house and walked up to the firemen.

Stella twisted around to get a better look. "I take it that was where you were staying? Why didn't we hear sirens I wonder?"

"Yes, and no idea. Bigger issue is, how did someone do that." Caradoc had one of his gizmos out and looked ready to run out of the van regardless of what Bart said. Finally, he sat back into his seat with a sigh. "They had to have used a spell to pull that off, I'm not picking up any tech readings." He put the gizmo back in his bag and looked across the street. "And Bart didn't like what he was told."

Bart came stomping back. "Good thing we still had our bags in the van, the front went up in seconds they said." He scowled toward the burnt house for a few minutes. "Plan B. We're heading out. I don't want to be around here at this point." He didn't wait for any responses, just started the engine and took off. "I have a friend who lives in Luton, he can get us a place to stay in his apartment building for a bit, until I'm certain no one is looking for us. One of you call Larkin and Jones and let them know to head out and go to the address I sent them. Guess I'm not flying back to L.A. anytime soon."

"There were bad guys?" Stella asked.

"Yes, but not sure who. The plane I borrowed blew up ten minutes ago. Had I left when I was supposed to, I would have been over the Atlantic when it exploded. The bomb was deep inside the right engine. The damage to this safe house was supposedly an electrical short in the kitchen. One that happened to take out half the house in an explosion. And leave everything else untouched. We would have been there had it not been for the recent underground invasion."

"That's not a house fire," Aisling said. Whoever caused the house explosion had been sloppy, it was too precise to have been an accident. Unless, whoever it was, they weren't concerned about anyone realizing it wasn't an accident.

"No, it's not." Bart got on the road out of the neighborhood and Aisling called Reece.

It took him a bit of time to answer, but he finally grabbed it before it went to voicemail.

"What's wrong?"

"Lots of things. Are you with Greely?"

"Not right now. Jones and I are looking for someone to drive us to the house. Greely vanished."

Aisling repeated that part to Bart and he kept a steady amount of swearing up as he merged into traffic.

"Can you get a car on your own? Not anything connected to any agency?" Aisling assumed that nothing was to be trusted at this point. Bart's nod at her words confirmed it. "The house exploded and so did Bart's plane. We're heading out of London."

Reece pulled away and was speaking with someone. He came back. "Jones can get us one. Bart will need to cover our asses though."

Bart heard him and raised his voice. "Done. Get to Luton."

CHAPTER TWENTY-EIGHT

"ARE WE KEEPING HARLIE WITH us? My friends aren't far from here." If Stella was concerned by the change in plans, she didn't show it. "They have a very secure home."

"I think we should keep him." Aisling looked down at her brother. Part of her would rather keep him with them in hopes they could help him recover. But an unconscious and possibly spelled person wasn't good to have with you if you were on the run.

"My friends are healers. And strong witches. They will help him." Stella sent a soothing smile toward Aisling.

She returned the smile. "There's a reason you run a comfort food diner, isn't there?

Caradoc? He's your brother too. What do you say?"

Caradoc had been peering down over the seat at Harlie, but finally looked up. "We have to keep him safe. Being with us and unable to defend himself right now isn't safe."

Bart sighed. "Detour it is. If you would give me directions?"

Stella called her friends to warn them they were on their way, laughed hysterically at something, then directed Bart down a series of increasingly smaller streets that looked less and less like London as they went. Londoners were fond of their small parks, even more so than the average fey obsession. But this was starting to look like an abandoned forest.

A massive, ramshackle house appeared at the end of the road.

"This is secure? Out of the way, I'll agree, but not sure about secure." Bart slowed down as he approached a small driveway. Huge house, tiny driveway. Almost like they didn't want guests.

"Oh, looks can be deceiving. We would have been stopped with force if need be, but persuasion would be the first option. These are natural, holistic, preppers." Stella shrugged. "If you will. They believe the end of the world is coming and only returning to nature will save us. They're good folks, though."

Bart frowned and raised an eyebrow but said nothing as he parked the van.

After a few minutes of sitting, two people in hooded cloaks came out. The capes were bright, beautiful, and reminded Aisling of hippies.

Hoods were thrown back, revealing a pair of tall elves, male and female, who watched the van carefully.

Stella jumped out and ran to hug them. Their faces lit up as they engulfed her. She led them over to the van and motioned for them to come out. "This is Jili and Arthero." She introduced Bart, Aisling, and Caradoc. "Their brother is the one who has been trance-spelled."

Both elves bowed in an old-world greeting then stepped forward to look inside the van.

"We can help shield him." Arthero smiled as he got a good look at Harlie's face. "I did not realize this was Harthinatle. We are honored."

Jili stepped forward and moved to touch Harlie's brow. "He will be safe with us. We will set shields once you have left."

"Full shields?" Stella frowned. "What do you sense?"

"Just a precaution. Harthinatle is known for his strength of mind. That someone brought him to this state is worthy of precaution." Jili smiled. "You made the right choice bringing him to us. Do not fear, the shield will always be open to you four."

Aisling had a twinge of misgiving at Stella's reaction. But shook it off once Stella relaxed. She trusted Stella implicitly, and Stella trusted these two. "You will have him contact us once he wakes up?"

"Immediately." Arthero tilted his head. "I believe you might need supplies." He waved his hand and a loaded cart came trundling toward them. That it didn't appear to have an engine moving it was impressive. "It is unclear how long you will be traveling, or if people are chasing you. But hopefully these will help."

Harlie was gently carried out and placed on a rolling cot. The boxes were quickly loaded into the far back seat and they moved some of the luggage up.

Stella hugged her friends. "Stay safe. There are dangerous things in motion."

"You as well. I hope we are wrong." Arthero and Jili spoke in unison and bowed. Then they retreated back into the house with Harlie's rolling cot.

They got back into the van.

"Was that a blessing? They hope they are wrong?" It had sounded like a blessing more than just conversation to Aisling.

Stella watched her friends vanish in the rearview mirror. "Yes. They are preppers, but oddly optimistic ones. They prepare for the end of times, but fervently hope they are wrong."

"As long as they keep Harlie safe and maybe help him, I'm good." Caradoc leaned back into his seat.

Aisling recognized a frustrated pout coming on. "Too many things on the mystical side and not enough on the technological one?"

"Yes. I feel like I should be able to do something, but almost nothing so far has been in my range of expertise. Although…" He unbuckled his seat belt and dug through the bag at his feet. "Just to make certain no one is tailing us. No idea who blew up your friend's plane, or that house. But something or someone is trying to slow us down or stop us." He fished around in his carry-on until he found what he wanted. A gizmo. Larger than some of his other ones.

"And what does that do? Track bugs?" Aisling wasn't as impressed with his toys as before; he'd been driving around with assorted bugs attached to his car and missed them all.

"Even better. Mott helped me increase the sensitivity after his little inventions got past me. This not only picks them up, it lets me trace it back to the owner." As he spoke, he pulled out a small scanner, connected it to his gizmo, and flicked a switch. Nothing.

"I think we're clean. This was waiting for us from Area 42 and had been—" Bart's comment was cut off as the gizmo started beeping.

"You were saying?" Caradoc grinned as his scanner pulled in information. Then his grin dropped. Then turned to a full scowl. "This isn't good. The bounce back isn't far behind us. We need to shake them long enough to get these bugs off."

"How much information are you pulling in?" Bart was on the motorway heading north. "Perhaps we can catch whoever it is?"

"I might be able to narrow it down, but you'd need to get off at the next exit." Caradoc started fussing with various knobs on the screen, looking behind them, then adjusting more. "Cheeky bastard, he's two cars behind us. Not even hiding."

"He wouldn't know you have the ability to reverse track him through his own bugs." Aisling looked back but traffic was heavy enough that spotting the suspect's vehicle wasn't easy.

"True, but if he knew me, he should have expected it." Caradoc seemed more cheerful now. "I'm locked onto him, so even if he shuts off the bugs on his end, we can still track him."

Bart took the next exit. "We'll go off here and try and grab him. At the least we can get the bugs off the van."

"Do you think they will put up a fight?" Stella sounded too excited about that option.

"We can hope not." Bart looked over to her. "You don't get out much, do you?"

"I am working on changing that." She grinned and kept looking in the side mirror for the car tailing them. "It's that dark gray one, right? They just switched lanes rather unsafely."

"That's the one my scanner is picking out." Caradoc smiled at Stella. "This is great, we caught a tail!"

"I think avoiding having people after us would be the best approach." Aisling looked between the two—too much excitement, not enough reality.

"That's the cop in you thinking." Bart slowed down, looking for less busy side streets to go down. "These two have never been law enforcement. And it shows." He put some weight on the last words, but neither Caradoc nor Stella seemed to care.

The gray car was still following but drifted further behind as the traffic thinned out.

"I know this has been fun, but I think I'm done." Bart swung the van to the curb, leapt out of the van, and pulled a gun on the driver.

The driver could have backed up, but they were awfully close to Bart and his gun.

"Turn off your car and get out very slowly."

Aisling's gun was in her bag in the back, but she, Caradoc, and Stella were all magic users. They got out of the van and moved to where they wouldn't block each other or Bart if things got weird. Would have been nice if Bart had warned them of his plans.

The person in the gray car was hard to see until they turned off the vehicle and got out.

Aisling started swearing first, but was followed quickly by Caradoc and Stella.

It was Nix. If he was upset or concerned about them seeing who he was or that he was at a disadvantage, he didn't show it.

"Keep your hands up, my lad." Bart's gun was steady. "If you're who you appear to be, and who my friends seem sure that you are, I could shoot you right now and no one would be sorry. Except maybe you."

Caradoc stepped forward with a pair of cuffs. Aisling had no idea where they came from but most likely they were something he'd invented. They almost looked like standard L.A. cop handcuffs, but they were thicker and there was a blue electronic arc crackling around them.

"If you have no objection?" He held them up in Bart's direction but didn't look away from Nix's face.

"By all means. I have no idea why he's following us, but he has a deeper connection to all of you than to me."

Caradoc stepped forward, his cuffs in one hand, his other lifted for a spell, he was a foot away when Nix started laughing like a mad man and exploded.

CHAPTER TWENTY-NINE

AISLING RAN FORWARD TO TRY and protect her brother, but he was too close to the blast. The explosion blew him backwards into Stella and the van. Then the gray car reversed and took off.

Aisling tried to stop the vehicle but only succeeded in running alongside long enough to see the grinning driver. Nix. The shock of him being there when she'd just seen him blow up and needing to get back to Caradoc stopped her and the car speed away. She ran back to her brother.

He was badly hurt; he most likely raised his right arm when the explosion happened as there were two bones sticking out. His left thigh had a piece of metal in it. Stella and Bart were holding him up, but he was slipping into shock.

"Let me." Aisling dropped down next to him as Bart stepped away. Caradoc clutched onto Stella with his uninjured arm.

"I messed up. Tech fail." He tried laughing but there were more injuries than the ones she'd seen, blood trickled out of his mouth. She'd prefer to get him somewhere safe to work on him, but she didn't think they had the time.

"I need you both to hold him still. Caradoc, I want you looking at me and thinking of every vile, nasty thing our mother has done." She gave a small smile. "I will be."

He bit his lip as Bart held him down, but he nodded.

Aisling slipped into a healing trance, one fueled by her own anger at her mother. And by the serious increase of magic now at her call. She vibrated with the power that flooded her system. Healing magic surged into her like a massive adrenaline rush as she focused on his arm first, a few internal injuries, and then his leg and minor slices. But she couldn't stop. He was healed, but the magic just kept coming.

"Can't. Stop." She got out through gritted teeth as more healing magic flowed through her. The spell felt wild, if she didn't stop it, the magic would start harming him since there was nothing to fix. Then it would turn back against her.

Stella released Caradoc's arm and threw herself at Aisling, knocking them both over. Aisling's magic lashed out at Stella, then bounced off a shield she'd raised and hit a tree. Stella stayed sitting on her until Aisling took a deep breath and nodded.

"I'm okay. Thank you. You could have gotten fried, you know."

Stella rolled to her feet and helped Aisling up. "Pish. I might not be as strong as you, but I'm wiser." She narrowed her eyes and dropped her voice. "I don't recall you having that kind of power before. Even when you focused on your mother."

"There have been some changes lately. I will explain later." Telling someone, even someone like Stella, that her mother had arranged for Harlie to block her magic when she was five, and that the block was now gone, wasn't something to be done on a London street.

Bart pulled a stunned and blinking Caradoc to his feet.

"He exploded? Where's the car?" Caradoc wavered a bit, but he was intact and upright.

"It took off after you went flying." Aisling paused. "It was Nix at the wheel and he appeared unharmed. He even grinned."

Stella went to the bloody mess where Nix had stood. "This is made up of shattered bones, tissues, blood. Someone died here."

Bart nodded. "I was watching him. He *was* the explosion. Probably hoped to take more of us out but was willing to settle for Caradoc."

"That doesn't look like enough of anything to have been a person." Aisling walked closer, but not as near as the others. Whatever just happened with Caradoc's healing had left her weak and dizzy.

"I think they are using clones of some kind—ones that aren't actually elves, or Nix. As much as I would love that bastard to be dead, that's not him." Caradoc stepped closer to her. "Thank you for putting me back together. I feel better than before I got hit."

"Yeah, something got away from me there. I wish Harlie wasn't unconscious right now." She rubbed her arms. Weak, dizzy, and now extremely cold. "I'm going back into the van." And put on every bit of clothing she could find.

Caradoc nodded and followed her. "I'm taking the damn bugs off of it. My tech worked, but I think we'd rather not be followed by homicidal clones." He held the door open for her. "Are you sure you're okay? You look awful."

Aisling laughed. "Nice brotherly love there. I think the spell just took too much out of me. If Stella hadn't stopped it by tackling me, I'm not sure what would have happened to you, or me." She'd thought having access to the power she'd been born with was a good thing. She was seriously rethinking that.

"That's not good. Stay here and rest; we'll be on our way soon." He patted her arm then went bug hunting.

———◆———

Aisling hadn't meant to fall asleep, but she had been in a dark void, no sound, no light. Then voices, low ones, caught her attention and the rumble of a vehicle moving brought her awake. "What happened?"

"We were hoping to get to Luton before you woke up. You look awful." Caradoc looked over to her and handed her a tissue. "And I think you were drooling."

"What?" Aisling wiped her face but didn't feel anything. "Funny."

"How do you feel?" Stella's concern came through in her voice and on her face as she looked back from the front seat.

"Probably better than I obviously look. At least judging by you two." She rolled her shoulders but, like the rest of her, they were stiff and achy. "Where are we?"

Bart looked back in the rear-view mirror. "Heading into Luton. My friend isn't home, but he set us up in a business rental unit and has his doorman waiting for us. Larkin and Jones are already there and will meet us in the lobby."

They turned down a side road to an apartment building.

"We're all going to stay in an apartment? For how long?" Aisling wanted a quiet room to herself, and a nice big bed. She might have fallen asleep on the drive, but it only seemed to make her sleepier.

"It's a penthouse, actually," Bart said as they pulled into a downwards ramp and the parking area. The building hadn't appeared fancy enough for a penthouse, but at that point Aisling didn't care. Food, shower, bed…that was her plan.

The parking level wasn't full, but if people who lived there worked, they probably hadn't come home yet. Her phone said it was four pm local time, but it felt so much later. Aisling started to grab her things, but Caradoc beat her to them.

"Yeah, still looking crappy. You saved me a lot of pain, time, and healing—least I can do is get your bags." Him being nice and giving her a concerned smile made her worried. Whatever happened while she was unconscious, it had involved speculation about her condition. Enough to concern her optimistic brother.

Aisling was too tired to argue and instead followed Bart to the elevator with Stella and Caradoc behind. Reece and Jones were waiting for the elevator at the lobby level.

Reece's eyes narrowed as he looked at Aisling. "What happened?"

"I look like shit. Thank you, I know." Aisling gave him a small smile.

"I wasn't going to say that, but yeah, you do." The snarky Reece she knew before she got to know the real him showed up in his smile and she realized that was as much a part of who he was as anything else.

"Thanks. I had to heal Caradoc when Nix followed us and things went to hell."

Reece looked to Bart who nodded. "I'll fill you in when we get inside."

The elevator stopped at what looked like the hall of a mansion, not an entrance to an apartment. There was nothing beyond a nicely ornate double door that opened into a spacious living room.

Aisling went to one of the plush sofas and dropped down. "I'm claiming the biggest bed. I'll stay awake while I can but recommend a quick debriefing." It had taken a lot out of her just to get this far. If Stella hadn't been able to break her healing spell when she did, she'd probably be in a coma now.

Reece didn't sit next to her on the sofa, but he did take the nearest chair to her.

"Okay, here's what happened on our end." Bart quickly told Reece and Jones about being followed. Then about Nix, his explosion, and Caradoc's injuries.

"I don't get it, so one Nix exploded in the hopes of taking Caradoc out, and another one drove away? Were there two when you turned on them?" Jones asked first, but Reece looked ready to ask the same.

"I'm pretty sure there was only one, when he came out there didn't appear to be anyone else in the car—but something was there. Or he blew up and then just recompiled himself in the car." Caradoc shrugged.

Stella held up an evidence bag. "I retrieved some samples of the remaining bits of the exploded one, but overall, there wasn't enough there to have made a complete person."

"Then Aisling healed me, got sucked too far into the spell, and Stella had to tackle her." Caradoc nodded over toward Aisling. "She's fading fast, folks."

Aisling pulled herself up from where she'd slumped forward. "I'm awake, but yeah, talk fast you two. Any updates?"

Reece ran his fingers through his hair. "The airport is claiming that it was an engine failure that caused the plane to blow up. Ignoring the fact that the engines weren't even on at the time of explosion and that there was a bomb detected. One they are now claiming was a mistake in their data. MI-6 has taken over that investigation, so not much coming out until they decide to rope in Area 42."

"Sneaky agencies don't play nicely together." Aisling glanced at her phone, but there was nothing from Maeve yet.

"And the Area 42 safe house having a fire of suspicious origin?" Bart asked.

"Under investigation." Jones shook his head. "Greely never came back around and the local office isn't saying anything."

"I can and will investigate the hell out of them," Bart said. "There was no way that the attack on the house was an accident."

"Since I really want to fall asleep right now, and we're not sure what exactly I did with that spell, I'm heading to bed." Aisling got to her feet, wobbled, and was caught by Reece.

"I'll just make sure you don't fall over before you get there." His smile was tentative as he held her up.

Aisling nodded. Siren spell or not, she missed him, and it felt nice to have him hold her up. The feelings she had been developing for him had sure as hell felt real on her end. They just needed to find out for certain.

He got her to the first bedroom and sat her down on the bed. "Are you going to be okay on your own?"

Aisling laughed. "You are not going to help me get undressed. But thank you for helping me get here."

He looked down at her for a few moments. "I really hope there hasn't been siren influence going on."

"Me too. Now go back out there before I do something stupid that I'll probably fall asleep in the middle of."

Reece kissed the top of her head, left the room, and shut the door behind him.

CHAPTER THIRTY

A ISLING FELT HERSELF RUNNING THROUGH the woods, but she wasn't getting anywhere. A voice cut through her odd dream. It was Harlie.

"Follow the necklace." His words were drawn out and sounded like a lot of effort came behind them.

"Harlie? Are you talking to me in my sleep?" Aisling stopped running but the trees kept flying by. Great, a dream with a tree treadmill.

"Follow the necklace."

"Are you all right?"

"Necklace."

"Harlie, can you say anything else?"

"No."

"You just did!"

"Just follow the necklace and keep your heart open. I will be okay. Stop Nix." There was a popping sound, the trees stopped, and Aisling found herself awake in the bedroom.

She had no idea what time it was, or how long she'd been asleep. She'd climbed into bed in a t-shirt and shorts, so she rolled out of bed, hit the light, and looked at the time before she changed clothes. She wasn't as bone-dead weary as she had been, but she could still go back to sleep if need be.

Three-forty-five a.m. on the dot. Leave it to Harlie to pick a witching time. Between three and four were said to be times when all the veils, not just the one to the old world, were thinnest. Harlie was a strong believer in the old ways. She rolled back into bed and massaged her temples. Follow the necklace. That made no sense, unless it was planning on pulling her around. A quick check verified it was still around her neck and not looking ready to go anywhere. Harlie's spell to keep the additional markings hidden was holding even though he was unconscious. It just looked like a high-end, silver Celtic knot. One that wouldn't go past her ears.

Stopping Nix was fairly obvious, but she wondered if Harlie's subconscious awareness, or whatever was communicating with her, knew about the recent attack and a way to stop Nix. So far he, or they, hadn't been causing trouble, beyond almost blowing up Caradoc. But she didn't think that had been intended. That clone, copy, whatever he was, had been assigned to follow them. The blowing up appeared to be a handy distraction after he was caught. And something the real Nix would do just to be an asshole.

Which brought her to her weird power surge while trying to heal Caradoc. It hadn't felt like her healing magic at all. In a way, it wasn't. This magic contained the potential her mother had blocked. And it kicked her ass.

She tried to let the thoughts go. But the feeling of pure panic when she'd healed Caradoc and her magic kept going deeper wouldn't vanish. Was that why her mother blocked it? That she had some wild magic that no one could control? Could her mother have done it to protect her?

The laugh that thought caused was almost loud enough to wake the others had they not been in a high-end place with thick walls. If blocking her magic helped Aisling in any way, it had been a side effect, not an intention.

She stayed in bed, but her thoughts kept running around too much for sleep. A flashing light on her phone caught her attention. It hadn't been there a few minutes ago.

A blocked number. That wasn't good. Caradoc's security system would have done its best to break down where random numbers came from, so one actually showing as blocked even after his system got at it was a concern.

Of course, MI-6 and Area 42 both could have probably bypassed his system. She didn't think anyone beyond Maeve would be calling her, and since it would be almost four am for Maeve as well, that was doubtful. There was no way she'd go to sleep with that light blinking—she was already too awake and curious. She hit play on the voicemail and almost dropped the phone.

It was her mother.

"Aisling. It is vital that you contact me. Do not tell either of your brothers, or anyone you're with, that I have called you. You are in serious danger, and I feel that Harlie has betrayed you. This is a secure line, call me when you get this message." Definitely her mother's voice, but the fear and concern sounded genuine and not at all like her normal condescending annoyance.

Aisling's immediate response was to delete the message, but the fact it had punched through Caradoc's security needed to be examined, so she saved it and shut down her phone. She'd play it for everyone in the morning.

A wave of fatigue smacked into her again, and since it was still too early to deal with anything, she gave into it, rolled over, and went back to sleep.

———◆———

The knocking sounded like it was coming from inside her head, but once Aisling fought to wake up, she realized it was the door.

"Hold on, let me get dressed." Her sleepwear covered everything, but she'd feel better fully clothed.

"Are you okay?" It was Reece, and he didn't sound okay himself. It was his voice, but pitched differently, like he was doing one of his undercover jobs. A slightly slimy one.

Aisling cracked open the door, kept mostly behind it, and peeked out. "I'm fine, why?" She almost shut the door when she saw him and déjà vu hit her from a few weeks ago. He was wearing low-slung sweatpants and no shirt and looked as groggy as she felt. And he looked good enough to eat. Damn him. That was the last thing her exhausted psyche or libido needed at this point.

"There's been an accident, back home. I didn't know if anyone had called you." He still sounded odd, and his normally gray eyes were light and vacant.

"No, no one. What kind of accident?" A chill went up her spine and she kept one foot braced against the door. It was morning, but not late. She couldn't hear anyone else in the living room.

"Caradoc's house blew up. Lots of damage. The entire neighborhood is gone. Where was Mott?"

His voice deepened, now not sounding as slimy as before, but flat and menacing. Whoever this was, he wasn't Reece. Or it might be his body, but he wasn't inside.

"Oh, Mott left for New York, remember? Caradoc will be upset that his place in the mountains blew up. Do they know how?" She kept her voice as flat as he had. Easiest to lie and see what this not-Reece's reaction was.

"Yes, the mountains, that was a nice place. I'd forgotten about Mott." He pushed on the door. "Can we talk? Just us?"

Aisling held the door in place. "Not right now, where are the others?"

"Sleeping." The grin was not Reece at all. He stopped pushing on the door, and she came forward as the pressure she'd been holding against vanished. Once she was off balance, he slammed the door open.

Aisling stumbled back but managed to stay out of his reach. She knew where she'd seen that smile before.

Nix's clone.

Reece/Nix came for her, but she kicked his chest hard

enough to send him across the room. He immediately came back at her.

This time she let him get closer, then wrapped her arms around his torso and forced pain filled anti-healing magic into his sides. She was more aware this time of the buildup of the additional magic in her system and pushed to keep it back. She wasn't sure if this was some sort of duplicate of Reece or if he was possessed, so she wanted to hurt, not kill. Not yet anyway.

She hung on tighter as Reece kept trying to pull away from her. His breath came in ragged gasps and finally he collapsed. The bruising around his chest and waist was intense already.

Aisling jumped away from him, ran to the nightstand, grabbed her gun, and aimed it at him. But he didn't move aside from the ragged up and down of his sides as he fought to breathe.

This was a problem. If he was faking it, he'd grab her as soon as she tried for the door. But if it was actually Reece's body, he was going to need help. Her shirt started tugging at her and she wondered if he'd gotten something on her while they fought. Nope, it was the damn pendant. Moving toward Reece.

"I wish Harlie were here, or if he could be a bit more forthcoming about his advice." The pendant pulled out from her shirt and was now pointing toward Reece as if it was some sort of deranged hunting dog. "I get it. You want me to go to him. Ya see, I don't want him to grab me, and to get you closer would let him do that." The pendant didn't care and kept tugging.

"Why would Harlie be involved?" Reece's words came out in gasps, she might have broken a rib or two. But the eyes that finally opened were Reece's. "What?" He lifted his head but didn't move more than that.

"You attacked me. You were acting weird before, but I'm not sure that you're really you now." She came forward a bit but kept her gun steady.

"I attacked you? Then why do I feel like a giant snake had me in a death squeeze?" He looked down, noticing what he was wearing. "I think I would get dressed before I attacked anyone."

The slamming of doors and pounding of feet told her the others had heard the fight. That, or this was a full invasion.

Jones got there first, dressed casually, and with his gun out. "What in the hell?" He glanced at Aisling first, then Reece on the ground. "Do I even want to know what you two were doing?" He lowered his gun but didn't make a move forward.

Caradoc, Bart, and Stella came running up behind him.

"Something or someone took over Reece. Or replaced him. I think he's himself now, but he tried to attack me. I think I broke a few of his ribs." Aisling kept her gun up and on Reece. The eye color change was noticeable, but it might have just been something to do with how the copy was made. If it was a copy.

Stella shoved the men aside and darted to Reece. She peered into his eyes closely, one hand raised over his head. Aisling couldn't tell what kind of spell she held in her fingers, but it didn't look friendly as it sparked and crackled. "Tell me your name. Your full name." She put a lot of weight into those words, most likely they were tied to the spell in her hand.

Reece didn't pause. "Reece Deon Larkin." He winced after he spoke. Yup, more than a few ribs were broken or cracked.

Stella dispersed the magic spell in her hands and rocked back on her heels. "Whoever he was before, he's himself now. Signs of a possession are in his mind. A deep one too. But they are fading quickly." She looked up to Aisling. "You can lower your gun and since you're the only healer we have, you probably need to fix your handiwork."

Aisling put her gun back on the nightstand and walked over to Reece and Stella. Her pendant wasn't pulling as hard as before, but still tugged a bit.

"Did you have any problems magically hurting him?" Caradoc stepped around Bart and Jones.

"No. I felt the magic try to get stronger, but hurting magic is different from healing magic." She shuddered to think what might have happened if she hadn't been able to stop the extra magic mojo from kicking in while she fought Reece.

"Great, you can hurt people but not heal them." Bart scowled down at Reece. "I can call someone from Area 42, but it will take a while."

Reece tried to get up, but Stella pushed him down with a single finger.

"I can help Aisling if she helps Reece. I got the feel for what her out of control magic was trying to do last time." Stella grinned and cracked her knuckles. "I'm ready for it this time."

Aisling looked to Bart and he nodded "Okay, Stella, you keep an eye on me. Caradoc and Jones, hang onto Reece if you need to. This is probably going to hurt." Not all healings hurt, but ribs were tricky.

"What is up with your pendant?" Reece said as she sat down next to him. The damn thing was twitching again.

"No idea. It started trying to get to you right after I'd chased off whatever was taking you over."

"Right after you cracked my ribs you mean?" He gave a half-smile. Still too sexy, even with his bruised torso.

Aisling focused on the spot between his eyebrows. No eye contact and it kept her from looking at anything else. "When I managed to fight you off without having to shoot you. You're welcome. Now hold still and stay quiet." There was a tingle of fear that what happened with Caradoc would happen again. But she did cause the injury, and taking him back to London wasn't a great option. They needed to get to Noth, sooner rather than later.

She took a deep breath and focused on healing magic, letting it flow into Reece and repairing what she'd just done. He was healing, the ribs knitted together as she worked. She was just pulling free when a void opened in front of her and pulled her through.

Her magic acted as a conduit to drag her across a threshold. She couldn't tell what it was, just that she didn't want to cross it. The pendant started to move but she couldn't tell what it was doing. Cold hands pulled on her, trying to bring her across the doorway, and terror filled her soul at what was on the other side. The pendant was trying to pull her away. Or was now trying to choke her to death as the pendant was pulling from behind which meant the chain was digging into her windpipe. Wherever she was, it was horrifying, even though she couldn't see anything beyond the threshold. She pulled away as cold hands grabbed her arms, but as they got warmer she realized it was Stella.

"Let go of her!" Stella's voice came in Aisling's head and in her ears and there was powerful magic behind it.

Chapter Thirty-One

———

A POPPING SOUND FILLED AISLING'S MIND and she was flung backwards. The room spun a bit and she had pulled Reece partially on top of her as she went back, but she was free.

"I appreciate that you didn't shoot me and did just heal me, but maybe this isn't the best position." Reece carefully removed himself from covering her body. The pendant tugged toward him briefly, then dropped back.

"That necklace of yours likes Reece. It kept trying to get to him while you were healing him." Caradoc helped Reece to his feet.

"Or something. If felt like it was choking me when I was…wherever I went." Aisling rubbed her neck. "Thank you, Stella. I couldn't get back out."

Stella nodded and got to her feet. Then looked at Reece and Aisling. "We might want to continue this over breakfast—clothed." The others weren't dressed for going out, but they were better clothed than Aisling and Reece. Not that he was hard on the eyes right now, but he was seriously distracting.

"Agreed." Aisling walked to the door to see everyone out. Reece was the last.

"Sorry I tried to attack you."

"Yeah, yeah. That's what all possessed men say. Go get some clothes on."

He flashed her a wicked smile. "You too." He left.

Aisling rolled her shoulders to break up the tension of the past ten minutes and quickly showered and changed. Her reaction to Reece was still normal, no idea what that meant. They needed to figure out if he was unintention-ally sending siren powers. Soon.

The others were clustered around the table, talking and eating. Reece stayed silent as Aisling filled them in. She didn't bring up mommy dearest's call as she wanted to deal with one crisis at a time.

Reece nodded. "And I recall nothing of what happened. I was asleep, dreaming about trees for some reason, then woke up bruised and beaten on the floor with Aisling looking to put a bullet in me."

"You weren't yourself at all. In fact, at one point your grin looked like Nix." Aisling kept her voice neutral but everyone exploded in questions and comments.

"Hold up!" Bart raised his hands as he yelled to be heard over everyone. "There's currently no proof of what or who got into Larkin. But we can assume this trick might be something new for Nix. We need to capture one of him alive."

"And figure out a dozen other mysteries and issues." Caradoc ran his hand through his hair. "Or that's what it feels like. They keep adding and we've no idea if they are connected or not."

"I have two more." Aisling didn't want to add to the pile but it wasn't like she could ignore things. She quickly told them about the tree dream she'd had—from the frowning nods from Reece, she'd described his dream too well. Then she brought out her phone. "I also got this message, sometime around 4 a.m. Came through as a blocked number. Better to just let you hear it." She played it back. Her mother sounded less like herself on this listen through. Of course Aisling wasn't completely awake when she heard it the first time.

"Can you play it again? There is something off about the call," Bart said.

"The odd part is that she's trying to sound like she cares. Our mother cares about power and money—nothing else." She played it again. Then once more when Jones pulled out a smaller phone to record it, placed it next to hers and nodded.

"Can I see your phone?" Caradoc held out his hand. He also pulled out a small tool kit. "That woman shouldn't be able to get through, regardless of the number. I have our phones set to block her voice. And no one should be able to get a blocked call through. I'll see what's going on." He almost dropped her phone when it rang before he could start ripping it apart. "Damn it!" He tossed the phone back to Aisling. "It's Maeve. Make it quick."

"Hey, interesting timing. You just almost shocked Caradoc."

Maeve laughed. "I'll try harder next time. Are you still in London? Something weird is going on with Area 42."

"No, we're not. Mind if I put you on speaker?"

"Sure. Hi all. Your Area 42 folks are having a shit storm. London, L.A., and New York but mostly London. My people are getting concerned and I was asked to touch base with you."

"Damn it, what's happened?" Bart moved closer to the phone. He refrained from grabbing it, but he looked ready to.

"I'm assuming you know about your plane, the safe house, and some weird underground invasion?"

"Yes."

"There's more. Ten Area 42 high level agents were found in a mass grave. They'd been there for at least a week."

"What? Where? Who?" Bart paled a few shades.

"I can text you the list. They were found in Hyde Park, buried in a distant corner of the tennis center. The royal family is not pleased."

"Was one of them named Greely?" Aisling asked. Something had been off about that man, and then for him to vanish? She ignored the look Bart gave her.

"Let me check…nope. Why, did he give you people trouble?"

"Not that much, but he's gone missing. If you could ask your people to keep an eye out for him, I can send you his public file." Bart didn't look relieved or upset at the news. Just extremely neutral.

"Any more news?"

"Just that I get to come work with you. Don't worry, if you tell me not to tell them anything, I won't tell them, and they know it."

"Any more Nix sightings?" Aisling would fill Maeve in on their own encounter when they got together. Maeve wasn't going to take it well.

"Not a one. I'm personally hoping he wants payback for what we did to him in California and will find us. Where are you?"

Aisling looked to Bart. They needed to investigate Noth, but London was having serious issues.

Bart sighed. "We'll be back in London by tomorrow. We're going to swing up to Noth, see if there's anything new. Then at least some of us will be coming back to London—it seems to be where the trouble is."

"Ya hear that? Stay put, we'll come to you."

"Will eagerly await your call. I'd forgotten how jovial and full of life most MI-6 agents are. See you soon." Maeve hung up and Aisling gave her phone back to her brother.

Bart started swearing a few moments later as his phone buzzed with an incoming text. "Damn it. Greely might not have been replaced; I say might because he's not acting like himself so he's still a suspect at this point. But his two partners at the house had been. The real Locke and Wastegirdle are listed as being identified in the mass grave." He rubbed his forehead. "And two more above Greely. Excuse me, I need to make a call." He left for his bedroom.

"This keeps piling up. We can't take care of anything." Caradoc had a huge pile of food in front of him but hadn't eaten it. Never a good sign. He started tearing apart Aisling's phone as if it having allowed their mother to call was a personal affront to him. Caradoc was usually able to keep a light heart about things, including the possible end of the world. That wasn't the case now.

"I think we need to split up," Aisling held up her hand before the protests could come in. "Trust me, I don't like it either. But with everything that's going on, sticking together isn't helping. And now our mother and her cronies, and I do mean the High Council, are possibly involved? We have too much to cover."

"I agree." Jones had been quiet, but he was clearly upset. "We can't trust Area 42 right now. What we need is someone with Harlie's abilities."

"Which is most likely why someone took him out." Reece started pacing. "We need one of Aisling's murder boards to see the connections. We're missing something."

"I'm surprised a super spook like you would be suggest something so old school, but I agree. If we could stay in one place long enough to set one up anyway. Not to mention finding one." Aisling did miss her boards. Her original one had been blown up when someone decided to destroy her home. The second one was at Caradoc's place. Both were too big to travel.

Caradoc was scowling at her phone, the guts of which were spread out in a pile in front of him. He looked up at her words. "I forgot about that!" He ran to a bedroom, and came back with a small laptop. "I've been lugging this all over, but didn't get a chance to give it to you." He put the laptop down in front of her like a proud daddy with his newborn.

"Thanks, but I have a laptop. A few in fact."

"No, no, no. Just open it." He stepped back. "Maybe put it on the floor first, open it, and step back a bit."

Aisling gave him a questioning look, but moved away. At first the laptop just sat there not doing anything. It looked like a laptop. "Okay, now wha—"

The laptop whirled at her touch and began unfolding. In less than thirty seconds, a mini murder board appeared in front of her. It even extended legs to stand on the floor. Although it was smaller than her previous two, it was still about four by five feet in size.

"Now that is impressive." Jones said as he and Reece came around to Aisling's side to look.

"But how do I draw on it?" Aisling was impressed at the ingenuity, the new screen in front of her was a single piece—no idea how Caradoc did that—and asking would probably just hurt her head.

"Touch the on button at the top. Then use the stylus. Or your finger, either work." Caradoc looked far happier than he'd been in a week.

She did so and grinned as a screen appeared. One that was clearly electronic but looked like an old-fashioned dry erase board. She took the stylus and wrote out, "What the hell is going on?" at the top, then turned back to him.

"This is amazing, Caradoc. Thank you." Aisling liked being able to see the issues in a large, cohesive format, it helped her find connections.

Stella came up to investigate. "This is wonderful." She turned to Caradoc. "I assume the details stay once it is collapsed back down?"

He tried to look affronted at her question but was still too proud of his invention to let it get to him. "Of course. It can even save multiple screens in their full state. And it has a locking mechanism so that if someone opens the laptop to search it, or by accident, it won't unfold, and will just look like a simple laptop. Am I good, or am I good?"

Aisling laughed and started writing down what they had so far—it was a mess. But now it was a mess on a board.

"I hate to break up whatever you have going on." Bart came out from his room and walked around to the front of the board. "Fascinating board, total crap intel on it. We need to split up." He waited for their response.

"Aisling already pointed that out. I assume the information you just got is making things worse?" Reece had started adding things to the board with his finger. Nothing major, but there were a lot of little events along with the large—there was no way to be certain which would impact major events.

"Yes. New York seems to have had a mole. It was Toril Kjai. He was killed in a gun fight once they caught him, and they're going through his computer looking for his connections. I knew that guy was an asshole, but he apparently was a larger one than we expected."

"Mole, or duplicate?" Aisling kept adding things to the board as well. Soon she and Reece would have it full and still no solutions in sight.

"Mole. They did blood work after he was killed. It was him. And yes, I asked about searching for possession. The seers found no signs of it. They hadn't been looking for possession prior, but I told them about Reece going after Aisling."

"It wasn't me," Reece said.

"I know. However, they got to you needs to be resolved. They got inside your head in a secure building. There are blocks against telepathic invasion here."

"Maybe they got him before he rejoined us." Aisling watched Jones as well as Reece. "They were left behind working with at least two duplicates."

Reece shook his head. "We don't know if there is a connection between the duplicates and someone pulling possession. Very different skill sets. Besides, you said I reminded you of Nix, and *we* didn't run into any of his clones." His look of concern was aimed at Aisling and

Caradoc.

Stella watched everyone and a frown appeared. "Look at you all, glaring at each other. We are not the enemy, but if they, whoever they are, manage to push us against each other, they win."

"We need a way to make sure everyone is who they say they are and that no one has been possessed. Anyone got that handy?" Aisling agreed with Stella. Bart, Jones, and Reece all seemed to be slowly moving to the walls.

Caradoc hadn't moved from the table. "And again, who do we need? Harlie. Whoever we are up against knows our strengths and weaknesses. Stella, can you check Jones for possession?"

"What? I'm fine. I have no idea how someone got in Larkin's head. But they didn't get in mine." Jones didn't pull out a weapon, but his body language said he was ready to.

Aisling held up her hands. "Easy there. Stella can check all of us, but then how do we check Stella?" She trusted her friend, but this was getting into some weirdness. She'd just finished speaking when a wall of darkness slammed her.

"Search. Here." Again it was Harlie's voice in her head but this time an image appeared. It was Mott and a small round box.

Chapter Thirty-Two

———

ISLING TRIED CALLING HARLIE BACK to her, they needed him and if he could reach out to her like this maybe they could strengthen the tie between them and get some answers. But he vanished and she felt someone holding her up and talking to her.

"I'm fine. Harlie popped in again." She opened her eyes to find that Reece was the one holding her. He helped to her feet. "I'm fine."

"You look awful. Seriously, sit down and have some tea." Stella pulled out the nearest chair. "Has he popped into your head before? I mean before this morning?"

"No. But he's also never been unconscious like this. This time he showed me an image of Mott with a little round box, does that ring any bells?" It didn't look familiar to her but hopefully, if it was something they could use, someone would know what it was. Not being able to clear everyone as not being possessed was going to make resolving things even harder. When everyone continued to look at her blankly, she sketched the box on the board.

"Did it have a small jewel, right here?" Caradoc pointed to the top. "Did you notice the color?"

Aisling was about to respond that it had happened in a split second, but then she nodded. The image still lingered with her. "It had a silver jewel there and the box was dark blue."

"Ha! I know that one; a pet project of Mott's, one he'd been working with Harlie on from time to time. Let me contact him." He dialed Mott before anyone could question him.

Aisling leaned over to Stella. "There's a gadget that can tell if someone has been possessed or not?"

"Not that I know of. But that Mott is a scarily smart individual. And if Harlie had been working with him… who knows? You are right, I can search everyone, but who would check me? If whoever is behind this knew about Harlie, they know my abilities as well. Not to mention we need something that can tell if someone's status has changed after the initial search. Unless we were planning on hiding out here until this blows over. Or blows up." She jumped to her feet as an idea hit her and ran to Caradoc. "Did you reach him? Can I speak to him?" She looked ready to rip the phone out of Caradoc's hand so he handed it to her.

"Mott? How are you doing? Very good. Now what did Caradoc tell you?" She paused then continued. "Excellent. Can it be made to adjust into subdural chips that can monitor possession or duplication? Ahh, it just picks up non-normal behavior—that will work if we can get the chips." A longer pause this time, and Caradoc was fully frowning at Stella. She finally nodded and smiled. "You are going to get so many cookies when I come back! Yes, let me have Bart give you the address. Thank you!" She bypassed Caradoc's extended hand and gave the phone to Bart. "He has something that will work and that he can modify into single chips that will let us know if someone has gone bad after our initial check. Or at least been changed, the bad part is an assumption. He'll have it sent mage-express, so we do need to stay here a few hours. Please do give him the address?"

Bart looked like he wanted to question what Stella was doing, but shook his head, took the phone, and told Mott the address. Then he held the phone up to Caradoc. "Did you have anything else to add?"

"I think that was it. Unless we need to know how to use these new gadgets?"

Stella grinned. "He already told me. Easy as pie. Actually, easier than pie—some pies can be extremely problematic."

"Thanks Mott, we're good. And thank you for getting it to us." Bart was about to hang up when Caradoc waved at him and reached for the phone.

"Hold on, Mott. I need you to increase the security on the house and perimeter. Don't go out unless you absolutely have to." He looked over to Reece. "Someone was asking about you and you might be a target. I don't think they know where my house is, but stay safe." Then he rattled off a series of numbers, letters, and what seemed like random sounds and hung up the call.

"Good thinking. It could have been something from Nix, or someone else. But someone definitely is after Mott," Aisling said.

"And didn't know where Caradoc's house is." Reece went back to the table after a final look at the board.

"Which is good," Bart said. "And even better that you are having him increase security. I know we're waiting for the new toys, but might not be a bad idea to have Stella check out Jones right off?" He shook Jones' off before he could complain. "You two were together. You were around at least two people who we know were replaced. And I am your boss."

Jones opened his mouth but shut it on the final one. That was the one that could not be disputed.

Stella motioned for Jones to take a seat. "It's a lot easier for you and me if you're closer to my height. Trust me." Her smile was broad but her eyes were serious.

Aisling was the closest to the two, so made sure she moved a bit closer. Her gun was back in her nightstand but hopefully she wouldn't need it.

Jones sat but didn't look happy. The other three came a bit closer as well.

"Seriously, I'm not going to grow an extra head or

anything." But even he seemed nervous. He did willingly hand over his gun.

"Considering that I had no idea there was something inside me, you never know." Reece turned to Aisling. "Anything beyond sounding weird and having a smile like Nix to look for?"

"Your eyes changed color. They were almost white with how light they were. That was the first indication I had that you were you—when they changed back to normal."

"Reece's eyes are light to begin with but everyone look for changes, they might be more subtle." Stella put one hand on Jones' face and the other held the red and orange sparking spell she'd had before when she'd searched Reece.

Aisling needed to ask her what that spell was when this was over. She and Stella were different types of magic users, but Aisling had never really tapped into her magic side beyond healing—maybe it was time. She'd see if Stella could train her after this was done. Harlie would be a good teacher, once he recovered. Except that he'd be looking at the deeper side of every spell, and Aisling wasn't a patient learner. Better to work with Stella.

Jones looked nervous as Stella peered at him closely and began her spell. Reece, Bart, and even Caradoc were nearby in case something went wrong. Reece and Bart had guns. Caradoc might prefer to play with his tech toys, but he was a powerful magic user if push came to shove.

"I think he's clean." The words had just left her mouth when Jones started twitching. "Or not. Damn them, they hid it too well. Anyone have a tranquilizer something that can keep him from fighting back, but conscious?"

Reece and Bart leapt forward and grabbed Jones' arms as he lunged to grab Stella.

Stella laughed and the spell ball in her hand crackled more. "Oh no, whoever you are. You don't get this one either. Tell us who did this." The spell ball turned redder and Jones shrunk back in pain.

"Not a tranq, but there is a healing spell I can try. I'm not strong in it though, it's tricky." Aisling stood closer to Jones. Like Reece, his eyes had gone lighter.

At nods from both Stella and Bart, Aisling took a deep breath and put her hands on either side of Jones' head. This spell was tricky and usually ended up with her knocking the suspect out. She'd stopped trying to do it on the job years ago. The turmoil in Jones' mind was impressive. The possession might have occurred a while ago, but his conscious awareness of it only hit when Stella prodded it. The search of Reece's mind happened after the possessing entity fled—this was still going on and it was a fight.

Aisling ignored the fight and focused on sleep and slowly added her spell. The effect, when it worked, would be like a strong sleeping pill. Before it actually put the person to sleep. In theory, it could calm difficult suspects but still keep them awake.

Jones started calming down, but the other being inside him still fought. Stella's spell was waiting for that and attacked the entity.

"Tell us who you are and how you got here." Stella's voice echoed from outside and within Jones' head.

The entity fought back, but a bit slipped up and Aisling could see who it was. Nix. The essence was so much like Nix, she almost released Jones' head.

"Destroy the possession." Aisling said it out loud and hoped Stella could hear her. She pushed through to completely knock out Jones.

"NO!" The shout came from inside, outside, and some-where beyond. And it was Nix's voice. He fought back. Aisling felt Jones' hand going back to where he kept his gun. When it wasn't there, he started trying to fight, but the others kept him pinned

Stella's spell pressed harder, and Aisling didn't let go on her end either. She grinned. "Get the hell out of his head." With magic that must have come from the repressed side of her skills, she flung Nix's essence out. At the same time, she found herself flung across the room.

Chapter Thirty-Three

N O HARLIE THIS TIME, JUST an overhelping burst of energy from Nix, Jones, or maybe herself sent her airborne and into the wall. Reece and Caradoc ran to her, Bart and Stella stayed with Jones.

"I'm fine, just might have overemphasized Nix getting the hell out of Jones." Aisling grimaced as they helped her up. "And yeah, it's him. No idea how he's doing it, but it's Nix doing these possessions. Probably why your smile looked like his when you came at me." She nodded to Reece.

"Might need someone taller to help move Jones to a sofa. He's sliding." Stella looked a bit haggard as she called over, her hair stuck up everywhere and her clothes were rumpled—but she was also grinning madly—she was enjoying this.

They got Jones on the sofa just as he started moving. He looked ready to wake up, his eyes fluttered, but then he gave a huge yawn, rolled over, and went to sleep.

Aisling shrugged. "I might have over done the spell I used. Never was great at that one. Surratt made me stop trying years ago."

"You got Jones' psyche out of the way, which helped a lot and kept him sane." Stella was checking his pulse, lifting his eyelids, and moving his arm around. "He's going to be fine. And I am glad for Mott's toy coming our way. If any of the rest of you are possessed, I don't want to know right now. That was way more excitement than I'm used to."

"Wouldn't being able to knock a suspect out like that

be handy?" Caradoc asked.

"In theory, but it means I'd have to be far too close to them, and the spell traps me in their head for a while. Even if I were good at it, it has limited applications. And I was never good at it." Aisling shuddered at the thought of the prior attempts. Other cops having to save her when the suspect didn't go under fast enough.

Bart looked down at Jones, but he was sleeping peacefully. "Maybe when this is over you could help agents who suffer from insomnia. For now, we need to figure out what in the hell is going on and how Nix is doing this."

"That was an extremely secure possession," Stella said as she sat. "And it felt unique. Too hard to explain at this point, but a possession that has jumped, and yes, they can do that, has a different feel. Even though Reece's possession had already been banished when I felt it and Jones' was right in the start of his—they were unique."

"But I felt Nix. He wasn't behind this?" Aisling hadn't sensed who had been taking over Reece, but he was too Nix-like for it not to have been him.

"He was. But he sent a possession to each of them separately."

"How?" Caradoc sounded more annoyed than anything else, but this was back out of his area of expertise. Which was making him cranky.

Stella shrugged. "How is he appearing in multiple places at the same time? I don't know that anyone has solved that issue. This could be tied to that."

A series of pieces slid into place in Aisling's head. "Could he have been pulled through the veil when he was sucked out of that tunnel in L.A.? And something changed in him?" She didn't like that idea any more than Nix just creating this stuff on his own. But there weren't a lot of options. Nix never had the type of magic skills for possessions, and she didn't know anyone who could duplicate themselves like he appeared to be doing.

"And he came back with super powers but the building is coming back in pieces?" Caradoc looked like he saw where she was going, but didn't like it.

"We have no idea what he came back as. If he even went." Aisling paced. "I think he planned everything and played us well. He set things up to happen; the bit in the forest, the iron death, the potential explosion of that drug. He was stopped each time. What if his contingency plans were actually part of his master plan and one was whatever busted through the veil?" That logic hurt her own head, but it also felt right.

Everyone looked at her in various degrees of *what the hell?*

"Each one easily leads to another if that one failed. They built on each other." Aisling went to the board, saved what they had so far, and on a new screen put what they knew of Nix's recent actions. "He grabbed Maeve because he was looking for a scroll." The narrowing of Reece's eyes reminded her she hadn't told him, Jones, or Bart about that part. "He wasn't even certain what he was looking for when he grabbed her and her stuff. But after we got Maeve back and took out his people, he fled. Then he set up trying to use the gnome tunnels under the city to disburse fatal amounts of iron death across L.A." She added that part to the board. "We stopped him. He fled again, then escaped by getting sucked up into a handy tunnel? And Area 42 goes missing at the same time?"

"It hasn't fared well for Area 42." Bart watched as she added things to the board.

"But if he *is* back, in multiple bodies, and can possess multiple people at the same time? It's worked well for him." Aisling frowned at the board as if that would make it point out what in the hell Nix was up to and how he was doing it. There was something to her theory, something valid. But there was also a lot missing.

"Not to mention, Nix was never one with the powers of possession. He's got some nasty magics, but possession was never connected to him." Bart scowled at the board.

"And you know if he had that power before, he would have used it." Aisling shook her head. "He had to have orchestrated being pulled through the veil. Either he killed millions and took over L.A., or he managed to get himself sucked through the veil. He probably didn't care which." She was making leaps that would make a professional hurdler green with envy. But it was right. She knew it. Just no idea the how or what of it. The why was simple with Nix—power. Everything he did was for more power.

The room was silent, but the worst part was no one could object to her theories. Part of Aisling truly hoped she was wrong.

"Then he meant for Area 42's building to be pulled through the veil? Why? How did that help him?" Caradoc asked. His eyes lit up as he made a connection of some sort. "Or it was a reaction to what he did?" He quickly saved Aisling's screen and started an intricate diagram on a new one. "All actions have to have opposite and equal reactions, right?" He circled a badly drawn tunnel and labeled it Nix. Then a building structure as 42. The drawings weren't great, but the representative distance between them was exact. At least with the detail and calculations he scribbled alongside, Aisling assumed it was exact.

"Area 42's building was pulled through the veil to counterbalance Nix being pulled through?" Now it was Reece's turn to scowl at the board. "They never taught us veil-physics in spy-school, but that doesn't seem right."

Something Harlie had said previously about oddly delayed spells and disrupted timing hit Aisling. "Maybe the events happened at different times? What if the Area

42 incident was already in motion, set up a while ago? And Nix knew of it and used when it happened to go through the veil?" She looked around but everyone was trying to digest her words—they really needed Harlie. "Think about it, everyone determined that Nix had to have somehow built up an immunity to iron death. But if the mass of it in that tunnel had exploded as he'd planned, no immunity could have protected him. He'd be dead like the rest of us." She paused. "Unless he was on the other side of the veil."

"Damn. I think that just added about ten more layers to our problems, but that might make sense." Reece ran his fingers through his hair. "I have no idea how any of that would work."

"Harlie had mentioned the time displacement spells a while ago. Something about a huge spell that had been hidden or corrupted somehow?" Caradoc shook his head. "While it did seem interesting at the time, we never asked him more about it."

Stella quietly nodded to herself. "Yes, that could happen. It would take a magic user of insane power though. The High Council forbade those types of spells because of the havoc they could cause."

Aisling and Caradoc shared a look.

"What if the person behind it was a member of the High Council? A very high, powerful, and psychotic one?" Aisling felt sick to her stomach.

"Your mother? Why would she, or anyone of the Council, push back a spell reaction? One that might or might not have been directly connected to Area 42?" Reece now got up and paced. He was smart, but usually let the brainiacs take over. "What if she, or someone with her, pushed back a huge spell years ago. Then they also wanted to get rid of Area 42 for some reason, so tied some part of the impact from the displacement to the building. And Nix found out and used it."

"Why did I just get a nasty chill at your words?" Bart shook his head. "We're accusing the High Council of treason. If your mother did do it, there's no way the rest of the Council didn't know. Which implies the High King and Queen knew. And then, somehow Nix knew?"

"I know. I'm freaked out about what our mother might have done—but as much as I hate her, I just can't see her working with someone like Nix. He's a thug and she's a snob." Aisling had no idea what could have been such an issue that her mother would have used a push back spell. Or if she'd only done it once. There could be more time-delayed spell reactions out there hanging around, waiting. With potentially catastrophic results. That was a thought she was shoving aside for a few hundred years.

"You just shivered," Reece said.

"What if this wasn't the first time this has happened? We have no idea what spell reactions she'd pushed back or for how long. Harlie thought it was about two hundred years ago, but he was only going on a hunch. Why would she have let the reaction to the spell loose now, and who knows if she did more before?"

"Could this somehow be related to the vallenians?" Caradoc frowned and drummed his fingers on the table. He didn't look happy about their family connection either, but he might also have a point.

"Great. No answers, but lots more questions." Aisling added the vallenians to the board. "Maybe? They keep pulling in boxes of the first families after all. All of which have someone on the High Council."

"Then why haven't they been back, aside from their trip to the first building drop? And they didn't bring a box that time," Bart said.

Aisling lifted her necklace. "If they are going to keep bringing things like this, we don't need them back. So far it hasn't done much but help, I don't like being chained to a piece of jewelry with a mind of its own. It was obsessed with Reece when Nix was inside him."

"Go over to Jones and see what it does." Caradoc had been closest to him but stepped back. Jones was now lightly snoring.

Aisling walked over and at first the pendant did nothing, then it slowly tugged toward Jones, then dropped back. "Maybe it only works on people who still have a taint of possession in them? Can you sense anything in Jones now?"

Stella went over to him then shook her head. "No. But I would have been surprised if there was anything. You did a good job knocking the possession out of him."

Jones turned on his sofa. "Why are you all in my bedroom?" He opened his eyes, then closed them again. "Actually, why am I in the living room?"

Stella pulled up one of the dining chairs next to him and sat near his head. "What's the last thing you remember?"

"Sleeping. Then something about Reece being compromised. Then waking up here. Damn it; I was compromised too, wasn't I?"

"Yup. That's what it looks like." Reece stood behind Stella. "Aisling and Stella kicked Nix out but he got you too."

"So we're sure it's Nix?" Jones started to sit up but winced and rubbed his head. "I need something or my head will explode."

"Why is he sending them now if they can be removed so easily?" Caradoc brought Jones some aspirin and a glass of water.

"Speak for yourself. I don't think being thrown across the room should be considered easy," Aisling said. "But it could have been more difficult, so you may be right. And he gave up Reece without a direct intervention."

"He doesn't know what Stella can do. Yes, Aisling and her necklace did their part, but he isn't familiar with

Stella," Bart said. "He took out Harlie, counting on that loss to stop us."

Jones sat up to take the aspirin, but looked like he'd just come off a three-day drinking binge. "But why not just kill Harlie? Wouldn't that have been easier? Not that I want anyone to do that, obviously."

"Nix, or most likely whoever he's working for, wants him alive. For whatever reason," Reece said.

Chapter Thirty-Four

———◆———

"ANY CHANCE THAT THE CALL from our mother isn't related? Any chance at all? Because that's where my mind is going and I would rather be wrong." Aisling sat down as a nasty series of connections linked up in her head. "She calls to warn me against Harlie, right before a possession-controlled Reece comes at me. Nix would have needed to be working with someone on the Council to get the information about a pushed back spell." She stopped. Just couldn't say it out loud.

"You think she's working with Nix? You said she wouldn't be." Caradoc had been adding more doodles to his Nix-tunnel-Area 42 building image.

"I might have underestimated her, or Nix. They wouldn't be working together because they wanted to, but because they needed to. Or one of them has some blackmail over the other." Those two working together was almost worse than the veil weakening. Almost.

"I think at this point we have to assume everything is possible, no matter how far-fetched," Bart said. "I never got to meet your mother, but just by reputation and power alone, she's not someone I would suspect of working with Nix."

Jones sat up but still looked out of sorts. "Now what?"

"We're waiting for a delivery from Mott," Stella said. "I can't go through searching everyone for possession and then who would search me? I have a feeling we discussed it while you were a bit out of sorts."

"We need to get this possession bit taken care of and get out of here. The longer we sit, the more of a target we are." Reece got up and walked toward his bedroom.

"I know you were the first cleared. But I'd feel better if we all stayed in sight of each other until we get Mott's toy. Eat up, just don't leave this room." Bart sat back at the table and loaded a plate. Reece sat back down. "And moving forward, until we're certain everyone is clear, we might not want to discuss anything about the case."

Aisling bit back what she had been about to add, mainly the information about the scroll Nix might still be hunting for. Bart had a good point; there was no way to tell what information Nix had already gathered.

Everyone was lost in their own thoughts when a buzz came from the front door speaker. Bart answered. "Yes?"

"We have a delivery for you. Would you like me to send one of my people up, or do you want to come down?"

"I'll come…" He turned to everyone watching him. "I'll be waiting up here. This is one of your people, correct?"

"Yes, my assistant manager, and he took it directly from the mage-express courier. We take our security seriously. He will be there momentarily."

That was one thing about mage-express, it was expensive as hell, but it was the fastest way to get things sent anywhere in the world. Or so Aisling had heard. She never had anything to send that would be worth the cost of the service.

Bart turned to the rest with a shrug. "Almost forgot about us all sticking together. This is too cloak and daggery even for an old spook like me. Who wants to wait behind the door with a gun drawn?"

Reece got up the fastest. "I will."

The knock came a few moments later and Bart cracked the door open. To get to this level a person would need to have a special key card. But there was no way to know if Nix heard some of the information about Mott or not. Or how easily he could possess someone.

"Yes?" Bart had his foot braced against the door and Reece was out of sight behind it with his gun raised. The rest were ready but trying to look normal.

"A package for you from a Mr. Linklinsphere?"

Bart turned back to Caradoc. After a moment of confusion, he nodded. Must have been a nom de plume of Mott's but not one Caradoc was expecting.

"Thank you." Bart took the package, but didn't remove his foot from the door. Reece didn't step out from behind it until the door was shut and locked. Bart sat the box down in front of Caradoc.

"Mr. Linklinsphere? Wasn't that a cartoon character when we were kids?" It had taken Aisling a few moments to figure out why the odd name sounded familiar. Memory finally kicked in.

"Yes." Caradoc looked over the box before he opened it. It took him a while and the use of a small knife as Mott had it extremely well sealed. "Mott used it when we first started working together. He thought it was funny since that character was always anti-magic. He must have decided it needed to come out again." The packing inside was extensive and meant there was no way the item could have been jostled in the slightest. "This is typical Mott." Caradoc lifted the item out and started laughing. "I think this confirms he sent it and this is for Stella." He freed a small note from the round box and handed it to her.

Stella carefully opened it, then started laughing. "He wants more cookies."

"How does this work?" Reece and Jones were hovering over the table.

Caradoc held it up, turned it over, and frowned at it.

"He added that you just need to flick the switch on the rim. The person holding it will be scanned for possession." Stella laughed again. "He added that you never believe when things are easy."

Caradoc lifted an eyebrow but then did what Mott said. The box whirled a bit, the lid opened, and a bright light smacked Caradoc in the face. "Damn it!" He hung onto the box, but barely.

"Keep your eyes open. It won't hurt you." Stella either recognized what the small machine was doing or there was more in her letter from Mott.

After another few moments, the light went out and Mott's voice came out of the box. "Clear, there is no possession here." It was definitely Mott's voice but it was low, menacing, and had a slight growl. The lid closed.

"Was he trying to sound scary?" Aisling recognized Mott's voice, but it sounded like it came from an old-time monster movie.

"Yes. He used to do that when he first started working for me too. I had him take it out of anything he did for me, but this was his own toy." Caradoc handed the box to Stella.

She put down her letter and triggered the rim. Same light, same weird Mott-spooky voice. No possession. Aisling and Bart both showed clear as well.

Reece took it and shrugged. "Can't hurt, right? And this way we can see what it does after someone has been possessed." He triggered the process. This time the light started bright white, then changed to a light green. "Former possession detected. Clear now." Mott's voice wasn't attempting to be scary on this recording.

Jones took it and had the same results as Reece.

Stella looked in the box the thing had come in. "There should be another envelope with my…ha!" She pulled out a cardboard tube then gently emptied the contents onto a clean napkin. Silvery shards, no more than a quarter inch long glinted on the fabric. Stella closed her eyes and held one hand over them. "That boy gets a lot of cookies." She opened her eyes. "These will tell us if someone has been possessed, or repossessed. I'm going to magically implant them into each of us." One of the shards raised into the air and slipped into her cheek. It glowed a soft gold color then vanished. "If it turns red or orange, the person has been compromised. The face isn't the best place, but harder to hide if something happens to one of us."

Aisling stepped forward and Stella sent one into her. She rubbed her face at the slight sting. "There's no way to prevent Nix from getting to us? Knowing he has taken over someone is better than not knowing, but stopping it would be even better."

Caradoc held still as the sliver went into his face then nodded. "Agreed, but not even this technology can do that. And it, along with Mott's box, is way ahead of any-thing else. Possession hasn't been used in hundreds of years."

"Although your brother might have been able to find a way." Reece shook his head.

"Yup, if anyone could have, it would have been Har-lie. Which is why our mother took him out and tried to convince me he's been compromised." Aisling got to her feet. There was no way anyone else could have done what was done to Harlie. It was either her or her work-ing with someone else. "We can leave after this, right? I think leaving here quickly would be a good idea."

A knock came at the door and everyone looked to Bart.

"No one else should be up here unless they cleared them through the lobby." Bart walked to the door and looked through the peek-hole. "All I can see is the top of someone's head. Who is it?" He raised his voice. Another knocking sound, but there was no other response. He called down to the front desk, but there was no answer.

"Damn it. This is the only way out, isn't it?" Jones had his gun out and so did Reece.

The hairs on the back of Aisling's neck stood up. There

was something extremely wrong.

"Yes. I thought we'd be safe here, so wasn't worried about it. Dumbass mistake." Bart nodded to Reece to come behind the door and Jones to stand in front of it with his gun raised. Stella, Aisling, and even Caradoc all had spells at the ready.

Bart opened the door and jumped back as a body fell at his feet.

Jones and Bart turned the body over and Reece stepped out from behind the door to cover them.

"It's the assistant manager. He's been beaten and his neck broken." Bart patted him down. "No explosives planted on him, but someone wanted to make a point." The bloody trail lead from the elevator but there was no one else in the entranceway.

"Jones and I will go check the lobby; I recommend everyone else stay here until we know what's going on."

Caradoc stepped forward. "And me. Sorry, too many weird magic things, and I may not like to use it much, but I can still fling a mean spell."

"And all of us. Didn't we just say that for now we stick together?" Aisling ran into her room and grabbed her bags.

Reece's forehead crinkled a bit and he shook his head. "I think we need to get the hell out of here, now." He gave a meaningful look to Aisling when she came back into the living room—he sensed something but couldn't explain it to Bart.

"I agree, we need to leave now. Together." Aisling stepped to the door and dropped her bags.

Sticking around to find out wasn't Bart's normal MO, but he was rattled like the rest of them. Didn't matter that both common sense and the feeling in her gut were saying to get out now. Even before whatever precog bit started kicking around Reece's head.

Bart went for his room. "Fine, everyone grab their stuff.

We'll need to take the stairs down."

They made their way to the stairwell. Bart checked first then went down. After he'd gotten a few steps, Stella followed, then Jones, Caradoc, Reece, and Aisling. Reece had wanted to bring up the rear, but Aisling pointed out that the magic users needed to be spread out. He wasn't happy but followed Caradoc.

They stayed silent as they went down the flights with either guns or magic at the ready. Or both in Aisling's case. Carrying her bags draped over her wasn't great for mobility, yet she needed her hands free. She wasn't ready to start relying on her magic to defend her or anyone else, but better to be prepared in case it was needed. Having access to more power was great, but so far it wasn't helping her much. Collapsing while using a spell in the middle of a fight was the fastest way to be killed.

Aisling kept feeling like there was someone behind her, but each time she turned there was no one. Spread out this way going down the stairs would make it safer against anyone coming out of one of the floors, but being the last meant she needed to make sure no one came out after them. She slowed down as the feeling continued. Reece looked back but she waved him on. There was no one behind her, yet the feeling persisted.

She approached the first floor, in the U.K. that meant the one right before the ground floor. The door rattled when she was a few steps away from it, so she stopped and held her gun trained on the space where the door would open. A chill went through her as the doors above her blew out with a bang.

CHAPTER THIRTY-FIVE

THE DOORS SLAMMING OPEN SOUNDED like some massive pressure was blowing them outward. As if the floors were collapsing. The crashing sound rattled the entire stairwell, and pushed Aisling to scramble down the stairs faster. The building started shaking as more floors pancaked to the one below.

Reece and the others waited at the bottom but she motioned at them to keep going. The others moved back and Aisling was tossed through the doorway as the floors above her collapsed. She scrambled to her feet and ran out of the stairwell.

The front lobby was a murder scene; at least three people were lying in pools of their own blood. But Aisling knew there wasn't time to get information as to who or what killed them. The building was crashing down on itself. Floor by floor was collapsing under some great weight. Reece and Jones had the front door open for people to escape and Bart was out in the street waving people away from the building.

"What in the hell just happened?" Aisling kept running to a small park across the street. She bent over and forced herself to breathe slowly, the dust and debris from the collapsing floors was choking her. She dropped her bags and put away her gun. A plume of dust rose high over the remains of the building. All around her, people who'd managed to get out, stood in shock.

Once her breathing was under control, she dropped into cop mode. Her L.A. police tat wouldn't mean a thing here, but attitude and confidence often did. She worked with the others to keep onlookers across the street as the apartment building settled.

Bart started swearing first once the dust cleared but was joined by everyone else. A huge piece of the missing Area 42 building had come down directly atop the apartment building and ridden it down to the ground. There was no way to tell who, aside from the assistant manager, had been murdered, and who had died in the destruction. A few shocked tenants were on the grass, but there could have been dozens of people in there when the collapse happened.

Sirens echoed in the distance and emergency crews came racing in. Aisling looked at the wreckage. She wasn't sure what they could do. Normally in a building collapse there would be searches for survivors, but there wasn't enough of the original building for anyone to have survived the collapse.

Bart looked around then dropped his voice low. "This might be a good time for you all to take off. I'll handle the officials, and will do what I can concerning our newest chunk of Area 42's building. But I don't want you to be bogged down here. And since the murders were most likely directed at us—getting out of here is best."

"I'm going back to London to pick up Maeve, check on Harlie, and see what other disasters have gone on." Aisling watched as more vehicles pulled in. Two seers came out of one truck and approached the building. Or rather, buildings. They kept walking around but neither looked like they sensed anything living.

"I'm not feeling anything odd about this chunk of building. There isn't any activity within it. Nor any goo." Caradoc didn't have any gizmo's out; he was using his magic. He'd probably used more magic in the past two months than he had in the previous five years. "I think I'll go to London as well. We need Harlie back. If it is our mother behind what happened to him, knowing that might help Aisling and I break through to him."

Stella watched the activity around the buildings. "I'll go on to Noth. I have an idea what Harlie was looking for, at least what he indicated he was looking for before we left L.A." She turned to Jones and Reece. "Boys?"

"It's up to our boss." Jones gave Bart a nod. He had a point; Bart was technically all of their boss. He seemed to forget it more than the others.

"What?" He'd been focusing on the emergency crews. "I pretty much figured you'd sort yourselves out. You all have done well free ranging before from what I've read. But yes, having people go to Noth now would be a good idea. See what you can find out about it. I'll be in touch." He nodded to them, then stalked over to a large black car.

"I'll get us train tickets back to London." Caradoc turned to the others. "You two going with Stella? Not sure where the closest train stop to Noth is."

"I'll go with you and pick up our tickets." Jones had been watching Reece but at his nod followed Caradoc.

Stella roamed over to the edge of the park and to watch the containment.

Which left Aisling and Reece.

"I need to go to Noth."

"I need to go to London." She smiled. "We'll join you up there."

He stared at her for a few moments. "I still wish I knew."

She stepped forward and hugged him. "Me too. This feels right. But sirens…"

"I know. Trust me, I know. I'm the one who loses if there is some DNA weirdness of mine affecting you. My feelings are real."

"Unless because you're a breed, and shouldn't have powers at all, they've mutated inside you and affect you as well." She hadn't said to him before this, but it had been there lurking in her mind. Both of their emotions could be messing with them because of Reece's family line.

He pulled back and looked down at her. "Is that what's wrong? You think *my* feelings aren't real? Sirens affect others, not themselves."

She shrugged. "Possibly? You have to admit, you're a bit of a magic freak. Who knows what your magic is doing?"

"I don't have magic. I have the ability to swim well, am precog to psychic events sometimes, and I know how I feel about you." He started to lean forward, but pulled back.

"I see it in your eyes, you're really not sure. That's okay, I'll wait." He gave an odd smile then went to watch the cordoning off of the collapsed building.

"Still messing with your head?" Stella was far too good at sneaking up.

"Yes. But on our list of problems, the weirdness between Reece and I is low on the urgency level." She checked everything in her pack, mostly that the spelled charging box was still secure, then put it back on and pulled the larger bag with the long strap back across her body. She wanted to be as hands free as possible.

"This scroll you mentioned?" Stella kept looking at the flattened building as she spoke.

"Yes. Long story, but Nix wants it, even though he might not know what it is he wants. He knows it's an item of power. Maeve was working on learning ancient elvish so she can translate it."

Stella turned to her. "Does she know what's on it? The real ancient scrolls shouldn't be messed with. Another bad habit of my late aunt." She paused. "Can't Harlie read ancient elvish?

"Not sure what it is. That's part of the problem. It looks old though, really old. He can, but it will only allow the person it was given to the ability to translate it. She even tried giving it to Harlie, but the scroll wouldn't let him read it."

Bart came jogging back and yelled for Reece to join

them.

"I have some reports on new issues in London. I already told Caradoc, but I'm swapping him and Larkin. I need an Area 42 agent in London." He held up his hand before anyone could say anything. "Yes, you're onboard as a consultant, but Larkin will carry more weight and I need him to look into things you might have trouble gaining access to."

Reece's face showed no emotion, but after their last conversation there were probably many going on. Bart briefed them on some of the issues to look for in London.

Caradoc and Jones came back a few minutes later.

"Might take a few stops for us three, getting to Noth isn't easy. But we're all booked. Aisling and Larkin are booked for London. Train leaves in an hour."

Bart said his good-byes and returned to the black truck.

Aisling and Reece started walking to the train station.

"Are you okay with this?" He kept looking ahead but there was uncertainty in his voice.

"I think we have to put everything aside at this point. Good or bad." She had a lot of thoughts running in her head that were not related to any of the crap going on. But she wasn't going to share them with him. "Let's pick up Maeve, see what's wrong down there, then check on Harlie and hope he's awake." She paused, but better he found out now. "Harlie was looking into whether your siren blood was making an impact on us. We should have told you, but…"

"But you wanted to find out what you're dealing with. I get it. Don't like it, but I get it." They'd been walking briskly, they could see the station, when he suddenly stopped and stared ahead.

"What?" Aisling looked but she couldn't see anything out of the ordinary.

"I just…it's…" Reece blinked a few times, grabbed his

head, then dropped where he stood.

Aisling saw at least three people on the station platforms also drop. "Damn it." She lifted his head up gently and first checked for any sign of possession from Stella's sliver. Nothing showed on his face. His breathing was rapid, his eyelids fluttering, and he was twitching. Another precog attack. "Reece? Can you hear me?"

Last time this happened he'd come out of it on his own, but he wasn't waking up this time. Judging by the yells for help coming from the platforms, the others who were struck down weren't responding either. Caradoc, Jones, and Stella would be coming this way at some point, but she didn't want to wait if there was something seriously wrong.

She took a deep breath, put her hands on either side of his head, and went into healing mode. The chaos of his mind almost pushed her back out. It didn't seem to be of his own making, but some elements felt like him. Like the ones fighting back against whatever was attacking him. And this was an attack. The prior times had been more an intrusion of something along the psychic energies that lived in the precogs. At least that was how Harlie had explained it to her.

Something else might have pushed open the door, but someone or something was going after Reece's mind with the intention to kill. This was vicious. She pushed aside as much of the mayhem as she could; she needed to grab hold of part of him to use her healing magic.

She used herself. Whether true or not, right now they had feelings for each other—and that was something she could hang onto. Grasping at his feelings for her, she pushed back at whatever was attacking his mind. The response was brutal and she could almost see claws raking into Reece's mind. She pushed back as hard as she could, but his breathing was slowing down, his heartbeat barely there. Whatever was attacking him was winning, and she couldn't stop it.

She tried coming at the fight from different angles, anything to get traction against whatever was killing Reece. Finally, she started to get the upper hand. His breathing steadied and the maelstrom in his mind eased up.

"How?"

That wasn't Reece's voice in her head—surprisingly not Nix's either as that was who she'd assumed was behind this. This voice was like nothing she'd ever heard before: deep, almost otherworldly, raspy, as if that single word had cost it much.

"You can't have him. I'm protecting him. You can't stay within him, or in any others." She tried to sound fierce, but something deep in that voice scared the hell out of her. Her increased healing magic flared up again and she fought to keep it under control.

"You died. You are dead."

Those words weren't expected, but there was a horrible truth behind them. This being knew who she was and knew that she was dead. Something to add to the pile of not-dealing-with-now and she shoved the terror in her head into a corner of her mind. Reece was stronger, but still felt like he could slip away from her at any moment.

"I'm *alive*. And I'm telling you to leave all the people you are attacking. Now." The newly tapped into magic fought harder to be released. But she couldn't take a chance it would overwhelm her. If she couldn't stop the connection, she would keep healing Reece until both of them died.

"Dead. We felt it. Dead."

Aisling kept enough healing available to help Reece fight against what was in his mind, but locked down the rest of it. "Not dead. Leave." An image of what the voice intended to do with Reece and the others slammed into her. They would be zombies to allow entry into this world. A sharp coldness ran along her neck. For a moment she feared it was killing her too. Then the chilling cold settled down to a gentle coolness.

The pendant.

"Take that off. Not yours." A trace of something new, fear maybe, lingered in the voice now.

That just won points for the pendant. Anything that this scary disembodied voice didn't like was good in her book.

"Not on your life." She let as much of her magic loose as she dared but directed it at the voice, not Reece.

"Not alive…" The voice faded and she couldn't tell if it was talking about itself or her. The pressure on Reece's mind stopped. His heartbeat grew stronger and his breathing normalized.

Aisling pulled herself free of his mind just as his eyes opened.

"That was not fun. However," he reached up and pulled her down to him. The kiss was quick but intense. Aisling found herself responding with the same intensity. He dropped back. "You saved my life. Thank you."

Aisling still wanted to be sure about him, but that kiss did not suck. Aside from being too short and while they were both sitting on a sidewalk. Her lips tingled as she shared a smile with him. Her hormones definitely weren't having a problem with any supposed magic mojo.

She shook her head. "Did you also hear that apparently, I'm dead? Or at least died at some point and should still be dead?" She helped him to his feet, but he didn't seem worse for almost dying himself.

"I missed that part. What was it that attacked me and said you were dead?"

"Aside from terrifying, I have no idea what it was." She rubbed her arms at the chill that hit just thinking of that voice. "It was something from beyond the veil that wanted to use you and other precogs as a gateway here. It would have killed you all and created a chain of some sort into this world—using your bodies. Then it got freaked out about my being alive once it realized who I was. Oh, and it didn't like the pendant either." She held it up but it felt normal now. She couldn't explain how she knew that thing had been from beyond the veil—she just did. Her soul felt it.

It looked like the attack on the other precogs in the area had stopped as well. People who had collapsed on the platforms were getting to their feet. Hopefully, unlike Reece, they wouldn't know how close they had been to dying.

"If you're okay now, we can try and sort it out on the train." Reece dusted himself off and started toward the station.

Aisling followed. She'd managed to heal without losing herself, so that was good. But the being dead thing hit her hard. There was a tiny corner of her being that believed the voice. She had died. How, why, and when were complete mysteries—ones she wasn't sure she wanted solved.

CHAPTER THIRTY-SIX

REECE TURNED TO ASK SOMETHING, then stopped. "Are you sure you're okay? You look like you saw a ghost. You know that thing that tried to kill me would have said anything to stop you, right? Lies work."

She forced a smile. She wasn't ready to admit the feelings she had about the voice telling the truth. "I'm sure that's it. I think the healing just took a bit more out of me than I expected."

They boarded the train and claimed seats facing each other—better to watch both ends. Paranoia was more his lifestyle than hers, but she was adapting to it.

"The voice you heard; it wasn't Nix?"

"Nope. It didn't even sound like something from this world. Voice was lower than the roughest giant or trolls I'd ever heard. And it didn't seem used to words, they came out harshly." She rubbed her arms as a chill ran through her. "I think whatever it is, it doesn't communicate with our type on a regular basis. But it was upset about the pendant. Since a vallenian was the one who put it on me, I think we can count them out as the ones who attacked you." She was going to keep pushing aside the fact that a murdering voice from beyond the veil thought she was dead. At least until she could find a rational way to deal with it. Maybe in a few hundred years or so.

Reece rubbed his head. "I think I'm beginning to feel how close to dying I was. When you first pulled me out, it wasn't bad, but now there's almost an echo of the pain."

Aisling looked around the train, it was a fairly full car and two others, a male and female elf were also rubbing their heads. "Damn it. Come to my side so I can check you without suspicions." It could be a precog reaction, residue from what just happened. If the others were like Reece, they had been minutes away from dying, whether they knew it or not.

Or this was the start of a second attack.

Reece looked ready to shake her off, then switched to her side once she moved to the window and glared at him.

"You were one of those kids who never admitted when he was sick, weren't you?" She didn't wait for an answer, just placed her right arm around his neck in a friendly manner and twisted her hand to touch the side of his head. She leaned into his shoulder so it would be a little less odd looking. His head was much better this time around and her healing magic found nothing to heal.

"You're clear. But you need to tell me if anything weird happens." She turned him to face her. "Anything. I'm serious, Reece. It's not just you, whatever was after you would have killed thousands of precogs and would have gained a foothold into this world. There are reasons the fey fled the world beyond the veil, and I think one of those is what went after you."

He sighed, then gave a slow nod. He might be loose about his own living and dying, but he'd devoted his life to saving others. "Do you think the prior attacks on precogs were from them as well?"

"I don't know. I do know that Harlie said the veil opening was causing the disruptions. Whatever was after you might have been testing things during those times, or those instances were unrelated to this one."

"I still have trouble believing the vallenians aren't behind this. I never got all the scary stories you full fey did growing up, but my mother would tell my brother and I some of them. Scared the crap out of me."

"I didn't even know you had a brother. I thought you

were an only child." He'd never spoken much about his family, but then, aside from Caradoc and Harlie, she didn't talk about her siblings either.

"Had. He vanished when we were in our early twenties. Two years older than me. Named Tomas." He paused. "We had been close growing up, then drifted apart as I went into law enforcement. He preferred the other side."

"He's still alive?" She watched as he carefully schooled his emotions.

"No idea. After all these years and no contact from him to me or our family, I've found it's easier to think of him as gone."

Reece had been Area 42 for a long time and they had an insane number of resources. "Did you ever search for him?" She had a hard time believing that if his brother were alive, he couldn't find him.

"I found him once. Three years after he took off. He was living in Chile on a farm, running drugs. He made it clear he didn't want to see me. I left and never looked again." There was pain in his voice, but he was trying to ignore it.

"I am sorry that you lost him." Aisling took his hand and squeezed it. "I don't like trying to one-up someone, but my mother might be trying to rule the world. And aside from Caradoc and Harlie, my siblings are helping her. I think we both got screwed on the family front."

He squeezed back and didn't let go. "Agreed. My parents don't even acknowledge him anymore. It's as if I was always an only child. Which is weird. He was a good guy once." He nodded. "Anything else about you being dead?" He'd opened up a lot for him, but clearly didn't feel comfortable about going further.

"Aside from the fact that voice was certain I was? Not you had been dead, but you *are* dead. That I obviously wasn't dead stunned whoever they were and I think helped the pendant chase them off. I'm not going to lie, they almost destroyed you and the others they attacked. If they hadn't backed off on their own, I might not have been able to save any of you."

"For which I am very grateful and I'm sure the others would be if they knew. But there was never a near death experience as a kid? Anything?"

"No, not that I know of. I'll call Caradoc when we get to London and I can have some privacy, but he didn't even realize I'd been taken to Nepal to see Harlie when I was five. I have a feeling if our mother didn't want anyone to know things that happened, they didn't."

"Once we're in London, call Stella too. She might not be as strong as Harlie, but she has a few more abilities than she ever let on."

Aisling nodded. "And possibly family connections." She quickly told him about Stella's late aunt and what she'd believed. And that Stella now felt differently about her death.

"That's interesting and not in a good way. The stories of when the fey came here never implied anything of leaving other fey behind. But if true, if there were people left behind on purpose—ones who should have been brought over, that's scary."

"Especially if the veil is getting thinner, and with the stuff that keeps coming out from beyond the veil, I'd say that's a given." Aisling watched the countryside race by as they got out of town.

"Excuse me. Excuse me." The voice was slurred but still familiar as it came from behind them. A man was staggering down the aisle and apologizing as he weaved from side to side. He had his head down, but the short red hair and pointed ears sent a chill down Aisling's back. She nudged Reece and tilted her head back. The man had stopped, still sounding and acting drunk, but now he was talking to himself.

"Nix?" Reece kept his voice low. At Aisling's nod, he

got up into the aisle and stepped toward the man.

"Slippery, slip, slip. Penalties must be paid." The voice could have been Nix's but sounded oddly distorted. He looked up and smiled at Reece. "Dead, dead, dead. Most be dead. Can't work if not dead." Nix started shaking and an image hit Aisling. Caradoc facing a shaking Nix clone. That was a clone and he was about to explode.

"Get him off the train! Everyone else go to the next car!" She yelled but most everyone looked at her and didn't move. "Undercover agent! Move now!" Technically she wasn't any sort of British agent, but right now they needed to get the hell out.

Reece tackled the Nix clone then pulled back. "He's squishy." Rivulets of familiar green goo started leaking out of Nix and Reece scrambled backwards.

Aisling pushed the other people in the car toward the connection to the forward one. She couldn't help them more than that, she needed to help Reece get this clone off the train before it exploded. It had already lasted longer than the one that had faced Caradoc.

"Damn it, what is up with that goo? How can we get him off this car?" Aisling pulled Reece further away as the goo oozed toward them. The image of the agents' skeletons from L.A. came to mind.

"We're the second to the last car, but I don't want him to get back there either."

"Do you have any exploding gadgets? If we can separate this car from the main train and that final car, we can at least give us more time to get rid of that thing." Aisling looked at the connector to the rest of the train. They'd need to push people even further back, but that goo could destroy everyone if they didn't cut it off.

"Only three small poppers. Mostly good for blowing doors. Not sure one could blow the connectors." Reece held out three small rectangles.

The Nix clone was still muttering to himself, seemingly unaware of the green goo leaking out of him.

"Give me one, I'll do what I can to magically enhance it, and try to get those people away from the connector. Can you get past our friend to that last car?" She and Reece would still be with the clone, but everyone else should be safe.

He handed her a small gray rectangle. "Just place it, enhance what you can, and get back on this side. I should be able to disconnect the last car with two of these. And I'm agile, I can climb over the seats." He flashed her a grin and demonstrated. For a tall guy, he moved well over the seats.

Aisling ran to the forward car and flung open both doors. "There's a dangerous contagion, I need you all to move as far from here as you can and brace yourselves. We need to separate that car." Surprisingly, everyone crowded out of the way, many even going into the next car up. Aisling darted back and placed the small explosive. She added a spell of healing. There was nothing to heal in the inanimate explosive, but it felt like it had more energy. She set it for three seconds and darted back into the car with the clone.

Chapter Thirty-Seven

———

REECE WAS JUST SHUTTING THE other set of doors when she ran in. "Hang on to something!" He threw himself across a row of seats and she did the same. The explosions weren't huge but they sounded that way in the car. Smoke billowed into the car, but also from the rest of the train pulling away. Most of the damage appeared to be on this end though as the door between cars was completely blown off.

Aisling looked up from the row she'd dove into. They had been going up an incline, and it looked like the car behind them was dropping back as well.

The Nix clone was now drooling green goo and stumbling about like a zombie. She just wished killing this one would destroy all of them.

"What next?" Reece was closer to the back of the car but was already working his way back to her,

She nodded to the gaping hole where the door had been. "Go outside and hope it follows us?" Aisling wouldn't mind if it stayed here, but the other car wasn't that far behind. It hadn't looked like there were that many people in it but they needed time to get them away.

"Best idea." Reece climbed over the final rows of seats, avoiding the oozing clone. They climbed out of the car and ran to the last one.

Aisling sighed as they got outside. They were in a large open field with no houses or businesses nearby. At least that was something. As long as they could stop the clone from getting out. She no longer thought he was going to explode, but that goo of his could kill.

There were only six people in the last car, all shaken but no serious injuries.

"What the hell did you do, mate? You blew up the train?" An older fey yelled out as soon as Reece appeared.

"I'm with Interpol and an explosive gas was released in the car ahead of you." Reece adopted a British accent, not heavy and not too posh, but enough to sound legit. "We might have saved your lives. But you need to get far from here before it blows."

That was it, all six scrambled for the door. One was a young male pixie flyer. "I'll go get help, the rest of you head that way. I'll send the police to you." He pointed toward some very distant houses. At least that would keep everyone far from these cars. With a nod to both Reece and Aisling, the group started running the direction the flyer had pointed toward and he lifted up and flew off.

"That's great, but now what?" Aisling looked at the car they'd been in. "That thing isn't coming out and the only way the goo has been stopped before was with heavy explosions…or an electrical charge. The airport attack was stopped when it hit the electrical panel for the boarding screen." Trains were full of magically enhanced and protected electrical parts. She smiled.

Reece grinned back as they ran to their car. "This car should have enough electrical juice to fry that stuff." He looked at the passengers still running across the field. The flyer was long out of sight. "I want to wait until they're further out, but before our winged friend brings the police in."

"How are you going to explain you're not British? Or is your Interpol identity from here?"

"It's under my name, my real one, so it's not British. But I figured they'd respond better to that." He finally turned back from watching the former passengers running; they were little more than specks now. "We work together pretty damn well." That smile was killer.

Aisling sighed. "That isn't the problem—never was. But you're right, we do. Now let's go fry Nix. Gods I wish I knew where these things were coming from." It felt good to be back to working with Reece, she just wasn't sure how she needed to handle it.

They looked into the open doorway of their car. The Nix clone was half the clone he used to be. The goo was eating away at the seats, frame, and anything else it could reach. Aisling grabbed her pack and slung it on her back. Reece tore apart a few panels at the entrance and came across a large enough collection of wires. With some twisting, turning, and fancy knife work he managed to get a section of electrical wire an inch away from the goo.

"You are so lucky there is magic shielding on all the electrical wires on these trains or you'd be crispy." Aisling had seen more than a few sparks go up even with the shielding. While her magic would help him if he did get toasted, she couldn't increase the already in place shielding.

"I know." He grinned and moved the wire a bit closer down toward the goo. "Be ready to dive out the second I yell. We have no idea what will happen when this hits that goo."

Aisling did better than getting ready, she grabbed Reece with one arm around his waist. "I move faster than you, remember? If that backlashes, and you can't get clear, you're dead." She could fling them out faster than anyone could see.

The goo oozed to the wire. The Nix clone was down to just a head, but while there hadn't been much life behind those eyes before, there was nothing now.

Aisling held her breath as an electrical spark flashed and Reece yelled. She pulled herself and Reece out of the train car and ran as fast as she could.

"I think we can stop now," Reece grunted as he was bounced around as she ran.

Aisling stopped, dropped him to the ground, and then bent over to catch her breath. "You're a hell of a lot heavier than you look."

He got up and dusted himself off. "Clean living." He grinned, then frowned. "I would have thought there would have been an explosion by now."

Aisling shook her head. The scene looked like nothing had happened. Just two disconnected train cars sitting a few feet from each other in a field. "I thought so too or I wouldn't have run so far. Damn it, I saw the spark."

They started trudging back, but Aisling had no idea what else they could try. Maybe just keep everyone away from it until Area 42 personnel could come in and secure it. Unless the London Area 42 was completely compromised. Maybe she could catch Caradoc, Jones, and Stella before they left for Noth. She was still trying to sort it out when the train car exploded.

Reece dove to cover her as debris flew in the air. Only a small amount made it out to them, but the explosion was impressive. The goo was fried completely, it looked like tiny pieces of dark green glass had been flung about.

"Thank you, but I think we're fine now." Aisling said from under Reece.

He scrambled to his feet. "The solidified goo is new." A piece had made it a few feet in front of them and he pushed at it with a stick. "Local office is going to hate us. They're going to have to cover this entire meadow and get all the pieces. In hazmat suits."

"It looks like stone. That hasn't happened before. Not even when Harlie crashed a car into it." They kept walking to what was left of the train car and were almost there when the sirens started. "You better go wave a badge and do some fancy talking. I'll call Bart while you deal with them."

Reece nodded and strode up to the arriving cops and fire engine.

Aisling called Bart.

"Did you two get lost already?" From the sounds in the background, he was still at the collapsed building site.

"No. But we kind of blew up a train." She quickly told him what happened as she watched Reece discussing a different version, whatever that was, with the officers. "We're going to need support and this entire area blocked off. There are three police cars and a fire engine here right now."

"Damn it. Okay, keep Larkin talking to them. I'm going to make calls and get someone I trust out there immediately. She's a flyer, her name is Narissa Jhali and has enough layers of rank to get everyone else to step back. Once she arrives, you and Larkin get the hell out of there. Get to London and find Maeve." He ended the call.

Aisling stayed back as Reece continued his discussion. She could only hear the tones of it, not the words, as she'd stepped some distance away to make her call. Reece was calm, everyone else was freaking out. With a sigh she walked forward.

"My partner, Aisling Danaan." Reece turned to her. "What did the chief say?"

"He needs everyone to back off until he can get someone here. This entire area is a crime scene and will need to be taped off, at least as far as that tree." She pointed just past where she and Reece had stopped.

"You're Interpol too?" One of the police stepped forward, obviously the highest ranking. The fire personnel were all staying back by their truck as nothing was burning.

"She works with us. Different agency, and not sharing which. You verified my badge, that's enough." Reece looked ready to go another round, but Aisling tapped his shoulder. A flyer was coming in for a landing. Tall and slender with deep green wings. And wearing a dark blue business suit. Impressive.

"The person we are waiting for is here. Bart sent her."

"Agent Larkin, Agent Danaan, good to meet you, not under these circumstances however. I'm Agent Jhali." She shook their hands then quickly turned to the police. "Thank you for your quick arrival." She flashed a badge that made the cop up front blanch even though Aisling couldn't see what it was. "If you could keep this entire area clear for at least a few days while we continue our investigation, that would be appreciated. We have already notified the train line and they will divert all trains from this section of track." She marched over to the fire crew and politely sent them on their way.

Aisling liked Agent Jhali.

The fire crew was driving off and the cops starting to establish the perimeter when Jhali turned back to Aisling and Reece. "Now then, please do call me Narissa. Have you looked inside yet?" She nodded to the train car. The walls were still mostly intact, the force of the explosion had gone up.

The three of them stepped forward to look. There were more of the green rock-like items here, still small, but very solid looking. Aisling was in the front so she started swearing first. Not only had the explosion gone up, it had also gone down. The tracks were twisted and the hole beneath them was deep.

"I'm surprised it hasn't collapsed." Narissa didn't step inside.

"I think what's left of the rails is holding it up." Reece took his look around and stepped back. "Have you been read in as to what happened in London? A large hole?"

"Aye. I was not happy to hear those hit London. The prior ones were all out in less populated areas. You think that's what happened here?"

Aisling walked around the car. "There's no other signs of ground issues. They couldn't have done whatever it was they did on a fast-moving train. Hopefully, that hole is just the result of the explosion."

Reece filled her in on the Nix clone, the goo, and how they stopped it. If Bart sent her, she could be trusted.

Narissa nodded. "Quick thinking. Damn, Nix was a pain in the arse before this. Now there are clones? Hate to say it, but I do hope I get to remove one or two of them. And I speak for most of the agents in London. That man is a bastard."

Aisling laughed. "There are many people who would agree on both those counts."

Reece darted into the train car and grabbed their luggage. Aisling had made certain to keep her pack with her, there was no way she was losing that scroll or her clan jewelry, but clothing hadn't been something to worry about when they were running away.

"Our bags were near the edge." He shrugged.

Narissa walked over to the luggage and closed her eyes. After standing there for a moment she opened them and smiled. "Just checking. There are no contaminants on them." She paused and stared at Aisling. "That is a most unique pendant. Is that trileium?"

Aisling reached up and tucked the pendant back into her shirt. That wasn't good that Harlie's spell on it was gone, nor that Narissa knew what the metal in it was. Few people who hadn't come directly from the old world would have a clue of the metal.

"Easy." Narissa flashed a smile and stepped back. "I won't tell anyone. I am far older than I admit to, and have heard tales of it. I won't ask how you came about it, nor tell anyone. But yes, do keep it hidden. These are strange times."

"Thank you. It's a family heirloom, but it's only a type of steel, not trileium." Aisling smiled. She knew Narissa probably didn't believe her, but for good or bad that pendant had exposed itself. She just hoped that Narissa was on the right side.

"I think we should be heading out." Reece lifted his bag and Aisling did the same. "Thank you for taking care of this, Narissa."

"I hate to say it, but if this is what you leave in your wake, I hope not to meet you two again." Her smile dropped. "But take care, this is a deadly time."

"I agree." Aisling nodded as she and Reece started off toward a row of houses in the same direction as the tracks.

"What happened to your pendant?"

Aisling pulled it back out. Yup, gold and trileium lines were back in place. "Damn it, I don't know. Harlie had a spell on it to keep the extra lines hidden. I hope this isn't a bad sign." She didn't like the pendant exposing itself, but the bigger issue was if something had happened to Harlie. She was pretty certain their mother was behind the collapse he had, but had she gone further?

"He's fine." Reece's voice cut into her thoughts. "One thing I have learned dealing with you three siblings, is that you are all far tougher than anyone would think. I know you hate your mother, and I don't blame you; I've never met the woman and I hate her too. But she made you all as tough as you are."

Aisling dropped the pendant back into her shirt. "I will never be grateful to her for anything. We wouldn't have had to be so strong, if she hadn't been so vile."

Chapter Thirty-Eight

———

THEY CONTINUED IN SILENCE, EACH chasing their own thoughts. The hamlet they came to did have a train station and luckily a train that had been stopped before it could continue northbound and was getting ready to head back south. It wasn't going directly into London; the track closure had messed up schedules. But it would get them closer and buses were taking people from its final stop into London. They quickly bought tickets and boarded. All around them were angry mutterings of who blew up the tracks.

Aisling listened carefully. Knowing what the average person thought could help down the line. So far everyone was determined it was an attack from the Human Liberation Front. That wasn't good. The HLF was a young group, only found in England so far. They mostly stuck to propaganda concerning the inequities between fey and humans and tried to fight for more studies into increasing human conception levels. As far as Aisling knew, they'd never done anything violent. And they hadn't in this case, but that wasn't anything they could share with the people around them.

A quick glance at Reece and his scowl told her he heard the same thing. They'd need to pass this to Bart so damage control could kick in. Just what they didn't need were rumors to make things worse.

The trip was non-eventful. Aisling had intended to call Maeve when they got to the station to give her a heads up on when they'd get to London, but a familiar face stood waiting on the platform once they got off the train.

"Aisling!" Maeve ran forward and engulfed her. Then grabbed Reece in a hug too. "Come on, I've got a car." She was smiling so hard that Aisling pulled back.

"How did you know where we'd be? Are you okay?" Damnit, she had Mott's box and a sliver with her in her small pack, but was it already too late? Maeve didn't smile like that unless she was drunk.

"I'm fine, just missed you both. Since this is where most of the London-bound trains are going, I took a guess." She dropped her voice to barely a whisper as she escorted them toward the car park. "We are being watched. Not sure who they are, but there are at least six scattered in the crowd. You have the box, right? Bart called ahead and told me. You'll see when you use Mott's gizmo, I'm me, but we need to get out of here."

Aisling glanced to Reece on the other side of Maeve and he nodded. He also had his gun hidden in his pocket now. Aisling mentally prepared to use her anti-healing magic if this wasn't really Maeve, and they got in the car.

Maeve shook her head as they pulled away. "I can see the gun, Reece, and I'm sure Aisling is armed physically or magically as well. I don't blame you. But I am me and there are…damn it. Whoever was watching us, they also had cars waiting. Two behind us. A delivery van and a white BMW. Just pulled out behind us."

Aisling looked back. Those two cars were behind them, but it was Maeve's word that they'd just pulled out. "Okay, so where are we going? Mind you, I'd like to stop before we get there." Not that there couldn't be people after them, but she needed to make sure Maeve hadn't been possessed.

Maeve started swearing and hit the gas.

"Whoever they are, they are definitely following us." Reece was watching Maeve and also keeping watch behind them. Aisling glanced back as well. This was only a two-lane road, but the two vehicles in question sped up and dodged around other cars to keep in range of them. Not a good sign.

"They might have followed me to the station. I was focusing on what happened to you, and they might have been more hidden about it than they are now. Damn it. Sloppy work on my part." She weaved around a slow-moving truck and dodged down a side road.

"Do you have a clue as to where this road goes?" Aisling didn't like the look of it—very rural. If it ended in a dead end, they were in for a firefight if those people behind them were really after them. Actually, considering the condition of the road, they had to be after them. She couldn't imagine too many people coming down this way, dead end or not.

"Nope, just wanted to see if they were following. Guess what? I was right." Another road, this one little more than a wide dirt road with stone walls along the edges, came up on the left side of the road and Maeve tore over to it at the last moment.

The BMW stayed on the prior road, but the delivery truck was still behind them, and picking up speed.

Reece swore. "I don't believe it. We thought they came out of their homeland before because of the iron death drug. That driver is Lazing, one I've seen before." The Lazing were a notorious east Asian gang, far older than any other criminal element. They rarely left their turf, but had shown up a few months ago when Nix started messing around in L.A.

"Why would they be after Maeve? Or us for that matter? What, they stay in the east for a few hundred years and now have decided they like traveling the world harassing people?" Aisling dug through her pack. Caradoc had given her a few gizmos. Maybe one of them… "Ha!" She pulled out two. One was a bug detector, the other, however, might work.

"I have one of Caradoc's mini mines. Not as impressive

as the one we blew up old town with, but if we're close enough, it should take out that truck. Or at least slow it down." She wasn't sure why in the hell the Lazing were showing up here, and she'd like to keep it that way. She turned to get in position to throw it out the window.

"How good is your aim?" Reece held out his hand. "I used to play baseball in college. Pitcher." He wiggled his fingers for her to hand it over.

"Fine. This will release the spikes that attach it to the target, they go off three seconds after you press it, so do it as you're releasing it." She handed it to him, then turned to Maeve. "Slow down, then punch the gas when Reece throws it. I have no idea how strong the explosive is, but we don't want to get caught in it."

Maeve hunched over the wheel, Reece rolled down his window, and Aisling hung on. Reece threw the bomb, Maeve punched the car, and they tore off. The explosion wasn't large and as the smoke cleared it was obvious the truck hadn't blown up, but the hood had flown into the air and the engine was smoking badly.

"Good shot! Ever think of playing cricket?" Maeve didn't slow down as the road curved. A familiar white BMW was coming right for them. At least they knew this wasn't a dead end.

Maeve veered to the right and drove through a field. The white car veered as well. Neither could go fast as there were holes in the ground everywhere. But it wasn't giving up.

"Okay, we'll do this another way." Reece rolled his window down again. "Can you turn on this side suddenly? Give me a chance for a shot?"

Maeve nodded and spun the steering wheel. Reece leaned out and fired but the car kept coming. He shot again, this time aiming lower and the car spun out as its tire blew. Aisling reached back and pulled Reece in before he fell out.

"They had a spell on the car—forgot to completely cover their tires though." He rolled up the window and slid back into his seat.

Maeve drove slowly until they hit the dirt road. Then she pulled over. "I think we're safe here and while I don't think we should hang around long, I want you both to believe it's me." She turned to Aisling and lifted her chin. "Do your worst."

Aisling laughed and took out the box. She held it up, it flashed Maeve in the eye, then Mott's voice came. "Not possessed."

Maeve sighed in relief. "I knew I felt like me, but you just never know, do you?"

"And now you get one of these." Aisling held up one of the slivers. This spell was a bit trickier, but after two tries the sliver vanished into Maeve's cheek.

She patted where it went in and looked in the rearview window. "Can't even tell it's there. I was going to take us right to see Harlie, but I think we need to stay low for a bit until we figure what the Lazing are after. I've got a flat in London where we can hide." She got onto the main motorway and headed into London.

"Any clue as to why the Lazing are chasing us? They weren't after us in L.A. before we left." They'd vanished after a helicopter of theirs was blown out of the sky over the ocean. Aisling wasn't sure if they were after Reece and her this time at all—they'd been following Maeve though.

"No idea," Reece said. "All my sources said they'd been in L.A. because of Nix, his power play to control the gangs, and the iron death drug. Those aren't here. It was thought they went back home."

"But Nix has been spotted all over the U.K.. And if they know Maeve, they know she is probably hunting him." Aisling watched her friend. "Either he still has something they want, or they just want to make sure he's dead this time."

"Then they would also probably know there seem to be a lot of Nix at the moment. As much as I would like to kill that bastard over and over, I can't just find him like that." Maeve snapped her fingers.

"But they might think you can, or that he'll find you," Reece said. "Or they might have been trying to grab you and hold you out as bait."

"Which means they were after something more than just the iron death drug when they were in L.A. Revenge would be one thing, especially if they felt he double-crossed them." Aisling wasn't sure how things were tying together and she didn't think she was going to be happy when she found out. "But the amount of people they had following us right now, not counting any others they had at the station, indicates more than just revenge."

"Damn it." Maeve rolled her eyes. "That could tie into the MI-6 issues. Some unknown sources were trying to find me, so MI-6 pulled me in. Then after asking questions about everything under the sun, they decided they didn't want me and let me go. I'm still supposed to report back anything I find, of course.".

"You think the Lazing were *asking* about you? A little direct for them. Not to mention I'd think MI-6 would be more concerned if the Lazing were involved than just asking some questions and then letting you go." Pieces weren't matching and from the look on Reece's face in the mirror, he felt the same.

Maeve sighed. "I have a confession; I am officially MI-6 but I'm a member of a smaller group. The Closen. Yes, like Area 42, they are mostly thought of as a myth, if thought of at all. I see that Aisling looks totally lost and Reece is trying to figure out what he's heard." She grinned.

"I can tell you both, you won't have heard much. Small, England only, not even in Scotland, Wales, or Ireland. We look at the weirder things than MI-6 wants to deal with.

When I wanted to leave MI-6 ten years ago, they offered me a position in this group. When I first got back here, I did meet with MI-6. They questioned me, but they knew Closen would be working with me."

"I've heard of them, but you're right, not much. For now, we're going to this flat to hide and wait? For what exactly?" Reece shook his head. "I get secret groups, trust me. But I don't know how much time we have. There are a lot of things going on beyond the parts of the building I worked in falling around the world."

Aisling wasn't sure how to process this revelation of Maeve's status. The larger shock had come a month ago, when she found out her partner was still MI-6. This could be dealt with later.

"That's the thing." Aisling turned partially in her seat so she could see Reece without using the mirror. "The building parts have only hit Los Angeles, southern England, and one in the Pacific and one in the Atlantic. Why? L.A. fine, it's where the building came from and makes sense that as it falls through, it's hitting the same general area. But why here?"

"That's what Closen is looking into. They won't leave London without coverage, but most of them are already in Noth. They're trying to find the connection, although not everyone believes the veil is thinning." Maeve turned down a narrow London road, one crowded with apartments.

"Nice place to hide." Aisling looked up. There were *a lot* of apartments.

"Hiding in plain sight works well." Maeve looked in her mirror at Reece. "I assume we're still clear?"

"As far as I can tell, no one followed us." He'd been sitting semi-sideways as well but it just looked like he was admiring London.

They pulled into the underground lot, then took the lift to Maeve's floor. She had to unlock three locks before they got in. The place was small, not dingy, just more like a low-end hotel room. But it was better than driving around.

"You could have left your bags in the car; we won't be here that long." Maeve looked at their luggage.

"Yeah, the last car we were in is now under a few tons of rubble, would rather not take that chance." Aisling lifted up her smaller pack. "And until such time that I can lock this up, it stays with me." She frowned at the bag. "How far did you and Harlie get in translating the scroll when you were in L.A.?"

"Not far. It's a calculation for changing something, like turning steel into gold, but we're not sure what changes. But even with Harlie's training, translating it is damn hard. Your people have a screwed-up language." She went into the kitchen, put a kettle on, and came back with cups and saucers.

Aisling shook her head. "Not mine, that language was dead before my people crossed the veil. We have to learn the basics as kids out of some perverse sense of history. My point is, what if Nix isn't the only one who knows something like it exists? If the Lazing knew he was after an ancient fey relic of some kind that you had, or in this case, a scroll written in ancient fey, they would be after you too, regardless of Nix."

Maeve brought out the tea, poured for all of them, then started swearing. "Damn it, that makes sense, if it does what supposedly it does, make people rich, they'd be after it. But if they never caught Nix, how do they know I have something? You said it yourself, Nix didn't know what he was looking for, just that he hadn't found it. The scroll is blocked, right?"

Aisling patted her bag. "Still in the sealed charging box. Whatever it is or contains, nothing is getting past that box unless I open it."

Aisling and Reece filled Maeve in on the incident in

Luton. She'd gotten the basics from Bart, but there was only so much that was safe to say over the phone—even with secure lines.

Maeve scowled. "Closen hasn't said anything about things coming up from underneath the ground. And that's kinda their wheelhouse. And what about this aunt of Stella's? If she knew about this ten years ago and was silenced for it? Damn it. What else aren't we being told?"

"Her mother called." Reece sipped his tea. "She wants Aisling not to trust Harlie."

"Which is ironic, since I'm pretty sure she's the one who spelled him. It would take a very strong magic user to take him out like that. That woman is a bitch, but she's a scary powerful one." Aisling leaned back and enjoyed her tea. It had been hours since she relaxed.

Maeve scowled. "That call doesn't sound like her though. Why warn you off Harlie? Do you think she's possessed?" The look in her eyes was a bit too enthusiastic.

Aisling laughed. "She's what possesses others, nothing could get into that dark soul." She paused as another thought hit. "But what if her warning me off had less to do with our case, and was more personal in nature? Harlie just broke the spell she'd had him place on me almost two hundred years ago. She might not have cast the spell, but she was connected to it. The odds of her not noticing what was done are slim."

"And she's just trying to put a spin on it? Is she that worried about what you think of her?" Maeve asked.

"No, I don't think she cares what anyone thinks of her, unless they have something she wants." Aisling shook her head. "Unless that's it. I have something she wants. Or know something she needs to know, or doesn't want others to know. Damn that woman!"

Reece nodded. "She's on Area 42's radar, but only at the highest levels. I haven't heard anything specific about her, but they are trying to watch her. She and the High Council have been on a list the higher ups have for over a year—which isn't a popular observation as you can understand."

CHAPTER THIRTY- NINE

—◆—

"WHY DIDN'T YOU TELL ME?" Not that Aisling was truly surprised. Harlie had found some evidence that their mother and her cronies were connected to something with Area 42—he just hadn't been able to nail down what it was.

"It wasn't pertinent at the time," Reece said. "And I only fairly recently found out she was your mother. Plus, I don't have any actual intel. It was way over my pay grade."

"I'm a target because of the scroll and possibly Nix. Aisling's a target because her mother had her magic blocked for some reason and now knows that block is gone." Maeve got up and paced. "It's not just releasing the block. I think we all agree that Aisling's mother wouldn't care if you knew what she did to you. Therefore, it's what she blocked that has her worried. Something your mother thinks Harlie could help you find out."

Reece went pale. "That whole you being dead thing. You said that spirit, ghost, whatever it was that attacked me on the way to the train thought you were dead—that you were supposed to be dead. What if your mother did kill you at one point? Your father has healing magic, right?"

Aisling leaned forward. "You think she *killed* me? And my dad brought me back? How? Why? And if she was supposed to kill me for some reason for this weird voice from the other side of the veil, why did she let him bring me back?" She was still pushing off the voice thinking she was dead as a mistake. Even though her gut said otherwise. But none of it made sense.

Maeve narrowed her eyes. "What if whatever it was that made you scream at night as a kid, was too much for her to stand, and in trying to shut you up, she accidentally killed you? Your father brought you back, then she took you to Harlie to block your magic that was causing the night screams. It could have been an accident." Maeve was trying, but the look on her face said she didn't believe her own words.

Aisling wished there was some nectar around so she could get gloriously drunk. The idea felt too real. It was as if once the connection had been made, the truth of it became undeniable.

"No…I don't know how, maybe Harlie's removing the block removed something else as well." She found herself shaking There was no way to deny it—her soul screamed the truth. "Somehow, I know she killed me—and it wasn't an accident. It was before Nepal, maybe a few weeks before." She closed her eyes as images and feelings flooded her mind. A dark room, her standing there awaiting her mother's orders. Even at that young age she knew she had to obey. Voices. None of them made sense. Then they were clear, even though she still didn't know what they meant.

"You've had your time. The agreement—" The voice that got cut off was low and guttural.

"Is not done yet." Her mother's voice was cool. But was that fear hiding under the words? Aisling's five-year-old self hadn't understood, but her current self did.

"We let you and the others do what you asked of us. Gave you the power to oppress your enemies. Now is time. The children must go. They were promised." The voice was now uncannily like whatever had spoken to Aisling before. The one surprised she was alive. And she felt deep inside that the term "children" did not refer to Aisling's siblings.

"You can't. These are our future."

"They mean our destruction. You will kill her. The others have already done so."

In the memory, her mother turned to her without pause, raised her hand, and Aisling died.

She woke up to a frantic Reece and Maeve hovering over her and calling her name.

"I'm fine. Damn it, she did kill me. The voice behind the attack on the precogs ordered it. Something about it being payment for prior favors." She rubbed her arms. "That sucked on many levels." She drank her entire cup of tea and held out her cup for more. "I didn't see who brought me back, but it had to have been my father. Then they hid my being alive by masking my magic."

"She did something *nice* by having Harlie block you?" Reece didn't sound like he believed it any more than Aisling did.

"Doubtful. There's something about me that my mother wants, something that voice wanted destroyed. Oh, and we need to see if there were a lot of fey deaths reported when I was about five. The children were all around my age." That had been a feeling too. Whatever was behind the voice, it had demanded the deaths of an unknown number of fey children—who most likely had not been brought back.

"There were more? Do we know what parameters we're looking for?" Reece asked.

"The voice said the others had already been killed. Maybe look at the High Council and all first families. If we don't find any connections there, we can branch out." Two more cups of tea and the chill was finally leaving her bones.

"Damn. I thought I had a rough upbringing. She really killed you?" Maeve went to the kitchen and brought out another pot of tea.

"I was dead. Hard to explain, but my memories ended

suddenly. She stopped my heart. One moment I was a confused little girl in a dark room, the next I was gone. I don't recall coming back, but clearly I did."

Reece put his arm around her shoulders. "That had to have been terrifying for you to go back and go through it now. I am very glad your father brought you back." He squeezed her shoulder.

"Gotta say, me too. Can we see if there's any connection in deaths that year? It's a feeling more than anything I heard, but the deaths were based on our age and some deal our parents made way before we were born."

Reece pulled out a laptop from his luggage. "This will get better intel than a standard internet search, but still not as good as if we had full Area 42 access." He looked up. "I don't think this should go through any agency until it absolutely has to. If this does tie to the High Council and the first families…." He let that thought hang, then started typing.

He was completely right. Whatever they were dealing with, a contract to kill a bunch of well-off fey children at a certain age would rock far more than just the involved families.

"Are you sure you're okay? You look far paler than normal." Maeve leaned forward. "Not healthy at all."

"Yes, no, who knows? It's been a weird couple of days. And how is all of this connected to what's going on with the veil?" She rubbed her temples. The fact was, knowing her mother killed her actually didn't make her angry. It made her want to know why. And if it was that important that Aisling die, why did she allow her father to bring her back? He never went against her wishes, and even the life of his youngest child, if he knew she had to die, wouldn't make him change that.

"I think we have a connection." Reece turned his laptop toward her and Maeve came behind them to see. "First family deaths are a big thing for the news services and the year you turned five there were a higher-than-average number reported. Yet, none of the news stories connected that all were the same age range or were from the first families. They reported each death individually as if unrelated to anything else. Most of the deaths were accidents."

Aisling watched as a list compiled of dead children. There were twenty-five. The only way there wasn't an investigation or at least a news story, was because the first families or High Council shut it down. "Mott. He's not dead either, but same age, same High Council connection. Maybe we can learn as much from who didn't die as from who did."

Reece saved his first list and started a second search.

"Could this be connected to the vallenians and those boxes? Although it seems odd that they would have saved you as an adult if they had demanded your death as a child." Maeve brought in a bunch of random snack foods and dumped them on the coffee table. "Help yourself, I've been eating out mostly."

"The three family boxes were all High Council. I'm not dead, Mott isn't dead, who was the third one?"

Reece looked up from his search. "The Hthia. One step ahead of you, their twin daughters are your age and not dead."

Aisling held up the pendant. "As far as I know, this wasn't connected to any family and considering the metal in it, it shouldn't be able to exist on this side of the veil. Pretty sure that it's not from here. Aside from still not coming off, it seems to be helping me. I just wish I knew why they put it on me. Could the others be protected as well?"

"Can it do anything? Maybe call the vallenians for help?" Maeve shrugged at the look Reece gave her. "What? They could have killed her four times that we know of. If they were part of whoever wanted her dead, they would have done so. Therefore, maybe they are on our side?" Her argument lost steam but she didn't look like she was going to back down.

"Or they have their own agenda that, while not supporting the child killers, is also not on our side." Reece went back to his laptop. "Well, of the sixty-five children who were from the first families in your age group, forty survived to their sixth birthday."

"And? There was an and hanging there." Aisling tried to look at his laptop but he wouldn't let her.

"And a lot of bad things happened to many of the families over the years. Out of those sixty-five, there are only ten left. Excluding you and Mott."

Aisling sat back. She didn't need the details, the look on his face said the bad luck that followed them was suspicious as hell.

"Then what's the connection?" Maeve looked at them. "Some of the first families got into a deal with a creepy group or being to give them power over something, somewhen. It involved killing a certain group of children at a specific age. The ones that agreed went on to stay successful and the rest had a horrible two hundred years? Did someone curse them?"

"I'd say more likely they had made a deal; a spell was cast long before two hundred years ago and then it came back to them." Aisling had a bad feeling this might be the spell Harlie had been talking about coming back. Which would explain her mother getting more aggressive now—whatever she and the others had pushed back so other fey wouldn't feel it was coming back with unknown repercussions.

Aisling's phone rang. Caradoc. "Hey, we were just discussing mother."

"That's a cheerful thought, any particular reason?"

"Long story, might be best to wait until we're in person—but she's worse than we thought she was." She wanted to tell him now, but not over the phone. This needed to be talked about in person. "What did you need?"

"Didn't want you to think you guys got all the excitement, we had a visitor at the apartment collapse not long after you left."

"Nix?" Aisling held up her hand as Maeve almost grabbed the phone out of her hand.

"Nope. We have another family box. I got to see my first vallenian. Bart didn't see him, nor anyone else. But they're back."

"Damn it. Did it do or say anything besides giving you the box? And what family name does it belong to?"

"Not a thing. It shoved the box at me, then literally ran through Jones, and vanished. Bart looked the name up, another High Council family. Flinth."

Aisling hadn't heard of that family name, but she'd never made it a job to know them all. The vallenians obviously thought they were important. "How long was it there? It said nothing to you?" To be fair, they'd only talked to her once. When they'd frozen a gang fight all around her.

"Not a word. Just the one, popped up, nodded to me, handed over the box, then poof. I didn't even get a cool pendant."

"Where are you now?"

"We're waiting for the bus to take us to our train. Your little explosion caused a hell of a mess to the train schedules. I'm assuming you two are okay and you found Maeve?"

"Yup and yup. We did get tailed, but we're not certain if they were after us or Maeve, The Lazing have sent people here. They followed Maeve to the station, then followed us in two cars. Tell Jones to keep an eye out, he'll probably spot them way before you would."

"That's not good. Nor is the fact you were willing to

discuss them on the phone and not whatever you were talking about our mother."

"It's bad. I'd either want to be in person, or have someone like Harlie running an interference spell. No offense to your gadgets."

"Understood. Okay, our bus is here, stay out of trouble. All of you." Aisling knew he wasn't too concerned about Reece, but there had been something growing between him and Maeve.

"You three, too. I'll call you when we check on Harlie."

Caradoc hung up. Aisling realized that if things were okay, he hung up without saying goodbye. It was when the shit was hitting fans everywhere that he said goodbye. Annoying, but good to know.

"We have another box?" Maeve settled down when it was clear there hadn't been another Nix sighting.

"Good guess." Aisling told them what Caradoc said. "It sounds like it was only there for a few seconds."

"Unless it didn't want Caradoc to see it before the handover. It seems like they chose when and where to be seen." Reece turned back to his laptop. "What family name this time?"

"Flinth." Aisling shook her head. "I don't recognize that one."

Reece typed a few inquiries, his scowl getting deeper on each one. "Are you certain that was the name?"

"It's a short one, and the line was clear, so yes. It's not in the fey database? All the first families were."

The first families were made up of a small group of fey who came through the veil before the rest. But they only came over days or weeks before the mass migration. That didn't stop them from being elitist about it. Most were also on the High Council.

"Not at all…wait a moment." Reece found something but it wasn't making him happy. "That line died out over a thousand years ago. They were a first family, but were killed in some sort of battle."

"A battle that wiped out an entire line? Did they all live in one village?" Maeve picked her way through the snacks.

"Sort of. It was a magic battle. One mage wiped them out and followed the bloodline. That box was held by the victors." He looked up with a wince as he found more information. "Your mother."

"She destroyed an entire family line by herself?" Aisling was finding out more than she wanted to know.

"No. Supposedly the Flinth started it, your mother and three other first family leaders took them down. According to the footnote, destroying the lineage of your enemy was an old way of doing things from before the crossing. It doesn't say what the cause of the fight was, though."

"Of course not. Not if the first families destroyed them. How did the high king and queen let this happen?" Aisling saw the same answer on both their faces that was in her head. They were involved in whatever had happened. "I wish the vallenians would stop dropping these boxes off with no discussion. There's no way to find out what they want, or what they are trying to tell us."

"That your first families are a bunch of assholes? Sorry, that's what this human mind is picking up." Maeve shrugged.

"I have to agree." Aisling's phone rang before she could add to that thought. "Hi Stella, anything wrong?"

"Not that we know of at the moment. Well, there might be, not sure. I just received a phone call from my friends, Jili and Arthero, where Harlie is staying. The good news is he's awake, the bad news is he appears to have gone berserk. They locked him in a meditation room, but he keeps yelling and pounding the walls. He appears to believe you are dead."

Aisling was getting a bit tired of this dying bit. "We can go over there; can you text me the address though?

I don't understand how they are keeping him in. His magic should be able to blast through their walls, let alone the door."

"That's the thing, he hasn't used any magic. Okay, sent you the address, good luck." She ended the call.

"What now about Harlie?" Reece was already shutting down his laptop.

Aisling filled them in on the little they wouldn't have heard. "I'm hoping that seeing me alive will calm him down."

Maeve grabbed her jacket. Both Aisling and Reece picked up their luggage. She raised an eyebrow. "Just because one building you were in got squished doesn't mean all will."

"No, but we might have to leave London quickly if there's something seriously wrong with Harlie. No idea why my brother's not using magic, but I think that if he does start, we probably don't want to be in one of the largest cities in the world."

Maeve sighed. "Good point. Hold a sec." She darted into a bedroom and could be heard frantically packing things.

The drive to the meditation retreat wasn't long, although the scarcity of street signs as they got closer did make it a bit more problematic than it should have been.

Jili ran out to them as they pulled up. Her cloak was askew and she looked rattled. "Thank goodness you're here. We've sent our clients away, as your brother is a bit disturbing. He's still locked up but that might not last long. Arthero went to get help."

Aisling got out and motioned to the others. "Stay behind me. I want to try talking to him first and even though he might not be using magic yet, he could still be sensing things."

Maeve and Reece nodded and dropped behind her.

"If you don't mind, I'll stay out here. I'm not a strong

magic user, and his screaming is hurting my soul," Jili said.

"I'm just sorry he's doing this. My brother is one of the gentlest people I know." With a nod, Aisling led the way through the small buildings. The gardens were lovely, lush and soothing and a deep wind chime echoed through. At least she could hear the chimes in between the increasing yelling.

Harlie was yelling sounds more than words, but a few words came through. Death. Destruction. Aisling.

Aisling picked up the pace and stopped a foot from the room. "Harlie. It's me. I'm not dead, nor dying. Something is wrong with you." She had to repeat herself twice before he stopped yelling.

"Aisling? Are you calling me from beyond the veil? I tried to protect you, little sister. I tried. I failed!"

She went up to the door. "It's me. Calm down and feel me." She put her hand in the middle of the door and tried sending healing magic his way. The magic slammed back at her.

She turned to Maeve and Reece. "Can one of you go ask Jili if they put an additional shield around this room? I'm not sure if this is them or Harlie, it's not the same as the one around the entire compound."

"You're dead. Gone beyond the veil with the others. The wee ones we couldn't protect. Gone." Harlie was wailing now and if she'd ever seen him drink, she'd say he was on a nectar binge.

"No, I'm not. Reach out, Harlie. I'm alive. Right here."

"It's a trick! You want me to cross the veil too. I won't. I know what's over there. You can't fool me."

Maeve came back from speaking to Jili and Arthero. "No additional spells used. They hadn't sensed anything else on the building."

Aisling closed her eyes and mentally reached out to whatever spell was around the small room. It was familiar, but so deftly woven she wasn't sure who…Harlie?

"Harlie, it's me. Your little sister. You built a shield into this building. I need you to lower it so you can tell it's me." She grabbed her pendant and readied a powerful healing spell. It would tap into the newer abilities, but hopefully Reece and Maeve could pull her back if needed.

Harlie didn't say anything but a wave of pain strong enough to drop her to her knees slammed into her. Harlie's grief was horrific, but there was more to it than that. He felt he had killed her. That she'd gone beyond the veil. Which was disturbing in itself as her people didn't see death as going beyond the veil.

Aisling stayed on her knees, easier in case another wave of pain hit, and gently reached out to him. "It's me. I'm not dead. I'm here." She kept sending that thought over and over while she let a trickle of healing magic flow through her words.

Finally, the pressure of the shield dropped completely, and the pain vanished.

"Aisling? Is that you? It was so real…so horrible." Harlie cracked open the door. He always looked a bit like someone who had spent a lot of time in a cave by himself. Now he looked like someone who should still be back in that cave under heavy sedation. He ran forward and picked her up in a hug. "It is you!"

Aisling hugged him back, then had to pound on his back. "Crushing me."

He gently sat her back on her feet and nodded to Reece and Maeve. "We found Maeve, good. What did I miss? I remember those beings coming from the ground, then nothing." He ran his hand through his hair and started untangling the knots. Whatever had made him think she was dead had vanished.

"There's been a lot." Aisling peered into his dark eyes closely. He looked rough, but it was her brother who peered back. They'd need to sort out his hallucinations, but right now he didn't look like he was aware of what he'd just gone through. Later might be a better time. "Maeve, can you bring me my small pack?" She was pretty sure this was really Harlie, but no reason to take chances.

Maeve handed her the pack and she took out the box. "I know you had a rough time, but we need to check something. Can you look into this box?"

His face lit up. "Mott's box, yes. You've had possessions?" He looked right into the box. The flash and words of being possession free caused his smile to widen. "That is good to know."

"It is." Aisling brought out one of the slivers. "This is a combination of Mott's work and Stella's; it will allow us to see if you become possessed."

Harlie beamed like he was a kid who was getting a treat. "Where?"

"Just turn your cheek toward me, doesn't matter which one."

"I wish to apologize to the owners of this place. I don't remember coming in, but it seems a place of calm. I can feel that I was not that." A brief flash of pain and sorrow crossed his face.

Aisling and the others escorted Harlie out toward the car. Jili was waiting. She kept smiling and didn't flinch, but there was caution in her eyes.

"I am glad you are able to walk out of here."

"I apologize for any problems I caused. I was not myself." Harlie still had hair sticking up all over and his clothes were a bit worse for wear. But his smile was sincere. "I will be leaving now, thank you for the shelter when I needed it." He bowed and a feeling of calm settled over everything.

Jili's eyes were wide as she clearly felt it. "Thank you, you didn't need to do that. You are still recovering... thank you." She felt what Harlie had shared. Judging by the looks on Reece and Maeve's faces, they did too.

"It is a small token of my thanks." His smile dropped. "There are dark times coming, and all who seek shelter might not respect it. Protect your doors and yourselves. I'd like to offer a spell of shielding if you don't mind?"

Jili nodded. "We would be honored."

The spell of shielding was more subtle than the one of peace. Aisling felt it but she didn't know if the others did.

"It is done." Harlie hugged Jili and then climbed into the back seat.

Aisling couldn't follow up that, so she just smiled and shook Jili's hand. "Thank you for everything. And Harlie is right about things changing. Be careful."

Jili smiled sadly and took Aisling's hand. "You're the one who needs to be careful. I see the armor of warriors on all of you.

CHAPTER FORTY

—◆—

HARLIE WAS HAPPILY BOUNCING IN the back seat, and the rest were most likely dwelling on Jili's last words. They all knew they were in a huge fight, but at least for Aisling, having it put so symbolically as armor was disturbing.

Aisling turned to Harlie as they drove out of the area. "I hate to bring it up, but you kept yelling about me being dead and it being your fault. There have been some odd issues about my "being alive" status in the past few hours. I doubt your attack, or whatever it was, isn't related."

Harlie had been happily smiling to himself, but the smile crumbled. "I don't know what happened, as I said. But a short while ago I awoke, but not in this world. Or maybe it was this place but through another's eye. I'll need to make notes. At any rate, this other world was dark and deadly—and you were dead. My job was to protect you, I failed. I felt like I killed you, but the details weren't clear."

"Might as well just say it." Aisling shared a look with Reece and took a deep breath. "Our mother killed me, probably a few weeks or days before she brought me to you to block my magic." She had second thoughts as soon as the words left her mouth. If Harlie lost it… maybe a moving vehicle hadn't been the best place to tell him. But considering what he just went through, he needed to know.

His face stilled. "I…you were alive when she brought you to me." He was never the type to be lost when it came to ideas or concepts, but this one hit him hard. "I know you were alive." His voice dropped. "Are you sure I didn't kill you?"

Reece leaned forward, appearing ready to grab Harlie if he needed to be subdued.

"No. I found the memories." She reached back and took his hand. "Don't worry, I don't recall being dead. And the dying part was painless. She stopped my heart as easily as you would put out a flame. But she did it because someone ordered her to. There was a deal of some sort made. That part wasn't in my memories though." Harlie stayed silent as she filled him in on everything from their mother's odd phone call to tracking down which families had lost children the year she turned five.

He sat there unblinking for so long, Reece nudged him.

"I'm okay." Harlie nodded to Reece then turned back to Aisling. "Are *you* okay? How did I not feel what had happened to you when she brought you to me?"

Maeve had been focusing on the road but looked back at him in the mirror. "I'd say you weren't sticking around in Aisling's head. You wouldn't have been happy to do what that bitch made you do. In those cases, it's always 'do what needs to be done, get out, and don't look around'." Maeve might not be a fey or a magic user, but she'd had enough unsavory situations in her life to understand Harlie well.

He nodded. "But I still should have known. We all should have known. Did father bring you back?"

"That's what I'm guessing, but not sure why she let him. Whatever that voice was, it must have tracked me through my magic. My theory is that I still was of value to her and that's why she had you block my magic."

"Or it was tracking you through whatever made you scream every night." Harlie appeared to be wallowing in his perceived failure. "Children of any species don't just scream for no reason. Something triggered it. You had only been doing it for a few weeks according to her when she brought you to me. Depending on the timing, it could be that the screaming marked a change which was what triggered her to kill you. Or the screaming was the result of her killing you." He leaned forward toward Aisling's seat. "Have you found a need to scream since I removed the block?"

He was definitely back to his normal inquisitive self. Aisling knew he still held guilt, warranted or not, about her death, that was just how he was. But he was moving forward to fix the problem.

"Not in any case that wasn't deserved. There have been a few of those along the way."

"Why is all of this coming up now?" Maeve swore as the street she tried to take was blocked by unmoving traffic. "These things happened almost two hundred years ago and the murder of Aisling and the other children was related to something that your mother and those other families made an agreement on hundreds if not thousands of years ago, right?"

"Probably." Harlie was still processing things in his head but nodded. "The High Council was even more power-mad when our people first came here. They settled down after we saved humans from the Black Plague, but I think they just kept their actions secretive."

"Again, why now?" Another car-blocked road brought more swearing from Maeve.

"The veil." Reece had settled back into his seat. "My agency is in denial even as they're looking into cases about it, but there is something wrong with the veil. That has to be the connection. It's weakening, and things are getting through."

"Then whatever killing me and the other children had been for, it was for someone or something on the other side of the veil." Aisling knew that had to be the case, but knowing it and saying it out loud were two different things.

"A deal made with something over there for the fey to cross here?" Reece shrugged. "That seems wrong since they were trying to escape whatever was over there."

"Not to mention that Aisling's birth and her fifth birthday were a few thousand years after our people came here. The timing isn't very good. Do we have any paper and a pen?" Harlie looked up. Aisling dug through her bag, then handed him a pen and notepad. "Thank you, just notes for later. Keeping most up in my head, but sometimes a few escape."

"We can do a data search to see what, if any, significant events happened the year Aisling and the others were born when we get back to the flat." Maeve turned down a third street. Also blocked by cars. She drummed her fingers on her steering wheel before moving to the side of the road and parking.

"London traffic is never great, but since they started reducing the number of cars with licenses to drive in the city, it's gotten better. Until today. I don't see any signs of accidents, but something is blocking every road to the center of town."

Reece got out of the car and walked over to the closest car sitting in traffic. The window was rolled up and the woman driver stared ahead. Reece knocked on her window. Nothing. He knocked again. Still nothing. He went up five cars; judging by the fact that no windows rolled down, they were in the same state as the first.

He came jogging back and leaned into Maeve's window. "Can either of you two magic users pick up on any spells? As far as I can see each car has a driver, but no one is moving or responding to anything. Some cars have passengers as well, but none of them react either."

Aisling got out and sent out her healing magic to the first car. And got slammed back into Reece's arms hard enough that both ended up pushed into Maeve's car.

Aisling rubbed her forehead. "Something is blocking them. My spell got smacked back into me." The pounding in her head was horrible.

Harlie got out of the car, took a deep breath, closed his eyes, and let a spell flow. Aisling felt it, gentle and stirring at the same time. He didn't get slammed back as she had, but the spell simply drifted away. He glared at the cars then sent the spell again. This time there was a bit more kick behind it.

Still nothing.

The pendant on Aisling's necklace started getting warm. She lifted it to eye level and noticed that a new line was etching its way in. Red this time.

"What's that?" Maeve yelled and pointed toward where the cars were facing. A massive, taller than the buildings, green ball, crackling with energy as it slowly expanded toward them.

"Something we don't want to reach us." Harlie's eyes were wide at whatever he sensed about the ball. "Get in! Get away from here!"

Reece and Harlie both jumped into the backseat.

The pendant grew almost too hot to touch. Aisling dropped it on top of her shirt and got back in the car.

Maeve backed up and tore down the street away from the line of cars and the growing ball. "Guys, it's still growing. What is it? What's it doing?" She swerved around slower-moving cars.

"I have no idea what that is. Actually, I might have one, but I don't know how it could be here." Harlie waved his hand. "It would be a long explanation and knowing will not make a difference—we can't fight it; we need to leave."

"Out of London?" Maeve managed to get on a wider road and picked up some speed.

"Yes, I believe that might save us."

Aisling and Reece both spun toward him at the same

time.

"What?"

"We can't let the entire city of London be destroyed! We have to tell someone, get people out." Maeve was still zipping around cars.

"It's too late, it's growing. But I don't think it is going to explode. That is a spell of containment. Someone or something is locking up London. You can call your people in the city, but I don't think that even the strongest spellcasters can hold out. I might have been able to protect the four of us for a short while, but that would have been it. And I am a very strong magic user." He wasn't bragging, he was one of the best. And if he couldn't hold back that green orb, probably no one could.

Maeve swore steadily as she picked up speed, got onto the motorway, and blasted out of town.

The ball was growing and cars heading into London were turning and trying to retreat as they saw it, but they were trapped by more cars heading their direction.

"For once I'm glad you drive like a race car driver." Aisling hung onto the dash and Maeve focused on getting out of town.

"Do we know how far this thing will go?" Maeve yelled to Harlie. "Not sure if we'll have enough petrol if it's too far."

Harlie looked back but shook his head. "That is a theoretical magical entity. No one has ever seen one larger than a baseball. I…wait. I can sense it. It's weakening. Keep going. It should have to fall back soon."

He might have said it was weakening, but it looked like it was still growing at the same speed from what Aisling could see.

"Either we're slowing or it's getting faster. It is catching up." Reece stared out the back.

"I'm going as fast as I can!" Maeve was racing the other cars all trying to stay ahead of the blob.

"I can feel it weakening. I don't understand." Harlie watched it come closer.

Aisling felt like the car was standing still, the translucent green dome was moving faster than they were. She grabbed her still hot pendant and focused a blast of healing at the green wall coming their way. The blob stopped.

"Thank gods it stopped. Getting off at the next exit; we can fuel up then go find the others." Maeve's voice was steady but her hands were shaking.

"I think Aisling and her friend helped." Reece turned around to Aisling.

She winced as she let go of the pendant. Yup, it had a brand-new red line in the celtic knot. And so did the palm of her hand.

Chapter Forty-One

"OUCH. DAMN IT. I WISH I wasn't the only one with healer magic," Aisling said. "This damn pendant burnt me." She could try to heal herself, but whatever blast she'd sent at the blob had wiped her out. She felt like a newborn kitten could beat her in a fight right now. With one paw tied behind its back.

Maeve looked over briefly. "If you do faint, please fall toward the door and not me. My nerves are a bit shot and it would be tragic to have escaped the London blob only to go off the road in a car accident."

"I won't faint, I'm just exhausted. And my hand hurts. Okay, Harlie, what the hell was that?" The green dome was fading behind them. It was still there, and who knew how many people were trapped inside, hopefully just in stasis. But at least it wasn't expanding anymore.

"It was a lincolica spell. Very old, extremely dangerous, both for the persons inside and the person casting it. To be able to create one that large, and have it hold is… unheard of." He looked terrified and fascinated.

"Could it be a group of magic users?" Reece still was glancing back but the green blob was little more than a quickly fading line at the speed Maeve was driving.

"It would take too much power to be able to connect even two spell casters to create this spell, let alone the number of them that would have been needed for something that large. There are variances that each magic user would exhibit that would conflict with each other and disrupt the spell." Harlie kept looking behind them. "Bart needs to be told."

Maeve started swearing anew, or she might not have actually stopped but just lowered the volume. "MI-6, Area 42, Closen, and untold other agencies are all based in London. Are we cut off from all of them?"

"There's a good chance." Harlie nodded and pulled out his phone. "I'm calling my friend in Noth, she's a precog and might have felt more than we did since she wasn't directly impacted." He called but hung up when he got voicemail.

"You don't want to leave her a message?" Aisling asked.

"Not right now. I'm not sure who or what can be trusted. I believe Bart is calling though." He looked at Reece who shrugged, he had his phone in his hand but hadn't dialed yet. Then his phone buzzed.

"Creepy, so you can sense phone calls?" Maeve looked back at Harlie.

"No, but it was a logical assumption. We had been in London and right now all of the agents who were not, are trying to reach those who were."

Reece mostly was answering questions, short, brief ones. That meant Harlie and Aisling might not be the only ones who didn't trust phones. "We're on the road to Noth now, we'll come find you. Larkin out." Reece ran his hand through his hair. He looked as tired as Aisling felt. "Bart says every office or agent inside London just goes to voice mail. The news choppers from surrounding areas are flying overhead and scanning, but it appears almost all of London proper is under that dome. The good news is that when Aisling and the pendant managed to freeze it, it did so everywhere. There are no cracks or holes that they've seen so far and no one has taken credit for the creating the blob—yet."

"In other words, no one knows anything. Do they think the people under that thing are alive?" Maeve kept her voice level. Her family had moved out of London a few years ago—but she still thought of it as home. Aisling knew how hard she was fighting to not whip the car around and try to find a way inside.

Reece must have heard it in her voice. "There's no reason to believe they're not alive. Right Harlie? This spell is unique."

Harlie started to say something, looked to Maeve, and instead forced a smile. "I would say the chances are extremely good that they are alive. The people in those cars were alive, just frozen, the spell must have started slowly, then once it was strong enough to build the dome, it expanded. Once we break the spell, everyone in London should be fine."

Maeve was silent for a bit, then looked in the rearview mirror. "You have no idea, do you? We could be driving away from millions of corpses."

"I don't know for certain, right now, no one except the caster of the spell would know. But based on my very long life, filled with observation and contemplation, I believe they are alive. And until proven otherwise, I will suggest we all do the same." Harlie sat back in his seat and folded his arms.

Aisling flashed him a smile. Harlie could be socially clueless sometimes, and other times brilliant. Maeve relaxed her death grip on the steering wheel at his words.

"I'm willing to agree with the wise man, how about you two?" Reece waited until Aisling and Maeve both nodded before dialing another number. "Narissa? Hi this is Reece Larkin from this afternoon." He quickly touched base with her. Not a bad idea since the majority of agents would have been in London when the dome encased it. After a few minutes of catching up on the disaster, he cut to why he called. "We're meeting up in the village of Noth. Agent Churchill of the New York office and a few other agents will be meeting there. I didn't know if you and your agents had a contingency plan."

Maeve gave Aisling a look of confusion, and Aisling

pantomimed wings. Maeve nodded and went back to seeing how many cars she could pass.

Reece and Narissa went back and forth a bit, he gave her Bart's contact information and ended the call. "She has five agents with her, she's pretty sure almost all of the rest were inside the city. She's going to contact Bart and get the word out for any free agents to go to Noth."

Maeve nodded. "My list is limited, but I will be calling any Closen and regular MI-6 agents I can when we get there. Closen should still have people there already. Do you think that is the reason for this? Cut down on the number of people working on these problems?"

Aisling shook her head. "There would be more strategic ways to do that, I'd think. But someone was trying to keep London shut." She left off that someone would probably be claiming responsibility eventually. This might not have ever been done before, but it was an act of terrorism.

"I'm going to keep calling any U.K. agents I have contact information for." Reece went back to his phone. "Oh, and Bart is glad that you're recovered, Harlie. He'd like it if you and Aisling can focus on anything magic connected that you noticed as we were driving further into London. I'd say as soon as Maeve started hitting blocked streets although it could have been before that."

"I already have been, but I will continue." Harlie scowled. "It was so subtle that I didn't even notice when I was walking around those cars. I originally thought someone had spelled them to get to us. That they managed to keep that large of a spell that well masked says much—none of it good."

"I'll try and search what I saw and felt, but I didn't notice anything either." The pain in Aisling's hand flared and she looked down. "Hopefully someone in Noth can heal this before it becomes permanent." She held up her hand. "I'm still too magically weak to heal it myself."

Maeve glanced over. "That looks bad. Is the pendant still hot?"

Aisling tapped it with her finger. "Not that I can tell." With her non-injured hand, she carefully lifted the necklace up. "It has added another line to the design though. Red this time, which is fitting since it felt like it was on fire."

Harlie leaned forward quickly and almost tore it from her hands. "Red…not good. I mean, not horrible, and not expected, but not good. Not that this is doing anything expected. And not as rare as the trileium. Oh yes, Hind's Blood." Harlie looked up at all of them. "It's not really the blood of a hind, it's actually a wood. Very hard wood." He drifted off as he stared at the pendant.

"And? I've never heard of it, is it from this world? Is it deadly? Will it poison me in my sleep?" Helpful or not, she wanted this necklace off. Who knew what it was turning into?

"It shouldn't hurt you." Harlie winced as he looked at her burnt hand. "More than it already did, that is. It's from beyond the veil, but the trees had grown here too—specifically in the British Isles long before they were British or even more than a collection of warrior states building walled fortresses. For some reason over the decades, the trees died out, and the ones remaining stopped growing. It shouldn't poison you."

"Don't think I didn't catch the word *shouldn't*." Aisling stared at the pendant. With the new line it was becoming quite pretty. It already had been but now it was dramatic. And unique. "I'm thinking the spell to disguise it fell off when you lost consciousness, but could we just make this thing look silver again? I'll try to keep it tucked in my shirt, but it does seem to have its own agenda."

Harlie shook himself out of his thoughts, reached to the front seat, took the pendant in his left hand again, then released it. "There" He flashed a smile. "Now, I will spend our driving time contemplating what just hap-pened. Many things were observed that were not taken in at the time." He gave a serene nod and closed his eyes.

Aisling made sure the necklace looked silver. Nice, but what you could buy in any jewelry shop in the U.K., then tucked it into her shirt again.

Maeve was locked in her own thoughts and still seemed focused on breaking the race time to Noth. Reece was quietly calling through to find London agents who might still be outside of it, but hadn't reached anyone after Narissa. Aisling closed her eyes and drifted off.

———◆———

To awaken to voices yelling her name. She opened her eyes. She wasn't in the car, but at the edge of a cliff. One with fire engulfing the land below her. It took a few terrifying moments to realize that it wasn't real, it was a nightmare. It was impossible to get that through her head, however. She looked down and her hands weren't hers. The clothing was odd, old fashioned, and nothing she'd seen before. Weird clothing in a nightmare wasn't too unusual. But the hands bit was disturbing. As she was trying to sort things out, the body she was in turned to a group of elves, all dressed like she was in flowing robes and tunics. She started yelling, but couldn't hear what she said. Yet she could tell it wasn't her voice.

That was worse than the terror around her. It was her mother's.

CHAPTER FORTY-TWO

AISLING FOUGHT TO WAKE UP. She couldn't hear her mother's thoughts any clearer than she could hear her words, but she knew that was the body she was in. It wasn't a nightmare, she didn't have any idea what it was, but she knew it was beyond the world of dreams.

"You need to know. This is who you are. You must know." This voice was clear, loud, and slightly familiar. It sounded both male and female, but wouldn't say anything beyond those three sentences.

"What am I supposed to know? What is this?" She yelled in her head but the voice stayed silent.

"Who are you? How did you get in my mind?" That voice was clear and loud—her mother directing her voice internally.

Aisling shut up and focused on getting out of whatever this was. Her mother kept asking who she was and Aisling stayed silent. Finally, she felt herself being shaken and could escape.

"Are you in there? What happened to you?" Harlie's face was inches in front of hers. The car was parked and he had the front door open. Maeve and Reece were crowded in close.

"I'm fine, thank you, I think you brought me out of it." She shivered. Dream, nightmare, or something else, she didn't want to go back to that place. Nor into her mother's thoughts.

"Nightmare?" Maeve asked. "You started yelling right before I pulled off to Noth."

"Sorry about that. I'm not sure what it was. I thought

it was a nightmare, but it was too real. And I wasn't in my body." She paused; it was hard to say. "I was in our mother's head."

"What? Could you see what she's up to?" Maeve got a bit closer.

Harlie looked concerned.

"No, it wasn't now. It was a long time ago—extremely long ago. I couldn't hear her thoughts; it was more like I was in her head along for the ride." She shuddered. "But they were doing something bad. It was her and a dozen or so elves; no other fey, just elves. All in robes and old-fashioned clothing. They were burning trees."

The fire could have been accidental, and the elves could have been running away from it. But in her gut, she knew that wasn't the case.

"What kind of trees?" Harlie helped her out of the car.

"No idea, they were burning. But she didn't know I was there until some voice said I needed to know and this was who I was. I responded to the voice and somehow she heard me. She couldn't find me, but if it wasn't a dream, she probably would have eventually. Thank you again for getting me out."

Reece came alongside of her. "Can you walk?"

"I'm back to looking awful again, aren't I?" Aisling certainly felt awful. She'd already been exhausted from over-using her magic, but now every joint in her body was ice, and the muscles and tendons were on fire.

Reece forced a smile. "I wouldn't say that—"

Maeve cut him off as she followed them. "I would. You look worse than that troll we brought in for drunk and disorderly a few years ago. The one who was coming off a two-week nectar binge."

"That good, eh?" Aisling let Reece and Harlie help her along a dirt path that led away from the car. "Where are we? I know we're in Noth, but specifically?"

"Bart found us lodging not far from the building drop

site, we can walk there once you're better." Reece ducked under a low hanging tree as they approached the door. "This cottage is for you and Maeve. Jones and I are next door on one side, your brothers on the other. They're small, but they'll work as a base."

Harlie opened the door and they escorted her to a lovely sofa.

"Any news? Beyond my nightmare?" She was almost certain it hadn't been a nightmare, but she felt better calling it that.

"Not much. All London based agents who happened to not be in town at the time of the attack are either coming here, or going to the headquarters in Edinburgh, or Dublin. There aren't a lot."

Reece wasn't saying what he thought—whatever was told to Maeve—by the tone in his voice, Reece believed everyone left in London was dead. Aisling wasn't going to say anything, but she agreed. From what she'd felt when she and the pendant had reached out to it, whatever had cut off London was deadly.

Caradoc stuck his head in the open door. "We leave you on your own for a short while and you lose Lon—What the hell happened to you?" He came over to Aisling. "Seriously, you look like a truck ran you over. The rest of you look fine, so something with the necklace?"

"Thank you for your concern. I'm recovering by the way." Aisling rolled her eyes. She hoped that she didn't look as bad as she felt. "The necklace, with almost all of my magic helping it, stopped the green blob over London before it could swallow us." Aisling held up her hand. "It did this and added a new line of color—Hind's Blood according to Harlie."

Caradoc looked over but Harlie shook his head. "You'll have to take my word for it. I had the oddest feeling when I cloaked it this time. I don't think we should be cloaking and uncloaking it, or it might just decide to remain uncloaked no matter what I want."

"It's alive?" Maeve asked.

"I wouldn't say alive as we know it, but I do believe it's sentient. I think it, not whoever put it on you, is controlling the changes it's going through. I felt a particularly stubborn mind this last change." Harlie scowled.

Bart and Jones came in with a distracted Stella and another equally short fey woman trailing behind. A harpy by the way she walked—the distinctive swagger was noticeable. Harpies were common, but they also hated large cities, so finding one out here wasn't surprising.

Bart looked around the small front room. "I should have found at least one larger house, meetings in any of these will be a mess, even worse when the others start coming in."

"I believe I can help on that, Agent Churchill." The woman with Stella stepped forward. Tiny, with wild gray hair, sharp blue eyes, and a wicked grin. Aisling liked her already. "I have a barn. Stella and I can fix it up, maybe with some more help." She smiled at Harlie. "I'm Dailten by the way. I feel like I know all of you from Harlie's calls and letters. And sendings. I really get a feel for you that way."

Harlie picked her up and lifted her high in a hug. Then set her down gently. "It is wonderful to see you again, my friend."

"I told you to just call me Bart." He actually looked embarrassed about it.

"I prefer Agent Churchill, makes me feel like I'm back in the old days." Dailten grinned and went around nodding and saying hello to everyone. She stopped in front of Aisling. "Oh, dear. I see what you meant, Harlie. Can I see the pendant?"

Aisling pulled it out and held it up.

"Oh, the colors are amazing. The Hind's Blood is new I take it?"

Aisling glanced down in surprise but the pendant still looked silver to her.

"Never mind child, it's covered. I have an ability to see beyond masks and cloaks." She gave Harlie a wink.

"Yes, the newest line created itself after Aisling managed to stop the dome over London from growing."

Dailten tiled her head and released the pendant. "You're exhausted magically, but also injured?"

Aisling held out her hand. Stella scurried forward at once.

"I can heal you, if you accept it?" A very old phrase once used by healers to ask permission before working on someone.

"If you can fix, this and hopefully the aches in my joints and muscles, I'll be in your debt for life."

Stella laughed. "Yours or mine?"

"Both."

Stella sat next to her on the sofa, took Aisling's hand, and closed her eyes. And fell over.

Caradoc was closest, and he grabbed her before she hit the coffee table, but it was a near thing.

Stella's eyes popped open and she shook her head. "That was very rude." That she said it to Aisling's hand didn't make it any less meant. "Now, behave." She sat back up, nodded a thanks to Caradoc, and dove in again.

Aisling would have stopped her, anything that punched back that hard might need professional help. But Stella was already in a healing trance.

It took a few moments, during which Stella grimaced and muttered swear words under her breath, but then her eyes popped open. "Ha! It thought it could thwart me. That is not going to happen, my friend." She patted Aisling's hand.

There was no longer a mark or pain. "Sorry that it was difficult, but thank you." She stretched and found that her joints and muscles all had recovered as well.

"You are most welcome. I'd gotten out of the healing game beyond minor injuries to the staff in the diner, those were easy to fix. This, however, was a very difficult issue. That pendant of yours knew damn well what would happen to you when it redirected your magic. And, had that mark remained, it would have given the pendant more hold over you." She shook her finger at the necklace. "Bad pendant!"

Aisling thought she saw a flare from the necklace, but it could have just been an odd bit of sun glancing off the metal. "I don't think I like that this thing is trying to take me over. Are we certain we can't get it off of me?"

Harlie shared a look with Dailten, then both shook their heads.

"I don't see how. The vallenians have their own magic, and that's what is anchoring it on you." Harlie frowned.

Dailten nodded. "From what I felt while looking at it, I'd say that is from beyond the veil. As in it is *still* beyond the veil."

"Wait, how can something that's here, also be there? Multi planes of existence?" Caradoc looked at Aisling like something to be taken apart and studied. She hated that look.

"That is a very good question, and one I wish I had an answer to," Dailten said. "This is a unique situation as far as I can tell. Even when we first crossed to this side of the veil, there was never a person, or thing, who was on both sides at once."

Aisling tucked the pendant back in her shirt. "Is there anything we can do about it now?"

Dailten and Harlie shook their heads in unison.

"While we were waiting for you, we did a brief check of the building site. It's is stable for now; I believe we need to focus on the attack on London first." Bart had remained silent during Stella's work on Aisling's hand, but was back in charge now. "We need to set up a base of operations."

Harlie nodded. "The energy that leaked through when the building crashed, is far weaker now. I agree, that that lincolica spell sitting over London is a bigger worry."

Dailten's eyes went round. "A lincolica spell? How—" She stopped and looked around the room. "We can discuss how that happened once we get started."

Harlie patted her on the arm. Since no one else knew what the spell even was, having a private discussion between the two heavy magic users made more sense.

Stella held up her hand. "But first, it's not that we don't trust you my friend…" She smiled at Dailten and nodded to Aisling. "I still have extra slivers, but I'll want the box first." Aisling gave her the box and watched Dailten.

Dailten seemed far more excited about the process than concerned about being mistrusted. She patted her check after the light declared her clear and Stella put the chip in. "This is amazing. I felt nothing and the box is a work of art. I'd like to meet this Mott person once this is over."

Bart nodded. "Now, to that barn of yours?"

Aisling felt much better, but Bart refused to let her help with setting up the barn meeting room. He browbeat her to a battered lawn chair in a corner. Fortunately, there was enough magic between all of them, along with physical labor from Reece and Jones, that a serviceable conference room was finished in a few hours.

Aisling felt it was a bit optimistic as there was a bank of stadium seating on one side that could fit a hundred or so people. She wasn't sure that many agents had escaped London.

Jones was working while listening to a news broadcast in an ear-bud, but he dropped what he was doing and turned around at something he heard. "There's been a claim as to who took over London. Our friend Nix has joined forces with the HLF. They want twelve billion dollars in gold, and all the fey out of London once the dome is removed."

"What?" Everyone in the room said at once.

Reece recovered first. "Why would he work with HLF? More importantly, why would they work with an established fey criminal? They want to raise human rights, not get rich."

"It has to be a ruse." Maeve stiffened at Nix's name and still looked far too tight. They might need to keep her car keys hidden from her in case she decided to go hunt down Nix herself. "He's using HLF to lend legitimacy to his crime. They aren't violent."

"That's a good point. Also, we still don't know how Nix could have pulled off that spell. Even if he is working with HLF." Aisling held up her hand to stop Maeve. "They are human and therefore not magic users. And Harlie said no group could do that anyway."

"And no single magic user would be strong enough." Caradoc was pacing now. "I felt Nix in that last fight, he's strong, there's no doubt, but not stronger than Harlie. And Harlie said he couldn't have done it. So who made that dome?"

"Damn." Aisling tried to shove down the thought that popped up, but it came forward anyway. "It can't be done by a group, because the separateness of them would shatter the spell, right?" At Harlie's nod she went on. "And no single magic user known is strong enough to do that." Again the nod. He knew where she was going and from the look on his face, he didn't like it any better than she did. "Nix and his clones. Same mind, same powers, lots of bodies. That's why he kept cloning himself." Unlike Maeve she didn't have the need to kill him herself, but she desperately wanted him dead.

The silence of the group wasn't comforting.

Finally, Bart nodded. "I think we have to assume that it a serious possibility. We can check to see if there have been any more spottings of Nix outside of London, but I have a bad feeling there won't be any recent ones."

Dailten seemed the most stunned. "I don't understand how…I know you told me of this person, but how can he do that?"

"That is a question I believe our network should look into." Harlie was already moving into solving the situation, one way or another.

"All I ask is that I get to kill him. The real him." Maeve looked like she was already sharpening her knives.

"We know." Aisling's comment was echoed by Caradoc, Reece, and Jones.

They set up a table with all of the laptops and a stand for Aisling's mobile blackboard. They were going to have to start backing up the original screens into storage at the rate they were adding new ones. But seeing everything spread out did make her feel better. There were a lot of connections lying under the surface, just waiting to be resolved.

"When you're ready, I can show the building drop site, but there isn't much to see. The agents who were here looking into it were called back to London a day ago." Dailten's face fell. "They are probably all trapped under that dome now, aren't they? That is very sad, they seemed nice."

Bart frowned. "Do you know who called them back?"

"No, a few were called back four days ago, then the final six were asked to return a day ago—not long before you got here. I thought you knew? I believe they left most of their things as they told the mayor they would be back in a few hours."

"That's not good," Caradoc said. "But it might explain why so few London agents have been found. If someone was working with Nix and was high enough up the pecking order to call agents back?"

Reece nodded. "And that would also tie into why some agents had been cloned or possessed. That way it was them who did the calling and the field agents would trust them. Greely must have been one too."

"We don't know for certain." Jones spoke up.

"Has anyone heard from him since he vanished at the house?" Aisling wasn't sure how she felt about Greely. "Honestly, he seemed too freaked out to have been a clone, replacement, or possessed. I think he was afraid of becoming one of those and took off after the attack on the house because he figured he was next." She might not have Harlie's mojo for sensing things, but she had intuition.

Bart ran his fingers through his hair leaving it stuck up. "You may be right and I should have worked harder to find him. He might know more than he was letting on, but was too scared to speak of it."

"He might be trapped in that dome," Reece said.

"I don't think so." Bart went to one of the laptops and started doing searches of some kind. "He was upset, he didn't trust anyone, because he knew some people had been replaced. But he wasn't sure who. Would you stay in town if everyone you knew could be an enemy?"

"No. But that just means he could be anywhere." Maeve peered over Bart's shoulder. "What's Langertown? I was born in the U.K. and never heard of it."

Bart grinned. "And you wouldn't have. It's shut down now, has been for over fifty years. But in the heyday of spying, it was where all the secrets were kept and worked on. There's nothing of value there now, they cleared it out decades ago. But if I were trying to hide, and I were Greely, I'd be hiding there. They had an underground bunker that was fully stocked with rations and water that would last a hundred years." He tapped the monitor. "If we want Greely, that's where we go."

CHAPTER FORTY-THREE

"I KNOW HE WAS YOUR FRIEND, but how much help is he going to be if he's that terrified?" Reece frowned. "I saw him in action, he was almost shaking when we were at the house that got pulled under. He probably does know a lot, but he won't trust us either." He joined Maeve in peering over Bart's shoulder. Disadvantage of being short, everyone could look over you.

"I think we have to bring in every resource we can." Caradoc was building another screen on the murder board laptop, but clearly still listening. "As I see it, there are two distinct situations going on." He expanded the screen. "Nix is over here. We have to assume he did get pulled through the veil when he escaped—whether it was his choice is another issue. He came back as clones of some sort and was working on gaining replacements of people in high places. He also either took over using a glamour, or persuaded the HLF to join him and made them more visible. You said they're not violent, yet they've been tied to some violent cases the past two weeks."

"But why pull them in?" Aisling asked.

"Because he's trying to gain control of the world and has decided to go start back at home," Caradoc said. "Increasing distrust between humans and fey could help him. His prior attempt was to remove the other fey, leaving him with power in a land of magicless humans."

Aisling looked at the board. It was twisted, but made sense. She took a marker and added, *Who on the High Council is he working with.* "Harlie said there had been evidence of a few massively delayed spells. Things Nix used to his advantage, but wouldn't have been strong enough to have created."

"It wasn't the spells that were delayed though, it was the reactions, the backlash of what they created with those spells. That was what they held back." Harlie moved to the screen. "Massive spells create a reaction throughout the natural world; someone delayed two that I can tell. One a few hundred years ago, the other even longer. It could be as far back as the first crossing to this world."

"Would there have been any advantage to have hidden the magic they used when they burst through the veil and crossed over?" Maeve was focused on Nix, but she could split her annoyance.

"I was there, young in age, but I crossed." Dailten also stared at the screen, but turned back with a shrug. "There was no magic on this side, nothing. That was one of the reasons our people chose it." She nodded at everyone's looks, even Harlie's. "Yes, you hadn't heard that had you? There are a number of worlds through the veil. Ours was dying and we were under attack from beings stronger than us. This one was magicless and beautiful. So the High Council selected it. But, the only reason to delay a spell reaction is to not let other magic users notice it. There were no magic users here when we crossed, so there would be no reason for a delay on the spell reaction."

"Excellent point." Caradoc stepped back from the board, scowling at something only he could see—or didn't see. "At any time, was there a large enough spell that someone would have wanted to keep hidden?"

"The only other large spell would have been when the High Council saved the humans from the Black Plague." Harlie added it randomly to the board. "I was born before then, and was old enough to understand that the humans were extremely ill. There were more of them than us by that point, we reproduced much slower than they did back then. By the time the High Council found a way to save them, they were less than half our population." He tilted his head. "But why would they need to hide that? All of the fey knew what the Council was doing. The spell to remove the plague almost took the lives of a few of the Council, but humanity was saved."

"And left almost sterile." Jones stood back from the board and folded his arms.

"Humanity was on the brink of dying out," Bart said. "And they are working on the sterility issue."

"Or are they?" Stella shook her head. "Along with her theories that we'd left fey behind the veil, my aunt had been looking into studies of the Black Death and the cure—not long before she was killed."

"The Council always gives a report on the status. It's slow going, but they are optimistic. I believe human conception was up again this year." Harlie looked like he was trying more to convince himself than anyone else.

"Yes, we're up to 2.7 percent." Maeve looked around. "I'm not blaming anyone here. But there is a lot of talk about feet being dragged in searching for a cure. People are getting angry."

"And we're back to Nix using that anger and pulling in the HLF." Aisling looked at the board. "How old is he? Nix, I mean."

"Random, but let me see." Caradoc pulled up a new browser window but swore as he had to go through a few attempts. "This information was hidden; but he crossed the veil as an adult."

Dailten came over to him. "Let me see his picture, please? I don't recognize the name, but it's not that uncommon." She swore at a level that Bart even blanched at as she saw his photo. "That one. He wasn't supposed to cross over. We did leave people behind, criminals who were waiting death." She glanced to Stella. "But I doubt that's what your aunt meant. This one, his name back then was

Nicolox Langhit. He was wanted for going on a murder spree a few years before we left." Her fist clenched and unclenched and she looked over to Maeve. "I won't fight you for the right to kill him, but I would like to help. And destroy his body to such small remains that he can never come back. He murdered many of my friends."

Stella took her arm and led her to one of the chairs. Dailten seemed stunned as well as pissed.

"I'm thinking we're finding out answers to questions we didn't know we had." Harlie sat on the other side of Dailten and patted her hand. "We still don't know what spell could have needed to be blocked. The effort to push a spell reaction back a few thousand years would be massive."

Aisling studied the board. Harlie was right, they were building more questions, but no answers. "We need to find the relationships. If Nix came through when the other death row prisoners couldn't, he had help. Whoever helped him is who told him about the spell reaction and enabled him to utilize it. But why, if he wasn't supposed to have left in the first place, would he want to go back, even for a short while?" Aisling looked over to Harlie, Stella, and Dailten. "Are there cases of people going there and coming back here? Ever?"

"No." Dailten was obviously still processing Nix's being here, but she answered quickly. "In the first years, a few did try to go back. Most were killed and their remains found on this side of the veil. A few vanished and a search for them on the magical planes indicated they had made it past the veil. The extremely powerful magic users were even able to make contact with some of them across the veil. All they knew was that the people who survived the crossing desperately wanted to come back to this world. But they couldn't. The veil wouldn't let them pass back."

"Yet, Nix appears to have crossed back and forth." Aisling knew this wasn't going to be a happy thought, but it struck her as true. "I'm not just saying this because I hate her, but pretty sure our mother and the rest of the High Council are working with Nix, probably have been from the beginning, and did some nasty spell of some sort 1700 years ago."

Caradoc scowled. "That was the Black Plague spell. One they had no reason to hide from anyone."

"Unless they added something to it." Aisling glanced to Maeve and Jones as the only two pure humans in the room. "Something that would keep the original owners of this world beholden to the High Council." She felt sick. Her mother was a nasty, vile, woman. But to have gone that far? That was beyond anything she could have imagined. But the pieces fell into place too well.

The silence that followed was heavy.

Even Harlie looked like he wasn't sure what she was saying. "Are you…"

"I think that when they were saving humanity from the Black Death, our mother and her people, all the ones in power, did something to change the way humans reproduced. They made sure that the fey would be the dominant species in this world. And humanity would be dependent on them. Isn't it odd that some humans can be assisted with magic to reproduce, yet they can't fix everyone?" She felt sick saying it and it was hard to meet Maeve's eyes. Maeve never indicated that she wanted kids, but Aisling knew many humans just ignored that thought altogether since the odds were so stacked against them. Getting the special conception treatment of magic took a lot of time and money. Even then it wasn't always successful.

Maeve looked pissed, but then she nodded to Aisling. "I think you're right. But just because some of your people, your mother, might have done this, doesn't mean all fey did. And if they pushed back the reaction to the spell they did to slow down our reproduction, they did it because they knew most fey wouldn't agree."

"This is huge. If it's true and it got out, there would be a war." As a breed, Reece was on both sides, and from the look on his face, both sides were terrified.

"Which would be a damn good reason to construct a long-time spell reaction delay." Stella shook her head. "I would have no idea how they did what we think they did, but the magic involved would be powerful."

"And I can't imagine any fey agreeing with that being done. Or how in the hell we can prove it if true." Caradoc looked ready to break something. Not a common reaction from him.

He had a good point. This was just a theory, but even if it felt true given what they were learning of the High Council, but there was currently no way to verify that was what happened.

Everyone stayed in their own thoughts until Aisling rattled them out of it. "We have some terrifying speculations of what might have happened back then, and while they might help us to figure out what we're up against, they aren't currently the direct source of our problems. If Nix is trying to create a human world that he can rule, he's not working with the High Council on everything. Most likely he's double crossing them. We need to look at what's happening now, and stop it." Not to mention, if her theory was right, it was too massive to face right now.

"And figure out why the veil is breaking through so much." Harlie said. "It's not just the magic of the first ones that keeps it closed, they did use spells. But it's the very nature of the veil that keeps it closed. If it fails completely, all of the worlds it divides will fall into each other. I don't have to point out how very bad that would be."

Bart watched the speculation, but stayed silent. He finally got to his feet. "I'm reversing my earlier assessment. I want everyone to see the building crash site, before we hunker in to save the world. Then I'll break everyone up into teams." He looked at his watch. "Narissa and the agents with her should be here soon. The others aren't flyers and she wants to stay together. I say we don't let anyone in on this newest theory until we know for certain and can prove it. Aisling could very well be right, but the news of that could destroy this world."

Aisling kept watching Maeve and Jones. Both had been furious at her theory—she had a feeling it was because deep down it felt right to them. She couldn't imagine why her mother and the High Council had gone so far. Yes, before the Black Death, there were more humans than fey. Had that continued, fey would be a massive minority right now. But to basically sterilize an entire species? Humans didn't have magic, so even as a much smaller population, the fey would be able to hold their own. The actions of her mother and cohorts were inexcusable.

Everyone except Harlie and Dailten walked down the road to the building drop. They were going to try reaching out to the other precogs they stayed in contact with and see if any of them had any information about the dome over London.

Dailten's barn/meeting room was only a block away from the building drop and Stella, Maeve, and Aisling walked down the road together.

"I thought you'd stay with Harlie and Dailten?" Aisling asked Stella.

"Naw. I do like Dailten though, she reminds me of my aunt. But those two have gifts I don't."

Maeve dropped one arm around Aisling's shoulders and hugged her. "I meant what I said by the way. If your theory does turn out to be true, it won't change how I feel about any of you here. Or any fey beyond the assholes who might have been behind that spell."

"Thank you. I still can't...damn it." Aisling hugged her back. "The entire time they've been working for a cure, and they might have been the ones who caused it." She stopped as a thought hit her. "Heike. She couldn't have kids when I first met her, then she joins the dark side and suddenly has three. They do have a cure, but are using it as incentive for humans who will help them. Damn it, this keeps getting worse." Heike had been a good friend in the police department years ago. Then the two drifted apart. She came back working for Nix. And trying to get Aisling killed.

Maeve tightened her hug and they walked forward in silence.

This building drop looked like the others, even though Harlie had tried to explain why it was different to her briefly before they left L.A.. She hadn't understood a single thing he said beyond that Noth was a nexus of magic lines and the veil should have been thicker here.

Dug into the ground before them was a piece of beige building, looking worse for wear, with cracks radiating out from it. Melted vehicles showed what had finally stopped it as there was rock hard goo trailing out from the hole to them.

Maeve stalked forward to the goo. "Is everything beyond the veil green goo? Didn't put it together before, but the building goo is green, whatever came up from underneath in London was green from what you said, that Nix clone you told me about melted down to green goo, and the dome strangling London is green. Did the fey flee because of an influx in green goo?"

Caradoc was off to the side, walking along the edge with one of his gizmos and scowling at some more petrified goo. "Unlike Dailten, I've never been on the other side, but it could be a chemical reaction to being here. The building was from our world, but going through the veil changed it." He looked over to Reece and Jones. "The first fall didn't have any goo, did it?"

Jones shook his head. "Not only no goo, green or otherwise, but the building was in a better state than any of the ones I've seen since then."

"My question is, what does our veil expert think?" Reece had his arms folded and watched Bart stalk around the hole.

Bart finally looked up. "Harlie is back in the barn, Dailten too."

"And Mott recognized you from a successful academic paper on the veil." Aisling joined Reece in the folded arms and glare brigade. It might have been a while ago, but the veil was still the veil. Maybe understanding more of how it was before could help them figure out what Nix had done to it.

"That was…fine." His defense fell as all of them looked at him. "It was a long time ago. I was fascinated by the changes in the veil since records started being kept. They are obscure and hard to find, but there has been a study of the veil and its functions since a few hundred years after we first crossed over to this side. Apparently, when the fey were on the other side, there was no thought or discussion about the veil. They could feel it, see it in ways we aren't able to over here. But it just was. They never thought about what might be on the other side until things started getting bad." He coughed. "I could go on about that for a while. But the pertinent points were that the veil was consistent, as far as these reports indicated, until about two hundred years ago. Then there were wobbles; little breaks, times when it got thinner, but then it would solidify again. My research paper was that these incidents of breaking down or thinning were getting worse and increasing in frequency. But there seemed to be no event or weather pattern, nothing to tie the issues to. They were random in all appearances."

"And then what?" Maeve asked.

"Then nothing. I had been on an academic track, aiming for full professor at NYU. Then my paper got buried.

It finally did get picked up by a smaller academic press. But my academic career was over."

"How could they do that?" Caradoc came closer. "That's important research, and they buried it? What reason?"

Bart looked to both Caradoc and Aisling. "The High Council felt it would cause panic in the general populace. My research was shut down by the high king and queen themselves."

"Damn. Good way to support the theory that we might be right and this all goes back to our parent." Caradoc leaned down to look at something stuck in the solidified goo, then jumped back. "I think it moved."

Stella went over and glared at the goo, which, as far as Aisling could tell, wasn't moving.

"Two hundred years?" Reece looked to Aisling.

"You think my death caused the veil to go bonkie?" Aisling had caught the two hundred years mention also. Damn thing kept popping up. But not everything could be tied to when her mother killed her. "That's a stretch, don't you think?"

"Or it's when our father brought you back." Caradoc moved away from the goo, but kept an eye on it.

Stella nodded. "From what I've heard, and what I learned from my aunt, death causes a ripple in the world and beyond the veil. Every death. It's natural and minor. Who knows what kind of impact coming back would have?"

"Might be on track," Maeve said. "Think about it, we don't know why she killed you, why your father or someone brought you back, or the repercussions. It's too bad none of you can safely go back through the veil—I think a lot of answers are on that side."

Reece had been close to an arm of the solidified goo when it liquified and reached out and grabbed his leg, pulling him off balance. Jones was closest to him and pulled him back, but he couldn't break him free. Nor stop the forward movement. The long arm of active goo was slowly, but determinedly, dragging Reece into the hole. Reece tried to fight, kicking at it with his other leg, but screamed as the part pulling his leg in started to smoke.

Aisling ran over to help, grabbing Jones and pulling as he had a good grip on Reece. But the goo kept dragging them forward. Caradoc ran to one of the cars, grabbed some electrical wire, connected it to the gizmo he had been using and swung it at the goo. The sections he hit froze again, but the rest was still liquifying, reforming, and reaching out.

Aisling let go of Reece and ran around the goo. She shoved aside the terror at what was happening to Reece and focused as much magic energy as she could at stopping the goo. It wasn't easy. The smoke around his leg had stopped but he still looked to be in a lot of pain. Forcing her eyes away from him, she pulled out the pendant, If the theory about the dome being connected to the goo was right, this should have the same result. But she kept her hand on the chain, not the pendant this time.

Caradoc ran to her and grabbed her hand. She thought he was trying to stop her, but then realized he was adding his magic to hers. A very tricky thing for any magic user and one they hadn't tried since they were kids and he'd accidentally flung her a few houses over. They were better matched now and his magic flowed along with hers and the pendant's.

Reece yelled as his foot was pulled into the hole. Aisling tried communicating with the pendant; if it was aware at all, she was going to make it listen to her. She felt it become aware, then furious at the goo. Primitive thoughts, but very pointed. They might both be from the other side of the veil, but they were not friends. The pendant took the magic she and Caradoc created, focused it, and blasted the goo.

The goo steamed, then exploded into blackened pieces of what looked like burnt glass. They shot high in the air, then rained around the entire road.

Reece was suddenly released and he and the others pulling on him were flung back a few feet.

Aisling and Caradoc both stumbled, but recovered. Unlike stopping the dome, Aisling didn't feel weak this time. The pendant had worked with her and Caradoc, not against them. It gave a soft humming sound; then whatever awareness was in there was gone.

"That was different," Aisling said with a smile to Caradoc. "Thanks for the assist."

"Reece isn't breathing!" Maeve yelled.

Chapter Forty-Four

Aisling reached Reece first, with Caradoc right behind her. Had she killed Reece in trying to save him?

Her heart was in her throat as she dropped to her knees and put a hand on his heart. She forced herself into a healer trance when her magic didn't initially respond to him. He was still there, but barely hanging on. His breathing was shallow and his heartbeat faint. Shoving aside the terror she felt at possibly losing him, she reached into his mind and grabbed that spark of him that remained and started mentally yelling at him as she worked on repairing his body. She needed him to fight back against dying.

"Don't you dare leave me! I will hunt you down and bring you back. Hang on—fight it!" His body had looked fine on the outside, but whatever power the goo had must have shot through him as they defeated it. His nerves and muscles were all fried. Which meant his heart stopped beating.

She focused on doing CPR externally as she worked on healing him from inside. And continued the mental yelling. "You can't leave me you fishy, annoying, superspy. Damn it. I don't care if you're a siren." She let everything she felt about him out in one mental shout. "I love you!" The force of her words, and the extreme anger she felt about him trying to leave her, surged her healing.

His awareness came back as his body responded to her magic rebuilding his nerves and muscles. Everywhere that had been burnt or damaged was healed now.

"I knew you did. I can sense these things." He kissed

her.

At first she thought everything was still in her head, then she realized his mouth was on hers. She opened her eyes and returned the kiss.

"That's great and all, but if you keep crying on him, you might drown him. And we do have a world or two to save." Maeve's voice had enough of a shake in it that Aisling knew she hadn't been the only one who thought they'd lost Reece.

Aisling broke off the kiss and wiped her tears off his face. "Sorry about that, you're a bit soggy."

He smiled and wiped as well. "A fair cost for getting you back—and the whole saving my life bit."

Bart nodded. "Good job, Danaan. I'd hate to have to replace Larkin right now. He is still a bit wet, though." If he was disturbed or surprised at two of his agents kissing each other, he didn't show it.

"Aisling is still shaking. How about I help you both up?" Jones reached down and helped them to their feet.

Stella walked over to them. Her eyes filled with worry as she touched them each on the cheek. She broke into a grin. "They're both fine now." She turned to Reece and shook her finger at him. "Don't do that again." Then she hugged them both and stepped back.

Maeve moved in after Stella and grabbed Aisling and Reece in a hug. "Damn it—no more dying, near dying, nothing even close. For either of you." She gave Aisling a nod, they'd talk later.

Aisling slipped her arm around Reece's waist at the same time he dropped his around her shoulders. All the uncertainty of the past weeks at what was going on between them fled when she thought she'd lost him. That he'd never had that uncertainty said a lot too. They'd deal with the possibility of him having siren powers after they saved the world. Or at least freed London.

Caradoc picked up a piece of the solid goo before anyone could yell at him to stop. He must have heard the gasps though. "Sorry to worry you all—but this stuff is dead. I want to look at it with my scanners, but it's dead now. I'd guess that electricity stuns it, but it takes a lot more to kill it."

Bart's eyes went wide as that implication hit him. He pulled out his phone. "Larkin, notify LAX they might have a new problem on their hands if that goo becomes active again. I'll call Driyflin and get her to cordon off the sinkhole. Jones, contact the New York office and get them to warn all the agents."

Reece had to release Aisling to make his call.

Maeve gave Aisling a smile and pulled her away from him a bit. "I know the world is ending again, but we've decided he's not showing siren powers now?"

Aisling shrugged. "I have no idea, to be honest. But when I thought I was going to lose him…I just don't think what I'm feeling is because of a siren. He's a pain in the ass, but he's my pain in the ass. I love him." She shook her head. "Awesome timing, right?"

"You were always a bit daft when it came to love." Maeve grinned. "But he's a good one. And he massively loves you. If we live through this you two can settle down and raise little sproglets. I do claim right of maid of honor and godmother to all aforementioned sproglets by the way."

"You are so jumping the gun. But I promise both positions of honor will be held by you. Providing we get through this and things get to that point. I just realized I am in love with the man for crying out loud."

"Deal." Maeve was focusing on someone past her.

Aisling grinned when she turned and saw it was Caradoc. "When are you going to make a move on my brother?"

Maeve started a bit. "Harlie's not my type, really, but thanks."

"Caradoc. I've seen the interest from you and him. He's also a pain in the ass, but a good guy."

Maeve's blushes weren't common. "I…yeah. He is kinda a hottie. And funny, and terrifyingly brilliant. Do not tell him I said any of that. I have to keep my focus on killing Nix, then life can continue." But her look wandered back to Caradoc as he collected a few more goo stones.

"I won't say anything." Aisling gave a sweet smile. "But you would make a great sister-in-law."

"Ack! Too soon." Maeve's face locked into a look of horror. "Oh gods, that would make your mother…"

"Your mother-in-law. Welcome to our hell."

Caradoc had gathered a handful of stones and was heading back toward the barn with Stella peering at them as they walked. Reece, Jones, and Bart finished their calls—none of them looked happy.

"What happened?" Aisling asked as Reece stepped over to them.

"It's not good," he said. "The airport goo had already reanimated a few hours ago, it killed three workmen before it was contained. They are using electricity to shock it back into dormancy, but it has already come back once. They have alc mages coming out, but it takes them a while."

Alc mages were extremely secretive and off-the-charts powerful magic users who lived in the furthest reaches of the globe. That they were being called out was almost as scary as what was going on around them.

Jones didn't look any happier. "New York reports three more building drops, all around the city, and far smaller than the ones on the west coast, or even this one. They have alc mages on the way as well."

Bart joined them. "Captain Driyflin was on her way to the sinkhole when I called her. Luckily Caltrans hadn't started on repairs but the goo came out and tried to attack the two Area 42 agents on guard duty. The alc mages will go there after they cleanse LAX."

Aisling kicked one of the goo rocks lightly. "Should we leave these scattered around? I'd feel better if they were gathered in some extremely reinforced and sealed metal container. And perhaps sent into the sun." The goo certainly looked solid, but it had seemed solid before. Maybe a nice bath in a live volcano would destroy them.

"I think gathering them is a good idea. But, your brother aside, I'd rather you all used shovels and wheelbarrows—not grabbing by hand," Bart spoke just as Jones bent down to grab a piece.

Bart went back to the barn. Aisling, Maeve, Reece, and Jones were on clean up duty. Finding shovels and wheelbarrows wasn't hard, they'd moved a number of both items out of the barn when they fixed it up.

"I'd hate to think of someone taking one of these home as a keepsake." Maeve chased a bunch of them around with her shovel. "But where are we going to put them?"

Dailten came out and looked at the collection. "Those really did get destroyed. Excellent. I am sorry they almost got Reece." She nodded to him. "But I think I know a perfect holding place for them. An old sealed up well. It's thick and strong, and has a lot of earth around it to reinforce the containment." She walked toward the side of the barn. Harpies were unusually attuned to nature, so she would have a good feeling for the strength of the earth around the well.

She stopped in front of a large underground well. It stuck up a foot or two from the ground. There was no way from here to see how large it was, but the heavy-duty lid on it was at least two feet across and had a large wheel on top to turn it. "Mayhap, you young ones can open it?" Dailten held up her hands and showed the slight bending in both. "Clean living hasn't stopped arthritis from making a visit from time to time."

Aisling tilted her head. She'd never seen a well of any sort look like this. "What kind of well was this?"

"Better not to bring that up, the ground is still touchy about it." Dailten grinned at the dirt. "I did apologize profusely. Never you worry, it's safe now."

It took all four of them, but they got the top off. The tank was huge and thick. After this was over, Aisling was certain Area 42 would send agents to gather the rocks, but for now this should keep them from causing any more harm. Whatever it had been a well for, it was intended not to let anything out.

Dailten smiled as they started dumping them in. "Harlie, Caradoc, and I are breaking from our prior studies to work on a way to detect the dead goo rocks, in case any were missed. We don't want any of them out and about." With a nod, she walked back toward the barn.

Harpies had a distinctive walk, their wings were larger than other flyers, and while they did fold back and become visually invisible, they still threw off their stride.

Watching Dailten, Aisling let out a deep breath as an old sadness hit her.

Reece turned to her. "What's wrong?"

Maeve knew and squeezed Aisling's shoulder. "Thinking of Forith, aren't you?"

"Yeah." Aisling nodded to Reece. "Forith was my partner before Maeve. She's gone now." She didn't want to go into it at this point, over ten years and the memory was still too fresh. It had been a brutal loss, and even though she'd run across harpies since, none reminded her of Forith the way Dailten did just now. "Just an old memory messing with me. We have enough to deal with." She mentally raised a blessing to her lost friend and went back to the rocks.

They finished dumping what rocks they could find into the well, even going out in a search pattern radiating out from the center to find more. If Harlie and Dailten could make a detector they should be able to make sure none were left.

Caradoc almost bounced out to meet them as they came back to the barn. "Great timing, sister mine!" He was too perky; which usually meant he'd discovered something deadly to create. "We have modified this metal detector to help with any missing stones. Just one detector though, so you'll have to take turns. We also have verified that the green goo is from beyond the veil. It's not a reaction to this world—it's actually bringing in components from the other side." He held up a heavy canister. "No idea if the pulverized rock dust will prove helpful for anything else, but it is secured now."

Harlie sat at the other end of the table. "Components, really, more so than aspects. I would love to get a sample of the dome, but the physical and metaphysical implications and aspects are huge. Something on the other side is forcing its way through. In the goo."

Aisling looked at the analysis Caradoc had up on his screen, but the chemical makeup meant nothing to her. "The pendant doesn't like the goo. There is some sentiency in the pendant, but it's not there all the time. Once I made it realize what we were fighting against, it got angry. That's what blasted the goo apart."

"Two entities from beyond the veil fighting each other on this side?" Dailten looked up from her own studies. "That seems a bit odd. But it would fit. You've said the vallenians appear to not be halted by the veil anymore. Trust me, those would have never been brought to this side. Could they now be helping us, and something else is fighting them?"

"Great, the monsters from our children's tales are now our heroes?" Aisling laughed but it felt true.

"On another front, we've reached out to our precog circle. All of them have felt something building. But none know what it is. Just a disturbance of great proportions."

Harlie looked to Maeve. "And I even picked up sendings from at least two people within the London dome. They are confused and foggy, their sendings little more than random mutterings as if asleep. But they are alive." He knew that news would be welcome by everyone, but mostly by Maeve.

Aisling smiled. "Thank you. That gives me hope for the rest trapped inside there. Any more news updates on Nix and his demands?"

Bart shook his head. "The timeline is still ticking, but no one has officially responded to them. And no confirmation or denial from HLF."

"Are the British king and queen still in Buckingham? Kind of hard to respond if you're in a slumber." Jones studied the screens and nodded. He was an action focused person, but understood a lot of science babble.

"No, they were in Edinburgh for a planned visit when the attack struck," Bart said. "I believe Nix and whoever he is working with might have felt taking London over was enough to motivate everyone; but locking in the royals might make getting what they want harder. This appears to have been extremely well planned."

"And that is why I wanted to remove you all before we got to this." Nix was standing right behind them.

CHAPTER FORTY-FIVE

THEY ALL SPUN TOWARD THE open barn door, but Maeve was the first to charge. She didn't pull out her gun, just raced forward with her bare hands curled into claws.

And ran right through him.

His image flickered as she ran through. "Oh, that was wonderful. Tell me you enjoyed it too? Come on, Maeve, you miss me. Admit it."

Maeve ran through him again, but all he did was laugh. "Yes, I've had my people push hologram technology further than anyone, even the great Caradoc Larfin. I'm not here, obviously, but just wanted to see how you all are doing." He leaned toward the table of computers and analysis equipment, but the others blocked him from seeing anything. He couldn't move from the spot that he landed in judging by the way he was twisting around but not taking any steps.

Dailten hissed and stepped forward. "Nicolox Langhit, you never should have crossed over with us. You should still be rotting beyond the veil." In her anger, her wings extended, their hooks looking ready to tear him apart if they could. She stalked forward. "I remember you from before we came here. I know what you did."

"Dailten? I'm surprised you're still alive. Still working on your potions and earth spells?" Nix looked bored. If he were flesh and blood, having a harpy come at him with wings out would end up with some serious pain. If not death. "I know technology isn't your friend, but you can't hurt me like this."

She stalked closer and the laugh would have been perfect in a kids' show on evil witches. "Oh, but I have friends now. And they do know technology. This won't hurt a bit. Actually, that's a lie, I hope it hurts you a lot. Rot in hell, you bastard." She was a few inches away from him when she threw a handful of what looked like dust at his hologram and spat out some dark spell words. The dust managed to go through the hologram and settle on him. He screamed as the spell forced the dust to sink into his flesh. He twisted to brush the dust off himself.

The spell she'd cast wasn't affected and appeared to be burning into his skin.

"I found you once, I'll find you again!" Then Nix vanished.

"Could whatever you just did have killed him? Because I would like him dead, painfully is preferred, but I was sort of hoping I could do it myself." Maeve didn't look as upset as usual when Nix was involved.

Dailten shook her wings and folded them back up. "Caradoc would be a better one to ask about that—that was his rock dust. I just added some magical assistance. Good to know ground goo breaks through holograms."

"Yup. I know we shouldn't mess with it, but Dailten had a hunch." Caradoc grinned at her. "Dailten's spell kicked it through. It should still be stinging him. Sadly, I think he'll survive the encounter."

"Is there any way to stop him from reappearing?" Bart went over to the area where Nix had been and kicked about the straw. "Does he know where we are?"

Jones shook his head. "I wouldn't think so. He was tagging on to one of us to appear here, not the location. He now knows we're inside a barn though."

"What do you mean he's tagging one of us?" Maeve looked around. "Do you think he planted something on someone?"

"I don't think we have a spy, but I think we've been

compromised." Jones looked to Bart, Stella, Caradoc, and Aisling. "The only time one of his clones got close to any of us was the one that blew up on Caradoc. My bet would be him, since he definitely was exposed directly. But it could have been transferred to anyone."

Caradoc dug into his bag of gizmos. "I was stupid. I should have thought to scan before we left the area. But first I was dying, then Aisling's magic went crazy. Things were a bit hectic. Still, no excuse on my part." The device he held up was large for one of his toys. Twice as wide as his hand and almost as long. "This might take a few adjustments, as I'm going to have to scan for all frequencies. We have no idea what he used." He first passed it over himself, then the other three who had been there, then the rest. "At this point, we're checking everyone."

Nothing pinged the first sweep, and the second sweep just pointed out the possession-alert-slivers all of them had. The third sweep, however, brought pinging when he swept himself, but then also Aisling, Stella, and Bart. The others were clean.

"He blew up one of his clones just to track you four?" Maeve asked once she'd been found clean.

"That's what it looks like." Caradoc adjusted the readings, scanned again, and got the same results on the four of them. "Aisling would have been hit the same way I'd been since she healed me. Stella pushed Aisling, so that connects, but Bart didn't touch any of us."

"In the air." Both he and Dailten said at the same time.

"Let's see what we can put together to remove whatever trackers he's made. *Before* he recovers enough to return. That bit with the dust and magic worked once, but I doubt it'll work again," Caradoc said as he and Stella took over two of the computers and started working. Harlie watched carefully.

The sound of cars pulling up caught everyone else's attention. Bart nodded to Reece and Jones and they stepped out of sight behind the open barn doors with their guns drawn. Caradoc, Stella, and Harlie stayed working. No one would get to them unless they got through Reece and Jones first.

The rest of them walked out to greet their guests.

Narissa was the first out of the foremost car. She nodded to Aisling. "Good to see you made it. These were the only agents I could find. Eight, besides myself."

Aisling nodded hello and Bart walked up to greet them.

"She's okay, right? Damn, how are we going to know who to trust?" Maeve whispered next to her. She wasn't grabbing her gun, but she was twitchier than she had been. Maeve might have downplayed Nix's appearance, but it had thrown her off.

"Yeah, she seemed fine." Aisling turned to Stella. "You have the box and the slivers, right? Do we have enough?"

Stella patted the side bag she wore. "We have plenty. One thing I've learned from years in the diner business, always plan for four times what you think you'll need. Once Bart has finished sniffing them out, *we* can check them all more scientifically."

Bart motioned for Stella to come forward. He had Narissa step up. Stella briefly explained what she was going to do, then held up the box. Even a bit back as they were, Aisling heard the "all clear". Then Stella put the sliver in her cheek.

Narissa nodded toward a tall human man. He was older, but moved like an athlete. He shrugged, looked in the box, passed, got his sliver, and stood to the side.

Three more agents were checked and passed, but Aisling got an odd feeling up the back of her neck as the next one—a gnome woman—hesitated before she approached. Aisling took a step forward. She didn't reach for her gun, but her hand was ready to do so. The gnome woman was an inch or two shorter than Bart, and didn't step as close to Stella as the others.

"Come on Nari, you know me. This is ridiculous." She turned her smile to Narissa.

"Dhila, everyone needs to do it. You might not even know if you've been possessed. Just step up and let her scan you with that box."

Dhila took a step back toward the car. "But I'm fine."

Aisling pulled out her gun and so did Maeve. "I would advise you to stop moving right now. Bart, there is something wrong with her."

Harlie came running out of the barn. "You've got a problem…oh, yes, you know. Her mind isn't right."

Dhila looked around but the two remaining untested agents moved away from her with weapons raised. "But I'm me. Just me." She was fast, but not faster than Aisling. Dhila had her gun out and raised as Aisling shot her arm, and the gnome's gun dropped to the dirt. The scream that followed was nothing a gnomish, or elven, voice could make.

Dhila, or what had been her, mutated as she stood there. Cracks crept along her skin and red flames appeared through them.

"At least it's not green goo?" Maeve kept her gun trained on the two untested agents.

"What in the hell are you?" Narissa had her gun out and was already extending her wings and lifting off the ground.

"Exactly." Dhila screamed again and fiery wings appeared from her back.

Chapter Forty-Six

——◆——

REECE AND JONES CAME RUNNING out of the barn at the first flap.

"Oh hell no. Everyone fire!" Bart yelled as he started shooting at whatever the gnome woman had become. Everyone, even the two agents who hadn't been tested yet, shot into the fire creature. The shots seemed to make little impact beyond damaging her wings, but the holes grew back each time. It was enough to keep her from getting any real altitude however.

Dhila drifted closer to Aisling as she fought to get into the air. Aisling stuck her gun in the back of her jeans and leapt for Dhila. Her skin wasn't as hot as she looked, but Aisling felt the burns starting on her skin. She quickly retaliated. Anti-healing magic flowed much easier now that her magic was unblocked—she just hoped someone could break her free before she died magic-locked with Dhila.

"What are you doing?" Dhila yelled between her shrieks of pain. "What are you?!" Aisling kept sending magic into her until they dropped to the ground. Dhila reached out and grabbed the pendant, then gave an ear-piercing scream and exploded into ash.

Aisling rolled away from the ash storm, checked to make sure the pendant was still there, and fell back panting.

"Damn it, Stella, heal her!" Reece was the first to get to her, even though he wasn't the closest. He lifted her head up. "She's awake."

Stella looked down at her with a grin. "That was a very

impressive show, my dear. But you need to use some caution. Let's take you inside and get you fixed. Bart? Can you test the last two?"

Stella chased off Reece, then led the way and got Aisling settled on the sofa. Her healing magic was less intense than before, but aside from feeling massively bruised, Aisling didn't feel that much worse for wear from her battle with whatever that had been. The burns she'd felt hadn't been real.

"What was inside her?" Aisling rubbed the back of her head. She'd fallen back harder than she thought. "I've never seen or heard of anything like that. The pendant didn't like her either. I could feel part of her mind, she thought the pendant would help her. It had other plans." She shuddered. Yes, it had been a life-or-death fight, but having your necklace blow up your opponent was disturbing.

Stella finished healing her then sat back. "We should ask Dailten to confirm, but I'd be willing to guess that was a full possession. Not something Nix made, but something he might have let come through. Or he might have nothing to do with it. There were beings, other Old Ones beyond the vallenians, who could possess souls. I'd say Dhila had been taken a while ago, possibly months for that level of control to have settled in."

"But do they have a name? And if Nix didn't bring it here, what did?"

"Logazins. Nasty creatures, the books my aunt had showed them as much larger when fully hatched—this one was forced to expose itself too early. Although this one had probably been inside Dhila for months, it still wasn't fully grown." Her tiny face went serious. "A fully grown logazin, in complete power, would have destroyed all of us. Even you, I'm afraid. Although your pendant there is an unknown entity, so there is that."

"That's so reassuring." Aisling looked at the pendant,

then tucked it back into her shirt. "Still not sure if it's on our side or the other side. But it's doing a damn good job saving our collective asses."

"I'd say it's on its own side." Harlie came into the room. "You do look much better by the way. The other two agents tested fine; it was just that one logazin. Nasty things. Glad you destroyed it."

"You knew what it was?" Aisling shook her head. "Never mind, of course you did."

Reece stuck his head in. "Bart is having all of the agents, excluding you two, go do a field search and make sure the area around here is cleared and we've checked any remaining civilians in the town. He and Maeve are staying here until Caradoc and Dailten can find a way to block Nix. You *are* okay, right?" The look on his face said he didn't want the others to be here right now.

Aisling smiled. "Just tired and trying to figure out my new best friend." She tapped the pendant under her shirt. "Stay out of trouble."

He nodded, then left. Harlie turned for the door as well. "I've actually been some help to them on the breaking of the trackers, I'll come get you when we're done."

Stella waited until he was gone. "Everything good with you and Reece?"

Aisling laughed. "Nice to know we're fighting for our lives and folks are more worried about my love life."

"It's a distraction of the non-threatening kind. And people care about you. So?" The way she leaned forward she reminded Aisling of a teenager getting gossip on a first crush.

"So when I healed him, I realized I love him and that it wasn't something a siren could make. Even if his genetics started it, the feelings are real now." She couldn't tell most people about Reece's weird hybrid powers, but she trusted Stella completely. So did he.

"Good. Magic is strong, love is stronger." Stella patted

her knee. "Shall we go see how the others are doing?"

Caradoc, Dailten, and Harlie were gathered around the computer filled table. Maeve and Bart were off to the side in some chairs talking intently. Aisling had meant to ask if Maeve had reached any MI-6, or Closen, yet. That Maeve hadn't said anything probably meant no.

"How goes the search?" Aisling stood behind them; the way they were darting back and forth between computers made her afraid to get too close. Stella stayed with her, probably for the same reason.

"This is quite interesting. Did you know that Caradoc has found a way to separate out individual psychic energies? Fascinating!" Harlie's enthusiasm was almost tangible.

"And this helps us right now…how?" Aisling was all for research, but things needed to be fixed quickly, not wandering off into other areas.

"Oh, it doesn't, not really. But it is interesting." He beamed at them again and went back to the computers.

Caradoc looked back. "Actually, it does help me separate out what is each one of us and what is the tracking agent. I already sent the specs to Mott for modification. It's a tricky one. However, I'm trickier. A bit more narrowing the targeting down and I should be able to breakdown the trackers on all of us."

"I don't think I want tracker bits inside me, diluted or not." Aisling tried to look at the screens but they were so full of computer code and magical notations that they were a blur.

"Well, in this case it's the only way to get rid of them. They were airborne as predicted but they settled on the skin. We have to break them down on the dermis level, but then the body will destroy the pieces through natural regeneration. Once we break it down, he can't track you anymore." Dailten had that same crazy happy grin the other two had.

Aisling shook her head. As long as they were happy and productive. "Great. So when? And is there any way to weaponize that dust or does it only work on holograms?"

Maeve came over at the end of her sentence. "I heard weaponize?"

"You two are spoiling our surprise. But yes, I think it can be weaponized. But no more about that until we get these trackers off and this barn resealed." Caradoc turned back to the others and they returned to working on more magic/cyber babble.

"It is interesting how tech and magic are working together on this," Maeve said.

"It is, but right now, I feel like everyone is focused on fixing things, and I'm still not sure what the hell is going on." Aisling was used to a more direct type of crime solving.

Bart came over. "None of us are. We're facing things no one has dealt with before. Harlie explained to me what that agent turned into. Those were supposed to be children's stories, not real."

"I think all of the old stories are right." Dailten stepped away from the bank of laptops. "I was young when we crossed, but not so young that I forgot what we left. The veil is failing."

"When Nix's hologram was here, you said you knew what he did," Maeve said. "What was it?"

Aisling knew Maeve didn't need another reason to want Nix dead, none of them did. But she had been curious as well.

"It's not a pretty tale, and when we've destroyed him for good, I'll share the full story. But, in brief, he slaughtered an entire village of harpies and gnomes simply to see how much energy he could draw from their deaths. I lost two cousins and an uncle in the murders." She clenched her fists and her wings briefly appeared behind her. Then she took a deep breath and they vanished again. "It took a few decades of isolation to get past the anger, but the fact he made it through to here, and is still alive is making things difficult."

"This confirms that he had help from the Council then, and is still working with them one way or another. There's no way he would have been able to have crossed during the migration without the Council allowing him and hiding him from everyone else." Harlie looked like he'd like a crack at killing Nix too—an extremely uncommon sight.

Silence filled the barn as everyone settled on their own thoughts.

"Ha!" Caradoc had been focused on his computers and finally started waving his hands in the air. "I have it. Let me just make one more tweak." He started muttering to himself as he fussed with one of his gizmos, then held it up in triumph.

"It looks like a giant bug." Maeve gave it a longer study. "Yup, a bug."

It was a foot long, appeared to have been created from a number of smaller gizmos, and had what looked like legs and antennas all around it.

"It really does look like a bug." Aisling didn't need to step forward, it was too buggy for her liking.

"But it works!" Caradoc aimed it at himself for a few seconds, grinned then aimed it at Aisling, Stella, and Bart. "You won't notice it, but it's breaking down the trackers. And, best of all, I can modify it to take out other trackers as well."

Aisling looked down at herself. "I feel the same. How do we know if it's working?"

Stella held the scanner gizmo of Caradoc's. "Mind if I demonstrate?" At his nod, she aimed it at Aisling. The pinging sound was still there, but growing weaker.

"That's one issue done, and I am glad none of you are calling Nix to us, but we do need to get a move on figuring out how to free London," Maeve said.

Dailten and Harlie had been quietly watching everyone, but both stepped forward.

"We're going to storm it," Dailten said proudly.

CHAPTER FORTY-SEVEN

EVERYONE WAITED FOR THE TWO to elaborate, but they just stood there smiling.

Bart shook his head. "A handful of agents and us are going to storm a blob that has taken over all of London. Do you two know how large London is or how insane that sounds?"

"Yes." Harlie smiled. "Six hundred and seven square miles for the greater area, but the area of the dome is a bit less than that. We've estimated only five hundred and two square miles to be currently covered. As for the insanity, yes, but we need to go far outside of what we know, to destroy what could not be." He nodded serenely as if he'd just clarified the meaning of life.

"You slipped into your mystic-on-the-mountain voice with that last bit," Aisling pointed out.

"He did." Bart narrowed his eyes at both of them. "I assume you two have a plan? Something that indicates how we storm it? Something clearly defined?"

"We use the fey and human forces. Most of the HLF is still outside the dome, and while not a military group, they are pissed that their name is being used in such a way—they are not involved with Nix." Caradoc had clearly been multitasking on both projects. "It appears their higher ups are missing and presumed inside the dome."

Maeve went to one of the laptops. "I can help encourage their involvement. I'm not a member, but I know a few people who are. But even if we get them and others to join, shooting it isn't going to take it down." She questioned their actions but Aisling noticed that she'd sent out a few emails and was composing more.

Dailten held up the case with the green goo rock dust in it. "We get enough of this made, use flyers to get it dispersed over the dome, then attack. The dust and spells will weaken the dome enough for us to take it down."

Noise from outside the barn indicated the others were back.

Reece, Jones, and Narissa came in first, the rest stayed outside. And it looked like there were far more people with them than when they'd left.

Reece came to Stella. "We need you, your box, and those slivers. We cleared the area, but found more agents from assorted agencies coming this way. Word got around that we're the place to be."

"How many more?" Bart was already heading for the door.

"Fifty-three. Once they're cleared, we can start trying to find more. Any luck in getting the tracking off?"

"Yep and yep." Aisling hooked a thumb over to where Harlie, Caradoc, and Dailten stood. "We're cleared and they've figured out how to save London."

Stella and Bart went to go check on the other agents, with Jones and Narissa going out as back up.

Caradoc explained a brief version of the plan to Reece.

"Will it work?" Reece looked over the schematics and notes, but didn't look optimistic.

Dailten nodded. "We don't have much choice. It's this, or Nix keeps London. At least until that lincolica spell he created collapses in on itself and takes everyone and everything inside London with it. Making the extra dust won't be a problem, we have a lot of stones and it's a fast process."

"We still won't cover all of the dome, but all of the cells for the HLF are converging on London already, I convinced them to work with us," Maeve said.

Reece ran his hand through his hair. "We need more people, even if this dust works and we can get enough magic using flyers up and over the dome, the fire power we'll have will be minimal. There's no way to cover the entire area. Can we use small planes or drones to disburse it?"

Caradoc scowled. "No. I already thought of planes and drones, but there is a static charge coming off that dome. In every computer scenario the drones dropped and the planes crashed. It's tech, not magic. Flyers won't be affected."

"I might be able to help." Greely spoke from the barn doors before anyone inside noticed he was even there. "Sorry I took off like that in London, no idea who to trust. But I picked up on the call for agents to come here. I like the testing for possession by the way, I wish we'd had that a few months ago." He sighed. "But I have connections to the Royal Army; I can get more forces on the ground and in the air."

Bart and Stella were still working through the crowd of agents with Mott's box, but Aisling knew Jones wouldn't have let Greely through unless he'd been cleared.

It was already after nine on an extremely long day. Once the agents had all been cleared, not a single sign of possession among them, people were settled down and told to rest.

Of course, that still meant sorting through the specifics of the attack, so Aisling and the core team worked until Bart finally pushed them off about midnight.

They had thirty flyers with them, with at least another eighty reported from the Royal Army. Luckily for them most flying fey weren't fond of massive cities like London, so they lived outside of it. They would all meet with the army and the humans at a set meeting spot tomorrow afternoon.

Stella bunked with Aisling and Maeve and they were

all settling in with a bit of tea to unwind. "I should have told Bart; he is our leader after all. But Reg and Grundog contacted me once the news of the dome on London went worldwide. They are either here in the U.K. now, or on their way. He's gathering the Ckiong to do their own attack on the dome."

Aisling shook her head slowly. "More fighters are good, but why do I think there's a problem?"

"Because, while Reg and Grundog like us personally, as a whole the Ckiong don't trust other fey or human organizations. Trying to get them to work with us would be problematic to say the least. I've tried calling Grundog twice in the past hour, but it goes to voicemail. There are over two thousand trolls in Ckiong, they would go a long way to increasing our ranks."

"Damn right they would." Maeve topped off their tea. "We have to get them on our side. If the HLF is working with us, they bloody can too." She grumbled, pulled out her phone, and started stabbing in a number. "I am tired as hell and we're going into battle tomorrow…hello? Reg? Good to hear you. This is Maeve. What's this about your people not fighting with us to free London?" She nodded to Aisling and Stella and stomped off into her room to continue the call.

"I didn't even know she had his number." Aisling watched the shut door.

"Me either. He must have taken a shine to her. And judging by the raised voice from Maeve, he might be regretting he gave it to her." Stella gave a small smile.

"Yelling sometimes is the best way to deal with a troll."

"I agree. That's why I didn't tell Bart. If anyone had officially contacted them, Reg would have been obligated to say no. He'll have a very hard time doing that to Maeve." She cleared away the tea. "I know it's late, and we're both tired. But I want to teach you some shielding spells. We've no idea what we'll be facing tomorrow."

Aisling started to shake her off. Her mother had tried to teach her advanced shielding, but somehow it never worked. Then she realized that with her magic released, it should work now. "Can we do it quickly? I'm exhausted."

"Yes, nothing fancy, just basic shielding for you and whoever is close to you. Probably can get a good ten foot spread each direction as long as it's short duration." She got to her feet. "Now, let's do it."

An hour later an exhausted but satisfied Aisling rolled into bed. She had some marks on her arms to show where Stella's tests had gotten through, but she could shield now. Maeve had tottered out a while ago, said she got the damn trolls to join the fight, then went to bed.

Morning came far too soon.

The knocking on the front door wasn't welcome nor quiet. She rolled to her feet and went to open it.

Reece looked far too awake, aware, and sexy to deal with after three or four hours of sleep. "Just wanted to see how you all were doing?"

She didn't miss the emphasis being on the word you and not all.

"Stella taught me to shield, Maeve got us some more support." She pulled him inside and explained both while she made coffee.

"That's amazing. Both things actually."

"What's amazing?" Maeve asked as she stumbled into the kitchen, claimed a mug, and got some coffee. She gave Reece a look. "You do not appear to have stayed overnight."

"Because I didn't." Reece laughed. "We'll need to coordinate Reg with the rest of the team, but that is amazing that you got him to join in."

"That is an issue. The Ckiong won't follow Area 42 or any other group. I gave him the full details. He and his people will *happen* to meet us there, then decide to join."

"But that...is very troll." Reece sat down the coffee

cup Aisling handed him. "I suppose Bart has to come here to learn of this, and we can't tell anyone else?"

"Yup." Maeve took a sip of her coffee, dumped it down the drain, and started some tea. "I love the smell, but can't take the taste."

Reece left with a quick nod to Stella as she came into the kitchen.

"That's how he's getting around Ckiong stubbornness. Good job, Maeve." Stella came in. "Are we ready for a battle that will go down in history?"

CHAPTER FORTY-EIGHT

THE MORNING WAS A BLUR as more agents filtered in, were checked by Stella and Dailten, then put into groups. The plan was to send the people they currently had to circle London, leaving coverage on the northern side to the army. The only exception would be the flyers—they would all have to meet Bart's group in Amersham to get their goo rock dust. Amersham was close enough to the northern edge of the dome, that it worked as a strategic base; the southern part of the town had been swallowed by the dome,.

Those who had been sheltering in other Area 42 locations had already been coming down and would circle the dome as well. MI-6 had lost the majority of their agents to the dome, but the ones still out, as well as the free Closen, would also meet in Amersham. So far there hadn't been signs of the enemy, but that didn't mean Nix didn't have his clones and other fighters ready to retaliate when the dome came under attack.

Only Maeve, Aisling, Stella, Reece, and Bart knew that Reg and his marching Ckiong army would also be in Amersham—by coincidence, of course.

The grinding of the dust had taken all night. But they now had over a thousand packets. They didn't have that many flyers yet, so Stella had harnesses made so each flyer could carry multiple packets. The ground assault would be first as a distraction, then the flyers would start. The spell that went with the powder was simple and all of their current flyers were fine with it.

"What sort of resistance are we expecting?" Greely

was helping load the last of the dust packets. He'd gotten commitments from just under a thousand Royal Army retirees. Even though the king and queen of the U.K. agreed something needed to be done, they wanted to wait things out before officially reacting.

Bart's crew didn't have the luxury of time. Aisling felt it on the back of her neck as she helped load dust as well. Watching the news, both official and what a few Area 42 agents who were outside the dome were sending back, didn't show any changes in the dome, but she felt it on another level. The dome was solidifying.

"No idea." Bart checked his guns and loaded them in a pack. "There's been no signs of activity around the dome, no sightings of Nix, and no more demands." He turned to Greely. "Unless the royal family has received some?"

"Not that any of my sources are saying, but the Royals do appear to be setting up Edinburgh as a fortress. No one in or out." Greely already looked better than he had in London.

Bart snorted. "That won't help them if Nix has the ability to throw another dome their way. He will find a way in."

"They never believed me about him either. Oh, the Royals recognized he was a dangerous criminal, but they doubted me when I said he was more." Greeley scowled. "What about the High Council and the fey royals? This is a fey situation after all." The British royal family was always human, it was an agreement made long ago. But the fey High King and Queen had no jurisdictional boundaries.

"They aren't responding." Bart gave a quick glance to Aisling.

The High Council had said they would be looking into it. But Aisling and the others were pretty sure they were extensively aware of things, and waiting to see how they played out. Her mother was somehow involved, which meant the rest of the Council at least knew, and might have been working with her on this. They'd agreed no one else outside of their immediate circle needed to know that.

Everything was mostly ready and packed when Reece came up to Aisling. "Can I talk to you for a moment? Alone?" His gray eyes were dark with worry.

Aisling nodded to Bart and followed Reece to the cottage she'd stayed in. He shut the door, then took her in his arms. The first kiss was quick and filled with an urgency far beyond passion. Aisling returned it, then allowed herself a look in his eyes when he pulled back.

"That was great, really. But?"

"I don't want to lose you." He smiled, but his eyes still looked worried. "I can't explain it, maybe it's that precog kicking in, but I just feel like—"

Aisling kissed him to cut him off. She put how much he meant to her into her kiss. They were going into a battle of unknown elements—there was always a chance one or both wouldn't survive.

They finally broke from the kiss. "I wish we had more time." He traced her cheek. "No matter what happens, save yourself."

"Only if you will." She kissed him again, running her hands up his back.

A knock at the door cut them off.

"Aisling? Bart says we're ready to go." Maeve could have just opened the door—chances were she'd seen the two of them go inside together.

"On my way." Aisling started to reach for the door, but Reece grabbed her hand.

"I do love you too, you know." His eyes didn't look as upset as before, but there was an intensity there. "Don't forget that. No matter what happens." He released her hand, opened the door for her, and they joined the others.

They might have only had two hundred people gathered here, but the number of weapons was impressive. Bart and Caradoc were driving a huge farm truck with what looked like a missile launcher strapped on its bed. Considering Aisling hadn't seen any such thing on the grounds before, odds were that Caradoc had made it.

She rode in a car at the back of the line with Reece, Stella, and Maeve. Jones drove the car behind them with Harlie, Dailten, and Narissa. All told, fifty-one vehicles wound their way south to Amersham.

There were fewer cars on the motorway than normal, but Aisling heard the radio crackle that they were being followed.

"Damn it." Reece grabbed the radio and contacted Bart. "I'm going to drop out and see if we can come up behind them."

"They might just be out for a drive?" Caradoc's voice responded.

"Doubtful. Jones, you want to stay or take off with me?"

"We'll go with you. Next right?" Knowing Jones, it had been far too long since he'd had a chance to kill someone and was looking forward to some action.

"Yup." Reece took the exit and picked up speed. Jones followed, and three of four cars behind them did as well. "Bart, the convoy still has one tail. We got three to follow us. We'll meet you in Amersham."

Aisling looked back at their new friends, but they were still too far to see well. "Can't tell who they are, anyone have a clue?"

Stella closed her eyes in focus, then opened them. "They are speaking Japanese. At least the last car is. The first two cars are silent."

"Lazing, again? Are they still after me? We're heading toward Nix; they can go find him themselves." Maeve turned and glared at the cars behind them.

"Who knows with them. I'm still…damn it. We're blocked in." Reece started swearing as a dead end appeared. "This isn't on the GPS. Jones, get your folks ready, we're going to have to come out fighting. Try and get your flyers in the air before they notice." He didn't wait for a response, but spun the car to face the oncoming vehicles. The first two cars blocked their exit—the last stopped further back and on a slight rise.

Gunfire came from the first two cars. Reece, Aisling, Maeve, and Jones returned it. Dailten and Narissa were up high above them and Stella had closed her eyes again. Harlie stayed in Jones' car but looked to be doing what Stella was—sitting with his eyes closed.

She opened her eyes and yelled. "Wait! Don't shoot at the last car!"

Before anyone could respond, the two front cars exploded and debris flew high in the air. Aisling ducked back into their car, but only smaller pieces came toward them.

The third car had blown up the other two.

Chapter Forty-Nine

———◆———

"THAT WAS DIFFERENT." JONES CREPT up to their car. "I didn't see what happened, but I assume none of you have a rocket launcher?"

"It was the last car. They didn't like something about the other two." Stella kept her eyes closed as she did her spying. "This was a setup to get rid of those two cars, but now they are debating what to do with us. And they *are* Lazing."

"We can't sit here forever, we do have a battle to get to, you know." Maeve scowled at the third car, but so far no one came out. "I can turn myself over to them if they will let the rest of you go."

"As honorable as that is, it will not be necessary." The unaccented voice cut in on the radio in Reece's car. "We are here to help."

Aisling was sure the look of shock and confusion on everyone's faces was reflected on her own. Before anyone could stop him, Reece put down his gun, and stepped away from the car.

"How?" He seemed far too calm as he faced the Lazing car.

The car door opened and a tall Japanese human male stepped forward. He reminded Aisling of Jones. He placed himself at the same distance from his car as Reece was from theirs. "The individual Nix has been a focus of our clan for over five hundred years. Different name, same person. However, we have become split in what we should do. Some wanted to bring him back, to get him to work for us. The rest of us believe he's too deadly for that and he needs to be killed." He nodded to someone in his car and the fires of the other two cars were repressed. It would have taken more magic to do that than to blow them up initially.

"I take it you're of the "kill-him-now" group? I'm Reece Larkin, by the way." He gave a nod and slight bow. One which brought a smile to the Lazing.

"Thank you. I am Mazuka Kenko, you may call me Kenko. Yes, we are, and we know who all of you are. Except for the small fey who has been spying on us. But she might have saved us unneeded bloodshed. We want to join in your attack on the dome, and the destruction of Nix."

"Let me talk to my superiors." Reece reached into the car, then paused. "The last car of yours still following the convoy?"

"It is on our side. There is a shachen mage in that car. They are masking the convoy from our illogical counterparts and anyone else who might be trying to locate all of you. We have more people waiting in Amersham."

Aisling had never met one of the shachen, but she'd heard of them. Like the alc mages, the shachen were loners, but mostly stayed in east Asia. Most magic users had one, maybe two areas of power. Changelings almost always had more and the shachen mages were like them in that regard. But unlike the changelings, the shachen mages were exceptionally powerful. One could easily wipe out a hundred regular magic users, three times that if they were extremely focused.

Aisling could tell Reece wanted to know more, but they didn't have the time. Instead, he nodded and called Bart. The call was short.

Aisling wanted to know about the shachen. That one of them left Japan was a massive statement as to how serious the Lazing took Nix.

Reece finished a short conversation with Bart, then

turned back to Kenko. "Our boss said anyone who wants to kill Nix is welcome to join us. As long as you understand that our main objective will be to drop that dome. And there are a lot of other people who want to kill him also."

"And that this is temporary and we will be expected to leave the United Kingdom once the current objectives are over." Kenko's smile was small, but looked sincere. "I did not listen in on your call, however the same would have been asked of you had our positions been reversed."

"True and good point." Reece got back into their car along with Aisling and Maeve. Stella never got out. She did lean down so Kenko could see her and waggled her fingers and smiled. He actually cracked a large smile and gave her a bow before getting in his car.

Reece and Jones took the lead with Kenko's car behind.

"Well, if he's legit and they do have a shachen mage with them, that alone is worth having them along."

"As long as they are really on our side." Maeve kept looking back to the two cars following them, but her focus was on Kenko's car. "Think of the damage they could do if they aren't?"

"They could have killed us, or at the least most of us, just now. They didn't have to tell us about the shachen mage either."

Stella leaned forward. "And I trust them. Well, at least the one we spoke to, but I got no feelings of hostility or duplicity from anyone in Kenko's car."

Maeve still looked concerned, but they all stayed silent the rest of the trip.

Amersham wasn't a large town, and it was looking overfilled with all of the agents and former military in the streets. Flyers were already getting fitted with the packs. Reece went down a side road. Jones and Kenko followed him. Good idea, since while Bart knew they were bringing in Lazing operatives, others wouldn't. If

Kenko was as high ranking as she suspected, some agents might recognize him as Lazing. Keeping him and his people nearby until the information of their collaboration came out would be a good idea.

"Where did that other car go?" Aisling asked as they walked down the side street to where Bart had gathered people.

Kenko smiled. "Waiting for me to show up. Most folks wouldn't know we are Lazing, but with this many agents on hand it was safer to be prudent." He and his people followed Reece and Jones to Bart. There were two other men and two women, all of them with the same neutral look Jones usually wore.

"Jones, are you sure you didn't go in for training with the Lazing?" Maeve asked, as Aisling wasn't the only one who noticed the similarities.

"No, but they are to be admired." Jones was walking behind the Lazing contingent and Kenko turned and nodded.

"Thank you. The same could be said of you."

A group of elves, former military by their stances, surrounded Bart, but took off at a run so fast it was hard even for Aisling to see.

"They'll be leading to the south," Bart said. "I am honored to meet you, Mazuka Kenko. And a bit surprised."

"The same to you, Agent Barthlinio Churchill. I know time is crucial, but I would like to share what we are bringing." He and Bart stepped aside from the mass of agents to keep their discussion private.

"Any idea when…. ahh." Aisling was about to ask about the trolls, but Reg, Grundog, and three more came into view. "Thought there were more?"

Stella smiled. "There will be."

The rest of their group left to help with Caradoc's massive weapon, but Aisling, Maeve, and Stella met Reg and his people.

Grundog's smile was huge when she saw them, but she refrained from hugging.

"Good to see you, Reg. What brings you out this way?" Maeve had made the contact, she got to play lead. Aisling saw Bart look over from his conversation with Kenko, but he just nodded.

"Very nice to see you, Maeve. As well as Aisling and Stella. We were meeting here to set up a base for attacking the dome." He looked around as if in surprise at the number of people around them. "I see that I wasn't the only one who saw this town as a good launch point."

He, Maeve, Aisling, and Stella went back and forth discussing the plans and strategies. Finally, Maeve nodded. "I know the Ckiong don't work under anyone else, but would you be agreeable to working alongside our forces? We do have a common goal."

Reg nodded, then turned to the three trolls with him and Grundog. Close up, it was clear all three were older and far more formally dressed than he or Grundog. They nodded as a single person. "I believe we can agree to that."

Reg smiled, keeping the tusk visibility at a minimum and nodded to where Bart was sending off another group. "I believe I shall go discuss this with your Agent Churchill." He left. The three older trolls also left, leaving Grundog behind.

She waited until they were gone, then took a deep breath. "Those are the Akeng Council—almost royalty among the trolls. They've been with us the past two days. Feels like I've been in a corset the entire time." She looked around, then picked up and hugged all three women. "Better."

"They don't approve of hugging?" Stella looked worried for her friend.

"Not so much that. Just trying to impress them." She looked around and bent lower to whisper. "Reg and I are courting and there are still some biases against those of us who aren't full troll. He's fine with my minotaur half, but until we are wed, I need to tread carefully." She smiled. "It is good to see you all."

"Agreed. These are trying times." Stella looked around the hustle. Groups of flyers and other fighters were heading out in waves. "I'm still not sure what this effort will bring about, but at least we're doing something."

Aisling looked around also. "Are you happy you got involved in this after all?"

"Yup. Someone has to keep an eye on all of you." She looked toward where Caradoc, Harlie, and Dailten stood. "Now, if you will excuse me, I need to get my harness on."

"You're flying?" Aisling was surprised. As a changeling, wings would be possible, but if Stella had never used them before she'd have issues.

"No, I'm going to be attached to Dailten. We made a special harness last night, she's strong enough to carry me, and this way we'll have twice the magic." The gleam in her eye wasn't reassuring.

"Make sure you two stay out of trouble." Aisling knew Dailten wouldn't have a problem with Stella's weight, harpies were a compact but extremely strong race, but she'd seen the two of them off laughing together back in Noth. She wouldn't put it past them to have their own agenda.

The ground started rattling not long after Stella and Dailten lifted off.

Two thousand trolls were marching down the road, not saying a thing, but their footsteps spoke for them. If pure might could get through that dome, they wouldn't need anything beyond the trolls. They stopped in the road, clearly at parade rest. Reg and Bart spoke some more, Reg nodded to the trolls, and most of them took off at a jog around the base of the dome. Trolls couldn't hit the speeds that elves could, but they could still get in a good pace once they built up steam.

"I still don't fully understand what guns are going to do." Maeve nodded toward Caradoc's machine as they walked toward him. "Or what that is."

It looked like someone had combined the weapons area of a tank, a trebuchet, and a massive body scanner. It also had two thick arms and eight long skinny metal arms.

"This is the answer to both questions." Caradoc said as they came closer. "We have enough firepower on the ground to make some dents on the dome, but we needed something to help de-stabilize it before the flyers hit it with their dust and spells." He patted the awkward looking thing. "That's what this is for. It uses firepower, electrical shock, ground vibration, and concentrated goo dust. Watch." He looked like a kid with a new toy on naming day as he pressed a few buttons on the remote he held. The machine rumbled forward and trudged to the dome's edge. It stuck out one of the heavy arms, but didn't touch the dome. Instead, the arm started pounding the ground right at the base. The vibrations shook the ground and nearby rocks hopped.

The dome looked solid, but intel indicated it wasn't. But it was so thick and dense, it was almost impossible to get through.

Until now.

As the first arm kept pounding the ground, one of the thinner, smaller arms went up about four feet and positioned a small explosive into the vibrating dome. It was slowly swallowed by the mass of the dome, exploded, and blew up a small hole. The inside of it was dark, but clear. Then it slowly closed on itself.

Caradoc switched off the machine. "That was a small test. When Bart calls for us to go, this baby and I will be punching our way through all along the rim. More of a distraction than a serious threat. But did you notice the color of the dome where we punched through?"

"It's lighter." Aisling leaned forward even though being that close to the dome was disturbing. "I can see the street on the other side. People are frozen."

"Yup. If I can make enough holes, I might do some lasting damage to it." After a brief time of doubting his powers, he was back to the cocky Caradoc she loved.

Aisling stepped back a few feet. "I don't get why Nix isn't responding. I know he's a cocky bastard, but there's a chance we'll drop this thing. He's not even coming out to defend it?"

Caradoc's smile fell. "My fear as well. We might have mobilized sooner than he thought, but he must have expected something."

Reece came over. "I hope you're ready to roll, Caradoc. It looks like everyone is in place."

"I am—"

The top of the dome opened and a dozen or more heavily armed people scrambled out. They wore odd boots that kept them on the dome surface even as the hole closed back up. Most appeared to be Nix clones, but there were others there too. They didn't even acknowledge the people on the ground but started shooting at the flyers.

Chapter Fifty

REECE AND BART STARTED YELLING orders. Caradoc swore and quickly reversed his machine, made some adjustments, and started firing at the top of the dome. Obviously it could do more than just rattle the dome, apparently he'd worked a large caliber gun into its design.

"All flyers get the hell out of here!" Bart yelled into his radio so loudly Aisling was sure they could hear him without their radios.

First one, then three more flyers couldn't get away fast enough and were shot down by the Nix clones. Three crashed to the ground. One hit the dome and Aisling watched in horror as the dome itself swallowed the body.

Elves were racing trying to catch the struck flyers as more were hit. Kenko ran up with a heavily robed person.

It must have been the shachen mage, but there was no way to see anything as even the hands were covered.

Kenko said something in Japanese to the mage, then turned toward the dome. The mage's words as they chanted reinforcement to their spells were heavy and reverberated in Aisling's chest.

Dark blue lightning shot out from the mage's hands and struck five of the people on top of the dome. Before the remaining flyers could return to the airspace above the dome, the top opened again and twenty more people, armed with guns, came out of the top. The mage's voice grew stronger and the arcs of lightning turned deep purple. A shachen mage should have been able to wipe out all of the people on the dome; they were still removing some, but more replaced them. Something was affecting the shachen mage's magic.

Caradoc's weapon wasn't doing as much good as hoped. Shot after shot was deflected by some unseen power and went wide over the dome.

A crack appeared in the dome right in front of them and a wave of Nix clones, plus a dozen more people stepped out and started firing. An odd gas came out with them.

"Back up and get on your masks!" Caradoc yelled as he slapped on his.

Bart called the order to get on the masks through to the others around the dome. The trolls didn't have masks, but those with Reg accepted the ones Reece handed out.

Caradoc fired his weapon at the crack. Part of the dome crumpled on itself.

The Lazing had their own masks and a shield appeared around the shachen mage. They kept sending spells to the top of the dome, but whatever was blocking them continued.

Aisling and Maeve ducked behind a car and returned fire, as all of the agents did. The dome had closed back up again and the clones and the rest who had come out were still firing but not trying to protect themselves. They went down quickly.

Two Lazing were near three clones as they fell, then the Lazing crumbled to the ground pulling at their masks and screaming.

"Stay back!" Bart yelled as the two Lazing twitched violently and then stilled.

"Caradoc, are these masks going to hold?" Aisling watched as the people and clones from within the dome were shot down. They appeared to just be a way to distract the attackers and get the gas out.

"Damn it, I don't know." He fussed with something on his machine and it started shaking the ground again.

The shachen mage stepped forward as the gas enveloped them. Their shield protected them, but they weren't firing spells anymore. Aisling shuddered at something strong enough to nullify a shachen mage.

Dailten and Stella landed hard behind them. Stella was unconscious.

Aisling ran and unbuckled the harness as she checked for a pulse. It was there, but Stella had a gash on the side of her head. She handed Dailten one of Caradoc's masks and put one on Stella's face.

"Will she be all right? I tried to pull back in time, but they tagged us." Dailten's right arm hung down uselessly.

"You can't fly like that." Aisling started to heal Stella.

"Why? It's not one of my wings." Dailten shook her feathers to demonstrate. "But I need you to fly with me. I can't release the powder."

"Stella is stabilized, I can protect her." Maeve squatted down next to Stella. "But if you get inside, don't forget, the real Nix is mine."

Aisling looked between Stella and Dailten. "I have no intention of going inside, but he's all yours." She looked up. "Someone needs to get the Lazing to pull back, their masks aren't working."

Maeve looked as two more Lazing charged the shield. "They know. They are bound now and will fight to their death."

"Damn it." Aisling turned to Dailten. "You sure you can carry me? I weigh more than Stella and am about a foot taller."

"Pish. Get the harness on." Dailten looked down at the unconscious Stella. "We'll win this, my friend."

Aisling put on the harness, attached both bags of dust and got buckled on to Dailten.

Reece came running up as they finished. "What are

you doing?"

"Same as you, fighting."

"Be careful, Nix can open the dome anywhere he wants. Harlie radioed in from the other side of the dome—he said for you to use the pendant."

Aisling shrugged. "Can't hurt. Hopefully." Anything else she was going to say was lost as Dailten pushed off and flew high above the dome.

"We have to get those people off the top. What kind of aggressive spells do you have?" Dailten's voice carried well even in the wind from flight.

"Nothing that will reach them."

"You have your guns on you?"

"Yes I do."

Dailten swooped low and Aisling managed to pick five people off the dome. The speed with which Dailten flew back up was impressive.

"Hand me some dust and we'll go for another run."

Aisling grabbed some dust, but left most of it in Dailten's good hand, then rubbed the rest on the muzzle of her gun. There was a chance that the bullets could carry the dust into the dome. Aisling figured it couldn't hurt.

They swooped low again, this time Aisling got eight of them and Dailten dropped her dust. Dailten and Aisling chanted the spell that would activate it.

If the dome were a living thing, Aisling would say they hurt it. It shook where the dust hit, causing more of the enemies on top to tumble. The people she shot this time fell back into the dome, causing more ripples in their wake. It seemed lighter also, but it could just be wishful thinking on her part.

"Good work!" Narissa and four more flyers swooped near them and also dropped their dust. One of the people on the dome got off a good shot before they themselves were shot and a tall male pixie crashed to the ground.

Aisling looked down but no one could catch him

before he hit the ground.

More flyers flew lower over the dome, some using guns after they dropped their dust, some flying away as best they could. Too many got hit.

But the dome was shaking and showing holes. A large one opened right below them and Dailten flew inside before Aisling could say anything.

Aisling swore as the air grew heavy around them. Their masks seemed to hold, as whatever gas was in here wasn't affecting them. Dailten got hit and crashed to the street. Aisling quickly released her harness so she could roll away as they landed.

Dailten was still alive, but had a huge tear in her right wing, and her eyes were rolling back in shock. Her wing was bleeding badly.

Aisling dragged her unconscious body behind two parked cars.

"Come out to play, little elf princess." That was Nix. Aisling wasn't sure how she knew, but it wasn't a clone.

CHAPTER FIFTY-ONE

NIX WAS DOWN THE STREET and close enough to a group of immobilized Londoners that Aisling couldn't shoot without risking hitting them. No one was certain they were still alive in here, but that wasn't a chance she could take.

The dome walls were vibrating harder now and windows appeared. Caradoc and his toy must be nearby.

"I will find you. This dome has almost finished its purpose, but I can keep you for much longer." He was closer now.

Aisling jumped up, checked for civilians, and when she saw none near him, fired.

The shot was clear and aimed right for his head. The bullet stopped in midair and dropped into his open hand.

"Oh dear, is that the best you can do?" He was next to her before she could move and knocked the gun out of her hand. She threw the rest of the dust at him but he was ready for it and waved it away with a flick of his hand.

He grabbed her throat and started squeezing.

Aisling fought to get her hands on him, but a heavy band spell was forcing her arms down. She kicked him away.

The dome near them shook even harder, but she kept his focus on her. She needed to find out what the dome's purpose was.

"It won't work." Nix waved at the dome. "Whatever your people are doing, it won't work."

As he spoke, holes started opening in the street behind him and green skeletal shapes crawled out. Unlike the creatures she'd seen before, these were having no problem moving about. They ripped apart a frozen gnome as she watched.

"What in the hell are you doing? Those things don't belong here."

"*We* don't belong here. But we're here, aren't we?" Nix's grin was nowhere near stable. "Did you know we can't go back? It changes us too much. Not the same… not the same." His voice dropped and a shadow covered his face for a moment. Then he shook it off. "But if we make this place more like beyond the veil, we'll be fine. This will be my kingdom." He nodded to himself again and Aisling leapt for him.

She focused all of the anti-healing magic she could gather as she grabbed hold.

Part of his arm where she was grabbing him was already turning black as the skin and muscles died. But instead of screaming in pain or pushing her away, he laughed and pulled her closer. "This could be fun. If I hold you right here, I can prolong killing you." He managed to get one hand on her throat again.

"Drop her, asshole." Maeve's voice was a damn good thing to hear.

"I will blow your brains out right now." That Reece was saying it, but not doing it, meant he didn't have as clear a shot as he was implying. Sunlight and a slight breeze told her Caradoc had opened the dome again.

Nix laughed. "If you kill me, the dome drops. If it drops without my control, it will kill the people trapped in here. However, my new friends will feast well on them before they move forth to the rest of this island."

Aisling kept one hand on his arm and one on his wrist, trying to keep him from strangling her. There was no way to tell if he was lying about the danger of the dome dropping, but the words *without my control* indicated there was a safe way to do it. The pressure on her throat was constant and she had no idea how long it would be before she blacked out. She was already seeing spots. He could have killed her; she had a feeling that would have been better than whatever he had in mind for her.

"You know your mother said I could kill you?" Nix ignored Maeve and Reece. "But she said I had to bring you to her first. You were lucky to have such a good mother."

Sounds of a fight came from behind her. Her vision was starting to fade, but she could move enough to duck. Nix followed but not low enough. Maeve leapt off a car, over some of the green skeleton attackers and swung a machete at Nix's head.

Aisling closed her eyes at the resulting splatter and crumpled to the ground rubbing her throat.

Reece held her up. "At least we'll be together for the end." The dome was starting to shake so hard pieces were falling from the top.

"Tell Bart to back away." Aisling forced the words out of her damaged throat. "Get everyone away from the dome."

He nodded and radioed Bart.

Maeve stood over Nix's headless corpse. "No way to be sure he was dead until his head was gone." She looked up as the dome shook harder and the skeletons moved away from the sides and toward the holes they'd come out of.

Reece was holding her close when her pendant started vibrating. Harlie had told Aisling to use her pendant, but not what for. It was pulling toward the wall of the dome. "Get me there." Aisling pointed toward the wall.

Reece and Maeve walked her over.

Aisling leaned forward, pendant in hand, and put the other hand on the dome. Then she pressed the pendant to it. Nothing happened at first. She focused her magic into the pendant. Healing energy, anti-healing energy, shield spells, any spell she'd ever known was funneled into the pendant.

At first it looked like it wasn't going to be enough. The dome was falling apart, but the gas within it was stronger, and the skeletal creatures had turned away from their holes and were coming for them.

"Think of your mother," Reece said as he held her.

That helped. Thoughts of all of the people who had died because of that woman's actions forced still more power into the pendant. It glowed so bright, she had to look away. But she hung on to it and kept it pressed to the dome wall. The shaking stilled. As she was about to pull away, it rocked hard enough to knock the three of them over and send them back a few feet.

Reece covered her and Maeve as best he could but the explosion that followed was massive. It came from the dome itself, as if in the middle of collapsing, it changed direction and burst outward.

Sunlight hit them as the dome vanished and millions of blackened pebbles landed around them.

The skeleton creatures ran back into their holes or fell to dust where they stood. The gas vanished, or it might have exploded with the dome, but the air was clear. The formerly frozen Londoners started slowly moving.

Caradoc came racing up and hugged them all as they sat on the ground.

Bart, Kenko, and Reg came marching up, looking around as medics ran to the formerly frozen Londoners.

"Good job folks, not sure what all you did, or how you did it, but you stopped him. And got rid of that damn dome." Bart nodded to them then yelled for a medic to get Dailten. She was conscious now, but not happy about it. Her wing would take a long time to recover.

"It was this pendant again—really wish I knew what it was doing though." At least it was becoming easier to speak now.

Bart looked from the headless Nix to Maeve to the

bloody machete at her feet, opened his mouth, then closed it and shook his head. "Good job, Maeve. I might have done the same."

Reece helped Aisling to a medic station. Aside from some bruising on her neck, she was fine.

Harlie came running to them and hugged Aisling fiercely. "You used the pendant, very good. The mystics found that Nix had used the Area 42 building to counterbalance his escape beyond the veil, then was using the pieces of it to bring through the underground creatures and other unsavory types to our side. You and the pendant stopped the dome from spreading and growing when it collapsed." He smiled.

"So no more building parts dropping on things?" Jones had his left arm in a sling, but looked like he didn't even notice.

"No. Well, we don't think so. Communication was hard until the dome fell. But we think no." Harlie hugged her again.

"How are Stella and Dailten?" Aisling had seen an awful lot of covered bodies as they came in, she hoped none of them were people she knew.

Bart stepped in to answer. "Stella is fine and off directing people. Big bandage on the side of her head, but it won't slow her down. Dailten should be fine, but it might be a while before she can fly again." He frowned. "We lost Greely; he went down fighting though. Kenko lost all of his people except the shachen mage, but the mage's powers are seriously drained. They will be in seclusion for years according to Kenko. But it looks like most of the people trapped under the dome will recover."

"I was thinking of taking everyone over to the base?" Reece asked, then clarified to the others. "There's an old Area 42 base about a mile from here. Nothing secret remains, so it gets used for local events. We've set up an area to get non-injured people fed and rested."

"Good idea. I'll radio if I need you. Go rest. Reg took some of his people there too."

Aisling, Reece, Maeve, Caradoc, Jones, and Harlie all rode over in a van. Aisling wanted to walk but she was outvoted.

They'd just sat down in the mess hall, when their radios crackled to life.

"Not all of the enemies were accounted for. There's a hostage situation in the back lab. The outer doors have been sealed—you'll have to take care of it." Bart's call was brisk and ended abruptly. Reg, Grundog, and a few other trolls were somewhere in the complex, but Aisling didn't think they had time to find them.

She was closest to the door and took off running. The lab was at the end of the hall, but there were no guards. She sent a text to Grundog; trolls might be a good idea right now.

Aisling and the rest ran into the room. She'd expected to see a group of desperate gunmen holding hostages. But that wasn't what awaited them in the dimly lit room.

"I didn't need all of them—just you. I might have been too dramatic in my cry for help. By the way, you should have let Nix have London." Her mother stood in the center of the room as an eerie light appeared from the back wall.

CHAPTER FIFTY-TWO

HER MOTHER SAID A SINGLE spell word, then frowned. "You should also be frozen. Why aren't you frozen?"

Aisling turned to the others behind her but they were all were standing locked in place. She could still move, albeit slowly. Her magic was deflecting her mother's spell, but not stopping it completely. Both of her brothers were frozen, and they were still stronger magic users than her.

"You used my magic when you had Harlie block it, didn't you?" Even though Aisling could move, rushing her mother right now wasn't an option. "I'm sure both Harlie and Caradoc could explain it better but you're using some of my own stored magic against me. Doesn't work."

The scowl on her mother's face told Aisling she was probably right. And that her mother hadn't thought of it. "I can still move faster than you right now, with or without magic. I wanted to give you one more chance to join us. Join the High Council and find out what power really is."

"This is still about power?" Aisling shook her head. This might be her only chance for answers—and maybe if she stalled, someone else might show up to help. "Did you change the humans? Back when they were dying of the Black Death, did you and other members of the High Council change them?"

"Not that it matters, but of course we did. We had no choice." Her mother's voice sounded as if it had been a drapery selection. "The humans were already out-breeding us and would have surpassed us in massive numbers within a few years. We didn't create the Black Death; they did that on their own. While we were making certain our people couldn't be infected, some of our scientists realized that changes could be made to the human physiology. We were able to save them *and* make sure we would be the dominant species on this world." She shrugged. "It was the prudent thing to do to ensure our survival."

Aisling was stunned. Even having a theory of what had been done didn't prepare her for the reality. "Our survival wasn't at risk. We have magic, humans don't. As that late idiot you supported was trying so hard to prove, it wouldn't take many magic users to rule humans."

"We could have killed them instead." Her mother looked annoyed. "Or let the plague do it for us." She glanced over to Maeve still frozen in place. "We didn't."

"You wanted a group of people subservient to you. They might not worship the fey anymore, but they are still dependent for reproduction abilities. You have to reverse the spell." Aisling looked at the others. They might be frozen, but their eyes said they were alive and pissed. She needed to force her mother to release the spell she held on them. It was more than just her magic; she never could have held both Caradoc and Harlie, let alone everyone else. Others created the spell and were feeding their magic into it, but her mother was the one who cast it.

"I want people to know their place. Look what happened in London. Humans and fey stormed the place and many died that didn't have to."

"They died because you let a homicidal sociopath have more power than he should have ever had. They died trying to stop him—something the High Council should have been doing."

The sound of a dozen or so heavy feet running was welcome to Aisling. She'd hoped reaching out to the trolls would help. If they could distract her mother, she might be able to break the spell holding the others.

Reg flung open the door and charged forward. Only to be frozen in place along with Grundog and all the trolls still out in the hall.

"Trolls? Really?" Her mother shook her head. "I shouldn't have let your father bring you back to life." She gave a grim laugh as she watched Aisling's face. "You already knew. How?" She might not be able to freeze Aisling, but she was still able to lift the pendant out of her shirt. She tugged, but it still wouldn't go over Aisling's head. "What is this?" She flicked her fingers and Harlie's spell vanished so the pendant showed in its full glory. "Someone has been naughty. And tricky." She didn't come closer, but she examined the pendant. "Not you. Nor your brothers. Who made this?"

Aisling smiled. "Something you don't know? Interesting."

"Where did this come from? Take it off, immediately!" Her mother was starting to shake but it appeared to be equal parts anger and fear.

"Even if I could, I wouldn't. This was a gift by a secret admirer and sadly it doesn't come off." She shook as a bolt of pain glanced off of her. The pendant bounced it back at her mother. "And it's very protective of me."

"That can't be on this side of the veil. It doesn't belong here." There was a rising note of worry in her voice.

"Do any of us? Technically this was the humans' world. We were taught that we came here in desperation. That might be partially true. But I have a feeling you and your cronies messed up things so badly on the other side of the veil that you had to find another world."

Before her mother could respond, the walls started shaking. Her eyes went wide in terror and she started backing up. "You have to take that off. Destroy it. Now!"

The pulling pressure from the pendant stopped and it

dropped back down to her chest. The shaking continued. Her mother had slowed her down but hadn't frozen her. If she pushed hard enough, she could get out. But there was no way in hell she was leaving Reece or her friends behind.

"Release them! It's an earthquake." She took a few steps closer to her mother.

"I can't. They are doomed, we're all dead now." She spat at Aisling. "I should have left you dead."

"But then you couldn't have pulled on my power all these years, would you? That was it, wasn't it? You had to kill me to honor the pact you and the other first families made with beings from the other side who helped you cast your twisted spell. Then you realized they would have tracked me through my magic signature. You had Harlie block most of my magic, which would change the signature, and you could siphon off what you needed over the decades. You hated me because I could have been more powerful than you."

The shakes grew stronger. It wasn't an earthquake unless one had grown legs. It felt like something massive was running for them. "Release my friends!"

"There's nothing we can do. Nothing—" The rest of her yell was cut off as the wall next to them burst open and a mass of skeletal beings came through. They didn't look right, aside from being skeletal, their bodies were out of proportion—no two were the same, and everything looked mis-matched. They moved to grab Caradoc, the closest to them, but Aisling moved in front of him. They stopped as soon as she blocked him.

"Protect me! They want me!" Her mother was throwing spells, but the creatures focused on her and slowly moved toward her.

A shriek came from the glass window behind Aisling and a portal to some new hell opened beyond it. Wild trees and dark ragged skies took the place of the quiet courtyard the window had looked over. The lead creature stopped its hunting of her mother and raised its hand toward Aisling. She was flung backwards into the glass and lost consciousness.

———◆———

Aisling woke up slowly and painfully, there was grit in her mouth and her clothing was torn in small tears as if she'd been pulled through glass. Which, if her memory was right, she had been. Whatever shoved her here had not been gentle. Every part of her body screamed in pain just from trying to sit up. She was so exhausted that even sitting upright took all of her energy.

The window shimmered in front of her—the glass she'd been pushed through was now back in place. It was shrinking, slowly closing her view of the room she'd been in. Her mother's freezing spell was obviously gone, as instead of standing locked in position, everyone was on the floor. Harlie and Caradoc were both closest to the glass as if they'd tried to run after whatever grabbed her, but were dropped in place. Reece wasn't far behind, sprawled out as if he'd been running when he collapsed and clutching his head. Maeve and Jones collapsed near the door where they had been frozen. Past them was a mass of unconscious trolls.

It was bloody where her mother had stood, and she was missing. A trail of blood showed where she'd been dragged off by someone—or someones—through the hole in the wall. Whatever had destroyed the wall was also gone. Considering how her mother had betrayed everyone, and what she'd been a part of doing to the entire human race, Aisling didn't care if she was alive or dead. Part of her still needed answers though.

Trying to move brought waves of agony and her body refused. Just sitting was brutal and painful. She yelled, unable to even crawl the short distance to the window.

Hopefully, the others were still alive and would wake up before the odd window closed. But the sound of her yell bounced back at her. She tried to heal some of her wounds, but no magic flowed through her. No matter what spell she attempted, nothing came forth.

A chill grew over her as the window to her world slowly closed—deep in her gut she knew where she was. Something had pulled her into the old land. Beyond the veil, not in a dream, or channeled visage. But in reality.

And she'd lost her magic.

The End

About the Author

Marie is a multi-award-winning fantasy and science fiction author with a serious reading addiction. If she wasn't writing about all the people in her head, she'd be lurking about coffee shops annoying total strangers with her stories. So really, writing is a way of saving the masses. She lives in Southern California and is owned by two very faery-minded cats. She is also a proud member of SFWA (Science Fiction and Fantasy Writers of America).

When not saving the masses from coffee shop shenanigans, Marie likes to visit the UK and keeps hoping someone will give her a nice summer home in the Forest of Dean or Conwy, Wales.

www.ingramcontent.com/pod-product-compliance
Lightning Source LLC
Chambersburg PA
CBHW030355200726
48286CB00014B/1417